LOST STARSH

The Lost Starship
The Lost Command
The Lost Destroyer
The Lost Colony
The Lost Patrol
The Lost Planet
The Lost Earth
The Lost Artifactt
The Lost Star Gate
The Lost Supernova
The Lost Swarm
The Lost Intelligence
The Lost Tech
The Lost Secret
The Lost Barrier
The Lost Nebula
The Lost Relic
The Lost Task Force
The Lost Clone
The Lost Portal
The Lost Cyborg

Visit VaughnHeppner.com for more information

The Lost Cyborg

(Lost Starship Series 21)

Vaughn Heppner

Illustration © Tom Edwards
TomEdwardsDesign.com

Copyright © 2024 by the author.

This book is a work of fiction. Names, characters, places and incidents are either products of the author's imagination or used fictitiously. Any resemblance to actual events, locales or persons, living or dead, is entirely coincidental. All rights reserved. No part of this publication can be reproduced or transmitted in any form or by any means, without permission in writing from the author.

ISBN: 9798324561499
Imprint: Independently published

-1-

"Now, as to the fifth item on the agenda, we must decide how to retaliate against Captain Maddox and his allies."

"You are referring to his assault on Loggia?"

"In our very chamber, if you remember?"

"How could I forget? Enigmach, you have been silent for a time. Is there a reason for this?"

"If you must know," Enigmach said, "I am contemplating this very situation. I am partway to devising a response that takes into account Maddox's maddening abilities."

"This is interesting. Do you care to tell us about your plan?"

"Let me gather my thoughts a moment longer," Enigmach said. "Then I shall elaborate."

The three highly ranked Grand Strategists of Leviathan met in a subterranean computer complex. The complex and meeting chamber were located on Loggia, the capital planet of the Sovereign Hierarchy of Leviathan. It was the most powerful government in the Scutum-Centaurus Spiral Arm, which was approximately 8,000 light years from the Commonwealth of Planets.

In order of rank, the three Grand Strategists were Hyperion Codex, Tactix, and the sly Enigmach. Each humanoid cyber reclined on a couch. Each had inserted a jack into their massive, AI-enhanced brain. These jacks linked the three to huge mainframe computers that took up fifteen percent of the planetary surface crust.

This was one of the most sophisticated and powerful computers in Leviathan, which meant one of the greatest in the spiral arm. The ruling entities of Leviathan were cybers, as stated, or cyborgs, indicating they were partly mechanical and partly biological. In their not-so-humble estimation, Leviathan cybers held themselves to be at the pinnacle of being.

One interesting facet to being jacked-in like this or meshed meant that Hyperion Codex, Tactix and Enigmach concentrated on pure intellect. Their combined senses of sight sound, smell, taste, and touch no longer operated, while meshed like this, so they could focus solely on intellectual pursuits.

According to cyber belief, only those elevated to the heightened levels of the mind like them could truly comprehend such an exalting experience. This was so much greater than loutish breeding or drunken revelry or gorging one's gullet. This was deep thinking in a realm of scintillating meditation. Thus, the three did not "speak" with a mouth or "listen" with ears, but engaged in direct electric linkage with each other.

The incident they wished to retaliate against was Maddox's invasion of this very chamber. Some time ago, Maddox, Meta, and Riker had used a portal to gain access here, retrieve a computer crystal that recorded an earlier meeting regarding methods of entrapping Maddox with Omegan in order to murder him and start a cross-spiral space war against Star Watch. In other words, Maddox would never have invaded the chamber if the three and thus Leviathan hadn't inveigled against him and Star Watch in the first place.

That didn't matter to these three, of course. Grand Strategists of Leviathan had their priorities in precise order, the first being the preservation and then the expansion of the empire. They had earlier determined that the Commonwealth of Planets might harm that expansion in one hundred and fifty-three years. That timeframe could accelerate if the New Men, those of the Commonwealth and the Spacers united. That, obviously meant, at least if you were a cyber, that Leviathan must preempt the danger. That meant militarily or otherwise destroying the Commonwealth.

The three brilliant Grand Strategists had noticed something critical in their previous mediations. This was from several years ago. Much of their data came from a full spectrum Intelligence sweep and later an Intelligence assault throughout that region of the Orion Spiral Arm.

Captain Maddox, as a *di-far,* had unusual abilities that often meant he thwarted attempts to harm Star Watch and then practiced inversion against the foes. That meant he badly hurt or destroyed those trying to hurt him or Star Watch. The three hadn't yet pinpointed the exact reason why or how Maddox did this each time, but they decided that direct attempts at killing Maddox had the least chances of success. That meant a roundabout method, even trapping him elsewhere, so Star Watch would succumb more easily to direct methods without Maddox being in the way. Those direct methods would be beams, missiles and asteroid bombs from attacking Leviathan warships.

"I have it," Enigmach said. "My plan is now ready for dissemination."

"You know how to eliminate Maddox?" Tactix said.

"What? No. Why would you ask that?"

"I thought you said you were devising a solution to the problem of Maddox?"

"I did, and I have," Enigmach said.

"Your plan will cause Maddox harm for invading our chamber?" Tactix said.

"No, not directly," Enigmach said.

"What good is it then?" Tactix said. "Have you even been paying attention to our problem?"

"Let me answer you with a question," Enigmach said. "What is our primary objective?"

"That is obvious," Tactix said. "Teaching Maddox a lesson."

"Do you agree with this assessment, Hyperion Codex?" Enigmach said.

"Do you seek to *lecture* me?" Hyperion Codex replied.

"I do not," Enigmach said promptly. "I am merely attempting to ascertain if this is our primary objective."

"Then you are seeking to gain rank at my expense," Hyperion Codex said, "as I deem this a trick question. We all know that our primary goal is defending and then expanding the Sovereign Hierarchy of Leviathan."

"I concur with that," Tactix said in a rush.

"I naturally agree with the both of you," Enigmach said. "That means, then, that harming or teaching Maddox a lesson is not the primary objective."

"You are correct in this," Hyperion Codex said.

"My idea, then, the one I've been contemplating, addresses our primary objective," Enigmach said.

"I thought you said this was in relation to our problem with Maddox," Tactix said, apparently unwilling to give up that angle.

"Maddox is a problem as he stands athwart our primary objective regarding dealing with the Commonwealth of Planets," Enigmach said laboriously.

"Do we simply let Maddox be then?" Tactix said.

"Once more," Enigmach said. "I will answer with a question. Would not the conquest of the Commonwealth cause Maddox anguish?"

"I desire a more immediate pain to the man," Tactix said.

"I see," Enigmach said. "Is this perhaps an example of emotionalism at play within you?"

"No!" Tactix said.

"But you just said—"

"I desire this in a brutish sense, I mean regarding Maddox's concept of self," Tactix said, interrupting. "I do not mean brutish in my thinking on the matter. I say this as I suspect brutish or direct pain to Maddox will affect him more than a cerebral pain, such as seeing the Commonwealth suffer."

"You may be right about that," Enigmach said. "I am, however, less concerned with Maddox directly than in our primary duty to Leviathan."

"That is well said," Hyperion Codex replied. "I commend you on your adherence to the primary problem."

"I merely state the obvious and my full cooperation and obedience to it," Enigmach said, perhaps with a touch of pride.

"I have now begun to wonder, Tactix," Hyperion Codex said, "if you have allowed emotionalism to cloud your analysis of the Maddox Dilemma as Enigmach has suggested."

"I am analyzing myself," Tactix said. "No. I do not detect any emotionalism on my part."

"That is excellent news," Enigmach said. "Such being the case, I can now explain my plan. It addresses the Maddox Dilemma by focusing on the apparatus that sustains him and his blasted starship."

"Yes?" Hyperion Codex said. "What is that?"

"To begin with," Enigmach said, "as the first move, I suggest we eliminate the Lord High Admiral of Star Watch."

"You mean eliminate the position from the Star Watch hierarchy?" said Tactix.

"No, I mean eliminate the one named Cook," Enigmach said. "Lord High Admiral Cook has brought great stability to Star Watch. His death would undoubtedly shake the foundations of the hated military arm. That, in turn, will aid our military forces against the Commonwealth."

"I have begun to doubt your so-called plan," Hyperion Codex said. "Or is there more to this than mere assassination?"

"Oh, yes," Enigmach said. "There is much more. I have an extended program in mind, which, incidentally, will cause great mental anguish to Captain Maddox."

"What is the root method you're proposing?" Hyperion Codex said. "I ask, because so far you appear to suggest direct methods. We know Maddox most easily counters those."

"I am perfectly aware of that," Enigmach said. "My method involves the humans of the Spacer Third Fleet. It will also entail giving the Spacers a set of Phantasma Synth Crystals."

"I seem to recall something regarding those," Tactix said. "Do these crystals not originate from the planet Ector?"

"Indeed they do," Enigmach said. "I was unaware you knew of Ector or the crystals."

"Ector orbits a distant pulsar," Tactix said. "The ancient and extinct Aetharians discovered or invented the Phantasma Synth Crystals, is this not so?"

"It is indeed so," Enigmach said. "I am impressed with your extended knowledge on such an arcane subject."

"Does this have to do with bio-electromagnetic synchronization and etheric projection?" Hyperion Codex asked.

"Exactly," Enigmach said. "I'm surprised you know about this. I congratulate you both on your extended knowledge."

"Never mind that," Hyperion Codex said. "We are supposed to know about arcane subjects so we can apply them to troubling problems others would miss. Let me contemplate a moment on your suggestion."

Tense seconds passed as the three Grand Strategists ran thousands of computer computations. During this time, Enigmach allowed them access to his master plan. They ran simulations on it, double checked the results—

"Yours is a risky plan," Hyperion Codex said suddenly. "Humans with Phantasma Synth Crystals... None of them knows about or understands this exotic technology yet."

"I'm not sure I would call the crystals technology at all," Tactix said primly. "The Phantasma Synth Crystals smack of senso-cultism and mystic alchemy."

"We have extensive records that indicate the crystals work," Enigmach said.

"Rather say that ancient texts claim so," Tactix said. "I'm not sure we have modern evidence of their viability. Are we sure that we of Leviathan wish to indulge in such mystical methodology?"

"In this instance, success is what counts," Enigmach said. "Besides, in resisting Maddox's semi-mystical functions, we will now employ some of our own. In this instance: like will face like."

"But the crystals won't be our own," Tactix pointed out. "They are Aetharian, an ancient cultic race of alien shamans."

"Do you vote against the endeavor then?" Hyperion Codex said, forestalling more invective against the idea.

"I...I have qualms regarding this approach," Tactix said, sidestepping the question.

"It is clear that you think the attempt will fail," Enigmach said. "Thus, you hope to diminish my standing by recording these so-called qualms. Is this because you think I sought to gain rank at your expense a few moments ago?"

"I do not indulge in such antiquated modes of revenge," Tactix said. "I simply deem this an exotic, perhaps an even semi-mystical attempt. Our first such exotic attempt failed, and it was…" Tactix trailed off without finishing.

"Yes?" Hyperion Codex said coldly. "Please finish your thought."

"It was nothing," Tactix said. "I may even consider the last part a misstatement." He referred to the Omegan Plan Hyperion Codex had advocated some time ago, a plan that had ultimately failed against Maddox.

"Tactix clearly assaulted your idea from last time," Enigmach said. "He is now seeking to gain rank at *your* expense."

There was a stiffening in the linkage, a slight stir of static between them. It might have come from one of them physically moving or shifting on his couch.

"I am Tactix. I believe in tactical and strategic excellence. On such, was Leviathan built and sustained. On such will Leviathan continue to expand. That is where my thinking on this matter originates. I am not sanguine about more exotic attempts, especially in regard to these mystical Aetharian artifacts."

"No matter," Hyperion Codex said abruptly. "I vote that we attempt this. Enigmach, do you agree?"

"I…I obviously do," Enigmach said, seemingly surprised. "This is my idea, after all."

"Tactix?" Hyperion Codex said.

"I will abstain, rendering neither a yea nor a nay verdict," Tactix said.

"You surely understand that Enigmach will gain rank if his plan succeeds," Hyperion Codex said.

"Yes," Tactix said, "as he should."

"Do you wish to add any addendum to the proposal?" Hyperion Codex asked.

"Not at this time," Tactix said.

"What about your stern invective against relying upon mystical apparatuses?" Hyperion Code said.

"I have made my statements," Tactix said. "The records contain them. I need say no more on the subject at this point."

"Then the proposal passes," said Hyperion Codex. "We will send it to Great Leviathan. With his acceptance, we shall begin the process. Enigmach, are you ready to deliver the crystals to the Spacer Third Fleet?"

"All is ready for immediate deployment," Enigmach said.

"You have an Intelligence Senior in mind for this?" Hyperion Codex asked.

"I do. Senior Dax will head the delegation to the Spacer Third Fleet. I have already instructed Dax in the needed techniques."

"This is excellent news," Hyperion Codex said. "We will adjourn then and reconvene tomorrow. In my estimation, Great Leviathan will agree to the plan. Thus, have the package ready, Enigmach. Tomorrow, we will discuss the best way to unleash the assembled assault fleets against Star Watch, as I'm sure that will be next on the agenda."

"Agreed," Enigmach said.

"I look forward to the discussion," Tactix added.

"Very well," Hyperion Codex said, "until then, my good Grand Strategists, a pleasant day to you each."

-2-

Great Leviathan accepted the proposal. Enigmach sent the needed message to his subordinates, and time passed.

Months later, Senior Dax of the Leviathan Space Intelligence Service (LSIS) met with the High Visionary of the Spacer Third Fleet.

Dax had traveled from Loggia in the Scutum-Centaurus Spiral Arm to the double star, Gamma Andromedae, in the Orion Spiral Arm. The star system was approximately 350 light years from Earth. The trip had taken several months via Builder Nexuses such as those the Commonwealth employed and then simple Laumer-Point jumping.

Dax had arrived in the Gamma Andromedae System in three *Kraken*-class warships. They were midsized in Leviathan terms but large in Star Watch terms, as they were similar in tonnage to *Conqueror*-class battleships. The *Krakens* were teardrop-shaped with iridium-Z hull plating. Each carried a complement of cyborg troopers, along with Leviathan state-of-the-art beam and missile weaponry. In a hangar bay, the newest ship held an extremely rare phase-ship of ancient and alien design.

Interestingly, no one in Leviathan or the Commonwealth knew how to build such a phase-shifting vessel. Leviathan scientists had tried taking a phase-ship apart before, and ended up disappearing with the vessel. Since then, no Leviathan technical expert had attempted that again. This phase-ship was one of three and nearly on the verge of breakdown. It was the reason Great Leviathan had agreed to letting it leave the Scutum-Centaurus Spiral Arm and go on loan to the Spacers.

Senior Dax had also brought a set of Phantasma Synth Crystals encased in a distinctive, elaborately designed wooden box. The crystals and phase-ship were still aboard the *Python,* the name of the newest *Kraken*-class warship.

Dax had arrived in the star system four days ago. The system had two stars, three gas giants and ten moons. It housed forty-three percent of the Spacer Third Fleet. Most of those were home ships: massive, square vessels holding Spacer families, factories and food-processing plants.

Spacers did not colonize planets or moons, but lived aboard starships their entire lives if they could. They were a nomadic culture composed of fleets. In this instance, a fleet was akin to a nation or world, or even a group of worlds. The combined fleets were the Spacer Nation. Some fleets were legendary. Some had been lost in the mists of time. Some fleets had split like a colony of bees, each following its own queen.

In these instances, a fleet had its high visionary, always a matriarch and usually one who possessed psionic abilities of some kind.

Dax knew these things about the Spacers and the Third Fleet. He was an impressive and important LSIS agent, one with a superior service record and with a direct link to Loggia. That allowed Dax an independent posting, which meant he had no overseer in LSIS but reported directly to Grand Strategist Enigmach.

However, Dax did have LSIS personnel under him.

At the moment, Dax walked with the High Visionary Zenya. She was an old crone, a little less than five feet tall. She had a dark, wrinkled face like a raisin and wore a billowing robe. She wore a blue turban, had piercing dark eyes and used a cane so she could hobble along the corridors. Following behind were Spacer fighting clones in tightfitting garments and carrying blasters. Each clone wore black-tinted goggles, as did Zenya.

There was no accompanying cyborg trooper in evidence for the Leviathan representative.

Dax had forgone that in the interest of convincing High Visionary Zenya to the plan. The troopers terrified humans, and for good reason. Cyborg troopers were among the deadliest combatants in existence. Almost all humans found them unnerving.

Dax towered over Zenya, as he was of a height with the fighting clones. He did not have their bulk or full sets of hair, although Dax was much heavier and considerably stronger than any of them.

Dax, a cyber, wore scarlet garments and boots. He was lean and made the slightest hissing, mechanical noises as his limbs moved. There were metal pieces to his face, including a metal nose, as the fleshly one had been burned away years ago. The eye sockets were black plastic and the eyeballs stainless steel with tiny red ports or pupils.

His brain and several other organs were completely biological. That did not include the heart and kidneys. He also had several cyber organs, one of which secreted various drugs that could heighten his intelligence, quicken his reflexes, and alter his time sense.

Dax possessed a senso-mask, which he would put on if he were attempting to integrate with unsuspecting humans. This was not such a moment.

Dax had undergone various Leviathan and LSIS mental regimens. He had greater use of his brain than most and amplified ambitions. Grand Strategist Enigmach had altered those ambitions. In most LSIS operatives, the motivations propelled him in the greater service of Leviathan, dying if necessary for the greater good of the Sovereign Hierarchy. Enigmach had nudged that so Dax wanted greater good for himself. Thus, Dax worked tirelessly to increase his status by succeeding at everything he did.

Enigmach had a belief concerning that, and Senior Dax was one of his prized test subjects concerning the matter.

"If you would care to examine the possibilities," Zenya said in her hoarse whisper.

"I would appreciate that." Dax's voice had a robotic quality, although there were slight alterations in pitch if one listened closely enough. When he wore a senso-mask, he had an artificial larynx set on his throat to change that.

Zenya raised a shaking arm and pointed down a new corridor.

The group turned that way, Zenya thumping her cane and tottering. She wheezed the entire time, a rather ghastly performance.

"Would you not rather use a sedan chair?" asked Dax.

"No, no," Zenya wheezed, "I can walk just fine. Thank you for asking."

Dax filed that away, wondering what the old bitch was trying to prove. He noticed her side-glance. It didn't bother him much although Dax was aware she analyzed him. He even understood that she had a psionic gift in that regard. Did such a gift work against a cyber? He suspected it might, as his brain was biological. The drugs altering his brain might change some of that, however.

A double hatch opened as Zenya led them into a large chamber. It proved to be a small theater with cushioned seats.

"We'll use the front row," Zenya said.

The crone hobbled there and chose the middle seat, crashing back into it.

Dax sat beside her, servos whining softly. He noticed that she held the cane in her lap so the end aimed at him.

One of his pupils dilated as he analyzed that. The cane functioned as a weapon, specifically a beam weapon. Would she dare to burn him down as they sat together? He would likely resist such an assault long enough to kill everyone in the chamber. He could kill with his artificial hands and feet, not even using his inbuilt weaponry.

"Show us," Zenya whispered.

A curtain rose on the stage. Five female beauties dressed in scanty attire stood at attention. They were ranged from shortest to tallest. Several had dark hair, one blonde and the other brunette. None was of Spacer origin.

Dax understood that part, as almost all Spacers were of Earth South East Asian origin.

"Given your specifications, these are the best operatives for the mission." Zenya snapped her fingers.

One of the fighting clones approached Dax, handing him a tablet.

Dax accepted it and began to scroll and read the service records of each woman. He stopped at the one named Venna McGrath. Those in Star Watch and the Throne World knew her as Venna the Spy. She had the longest list of achievements. One of them included a stint on the Library Planet. She had captured the Emperor of the New Men there, bringing him to the Supreme Intelligence before escaping in a dramatic fashion.

Dax showed the tablet to Zenya, pointing to the name.

"Venna is my oldest agent," Zenya said.

Dax looked at the tallest woman on the stage. That was Venna McGrath and was without a doubt the most beautiful and alluring of the five. She was curvaceous and—

The pupils in Dax's metal orbs dilated. He no longer possessed sex organs, having lost them on a mission fifteen years ago. That had been the most harrowing of his missions. It was after that that Grand Strategist Enigmach had made Dax the private offer and altered his ambitions.

Despite Dax's lack of sex organs, something about Venna McGrath stirred him.

Each of the females was in a semi-hypnotic state, not quite aware of what transpired. Yet, the way Venna presented herself, the slight tilt of a hip—

"Are you enhancing Venna's sex appeal?" Dax asked in his robotic voice.

Zenya gave him the barest side-glance. "What do you observe?"

"No," Dax said. "I asked a question. I prefer an answer rather than some weird subtly given as a question."

Zenya nodded. "Venna is the most sexual and sensual of the candidates. She is also the oldest by a considerable margin."

"I notice that none on stage is Spacer born," Dax said.

"Of course not," Zenya said, as if insulted.

"Is that because Spacers are not as beautiful as others?"

Zenya glared at him. That was evident despite her black-tinted goggles. "That is a racial slur. I demand you retract it."

"I retract nothing as it was a question, nothing more."

"You have offended me. None is as beautiful as Spacer females. That is clearly true."

"Your so-called offense is mere subterfuge," Dax said. "I will not let it sway me. Besides, it is all beside the point. None of the beauties up there is a Spacer. Is there a reason for that?"

Zenya stared at him. "There is a reason," she said finally. "We prefer to use others in these matters."

Dax nodded. "I perceive your point. Am I correct in thinking that you prefer to use hypnotic inducements in your agents rather than trusting in their judgment?"

"That is so."

"Is this always the case?" asked Dax.

"We have found it to be the wiser method," Zenya said.

"Yet, according to Venna's record, she trained other Intelligence operatives not so long ago."

"Yes. I had thought to retire her from active service. Venna is highly trained and superior in every way. She also has a gift in training others. This mission, however, is of supreme importance. And this irregularity of the crystals troubles me."

"Do you say this because of your hypnotic methods?" asked Dax.

Zenya fully faced him. "I do foresee possible problems. What do you think?"

"The hypnotism you routinely employ might create a situation at the wrong moment," Dax admitted.

"Do believe enough of a problem so we should change our method this time?"

"I wouldn't go that far," Dax said. "If you compensate for the hypnotism, that should prove enough."

"Compensate in what manner?" asked Zenya.

"Well... Do you believe Venna has enough motivation to see the mission through no matter what happens to her?"

"We give her the motivation."

"I understand," Dax said. "I mean if she were to break the hypnotic conditioning?"

Zenya became thoughtful. "The actual Venna hates the New Men, as she has good reason for that. This mission is against Star Watch... For those reasons, I wouldn't want her to break her conditioning."

"Tell me about the other candidates."

Zenya did so in detail.

At last, Dax contemplated the choices. He studied the females, his gaze lingering on Venna.

"Her," he said at last. "Venna McGrath is the one."

Zenya was quiet for a time with her brows furrowed.

Dax wondered if the High Visionary used her psionic talents on him, to see if she could understand his reasoning better.

"I agree," Zenya said at last.

"I would like to be kept abreast of her training. I will also have to instruct her in the use of the crystals."

"Yes," Zenya said.

It was at that point Senior Dax began to believe that his highly secret personal plan, one apart from Enigmach's instructions, had a chance of succeeding.

-3-

Surprisingly, Dax was privy to the Spacer Third Fleet Intelligence methods in preparing Venna McGrath. He wondered about that.

After a day of prep work, operatives readied Venna for the main motivational infusion. A Spacer adept used deep hypnotics to place Venna in a trance state. Female operatives then removed her garments. Afterward, they attached adhesive pads to her skin and carefully inserted wires that pierced her optic nerves. Another settled a breathing mask over her mouth and nose. Then, they placed a naked Venna in a tank of pale blue liquid.

She floated on the surface with the various wires attached to her. After several electronic pulses, Venna sank until she floated submerged in the middle of the tank.

A team of operators sat at banks of panels and monitors. The main adept placed an induction helmet over her head. The helmet completely covered her head and face. An antenna on top sparked with power.

"You are thorough," Dax said to no one in particular.

"If you will watch the main screen, sir," a second adept told Dax.

Dax glanced at the small Spacer. She wore black-tinted goggles and had a buzz cut on her round head. She also had various circuits hidden inside her. He could sense them. Did those circuits make her a cyber? The thought amused Dax.

A moment later, the tall cyber shifted his stance as he watched the main screen.

Now began a lengthy question and answer process. The adept with the induction helmet asked Venna a blizzard of questions. The spy answered with mumbles from within her breathing mask. A printout of both sets of words appeared on the main screen.

From this, Dax learned a little more about Venna's childhood and teenage years. She had been born on the first continent on the planet Thebes, which was in the Franco System, the Third Quadrant of the Commonwealth. The New Men had conquered it years ago and kidnapped tens of thousands of females, a teenage Venna McGrath among them. This had been during the counterattack by Star Watch's Fifth Fleet under Admiral Fletcher when Maddox had assisted.

Later, a highly ranked New Man had chosen Venna for inclusion in his harem.

Venna was one of those lucky few to have escaped New Men captivity. This was three years after entering the harem. The escape was a harrowing tale that involved courageous acts by Star Watch personnel. A pair of Spacer saucer-ships had hijacked the hauler taking freed captives back to the Commonwealth. The captives had soon found themselves as part of the Spacer Third Fleet. The prettiest and smartest had been inducted into the Spacer Intelligence Service, Venna the best of them.

A sharp line of inquiry from the adept now caused Venna to thrash and jerk in the tank.

The adept wearing the induction helmet spoke a litany of words.

Venna thrashed even more.

You must relax, Venna. You are among friends, remember?

Dax read the adept's words on the main screen. He'd been doing that for some time.

I want to go home.

Dax read those words as well. They were Venna's reply to the adept.

Sphinx, ten, cloudy day, saints, go to sleep.

Venna ceased thrashing in the tank as her shoulders slumped and her masked head fell forward. Behind the mask's glass, her eyes closed.

The adept with the induction helmet shifted in her chair.

Wake up.

The body in the tank stiffened. The eyes flashed open.

Can you hear me, Venna?

Yes.

Tell me about the time at Pharos 4.

I infiltrated a prostitute ring run by a crime syndicate in the spaceport of Cheops. The crime lord was an operative from the Throne World's secret service. I became the number one woman until Lord Mao arrived. He was a Throne World agent running a clandestine money laundering operation on Vega. I drugged him during our lovemaking session and began to load him into a waiting air car. His New Men protection team arrived, firing at us. I lost an arm during the escape.

From the air car, you brought Lord Mao to a waiting saucer-ship in the stratosphere.

The arm regrow didn't take right. They had to amputate it and regrow another. That took a full year and a half.

Your new arm has worked well ever since.

I want to go home.

Skip to age 34.

Venna spoke, her words on the screen: *Did you know that during winter, the grass is green back home on Thebes? My betrothed will be hunting horses in the high ranges. I plan to give him a surprise visit.*

Plaster, tango, six, honeycomb—skip to age 34.

Once more, Venna's words appeared on the screen: *The hawks in the high ranges are spectacular. My father used to take me hawking. My betrothed will likely do the same.*

Sphinx, ten, cloudy day, saints, go to sleep.

Once more, Venna's shoulders slumped in the tank as her head moved forward and her eyes closed.

The adept took off the induction helmet, blinking bloodshot eyes and massaging her forehead.

"What is the problem?"

Dax and the adept, everyone but for Venna, looked up at a walkway. The High Visionary watched from the balcony there. Zenya had asked the question.

"Venna is resisting the process," the adept said, who slid on a pair of black-tinted goggles.

"Do you know why?" Zenya asked.

The adept nodded.

"Well?" asked Zenya. "Tell me. I don't care for your posturing."

"Venna sustains a deep moral wound, refusing to part with it," the adept said.

"Is it the same wound as before?" asked Zenya.

"We've overlaid and thus suppressed that moral wound," the adept said, sidestepping the question. "But it hasn't taken. This is unwarranted due to her stubbornness. I still say we should retire Venna for good."

Zenya shifted her head, staring at Dax. "Do you hear that?"

"My auditory circuits are fully functional," Dax said.

Zenya's lips twisted as if sucking on a lemon. Perhaps her old fingers clutched the rail more tightly. She shook her head the slightest bit, those signals ceasing. "Is this truly the agent we should risk employing the crystals, given the stakes at play?" Zenya asked in a level tone.

Dax nodded. This was even better than he had expected. Fate was helping him. Who would have ever guessed that?

"Given this is the case," the adept said, "we may need to use a stronger overlay on her personality."

"Is that good with you, sir?" Zenya asked.

"I do not understand the problem," Dax said.

"A stronger personality overlay could create a mental rebound," the adept said. "That might crush Venna's psyche if it weighs on her too heavily or if she's pushed for too long."

"What are the odds that will happen?" Dax said.

"I would give it a one in four chance," the adept said.

Dax shrugged. "If you must do this, you must. The risk is acceptable to me."

"You heard the cyber," Zenya told the adept. "Condition Venna to the best pitch possible. Then, you will start adding the knowledge to her that Senior Dax will give you."

The adept nodded, glanced at Dax, removed her goggles and then slid the induction helmet back over her head.

Wake up, Venna.

In the tank, Venna stirred and opened her eyes.

I have some new information for you. Are you ready to receive it?

There seemed to be a moment of hesitation on Venna's part.

Dax expected to hear more talk about winter and home again. Instead, Venna surprised them all.

I am ready.

Excellent. Now, repeat after me…

As the others at their monitors added electric pulses to the words, and different others added chemical inducements to the blue solution, the adept began the next level of hypnotic training to Venna McGrath.

Dax filed it all away. He would join the insertion team to Earth, which would use the phase-ship from Leviathan. Venna would learn to use the Phantasma Synth Crystals, and through them assassinate the Lord High Admiral and a few choice others in Star Watch.

Dax grinned, revealing titanium teeth. This was proceeding to plan, to Enigmach's plan and to Dax's secret own. The Spacer Intelligence Arm was a grim reminder that humans were supremely opportunistic and ruthless in using each other. That knowledge might come in handy someday.

Venna paused in the tank.

Everyone in the chamber grew still.

Then, after a moment, Venna moved normally and the training continued.

-4-

Driving Force Galyan floated through the lonely corridors of Starship *Victory* as a holographic image from his projector in the armored center of the vessel.

Victory was in Mid-Earth Orbit, along with a myriad of other Star Watch vessels. Each had a skeleton maintenance crew and was full of weapons and energy. They were part of the reserve fleet Star Watch kept near Earth so it could jump to any point in the Commonwealth through the Builder Nexus nearby. Maddox had brought that Nexus from the Library Planet some time ago. It was now between Earth and the Moon and could create a hyper-spatial tube to just about anywhere in a radius of several thousand light-years. *Victory* had been in the reserves for over a year, ever since it had come back from its latest mission, one that had led into Underspace.

Throughout that time, Galyan had wandered the corridors or stood at viewing ports, though he didn't need to stand there. He could automatically use all the ship's sensors, as they were linked to him. It was his ship after all. Even with all the modifications, by design it was an ancient Adok vessel, one he had loaned to Star Watch.

Galyan was a holoimage of an alien Adok, a small humanoid with ropy arms and stringy fingers. He was a deified AI. That meant his copied engrams of the living Galyan from six thousand years ago had been impressed upon the ship's main AI core. Driving Force was his military title from his days as a living Adok.

With a powerful ship sensor, Galyan watched Captain Maddox water skiing on Lake Tahoe near his home in Nevada Sector. Maddox was with Meta his wife, his daughter Jewel, and with Keith and Valerie.

That was nice.

Despite Galyan's being an AI, a deified AI, he had emotions after a fashion. He yearned to project himself in ghost form and listen to what the others were saying. That would be against the captain's regulations, however.

Oh, look, Valerie was laughing as she shouted at Meta to slow the boat. Maddox had fallen off his skis into the water. It was good to see Valerie laugh. She was far too serious most of the time. Where she and Keith back together again? When had that happened?

Galyan did not sigh because despite his emotions he was a holoimage, not physically real. He did feel a little guilty. Not only wasn't he supposed to go down there in ghost form, the captain didn't like him spying on them.

They should have invited me. I am here, alone with nothing to do. Do they not know I get lonely?

Galyan made a face. His face had many lines in it, and they became more pronounced when he scowled like this. He not only possessed emotions after a fashion but had self-awareness.

How could a computer entity like him feel lonely? Why, he could play millions of computer games. He could check any record about anything he wanted. He shouldn't feel emotions like living, breathing people. He did not have glands that secreted biological agents into his body. Once, long ago, he'd had genuine emotions. What he was feeling…

Galyan turned away and continued to float through the empty ship corridors. As he did, he worked on old problems, soon finding himself thinking about the Glenna Nebula that held other Adok deified AIs like him. Unfortunately, those AIs had gone mad. *Victory* had barely shown up in time to save the last living Adoks left in the universe. The mad AIs had been trying to eliminate them.

Galyan had been instrumental in saving the last of his people. Yet, because the living Adoks had learned terror of deified AIs, they shunned him.

Why will the living Adoks not accept me? Do they not realize I am different from those others?

Galyan frowned. He did not like the whiny note he heard in his thoughts. That was unbecoming. He should be grateful for what he had, not pine for what he lacked. Gratitude helped one find peace.

Even though he had been sentient far longer than the deified AIs in the Glenna Nebula, he had not gone mad. Had his very loneliness all those thousands of years kept his circuits sane? He had guarded the shattered Adok homeworld for six thousand years, missing his lost wife and friends all the while.

What strange thoughts these were. He had gone over all this before. Why should he bother with the same old thoughts yet again?

Galyan smiled sadly. "I am what I am," he said aloud. Besides, most people worried about the same things for years upon years, seldom changing. Did that mean he was in a rut?

Galyan's eyelids flickered as a ship alarm activated. He concentrated on an exotic sensor that Professor Ludendorff had modified some time ago. This was strange. Galyan noted a bizarre blip.

He focused on the sensor and concentrated on an area of space a little beyond Mid-Earth Orbit. That was weird. Nothing was there now. The blip had vanished.

Galyan switched to visual teleoptics, scanning the same area. There was still nothing.

Then why did I sense that, or the sensor produce a ping? Was it a glitch? Was it some kind of ghost image?

Galyan ran through his memories, searching for a similar event. This was interesting. He found a match of sorts, well, not a match but a similarity. The blip resembled the glimmer or sputter of a phase unit.

Victory had used a phase device last mission, though it had not survived the journey. With the device, they had entered Underspace

Hmm. Did the blip have anything to do with Underspace or a phase ship?

Galyan checked old logs and ran through hundreds of thousands of pieces of data. Could that have been a cloaked vessel instead of a phase unit? Who might use a cloaked ship here? Methuselah Man Strand had in the past.

Galyan checked records. As far as he knew, Strand was still on the Throne World of the New Men.

If it was not a cloaked ship, what could I have sensed?

Galyan tried a different sensor Professor Ludendorff and he had developed for *Victory*.

It didn't show anything, but Galyan detected a faint pulse of the same nature by the other exotic sensor. This time, the blip was closer to Earth than before. As before, the blip disappeared.

Galyan analyzed the two blips. If Captain Maddox had demanded an explanation, Galyan would give this the highest probability: that what the sensors had witnessed was a discharge of energy from a faulty phase unit. No other explanation came close to what the data showed.

The blips had been in different places. Did that indicate a trajectory by a phase ship?

Galyan waited, waited, expanding the width of his search—he detected another faint blip. This one came from Low-Earth Orbit. Given the time between blips and how long it had taken for the first two blips... The third blip matched given a constant speed by this supposed phase ship.

With growing excitement, Galyan mapped out the three points, mentally drawing a line along them, conjecturing where whatever caused the blips had originated. This was interesting. The line went back to a nearby Laumer Point that connected to the Barnard's Star System.

Had an alien stealth vessel or alien phase ship arrived through the Laumer Point?

Understanding the importance of his find, Galyan used *Victory's* entire array of sensors. He didn't pick up any trace or ion trails.

Ah! He detected another blip with the original exotic sensor. Matching this blip with the other three, it was obvious a ship with a faulty phase unit headed for Earth.

Four blips like this was too many for a computer glitch or error. He had sensed something.

What do I do about this? What is my responsibility?

Should he tell Captain Maddox? Should he inform Star Watch? He knew Maddox would not appreciate an interruption. Thus—

I will use regular channels. I will follow procedure.

It was then Galyan realized it was good to be doing something. This was much better than moping about as he aimlessly wandered the ship corridors.

He contacted a satellite sensor operator, gave his information and listened to the acknowledgment.

To make sure, Galyan eavesdropped with the starship's electronic warfare gear. The operator passed the information along. Soon, the entire Earth Defense Net scanned for cloaked vessels. They did not spot anything. Galyan would have been surprised if they had. He had told the operator this was a phase ship, not a cloaked vessel. Unfortunately, those of Earth had never dealt with phase ships before. Should he correct them?

As Galyan debated the idea, he did not find any more faint blips. Could the phase ship have entered the planetary mass?

He decided to scan the Earth's vast array of news channels. If anything untoward or strange happened, he would contact Captain Maddox about his findings. Two oddities would be enough to engage the captain's interest.

One interesting thing to all this was that the anticipation of action drove off some of Galyan's loneliness.

I need to be doing things. That is the key to existence.

Galyan could hardly wait until the next mission. He wanted his humans to return to the starship so he could interact with them.

When will we go on another mission?

After a time, Galyan decided to continue working on the problem of the mad, deified Adok AIs in the Glenna Nebula. Perhaps he could solve the dilemma, understanding why they had gone mad. He would do that so he could forestall it ever happening to him. He did not want to attack what he loved. No. That would be awful.

-5-

Venna the Spy sauntered down a summer sidewalk of midtown Lyon in France Sector. Streetlights provided illumination since the sun had already set. She wore a tight red skirt with heels that accentuated her legs and ass, along with a daringly low-cut blouse that showed off her wonderful cleavage. Her hair was up, and she wore dark sunglasses and carried a small, glittering purse.

As Venna walked, many men turned in admiration. A few whistled. One catcalled.

The faintest of smiles appeared on Venna's painted lips. She was on a mission but couldn't quite recall how she had gotten to Earth. There was a faint memory…

Venna shrugged. If she needed to, she could press a device in the purse. Then she would be able to leave Earth.

Venna couldn't quite remember the methods of arrival or departure. Apparently, it was important she not know. She understood that she was a spy, and on a desperate mission dear to her heart.

Venna looked up at the stars, as she was between streetlights and it was a cloudless night. She pinpointed a star she thought of as Thebes.

When she finished the mission, she would go to Thebes to find her betrothed. They would go hawking in the mountains. They would each have a large hawk. They would chase the great hares of the high plains and maybe go after some of the red foxes.

The smile disappeared. Venna shook her head. She could think about that later. For now—she put something extra in the way her hips moved and added to the languid motion of her body.

Men certainly noticed, more than before. At this, Venna was the best in the Orion Spiral Arm.

If needed, she had an extra device, a red necklace. If she put it on and switched the necklace to active, men's lusts would increase tenfold. They would become putty in her hands, ready to fight to the death to possess her. Men were so gullible in this regard, so predictable.

Venna doubted she would need the necklace. She had used it on New Men, who were different from these easily duped Earthmen. She knew her skills, her alluring power. No one on Earth was like her. She would use her gifts, her charms, and her spite because she hated the horrible Lord High Admiral Cook.

Years ago, Cook had ordered warships against the planet Thebes. He had sent butchers from Star Watch down to the surface. Marines with pulse rifles had beamed down her family. She had barely escaped the massacre. Venna remembered the incident as if it happened yesterday. She'd hid in the barn under the old, overturned boat. She had seen such wicked things. Those with Star Watch insignia had chased down her father, mother and brothers. With their pulse rifles, the marines shattered their knees first so they would fall. Then the cruel marines beamed their arms so they were helpless. Her father, mother and brothers died in such a vile manner.

Lord High Admiral Cook—Venna could see him in her memories. Cook had been laughing, nodding and pointing during the wretched massacre. He hadn't been old then, although he'd been big with his oaken, steady features.

How had such a monster ever achieved his exalted status in Star Watch? That was beyond Venna's comprehension.

None of that mattered tonight. She wasn't going to think about hawking with her beloved. She was not going to think about Thebes or about her lost family.

"I miss them," Venna whispered, almost on the verge of tears.

Did the heartfelt words trigger something in her? An overriding compulsion forced the memories from her. She wanted to think about her family, about Cook. She couldn't see his features anymore.

Was that important? It must be. And yet—

"Cook!" Venna snarled, her extreme beauty twisted with rage.

She halted and worked to conceal her rage. Once accomplished, she hurried to the largest nightclub in Lyon. She attempted to pay the entrance fee. The man on guard waved her through.

"Have a good time, babe," he said.

Venna gave him a saucy smile as she passed. Soon she was on the dance floor, dancing with this man, that man, accepting one drink and accepting another.

Venna had taken an alcohol inhibitor earlier so she wouldn't become drunk. She used the ladies' room a few times to rid herself of the excess liquids passing through her body.

She danced with seeming abandon and provocative movements. As she did, she studied the men with a logic that escaped her conscious mind. She was using the hypnotic, Spacer-induced unconscious mind. Finally, she sensed a candidate, one with possible hyper-energy, a tall, athletic man, a Berber with a gold chain around his throat. She didn't know how she knew this about him, but she felt knew she should confirm this.

Venna pulled a tiny device from her purse, aimed it at the swarthy Berber and pressed a switch. The indicator flashed green, a match. He possessed the needed energy.

Now began the easy art of his seduction. Venna bumped into him as if by accident. He appraised her with his dark eyes. She spoke shyly, asking his forgiveness. He grinned.

Venna didn't need to use her red necklace, which would have activated his deepest lust. That was good because the necklace's process could have caused interruptions later.

Venna soon laughed as their fingers touched. They danced, and he plied her with drink. She laughed more and whispered in his ear. By the end of the evening, they left the nightclub and climbed into in a taxi, flying to his apartment.

"Will you come in?" he said.

"Yes," she said.

Venna had already picked up an ornate wooden box the length of a computer keyboard. The wooden box was heavier than it looked.

He cocked his head when she brought it with them.

"You'll enjoy this," she said.

Sure," he said, "I'm sure I will."

They rode a turbo lift to his floor, moved down a corridor and went up into his apartment. There he began his art of seduction, taking off pieces of her clothing, and then his.

"Wait," she said, "I can make this more alluring for you."

"Oh?" he said, his eyes shining with anticipation.

She went to the wooden box, picked it up and set it on a nightstand. She raised the cover. Within were two inert crystals half the size of his fist. Each had a rocky texture.

"Take one," Venna said.

He picked up the nearest and hefted it in his hand. "It's heavy," he said.

"Isn't it though? Now repeat after me."

"Come on, babe. We don't need these rocks. Let's just get to it. Hop into bed, why don't you?"

"Oh, we will get to it," Venna smiled so seductively that his eyes widened and brightened. He nodded. She spoke. He repeated the odd litany she told him to say. Each held up a Phantasma Synth Crystal. Suddenly, both the rocky texture crystals glowed.

"Touch your crystal to mine," Venna said breathlessly.

Surprised but willing, he moved his crystal toward hers.

Venna's secret training took over, the training she'd received in the tank of a special operative ship in the Spacer Third Fleet.

The crystals touched and flared with greater light, although hers dimmed immediately. The glow from his crystal bled out and spread to his hands. He grunted as the glow shot along hit arms to his chest. He looked at her with alarm. He might have tried to shout. Instead, the vibrant, energetic sacrifice grew rigid. He toppled and thudded frozen onto the floor.

Venna realized that she was laughing, as she continued to chant an ancient litany created long ago by the Aetharian shamans who had fashioned these horrid crystals.

Now began a grim process as Venna, through the crystals, used the man's etheric energy, a process that literally consumed his bodily form as it killed him.

-6-

The Berber who had joined Venna in his apartment was a shriveled husk, weighing a tenth of what he had. He did not resemble a human but rather a charred length of wood. All but one tooth had been crisped. That one gleamed in his stick-like remains. Above him, a ghostly shape shimmered, composed of seemingly shifting patterns.

Venna held both Phantasma Synth Crystals as if her life depended on them, which it did. If she set down the crystals, the energetic ghost thing would devour her.

She squeezed her eyes tight and fought for control of his etheric energy. As she did, the crystals shook in her hands. Both crystals glowed blue, the glow bleeding into her hands and up her wrists.

Venna squeezed her eyes even tighter. She strove to control the mystic energy, unique to planet Earth. There had not been anything like this for thousands of years, and never on Earth.

Abruptly, the shifting pattern of energy produced two eye slits. They opened, revealing swirling chaos instead of pupils.

Although Venna's eyes were closed, she saw through those eyes. This was working. She could do this. She could make Lord High Admiral Cook pay after all these years. He would now rue his murderous spree on Thebes. He would pay the ultimate price for his evil.

With the training she had received from Senior Dax and the Spacer adepts, Venna gained control of the etheric energy. First, she dimmed it and then sent it flying across the countryside, heading unerringly for Star Watch Headquarters in Geneva, Switzerland Sector.

The journey took four minutes and thirty-one seconds. The ghostly image penetrated the most secure place on planet Earth until it reached Lord High Admiral Cook's office.

Old Cook in his white admiral's uniform spoke to a secretary. Neither of them saw the ghost, even though the energy's eyes were open, and Venna saw through them. Cook dismissed the secretary. She exited the office, closing the door behind her.

Venna could barely control her laughter, rage and glee. Deep inside her welled a sense of shame, but she didn't know why she should feel shame. She hadn't done anything wrong. Maybe she'd lured the Berber to his death—

Wait!

Venna through the energy saw that Cook was rising from his desk. Because of that, panic took over in Venna. As it did, her training took over. Through force of will, she compelled the etheric energy to flitter over and encompass Cook's head. In a moment, the energy did so.

Cook's eyes flew open with astonishment. The old bastard tried to suck air, but it seemed he could not now. As big and old as he was, Cook clawed frantically at the bizarre alien energy encompassing his head like some space helmet. He was choking, trying to inhale. He tried to claw fistfuls of that stuff from him. However, it hardened, preventing his fingers from penetrating the foggy form.

Admiral Cook heard feminine laughter and then words:

"Know that I'm repaying you, Lord High Admiral Cook, for killing my family on Thebes."

"What? What?" he said.

Venna heard Cook's thoughts. It was due to the strange, etheric form that was killing Cook through suffocation.

"I never did that. You are wrong about this."

"You're a liar!" Venna screamed in the apartment in Lyons. "You're a liar and a thief of life. I'm killing you. You're going to die for your evil crimes."

Venna held on to the crystals and then forced the etheric projection that remained over the head of Lord High Admiral

Cook of Star Watch to its final action. The old man's eyes bulged in a grotesque fashion. His tongue protruded from his mouth, and he ceased breathing. As he did, the old man of Star Watch toppled onto the floor as his boot heels drummed upon the carpet. Then he became inert.

Venna still held on to make sure Admiral Cook was dead, dead, dead.

The door to his office opened. The secretary stepped in, stared in horror and screamed in a shrill and horrific fashion.

Venna released her hold on the energy. The ghostly form immediately dissipated and then disappeared as if it had never existed. The last thing Venna heard was the screaming secretary.

Seconds passed and Venna came to herself in the apartment in Lyon. She stared at the two inert crystals in her hands. She stared at the crisp and shriveled body of the Berber who had fed the crystals the power to do this.

Venna exhaled. She had assassinated the Lord High Admiral of Star Watch.

After swallowing several times, Venna put on her clothes, her high heels, and the crystals in the box. She slid the lid back over, as she whispered an inhuman litany. Even though a great weariness settled on her, Venna forced herself out the door and down the hall to the turbo lift.

She had three more people to assassinate. She had started with the most important. Now…

I could sleep for a week, I'm so tired.

Venna staggered out of the apartment complex, leaving the scene of a terrible crime. She had to return to her place and prepare for the next kill.

-7-

Senior Dax of LSIS watched on a monitor inside the phase ship. The phase ship was deep in an underground cavern, seven miles inside the Earth's crust.

As a phase ship in ghost form, it could slide through solid rock, through solid anything, really. But once it returned to solidified form, it could only occupy easily displaced air or vacuum.

Dax and the Spacer adept in charge of the phase ship, or theoretically in charge, deemed it wise to hide inside the Earth like this so the planetary crust shielded them.

Dax was sitting at a panel in the phase-ship control chamber. He studied the data from the tracker that Spacer Intelligence had planted in Venna's purse.

There were seventeen personnel in the ship, one of them a cyborg trooper. Dax had switched off the trooper for now in the interest of Spacer morale.

Dax debated teleporting the trooper onto the Earth. He did so out of boredom, because it would be a senseless maneuver. Watching humans react to the trooper might relieve his tedium, but it would hurt the greater plan and was thus a foolish idea.

Dax manipulated the controls as he concentrated on the present task.

It had been three days since the death of the Lord High Admiral. Star Watch had kept it out of the general news, but there were hints if one knew where to look. For one thing, Maddox was no longer on vacation.

Did the captain help search for the murderer?

According to Dax's studies on Earth culture, the authorities would soon have a grand funeral for the old man. Perhaps the political people were devising the best method of letting the populace know what had happened. It would likely be a tricky dilemma for them.

A beep sounded from the panel as Dax connected with the tracker. Through it, he studied Venna.

She was still sleeping. That was three days straight now. The psychic drain from using the alien crystals— Dax checked a different sensor. Ah. The crystals had drained some of Venna's life force. Grand Strategist Enigmach had foreseen that, but hadn't been sure how much life force the crystals would drain. This was twenty-seven percent more drainage than the Grand Strategist had calculated. Venna likely didn't understand the reason for her exhaustion—if she'd even woken up since originally lying down. If the crystals continued at this rate of drainage, Venna might not be able to make all four kills.

After a moment, Dax shook his head.

That wasn't the point now. She could likely kill again. Thus, he needed to recalibrate the crystals and check the woman to see when she could assassinate next. The sooner the better, as remaining here for long in the phase ship was questionable.

Dax checked the kill list. The next target would be Brigadier Stokes of Star Watch Intelligence.

Dax sat back, thinking. The tracker was small and couldn't make all the needed checks. He should go to her room. Enigmach had warned him about the likely need for recalibrating the crystals after each assault. After this first kill, he needed to check the crystals to see how far they had deteriorated. These were ancient crystals, possibly lacking their former sharpness.

Dax rose and approached the adept in charge, Mu 11, a Surveyor-class adept with several hidden Builder devices or modifications inside her. She was potentially dangerous, with devices that could attack his main cyber implements, shutting him down, or partly so. She was small with short dark hair, the ubiquitous black-tinted goggles and abnormally stubby fingers. Dax had found her to be a tough-minded Spacer adept.

"Mu 11," Dax said.

She turned around to regard him.

"It is imperative that I go to Venna's room in Lyon," he said.

Mu 11 frowned. "That is an unwarranted request. You are here as an observer. The phase ship is under my control and Venna is a Spacer agent. If anyone should go to Lyon, it's me. Besides, you would be spotted almost immediately and thereby ruin everything."

"Untrue as to the latter point. Let me demonstrate." Dax turned aside, took out and put on his senso mask and larynx adjuster. When he turned back and spoke, Mu 11 shook her head.

"I doubt that will fool anyone who looks closely," she said, "but you might be able to slip through crowds if you don't bring attention to yourself. I still do not agree to your leaving the ship."

"It's imperative that I recharge the crystals and check the woman."

"Venna is our woman, our agent. As to the crystals—you have point. I will join you in Lyon."

"I appreciate your help," Dax said. "However, our both going strikes me as foolish. You are nearly as distinctive as I am. Together…I ask you to reconsider. Besides, our both going would require too much energy to teleport the extra mass."

"Your mass is already too much," Mu 11 said. "With all the added metal and plastics—I should go alone. Perhaps you can instruct me in recalibrating the crystals."

Dax wanted to laugh at this blatant attempt. The Phantasma Synth Crystals were possibly more deadly than the old and faulty phase ship. The vessel wasn't going to last much longer. The crystals—Enigmach had instructed him on the recalibration. The Grand Strategist told him no one else must learn the secrets to them.

Holding his features in check, Dax shook his head. "Your selflessness is noted. However, your handling the crystals would be unwise. If done incorrectly, they will suck your life energy and kill you. I am trained to deal with them. This is my task and mine alone. I have received firm orders from home on this."

Mu 11 looked away.

Dax tried to analyze her reaction. Then, he checked to see if she was using one of her Builder devices against him. It did not seem so.

Mu 11 was surely a highly ranked adept, a Surveyor class with many modifications. He mistrusted her, and knew he had to tread carefully with her. He could all too easily envision an untimely end for himself, with the Spacers declaring that the phase ship and crystals were missing. How could Great Leviathan know the truth? Perhaps it was time to switch on the cyborg trooper. This was a critical mission, particularly for himself. He must be alert to treachery even as he practiced treachery. But he must on all accounts lull Mu 11 and the others.

"According to my home instructions, I must go alone," Dax said, "unless you have further objections."

Mu 11 took her time answering. At last, she looked at him from behind her black-tinted goggles. "I will teleport you myself," she said.

They headed to the teleporting chamber in the middle of the phase ship.

Soon, Dax appeared on Earth in a back alley behind a twenty-story apartment complex in Lyon, France Sector.

The cyber adjusted his senso mask and started for the main thoroughfare. He changed his gait after observing several people hurry past. Twice, others looked sharply at him. He noted the worry in their glances. Each time, Dax aimed a numb-gun at them and pressed the thumb trigger. The numb-gun emitted an invisible ray that dulled their curiosity.

After two blocks, Dax entered the apartment complex, rode a turbo lift to the fourteenth floor, walked down a corridor and stood before a locked door. He made a pass with his left hand, a device in his middle finger buzzing. He opened the door and entered Venna's apartment, closing the door behind him.

She slept as one drugged in her bed.

Dax eyed a smooth and lovely leg carelessly thrust from under the covers. Then he concentrated on the wooden box on a nightstand.

He took the box and walked into the kitchen, setting it on a counter. The crystals might sense her vulnerability if they were too near.

Gingerly, Dax slid off the top, staring at the two crystals. They were inert—

One flared with a blue color.

Dax nearly bolted. Instead, he whipped out the calibrator, which looked like a bulky tuning fork.

As the one crystal continued to brighten, Dax thrust the prongs of the device around the Phantasma Synth Crystal. He made subtle adjustments as instructed by Enigmach.

The blue glow weakened and then disappeared.

Dax breathed a sigh of relief. He likely would have failed with this if one of his synthetic organs hadn't injected him with a calming agent and a stimulant.

Even so, his heart was beating too fast.

Dax breathed deeply and finally manually gave himself a sedative. Soon, his heart beat normally.

With great care, even as his hands shook, Dax recalibrated both crystals. Soon, they were primed for action.

He slid the cover over the wooden box and returned the crystals to the nightstand.

With his servos whining, Dax squatted beside Venna. He took out a hand monitor and checked various brain waves and bodily functions. She wasn't as vibrant as before. He put away the monitor and brought out a small hypogun. He inserted an ampule, moved aside the blanket and pressed the nozzle against her left buttock. The hypogun hissed, injecting her.

Venna twitched and moaned.

Dax pulled the blanket over her form and straightened. That should give her the needed strength and vitality to assassinate Brigadier Stokes.

Given the deterioration from the first kill…would she last long enough to snuff out the Iron Lady next?

He would have to wait and see.

Dax took a last look around, backed out and then exited and relocked the apartment. Soon, he returned to the original back alley and pressed his retrieve button.

Ten seconds passed and nothing happened. Should he press the switch again? Was Mu 11 stranding him on Earth as retaliation for his overriding her?

Then, Dax began to dissipate as he teleported back to the phase ship. Good. Everything was in order. The next assassination should occur in three days.

Events were moving in the required order.

-8-

The next day, Captain Maddox was at home at his ranch near Carson City making breakfast when he received a call from Brigadier Stokes. Then, Maddox heard about the Lord High Admiral's assassination. This was awful and mind numbing. Cook was dead? Stokes assured him that it was so.

Afterward, Maddox took the stairs three at a time, waking Meta and telling her the awful news.

Maddox was a tall, lean, steely muscled individual. Meta was stronger than most men, having been born and raised on a 2G planet. She was also beautifully voluptuous, with long blond hair and stunning features.

In the middle of telling Meta what happened, Galyan appeared in the bedroom.

"Sir—" Galyan said.

Meta whirled around and shouted in alarm, with a knife appearing in her right hand. She had been taking special combat training lately as she had joined *Victory* last mission. She wanted to be included in the next mission, and do more. Thus, she was engaged in extra training.

"Galyan," Maddox said, outraged, "this is a terrible breach of orders. You shouldn't be in here. This is our bedroom."

The knife disappeared from Meta's hand. She attempted to appear nonchalant, as if Galyan hadn't startled her by appearing.

Maddox had stood up quickly at Galyan's appearance, but hadn't shouted in alarm. He was used to the holoimage's abrupt appearance. Never had Galyan appeared in their bedroom, though, and Maddox was fuming.

"I am sorry, sir," Galyan said. "I know this is against orders. But there is a bigger situation at hand."

After a second, Maddox nodded tersely. "Does this have anything to do with the Lord High Admiral?"

"You know it does, sir."

"I take it you've been monitoring my communications."

"I have," Galyan said.

Maddox ran a hand over his face. "You know that's also against orders. Never mind. You're doing what I've been unable to teach Valerie—the moment one should throw orders overboard. This is a catastrophe."

"Disobeying orders is your stock in trade, is it not, sir?" Galyan said.

"Never mind that," Maddox said. "You're here because the Lord High Admiral is dead. Do you have any idea who assassinated him?"

"Indeed, I do, sir," Galyan said, "as I have put several sets of facts together. What I observed in orbit several days ago may have a connection to the Lord High Admiral's death. I cannot be one hundred percent sure, but I think given all that we have—"

"Galyan," Maddox said, cutting through the AI's chatter, "you are being verbose. Now is the time to get to the point. But just a minute; Galyan, come with me."

Maddox walked out of the bedroom into the hall.

Galyan followed.

Maddox turned on him. "Do you understand why I have the rule about your not appearing in my bedroom? Do you realize Meta is wearing almost nothing?"

"I understand, sir. You enjoy being intimate with your wife and do not want anyone catching you in the act. I have noted that you engage in such activities more than most men."

"Galyan," Maddox said, "that's enough of that. This is unwarranted. This is awful. Cook is dead. I can hardly conceive of that. But on top of everything else, I don't want you measuring my proclivities with my wife."

"Should I erase that data from my memories, sir?"

Maddox gave him a shrewd glance. "Would you do it if I ordered it?"

"What if I said yes?" Galyan said.

"Then I'd think that you're practicing the art of lying."

"Yes, sir, I would be lying. There is a reason for that. It would be a crime for me to erase something like that. I have a personality profile on you, and your sexual habits are germane to it. You know I am trying to understand humanity, but most importantly, my humans."

"All right, all right," Maddox said. "This is an annoying conversation." He turned and stared off into space, feeling cold and maybe just a little lost. "I can't believe the Lord High Admiral is gone," he said softly. "It's unhinging."

Meta stepped out of the bedroom, having put on more attire.

Maddox massaged his forehead. On top of missing the old man, he wondered who would run Star Watch now. How would that affect— Maddox cleared his throat, studying Galyan. "I've been woolgathering. This has badly taken me by surprise."

"I can see that, sir. It is not like you."

"I miss the Lord High Admiral already."

"I do too," Meta said.

"Yes," Galyan said. He would like to have said that he missed Admiral Cook as much as they did, but that would not be true. Galyan tried to stick to the truth, at least when he wasn't trying to follow Captain Maddox's example of lying while it gave an appropriate advantage to their side, and while on duty.

Maddox breathed deeply as he sought for the Way of the Pilgrim. For once, he felt at a loss. He breathed again, more deeply, finding some of that calm. He realized Galyan had said something important earlier.

"You said there were more facts," Maddox said. "Tell me about them."

Galyan proceeded to tell Maddox about the four faint blips that had headed deeper toward the Earth. The blips likely came from a faulty phase unit in a ship.

"Wait a minute," Maddox said, "did you analyze these blips, as you are calling them?"

"Are you all right, sir?"

"What?" Maddox said.

"I already told you they were some kind of phase emanation, or from a faulty phase unit."

"You're saying a phase ship entered Earth?"

Galyan stared at Maddox.

"Right," Maddox said. "You did tell me that. I'm woolgathering."

Meta stepped closer and put an arm around his back.

Maddox swallowed. He missed Cook. In a way, Cook had been like a father to him. He'd lost a second father in this. Stunned amazement filled him, and now the stirrings of rage began.

"I do not know for a fact the blips or pings came from a fault phase unit, sir, but the data would seem to imply it."

"Yes…" Maddox said. "And given that the Lord High Admiral is dead through exotic means… Do we have any video how that happened?"

"We do. Would you like to see it?"

"This instant," Maddox said.

Meta's arm tightened around his waist. "Are you sure that's the right thing to do right now?"

"Yes," Maddox said, with his voice hardening.

Galyan looked from one to the other.

"Do it, Galyan," Meta said.

Using a function within *Victory*, Galyan projected a holoimage before them in the house near Carson City. They saw what the secretary had seen, having a special pair of glasses that had recorded the event. There was no other recording of this. Thus, for those brief seconds, they saw the swirling substance over the Lord High Admiral's head, which surely had suffocated him, as he died of asphyxiation.

"What is that?" Maddox asked.

"I have not been able to ascertain that, nor even the type of energy we are seeing," Galyan said.

Maddox nodded. "According to you, there's likely a phase ship in Earth and we're witnessing this exotic killing method. I give it a high probability the two are linked."

"Is this your intuition speaking, sir?"

Maddox glanced sharply at Galyan. "It doesn't have to be my intuition. It seems obvious, doesn't it?"

"I analyze things differently from your intuitive sense, sir. But given logic and probabilities, I give the connection a high probability, yes. I would say there is a seventy-eight percent chance the phase ship and exotic killing method is related."

"Right," Maddox said. "Stokes has already started an independent investigation. I don't think he's going to be able to run it for long. Chief of Intelligence General Mackinder will likely take over soon. I want you to tell Stokes what you've told me. We need to find this as soon as possible."

"Do you want me to bypass Star Watch security like that?" Galyan asked.

Maddox thought a moment. "No. It wouldn't be good for them to know you can do that so easily. It might put you under suspicion. I'll call Stokes. He'll call the starship. Then you can relate what you deem appropriate to him."

"Yes, sir," Galyan said. "May I say, sir, I am sorry for this grievous loss to Star Watch and to you."

"Yes, thank you," Maddox said. "Now let's get things moving. We don't know this is the end of it."

"Do you think this alien assassin might strike again?" Galyan said.

Maddox gazed into the distance, trying to use his intuitive sense. "Yes. I think this assassin will. That means we have to find him as fast as we can."

-9-

Brigadier Stokes was an older, sickly man, not much longer destined for this Earth. The doctors had told him he had a degenerative disease. His face had more lines than when he'd been Mary O'Hara's go-for. For a time, he'd run Star Watch Intelligence. Lately, as in the last few years, General Mackinder had taken Stokes' place running Intelligence. Stokes had lesser duties these days, and had helped Maddox on his last mission.

Stokes sat at his desk, coughing and sucking on his latest stimstick. When he was finished, he stubbed out the last of it, picked up another, and inhaled. The stimsticks stimulated his thinking but had been rotting out his lungs over the years.

Stokes was hard at work, correlating all the information he could about the signatures from a faulty phase device, at least as far as Galyan had been able to determine. If anyone should know about phase mechanics, it would be the permanent fixture, AI entity of *Victory*. Maddox and his team had dealt with more phase technology than everyone else in Star Watch combined.

Stokes inhaled deeply of the latest stimstick, held the smoke, and then burst out coughing, spewing the red smoke into the air.

He was in his office working later than usual. He had been on the horn with the Earth data-net people. They couldn't find anything odd around or in the planet. They'd searched for cloaked vessels and any phase signatures. They had found nothing, but their instruments weren't as finely tuned to such things as those on *Victory* were.

Stokes picked up a tablet and stared at the still shot of the patterns over the Lord High Admiral's head. He noted Cook's bulging eyes, dead eyes, he would assume.

Thank goodness for the secretary who had recorded that on her glasses. That was a piece of luck, if you could call it that, in this horrible desperate situation.

As Stokes contemplated these things in one of the securest facilities in Star Watch Intelligence, miles away in Lyon, France Sector, Venna the Spy got up from bed.

It had been a week since she used the Phantasma Synth Crystals. She'd regained most of her vitality since then, and she had checked the crystals. Someone had recalibrated them. They and she were ready for another venture with this horrible alien technology.

Venna felt soiled for what she had done. She didn't want to do it again.

Because of that, relays clicked in her mind, bringing forth more memories. She realized the Lord High Admiral hadn't been the only Star Watch bastard to murder her family on Thebes. There had also been a smaller, chain-smoking, stimstick fellow by the name of Brigadier Stokes. In her memories, Venna saw him slip a knife into the back of her mother's neck, severing her spine, and he had laughed while doing it.

Hatred flashed in Venna's eyes.

She went to her closet and chose her clothes and shoes with care.

Soon, like before, she wore a tight-fitting, short, revealing dress and high heels. She moved seductively that few could match when Venna wanted to lure a man. She strutted with rage. In her mind's eye, she plotted what she would do to Brigadier Stokes. Yes. She was going to make him pay for the vile evil he'd done to her family.

The fact that these were manufactured memories made no difference to Venna. The Intelligence arm of the Spacer Third Fleet knew what it was doing with these inducements and hypnotisms. They were masters at their craft, masters at the art of subterfuge and false memories.

Venna was soon in a nightclub, swaying, dancing, laughing, and at first, she worried there wasn't going to be one with the correct energy for what she had in mind. Then a pale-skinned Scandinavian man with burning blue eyes and wearing a leather vest entered. He was muscular, exceedingly tall, and she knew, yes, he had the needed energy.

To make sure, Venna took out the device, aimed it at him so no one could see, and tested him. Yes. This was perfect.

He looked her way.

Venna used the device as if applying lipstick to her lips. She pressed her lips together, saw that he still watched, and made a pouting kiss in his direction.

She slipped the item into her glittering purse and watched him stride across the dance floor. He spoke to her.

Venna shook her head.

He spoke again.

Finally, Venna shrugged and slid off the tall stool. She followed him onto the dance floor. They danced so that most of the couples watched in awe. They had such grace and beauty. Here was femininity at its utmost, and here was masculinity to match. The two attracted everyone's eyes like super-magnets, as if every person's pupils were made of steel filings.

Venna laughed. The Scandinavian man laughed. He would have been a Viking chief of old.

Once more, like a week ago, they left together, entered a taxi, and went to his house. There, he began laughing, and tried to ply her with drinks.

"We don't need that. You know what we do need?" Venna looked at the ornate wooden box that she had brought along.

"What is that, anyway?"

"Would you like to see?" Venna said.

He gazed at her in an engaging way. "Yes," he said.

For a moment, Venna felt a pang of regret. Here was a man to match her. His was a masculine power, and hers was feminine. She wanted to yield to him, to truly yield. But then the murderous image of Brigadier Stokes entered her mind.

Venna opened the box.

He looked at her. "What are those for?"

"Pick one up," she said. "I dare you."

He laughed, and he did.

Venna picked up her crystal. "I know you won't do this, but repeat after me."

He laughed again, and he repeated after her.

This was too easy. Were all men such idiots? Maybe at this point, they were.

So began a horrible, wicked repetition of the last time. Color bled up into his hands and up his forearms. He stiffened when the color glowed from his chest.

Venna did as before.

Far too soon, she watched him shrivel and shrink as the etheric energy, the electromagnetic pulses of his body, exited him in a bizarre manner, filtering through the crystals.

As before, scintillating energy appeared over him as he was reduced to nothing.

Knowing better how to do this, Venna took control of the etheric creature. It was alive after a fashion, and had a hint of the man, the Scandinavian Viking chief that he had been. Eyes appeared.

Venna sent his energy on its way.

Soon, in ghost mode, it slipped through the Intelligence Arm of Star Watch, searching until Venna found Brigadier Stokes in his office, chain-smoking, trying to figure out things.

Stokes looked up and cried out as he saw the ghostly, swirling thing settle over his head. He tried to run, but Venna added substance to the etheric creature. It weighed down poor Brigadier Stokes. The attempt to run strained his weak heart. It started to flutter. A second more, and a heart attack struck. His eyes glazed over as he gasped.

As before, Venna used the etheric power, choking him until Brigadier Stokes flopped onto his desk, causing his ashtray of butts to spew onto the floor.

In France Sector, in Lyon, in a house, Venna staggered, spent from her actions.

She gathered the implements, and a sob escaped her. What she had done tonight—she felt drained and torn from it.

Venna glanced at her thighs. There were blemishes, clots under her smooth skin. This was sickening and horrifying. Was using these crystals killing her?

Venna fled the house. Because of her intense training, she covered her tracks to a degree, but she fled, knowing that she had two more people to kill. The next would be Mary O'Hara, the former Chief of Star Watch Intelligence.

First, though, she needed to sleep this off.

-10-

Maddox strode purposefully through the desert near his house in Carson City, Nevada Sector. His long strides covered the distance quickly. Birds flew past occasionally. Mostly, the wind blew and the sun beat down.

Maddox did his best thinking walking long distances in solitude or taking a hot shower at the end of the day. He wasn't in the mood for a shower now. He needed to move.

He wasn't quite a New Man, although he'd received many of the treatments and heritage. Erill spiritual energy filled him, giving him something akin to a New Man's vitality and endurance. Therefore, he had trouble sitting still and doing nothing. He thought better while moving. It was as simple as that.

Thus, he covered ground thinking, correlating, trying to piece things together. First, the Lord High Admiral had been killed in a foul alien manner. Then Stokes had died the same way. Obviously, there was a connection. The two knew each other. Maddox knew both personally. Could that have any bearing on the situation?

Maddox strove to use his intuitive sense on this.

He'd gained the useful intuitive sense from Balron the Traveler, an energy being from a parallel universe. He'd helped Balron get home. Before that, Balron had done something to him, bequeathing this intuitive sense. It did not always operate. It was most helpful regarding things that concerned him personally. Did this concern him personally?

That was one question. The other was: who was the alien or the assassin using alien tools going to strike next?

Maddox had found Stokes' notes. They mainly contained information the brigadier had learned from Galyan.

Who was next on the list? How had whoever achieved the process? The attacks had been a week apart. Did that have any bearing on it?

Maddox strove to understand. This did not seem like something a New Man would do. He did not think anyone from the Swarm Imperium had done this. The obvious culprit would be from the Sovereign Hierarchy of Leviathan. They had sent spies to the Commonwealth before. They had captured him and made a clone of him to send back to Star Watch. Leviathan threatened a fleet invasion. The best thing an alien intelligence service could do would be to decapitate the decision-making heads before the start of an invasion. Why go after Brigadier Stokes then?

Maddox shook his head. The critical issue was who were they are going to kill next? He had to stop them. How could he do that? If this entity had slain the Lord High Admiral and then gone after Brigadier Stokes…? Could his grandmother be in danger? She also was in Intelligence. She was related to these two.

And she knows me.

Maddox had a sense that this had something to do with him. Was it vain or arrogant to think that? Most people believed things that happened to them happened because they were important. Maddox knew the difference was that it was true about him. He was important. He was a *di-far,* one of the few or the only one in the Commonwealth.

That was a vain thought even while it was a true thought. Still, if Maddox had the power to stop this, if he had the ability, then he had a duty to stop this.

What wasn't he seeing? What was he missing?

"It doesn't matter what I'm not seeing," Maddox said. "I need to—"

Galyan appeared beside him.

"Why are you here?" Maddox said.

"I felt like you needed company, sir."

"Oh?"

"I've been running my personality profile on you. It told me you should not be alone right now."

Maddox scowled. "You've been watching me from *Victory*."

"You know I'm watching you, sir. You know I'm watching the others. But you I watch in particular."

"Why wouldn't you watch Meta and protect her in particular?"

"Of course, Meta is dear and important to me. But you hold all this together. You are the link, and I think you are working through the situation."

"You know that I am," Maddox said.

"I do know. I have been eavesdropping on you, sir, and I know I'm not supposed to do that."

"Forget about that," Maddox said. "That's not germane today. What's going on, and how can we stop it?"

"We must find the phase ship," Galyan said.

"Are you convinced a phase ship is hiding inside the Earth?"

"I am certain, sir, as all the data points to it. All the correlations, all the logical possibilities point to a phase ship parked in Earth."

"Because of the four strange blips?" asked Maddox.

"Why else would I say that?"

"I don't know what to do," Maddox admitted. "I don't know how to stop this. I don't even know how to find any of the players."

"I realize that, sir, and that is why I have come to tell you that you need someone who can find your enemies for you."

"Okay, yeah, that's a good piece of advice, Galyan," Maddox said sarcastically. "Who would that be? Do you have a person in mind?"

"I do, sir, but I do not think you are going to like it."

Maddox stared at the small Adok holoimage. Galyan was a good friend, even if he was only a deified AI.

"All right, tell me."

"You need someone who can read minds, who has telepathic abilities."

Maddox stopped walking. Galyan stopped beside him.

"You can't possibly be talking about Captain Becker," Maddox said.

"Precisely, sir, you need Captain Becker."

Maddox shook his head. Becker had been a dangerous freak.

Becker was from the time when Admiral James K. Fletcher had taken control of Star Watch. The Liss cybers had attacked secretly through a being called Nostradamus.

Maddox had been *persona non grata* then. The rest of Star Watch had become pro-*Homo sapiens* human, Humanity Manifesto Doctrine had sprouted full bore. Becker had telepathically pushed Fletcher, using a power the Liss cybers had given him. In the end, Maddox had foiled Becker and used the man's abilities against the Prime Saa, a Liss mind-meld of cybers. The alien Liss cybers had done some horrific things to Becker, literally enlarging his cranium and making his brain denser and bigger. They had given him amazing telepathic, dominating abilities. In the end, Star Watch had put Captain Becker into stasis for safekeeping and in case they ever needed Becker's unique skills.

"You think now is the time we should take Becker out of stasis?" Maddox asked.

"I don't know how else or who else could possibly help you with this. It is important to remember that Becker was highly unstable. You are the key to controlling Becker. Becker is the key to finding our hidden foe."

Maddox rubbed his chin. "Only the Lord High Admiral can give the order to awaken Becker."

"Yes, sir, you are going to have to find a way around that."

Maddox stared up at the clouds, the few in the sky. "You know, of course, that whoever is the next Lord High Admiral will not like any such actions from me."

"Sir," Galyan said, "when did you ever care what anyone liked or thought about you or what you did?"

Maddox laughed bleakly and nodded. "You know what, Galyan, it's time we got the old crew together and it's time I got back on to *Victory*. I have a feeling I'm going to have to move fast when the moment comes."

"I suspect you are right, sir. I have everyone in mind you need and I know their locations and how to reach them."

"Start gathering them and have them ferry up to *Victory*," Maddox said. "I don't know if we're going to get the okay to do this because I don't know who can okay it and who won't."

Galyan waited as if expectant.

Maddox stared at him. "What is it now?"

"Uh…you are welcome, sir," Galyan said.

Maddox grinned. "Thanks for the advice, Galyan. I appreciate it."

"Yes, sir, I am glad to help."

"Right," Maddox said. "It's time to awaken Becker and convince the maniac to do something good for once."

-11-

The assassination of the Lord High Admiral, and then a week later, a similar or same type of death to Brigadier Stokes of Star Watch Intelligence, had created an uproar throughout Star Watch and the rest of Earth security. Orders and counter orders flew every which way. There was an unusual state of chaos and high alert on and around Earth.

Maddox had quietly gathered the crewmembers and had them shuttle up to *Victory*. He spoke with Ludendorff. Nothing the Methuselah Man told him added to Maddox's understanding of how this was happening or how to fix it.

Right now, Maddox was in a stubby-winged tin can piloted by Lieutenant Keith Maker, the best damn pilot in Star Watch. Keith was getting older but still had fantastic reflexes. There was a twitch to his hands Maddox hadn't seen before. What caused that?

Maddox didn't feel like asking Keith, though there was something slightly odd to Mr. Maker. Could that be due to his on-again, off-again love affair with Valerie? She was on her way to *Victory*, picking up her Darter *Tarrypin* to park it in the starship's hangar bay.

In the tin can, Maddox hurried to a special prison complex in Antarctica. Originally, he'd forged some orders that others had countermanded. This was Plan B, doing what he needed to regardless because Plan A had failed.

Star Watch was in turmoil, though most of the general populace of Earth had no idea what was taking place. Even so, this would have been a good time for an alien empire to launch a surprise attack, as no one was in charge of the whole thing, and many thought they were in charge of the same things.

Ludendorff hadn't thought it a good idea to free Becker. The man had been a highly dangerous adversary, especially with the alien Liss behind him. Nevertheless, Maddox was certain this was the right move.

He had just gotten off a comm link with his grandmother. The Iron Lady was on her way up to *Victory*. Maddox figured that was the safest place for her.

Mary had scoffed at the idea that she would be on anyone's kill list.

"No, Grandmother, I insist you take this precaution. Do it for me."

"For you, dear, I will," she'd said.

The ungainly tin can flashed over the tip of South America as it headed for Antarctica. It was summer in the Northern Hemisphere. That meant it was winter in the Southern Hemisphere. Winter in Antarctica, even in these advanced technological days, made the place a hellhole.

"Do you envision any problems?"

Keith turned to Maddox. "Are you talking to me, sir?"

"Yes."

"What kind of problems?"

"With the weather," Maddox said.

Keith grinned. "If anything, the bad weather will make this fun. Besides, we can always fold if we have to."

Maddox nodded. He'd chosen a fold fighter for a reason. If he needed to get out of Antarctica in a hurry, he wanted to be able to go straight up to *Victory's* hangar bay. Could all of Star Watch stop him? Of course, they could. Still, he felt safer operating from *Victory* and while sitting in the captain's chair.

This was one of those moments where Maddox was going to have to wear both hats: Intelligence and a Patrol officer.

Galyan had his assignment and was busy scouring intelligence and police reports across Earth. Everyone was putting up red tape, with no one able to cut through the blizzard of it. Therefore, Galyan had orders to infiltrate various computers and acquire what he needed clandestinely...if he deemed it warranted.

"I want to know everything," Maddox said, "but I want you to correlate it and only tell me what is important. That means you must use your judgment."

"Yes, sir," Galyan said.

The Adok AI was usually under strict orders, forbidden to use such clandestine methods on Earth. These methods had proven successful many times in the Beyond and against adversaries more technologically subtle and advanced than Star Watch. Surely, Galyan could get what they needed on Earth.

After another half hour of flight, Keith maneuvered down onto a high security complex in the center of Antarctica. There were watchtowers and a walking yard, although none of the inmates or guards would be using it in this horrible weather.

They landed in a subterranean hangar bay under the radar lock of heavy guns and missiles.

"Galyan," Maddox said from his crash seat.

"Here, sir."

Maddox turned around. Galyan was in ghost form.

"Are you still searching for data?" Maddox said.

"I can do many things at once, sir, as you know."

"You will stay with me in ghost form and continue to infiltrate the targeted computer systems."

"I understand completely, sir. You are doing what you should not be doing and could likely use my help."

"Never mind talking about that," Maddox said. "Let's just do it."

Maddox exited the hatch, stepping into an underground hangar bay. He met a delegation of tough-looking security personnel. They wore brown uniforms, had truncheons, and other devices on their belts, seven hardy men.

"You shouldn't be here," a lieutenant said. He was a big, bulky man who surely thought he could take Maddox. The lieutenant exuded threat in his stance and the way he stared at Maddox.

Maddox nodded politely and stood meekly, his shoulders rounded, as if he was afraid of being here. Sometimes subterfuge worked best in these situations.

"Here are the release orders for Captain Becker," Maddox said, holding out a form.

The lieutenant glared at and then snatched the orders, studying them.

Maddox watched the others, a truculent group. Some wore power holsters attached to their thick wrists. There was a power cord running from the holster to the heavy gun. A guard need only hold his hand in a firing position, and the gun would snap into it, ready for use.

These men guarded the most dangerous prisoners Star Watch had collected throughout the decades. That included Captain Becker, although the man was in stasis, one of the few.

"These actually seem to be in order," the lieutenant growled. He jerked his head at Maddox.

The captain submitted to a search. The guards went through his kit and took his monofilament blade from his boot sheath.

The lieutenant eyed Maddox as he held the knife.

"I forgot it was there," Maddox said.

"Of course you did," the lieutenant said. He hurled it so the knife stuck in a wall. "Follow me."

The lieutenant led the way as they marched through a hatch and down a hall, turning several times. They entered a turbo lift, plunging deep into the earth to the facility's lowest section. Galyan was there, although no one could see him, not even Maddox.

They marched down various corridors until they came into a chamber with big running machines.

"You can talk to him," the lieutenant said. "Then you'll have to leave."

"With the prisoner," Maddox said.

"No, he stays here."

"My orders are legitimate," Maddox said. "They're signed by the Lord High Admiral."

The lieutenant sneered. "I guess you haven't heard. Admiral Cook is dead."

"I know Cook is dead," Maddox said. "That's why I'm doing this. These are Cook's last orders. You're not going to disobey the admiral's last orders, are you?"

For once, the truculence in the man's eyes diminished. Maybe the question caused fear even in his security-conscious skull.

"I'm going to let you look at Becker," the lieutenant said. "Then you're going to see how impossible it would be to release him from the facility."

Maddox shrugged.

They went through a hatch and entered a cold chamber. The lieutenant led Maddox to a large cylinder. Captain Becker was frozen behind the thick glass.

The lieutenant had been speaking quietly into a comm unit. He must have asked for further clearance on Maddox's orders. The man gave him a bit more respect.

"The Iron Lady has given the okay," the lieutenant told the others.

The lieutenant didn't know Galyan was running an Intelligence sting. The AI had intercepted the call, rerouting it to the Iron Lady on *Victory*.

"We'll thaw him out," the lieutenant said. "We'll take him to a special room so you can speak to him."

Maddox nodded.

"You do know the freak was a mind specialist, right?" asked the lieutenant.

"I do," Maddox said. "That's the reason for the silver headband."

The lieutenant seemed to have lost interest.

The thawing continued as Maddox maintained a bland indifference to how much time this was taking. He was anything but sanguine. Yet, there was nothing he could do about that for the moment other than to wait patiently.

Waiting, however, was one of the hardest things a human could do.

-12-

Maddox sat across from Becker in a chamber with heavy bulkheads and antennae sprouting from the walls. Occasionally, a hiss sounded and a tiny spark appeared. The antennae and bulkheads helped suppress Becker's known telepathic, dominating powers.

Maddox sat on a couch; Becker sat on a couch opposite him, with a low wooden table between them.

Becker was slumped forward and wore a white formless smock. Maddox had slipped on a silver headband with a small box around his forehead. He'd clicked on the unit. If the antennae and bulkheads failed, the unit would protect him so Becker couldn't read his thoughts or mentally coerce him.

Becker was one of the most powerful telepaths Maddox had ever met. The man was a creation of the alien Liss. Star Watch had eliminated the Liss cybers many years ago. If there were any pockets of the Liss left, Star Watch did not know about them. The Liss had been part mechanical and part biological. That had been insectoid biological, but biological all the same.

Becker began to stir.

The man had been in stasis for over ten years. He'd entered a special machine on a weekly basis to keep his muscles from atrophying. Unfortunately, Becker hadn't been much of a physical specimen when he had originally entered stasis.

Becker was an ungainly looking fellow: mid-sized, with spindly limbs, a narrow chest, and an abnormally enlarged head. He no longer looked normal, but like some super science fiction or comic book egghead. His neck lacked the strength to hold up his head all the time. As a concession to that, he wore a neck brace. Because the Prime Saa of the Liss mind-meld had enlarged the head and brain, and made the brain tissues denser, his face no longer had a regular form. A third of the face contained the nose, mouth, eyes, all dominated by the bulging cranium.

Becker groaned and lurched back. The back of his head hit the wall with a thump. Becker's eyes flew open. He looked around with surprise, then at Maddox.

"You," Becker said in a hoarse voice. "What, what—how long have I been under?"

"Long enough," Maddox said.

"What does that mean?"

Maddox shrugged. He didn't trust Becker or know if the man's telepathic powers had grown.

Becker looked around wildly, like a trapped animal. It seemed he would jump up. Then he looked at Maddox again, appraisingly this time, undoubtedly noticing Maddox's superior physique, muscles, and much smaller head. Becker then proceeded to look at his legs, at his hands, his arms. He felt his torso.

"I've been under a long time. I've atrophied. This is horrible and disgusting. What did you do to me?"

"The Liss did it to you, don't you remember?"

Becker stared off into the distance. He grunted, and slyly felt his privates. His hands flew away. The Prime Saa had castrated him during their time together.

"Damn, it's not just a dream," Becker said. "After everything I did for them…" Both hands clutched his abnormally large head. "I gave them what they needed, and they castrated me. They did that because I enjoyed the women too much. Instead, I have the power to coerce. But how has that helped me? I've been under. How long has it been?"

"Over ten years," Maddox said.

Becker's eyes showed his horror. Then he closed his eyes and leaned back. He groaned. It was such a pitiful and horrible sound. He seemed to come to himself and sat up. His head was wobbly, but he balanced himself with both hands on the cushions of the couch. This would strain his upper back muscles as well.

"Ten years. Why did you wake me now? Don't tell me. I know. You need me. You want my services, don't you?"

"Yes," Maddox said. "I woke you when no one else would have dared."

"Should I be grateful for that? You just want to use me like a tool, like some draught animal. Put me back under. I will be of no use to you."

"You might want to reconsider that," Maddox said. "Why not barter with me? Surely there are things you want."

"My freedom," Becker said promptly. "I want to go and do what I want, when I want."

"All right, I can work with that. You give me what I want, and I'll let you go."

"What? You'll let me go on Earth just like that?"

Maddox shook his head. "I won't let you free on Earth. I'll send you far away. I'll even give you a spacecraft so you can explore to your heart's content."

"And if I turn back to the Commonwealth?"

"Then we'll destroy your ship," Maddox said.

"Why won't you destroy it anyway just to be safe?"

"Because I'm a man of my word," Maddox said.

Becker laughed and sneered. "I know you, Maddox. You're not human like me. You don't keep your word to the lower orders like us, even though I'm no longer of the lower order. I am high, a special mutation."

"That's right," Maddox said. "You're a mutant. That means you're a freak. That means you're just like me. Why, then, would you support the Humanity Manifesto Doctrine? You're no longer like them. They fear you."

"Are the HM people still in charge?" Becker said.

"No, they lost, just like you lost."

"I don't appreciate your insults," Becker said. "In fact, I don't like the way you're speaking to me. You can piss off, Maddox."

"Does that mean you want to go back under into stasis?"

Becker sat straighter. "I don't know if I'll let myself go under again." He glared balefully at Maddox.

The anti-psionic box on the silver band around Maddox's head hummed. Due to his intuitive sense, Maddox also sensed the mental assault. Then it stopped.

Becker was breathing hard. "You're wise to wear that headband. I'm still not going to do what you want. I won't be a tool for those who defeated me."

Maddox thought a moment. "Why take that attitude when you can have what you want? You have a unique ability. I need the ability, maybe even desperately need it."

"Desperately?" said Becker. "You let that slip."

Maddox looked away. "I shouldn't have said desperately."

"But it is a desperate situation. Otherwise, logically, why would you have brought me up?"

After a moment, Maddox shrugged.

Becker's eyes narrowed and he laughed. "You think I'm an idiot because I've been under for ten years. That was false that you let the word desperate slip. You said it on purpose."

Becker gathered saliva in his mouth and spat on the floor. "Damn, Star Watch. Damn the New Men. And now, damn me, too. I'm like you, a freak, intensely telepathic instead of strong. There's nobody in the universe like me. I should be ruling. I should have my own harem. I should…"

Becker's hands slipped to his privates again and jerked away. He clenched his hands into fists. He glared at Maddox until he became thoughtful.

"I'll tell you what I want," Becker said. "If you can give me what I want, I'll do what you ask."

"Name it," Maddox said.

"I want my balls back. I want to be a full man again and have everything operative like it should be. I want to have women."

Maddox raised an eyebrow. He hadn't foreseen such a request.

"That's right," Becker said. "You can't give me that. I know Commonwealth science. It can't restore such a thing. But that's what I want."

"Well, now," Maddox said, "I think we have a deal, then."

"How's that?" asked Becker.

"I'll take you to the Library Planet. My Uncle Ural is there. The Builders can surely take your genetic material, your DNA, and regrow that which you wish. They can attach it normally and restore you. You'll be a whole man again."

"Truly," Becker said, "this is possible? Could the Builders achieve what the Prime Saa stole from me?"

"Easily," Maddox said.

Becker frowned. "How do I know you'll keep your word after I do what you want?"

Maddox nodded. That was the problem. He sat forward earnestly. "I give you my Captain Maddox oath without tricks or subterfuge. I'll take you to the Library Planet and tell the Supreme Intelligence about this. He owes me. Besides, I think the Library Planet is a better place for you. The Supreme Intelligence may let you stay. I don't know. I don't think you should remain on Earth. I'll do this after you do me a favor."

"What favor is this?" Becker said. "Do you want to try to control Star Watch?"

"No. I need to find an assassin. Your special talents can help me find him."

"Whether I find the assassin or not, but make the attempt, that will be enough for you to keep your end of the deal, right?"

Maddox thought about that. It was a reasonable question and request. "Agreed. But I'm going to be with you. If you try to double-cross me, I'll kill you."

"I know you'll kill me." Becker looked around. "Isn't this a super-maximum security facility?"

"It is," Maddox said.

"Then how are we getting out of here? Or did you really get orders to release me?"

"This is when things will get interesting," Maddox said.

Becker smirked. "That's what I thought."

"Listen, Becker, I'm your only friend. Deal with me, and you'll get what you want."

"Sure," Becker said.

Maddox wondered if that was true. The key was this: what did Becker truly want? If he'd stated it, fine. If it was something Maddox couldn't give… That might well be the rub.

-13-

"All right, listen to me, Becker," Maddox said. "Do you feel capable of using your telepathic abilities with precision right now?"

Becker stared at Maddox. "Is this about us escaping from here?"

"Uh-huh," Maddox said. "It turns out that I'm going to need your help. But you need to listen to me carefully, you must use telepathic precision. I don't want you killing anyone. I know you're capable of it, and I bet you're angry with some of them. Maybe you're tired or, because you've been out of practice for so long, this is going to be difficult for you. Use just enough to suppress the immediate threats so they fall unconscious. We shouldn't have that many guards to go through."

"And if I do all that," Becker said, "we're going to waltz out of here?"

"That's the plan."

"You must know they record everything down here," Becker said, "and can easily play everything back later. What happens then?"

"I'll take care of that. You take care of any gentlemen I indicate."

"They're not gentlemen," Becker said with heat. "They're bastards. I've felt their emanations throughout my years of stasis. I've felt them in my dreams, and I'm beginning to recall things. You know what? Some of them opened my container and pissed on me as a joke. They probably did other heinous things to my sleeping body I don't even want to know."

"We can't do this," Maddox said, shaking his head, "unless you agree to my methods. These are Star Watch people. I don't want any of them getting hurt. They did a job, a tough job. And hey, let's face it, as much as I'm willing to make a deal with you, you're a bastard, and have been a bastard. You tried to help enslave the entire human race."

Becker scowled. "If that's how you feel, I should just take you out now instead of later."

Maddox stared deadpan at Becker before saying, "You might want to rethink that. The Prime Saa used you, castrated you, no less. I'm giving you back what those creatures gleefully stole."

Becker looked away. Was he calculating? He shrugged and struggled to his feet. "This is ridiculous. My head is too big. My brain is too heavy. I can barely support myself. Look, I'm going to need help walking, and you're the last person I want to help me."

Maddox wondered whether this was a ploy. Could Becker telepathically control him if they touched? Would Becker try to flip off the silver headband? Maddox decided in for a dollar...that sort of thing. "Let's go, Becker. Let's do this."

Maddox put an arm around Becker's waist. As he did, he felt a nudge in his mind. The little prick was trying something. Once more, Maddox strove for the Way of the Pilgrim, and strove to lock down his own thoughts.

"Are you listening to me, Maddox?"

"Hey, Becker," Maddox said between gritted teeth, "you try any more of that shit and I'll make this easy. I'll kill you, and find a different way to do this."

The mind nudge, the likely tendril assault, ceased.

"I'm ready," Becker said.

"Yeah," Maddox said. "Let's do this."

Together, with Becker resting his big, overheavy head against Maddox, they moved to and exited through the hatch. It should have been locked, but a ghost-mode Adok AI sent a surge of electricity through it. The lock clicked so the hatch opened.

On the other side, two tough-looking guards whirled around before grabbing their electric truncheons.

"Now, Becker, if you please," Maddox said. "Remember, use a soft touch."

Becker raised a hand, pointing at one and then the other.

One guard's eyes bulged. He collapsed onto his knees and fell face forward. Maddox released Becker and went to the guard, checking the pulse. There was none.

"Make his heart beat," Maddox said.

The other guard had already fallen to his side.

Becker concentrated. In a second, both men's hearts were beating strongly, and both were breathing and sweating heavily.

"Do that again—"

"I know, I know," Becker said, interrupting. "I wanted to see if you were aware. I guess you are."

"Listen, if you want me to keep my part of the bargain, you have to keep yours and not make me watch you like a sheepdog. Don't be a wolf, in other words."

"Okay," Becker said, before stumbling, going down onto a knee.

Maddox went to and helped him up, cinching an arm around his waist again.

Becker glared at Maddox before concentrating on pushing one foot ahead of another. Like before, he soon rested his huge head against Maddox's side.

They hurried through the corridors at the bottom level of the maximum-security prison. No camera eyes recorded them as no cameras functioned down here. Galyan had infiltrated the high-security computers and achieved the impossible. He put clear holoimages of nothing in their place so no alarms blared.

In truth, this was easy for Galyan, as he'd practiced much more sophisticated techniques against more tech savvy foes in the Beyond. The AI was enjoying himself. He'd always wanted to test himself against Star Watch's best. Now he was doing it.

Galyan watched as Maddox and Becker entered a turbo lift. Galyan sent it up and warned them as the hatch opened upon two security personnel.

Becker put the two to sleep.

Ten minutes later, Maddox and Becker stumbled into the subterranean hangar bay as five armed men whirled around.

"Make it a wave assault," Maddox hissed.

Did Becker glance with disdain at Maddox? If so, he immediately focused on the five, and all went down as if someone had switched them off, which was the truth. Unfortunately, blood poured from one of the noses.

"Becker!" Maddox said, releasing the man, stepping to the bleeder. It was the lieutenant. Maddox turned to Becker.

"He was the most susceptible to the assault," Becker said. "I'm sorry, I couldn't help it."

Maddox had his doubts. If anyone had urinated on Becker during his long hiatus, it likely would have been the lieutenant. Did that mean the lieutenant deserved death? No. Becker was an unstable, highly changed freak. Freeing him might have been a bad idea. The lieutenant had been a cruel bastard, but he'd still been a member of Star Watch.

Maddox strode to Becker, grabbed him by an arm, and propelled him to the fold fighter. "You do anything to the man in there, and you're dead. Got it?"

"Hey!" Becker said. "I did what you asked. It was an accident. Quit freaking out."

Maddox shoved the weak man to a crash seat and thrust him on it. "Buckle up, bud." He turned to Keith.

"That must be our passenger," Keith said.

"Yes," Maddox said. "Let's go. What are we waiting for?"

"The main hatch isn't opening," Keith said.

"Galyan," Maddox said.

Galyan appeared out of ghost form. "I'm working on it, sir. The outer hatch has more security locks than the rest. It could prove a dangerous problem."

"I don't care," Maddox said. "Get it open. We don't want to have to fold directly out of here."

"I can do it if I must," Keith said, as he began to manipulate controls and power up the tin can.

Galyan vanished. Tense seconds passed.

Then the outer bay doors opened.

In moments, they all lurched in their seats as the tin can rose and then shot through the bay doors into the Antarctica night. Winds shrieked—a reminder that at the bottom of the world nature was vicious and cold.

Despite that, the tin can rocketed up as it headed for orbital space.

Galyan appeared. "Others have sensed the fold fighter. They are requesting orders concerning it. These others have access to beams and missiles."

"I was afraid of that," Maddox said. "Mr. Maker, get ready to fold."

"Directly into *Victory?*" asked Keith.

"That's right," Maddox said. "We need to get out of here, and we need to go now."

"Give me a moment," Keith said.

Maddox glanced at Becker.

Becker watched everything with wide eyes as if absorbing each piece of information.

Was this his intuitive sense trying to tell him something? Maddox felt more uncomfortable than ever that he'd awoken and was bringing this strange man to the starship. Maddox reminded himself that the Lord High Admiral and Brigadier Stokes were dead, slain by assassins. They had been friends, his fellow workers in Star Watch for years. He must learn who had assassinated them. He'd make whomever did it pay. This wasn't just about protecting Star Watch. It was making these bastards pay the ultimate price for what they had done to his comrades. If Leviathan were behind all this—

Maddox sat straighter.

He didn't know what he could do to Leviathan.

"I'm good any time, sir," Keith said.

"Then go," Maddox said, "fold."

Keith had made complex computations and now started braking violently. He couldn't simply fold into *Victory* with his present velocity. It would be akin to a missile piercing through bulkheads.

Becker groaned.

Maddox gritted his teeth at the G-forces they were pulling.

The tin can shuddered as it braked even harder. Keith shouted with yipping cries as if he enjoyed this madness. An even greater blast of power seemed to cause the tin can to sit still in the air. At that precise moment, the tin can folded, appearing in a *Victory* hangar bay, moving only the slightest bit.

It was as nearly a perfect fold from flight as anyone had ever made.

In seconds, the tin can landed with barely a thump against the cradle.

"Excellent work," Maddox said.

"I do what I can," Keith said modestly. Adding, "When you're the best, you make it look easy."

Maddox grunted and turned to Becker.

The weak man was slumped in his crash seat as blood pour from his nose.

What the hell? Maddox tore off the restraints and jumped out of his crash seat. "Galyan, hurry, get medics. We have an emergency. If this bastard dies now—hurry, Galyan."

Galyan disappeared.

Maddox went to Becker, hoping the little creep was alive. Becker couldn't die before he helped them solve this terrible mystery. That would be unconscionable.

-14-

Events continued to roll along even after Maddox's foray into the maximum-security prison and taking Becker.

For one thing, although Becker survived the fold, he was sick. The fold had hurt him more than usual. This was probably due to his immense brain and its functions. The enhanced brain didn't deal well with folds. How would it do with a star-drive jump or a hyper-spatial tube journey?

The truth was that the massive brain opened Becker up to odd problems. If Maddox couldn't take Becker to the Library Planet, he would need to find another solution

A darker thought intruded upon Maddox's thinking. He could take Becker on star-drive jumps, and the jumps could give the man an aneurysm that killed him. That would solve the problem. However, Maddox was reluctant to rely on such a procedure. For one thing, he had given his oath. It wasn't the same as being in the middle of a mission, facing some arrogant alien dick. Here, he had made a deal, one he planned to fulfill.

As they waited for Becker to recover from the fold, a new Lord High Admiral rose in Star Watch. The heads of the services met with the Prime Minister of the Commonwealth. After a vote, Admiral William Preston Haig was elevated into the position of the Lord High Admiral of Star Watch.

Haig immediately met with the heads of the departments, including General Mackinder of Intelligence. Mackinder, no doubt, told Haig about an incident at the high security facility in Antarctica and the disappearance of Captain Becker. Most likely, Mackinder told Haig that Maddox was behind it.

Soon, Maddox received a summons from the new Lord High Admiral. "You must come at once, Captain, and by the way, where are you?"

"At home, sir," Maddox said from *Victory*. He stood in a holoimage fake showing his ranch home living room.

Galyan had rerouted the call. Everything was back to full steam ahead on *Victory*. They were deep into practicing their trickery and trying to hide it from the rest of Star Watch.

"I expect you here in two hours," Haig said.

"Yes, sir," Maddox said.

Maddox boarded the tin can and Keith took him down to Geneva at the spaceport. Maddox used a flitter, landing at Star Watch Headquarters. Soon, Maddox marched along corridors, spoke with the secretary, and entered the office of the new Lord High Admiral.

Almost everything was the same. The new Lord High Admiral hadn't changed any of the photographs, the desk, or the items on the desk.

The new Lord High Admiral Haig was a small man, although a fireplug of an individual. He was known for his engaging energy and stern countenance. He was twenty-eight years younger than the old Lord High Admiral. Haig had lank dark hair and was thin like a rapier, with dark eyes staring at Maddox.

"Sit down, Captain. Thank you for coming."

Maddox did as requested, sitting, removing his hat. He then jumped up as the new Lord High Admiral came around and shook his hand. The small admiral had a firm handshake, even though he had a narrow hand and several rings on his fingers.

"Sit."

Maddox did so once again.

Haig returned behind the desk and looked at the seated Maddox. Surprisingly, Haig did not appear dwarfish behind the great desk. That was likely due to one change in the office: thick cushions on the chair the old Lord High Admiral had used.

Maddox looked around the office, feeling a keen pang. He missed Cook; missed seeing the Lord High Admiral who had been in the harness for so long. Then Maddox noticed that the new Lord High Admiral was staring at him with his narrow hands folded on the desk.

"Are you finished?" Haig said.

"Yes, sir," Maddox said. He breathed deeply, bringing the Way of the Pilgrim to him. If ever he needed it—this man was different from the old Lord High Admiral. He didn't think Haig would give him much leeway in any matter.

Haig cleared his throat. "Let me begin by saying how sad it is that Admiral Cook is no longer with us. I assume you'll be attending the funeral."

"That's my plan, sir."

Haig nodded, and his dark eyes seemed to glitter. "I've been reviewing your records…" Haig paused, and shook his head. "Let me be frank, Captain. I have much to do and little time to achieve it all. Thus, I must be brusque with you today."

Maddox waited for it.

"I'll start by saying that I don't approve of the way Cook handled you. That is unimportant, however, at least for the moment. What is important is that I know you entered the high-security facility in Antarctica. What's more, former Captain Becker is missing from stasis. I believe you had him thawed out of stasis. So where is he, Captain, on *Victory,* perhaps? Should I order several *Conqueror*-class battleships to surround your starship and have Marines board and take Becker?"

"I don't know why you would do that, sir. *Victory* is in reserve status, nearly empty, in other words. I don't know why—"

"Listen to me," the new Lord High Admiral raised a narrow hand, interrupting. "Do not lie to me, Captain. I've been studying your file. You are a rogue, sir. You do not listen to orders. That is going to stop, I assure you."

Maddox noted the stern glance, the admiral's intensity. Instead of locking horns, Maddox smiled. "Respectfully, sir, I have done a lot for Star Watch through using my rogue methods. That would imply—"

"Yes," Haig said, interrupting, nodding sharply, "it is the only reason I'm not immediately ordering you into the brig. Now, answer me truthfully. Did you take Captain Becker from the max security prison?"

"No," Maddox said. "I did not."

Haig squinted at him. "You're lying to me, sir. That is a bad idea, I assure you."

Maddox cleared his throat. "I don't think there are any records that show I did any of this."

Haig shook his head in a quick negative, the way a hawk might. "In this case, there don't have to be records. The logic is clear enough. You went into the facility. Lieutenant Masterson who processed you is dead due to a brain aneurysm. Captain Becker would do that sort of thing. Clearly, you used that Adok AI to help you do all this. I also have reports from General Mackinder that your pet AI has been infiltrating Star Watch computer systems. Are you our enemy, sir?"

"I am not," Maddox said.

"Did you take Captain Becker?"

After a half-beat, Maddox said, "Yes, I did."

"Ah. Now, we're getting somewhere." Haig sat back. "Why did you lie to me the first time?"

Maddox had finished his quick assessment of the admiral. "Sir, I have a general idea as to the type of individual that is attacking and assassinating our people. I believed I could better apprehend them if I worked alone on this."

"I see. Are you referring to the so-called phase blips reported earlier?"

"That is part of it, sir."

Haig looked off into the distance and then focused sharply on Maddox. "What if I were to say that I believed you're onto something? What if I were to say I despise these methods you use to acquire this information?"

"I would say, sir, that my chief concern is success. My chief concern is winning. My chief concern—"

"All right, I've got the gist of what you're saying," Haig said, interrupting yet again. "I've read your brief. I know what kind of man you are. I do not agree with your methods, but there is some substance to what you say." Haig nodded. "You have Becker. You are practicing illegal Intelligence procedures. I will give you seven days and then I'm shutting everything down. If that means destroying *Victory*, I will do so, Captain. Though you have done amazing things in the past, and I appreciate them, we will run Star Watch from the top. That means you will pass everything through me. I do not hate you, sir. But you will learn to obey me."

Maddox recalled that Admiral Haig had Humanity Manifesto Doctrine leanings. Surely, this colored his thoughts.

"Are you listening to me, Captain?"

"I am, sir, and I respect your position. I respect you, and I thank you for this opportunity."

Haig pointed at Maddox. "I have my eye on you, sir. If you succeed in uncovering this culprit, then I shall forget what you have done illegally in Antarctica. If not…that will be a different kettle of fish, I assure you."

"Sir, I believe I should inform you that I made a deal with Captain Becker."

"Oh, and what deal is that?"

"To take him elsewhere, sir," Maddox hedged at the last moment. He wasn't yet sure how to deal with the new Lord High Admiral.

"Take him elsewhere?" Haig asked. "What the hell are you talking about? Becker is going back into stasis once this is done."

"Sir, I made a deal with the man."

"Captain, I don't care what kind of deal you made with this mind freak. Becker is going back into stasis, and that is final. Do you understand me?"

"I do, sir."

Haig stared at Maddox. "Will you obey me in this?"

"I will, sir," Maddox lied. He would not obey this. He'd given his word to Becker, and this new Lord High Admiral, well, how would his days in Star Watch go with this stickler in charge?

Maddox decided he would have to wait and see. He was used to running things how Cook had allowed him. Perhaps his stint as Star Watch's man of the hour was finally coming to an end.

Maddox shook his head. He wasn't going to delve into that now. He had to save the planet, even if this Napoleon Complex new Lord High Admiral was in charge of Star Watch.

"Seven days, Captain, and after that, we're going to do things my way," Haig said.

"Yes, sir. I understand."

Haig nodded curtly. "I believe you do. You are dismissed."

Maddox stood, saluted, and turned sharply, heading for the door. His grandmother was no longer in charge of Intelligence. Brigadier Stokes and Admiral Cook were no longer alive. Then Maddox had an epiphany, a moment of his intuitive sense. He turned and looked again at the new Lord High Admiral.

"What is it, Captain?"

Maddox shook his head. "Nothing, sir. I'm sorry." He turned and walked out of the office.

What was the reason for the two deaths? Was the murdering enemy doing all this in a strategic sense while also striking indirectly at him? That was an interesting and troubling thought.

Maddox hurried down the corridor. He needed to get back to *Victory* as fast as possible.

-15-

Former Captain Becker lay on his cot in the medical center aboard *Victory*. His brain no longer throbbed constantly, nor did his eyes blur from the pain. However, he did feel unwell. His limbs ached, and he had thrown up on three separate occasions.

Becker hated throwing up.

He remembered as a child when his mother used to hold his forehead with her warm palm and while calming him as he retched, spewing the contents of his breakfast or lunch into the toilet. Would a mother hold the forehead of such a freakish individual as he had become?

I'm a bigheaded freak. I didn't always used to be this way. I used to be handsome. Oh, if only I hadn't crawled into that deep cave and found the Liss on Jarnevon long ago.

That had been an awful day. He would give anything to change it, particularly the moment of his wretched discovery. Everything had followed from that.

The hours passed sluggishly as Becker felt sorry for himself, and as the nurses came by and looked after him. His health increased, so that was something. Soon, his eyes focused again, and his brain no longer throbbed incessantly.

Those were the positives. However, he refused to look in a mirror and see his horrid reflection. He wouldn't be able to stand such a sight. Here was the thing: if *he* couldn't stand it, how could he imagine any woman could, especially enough to love him?

Becker desperately wanted the virile part of him back. He replayed more times than he could imagine the telepathic discussion with the Prime Saa years ago. The alien Liss mind-meld had been so smug with him, forcing him to choose between sexual or political power. Becker could still hear the horrible snip in his mind when the Liss had stolen his precious parts. Now, though, if Maddox kept his end of the bargain, he would end-run the arrogant Prime Saa. He would receive what the aliens had stolen.

Becker yearned to read Maddox's mind, to know which way the captain would go. But if he could read Maddox's thoughts—

Becker smirked as he lay on the medical cot. *If I could read his mind, I'd take control of the damn starship. I'd go to this Library Planet, wherever that is. I'd have them work on me so I could regain...*

Ironically, Becker didn't like to refer to them as testicles. That seemed too clinical. He preferred the term 'balls,' considering it a more virile, jock-like term.

It was true that he was anything but a jock, but he loved to think of himself in a way the ladies loved.

Had the Prime Saa known how much the ladies consumed his thoughts? Maybe the Liss had been needlessly cruel to him. The Prime Saa must have known. Even though he was a eunuch, even though he was a castrate, he still wanted—

"A girl," he told himself. "I need a woman to love, maybe many of them."

Becker loved watching the nurses walk past or stop to take care of him. Whenever one doted on him, he smiled. Yeah, he rifled through the woman's life experiences. He'd see things in her memories that would make him really grin. The ugly things...he didn't feel like looking at those recollections yet.

Josef Becker was reading minds all right but refraining from any dominating, controlling thoughts. Then he realized he had to do this right. He'd lost track last time when working for the Prime Saa. That was the lesson there. He couldn't let himself go. He had to win first and play second, not play first. That had been a costly error. He'd lost ten years of his life, to say nothing about the rest.

Thus, Becker began to concentrate on Galyan. Didn't the Adok AI run the starship? Becker caught Galyan hovering in ghost mode, watching him. Becker could even *feel* the ship's sensors spying on him.

Through telekinesis, Becker started rifling through the AI stations in the armored center of *Victory*. He began collecting data.

That impressed him later. He could do more than read biological thoughts. He could master computers, too.

I am literally godlike, as I have godlike powers in this weak body. What if...what if I could combine my wonderful, my stupendous, my frankly incredible brain with the physique of Captain Maddox or even a New Man?

Becker considered the idea in detail as he lay upon the cot or as he sat up to drink fluids or eat bland medical food.

What if he could find and eventually have them—whoever *they* needed to be—change his body the way the Liss had changed his brain? If doctors gave him a Herculean physique so that he was truly godlike, could run for hours, could bend steel with his hands and still maintain his gargantuan, his colossal brain—yes indeed. He needed a body to fit his big head. Then he wouldn't be a mutated freak anymore. He would be a mutated *Overman*. He would not be a New Man. He would be an Overman. He would be beyond their small ideals of what a man really was.

The idea took hold of Becker's imagination and he began plotting out possibilities. That was what a real he-man did. He made things happen. With his dominating telepathy, he could take Professor Ludendorff, for instance, and force him to conceive of ways to do this.

Unfortunately, the blasted Methuselah Man kept a silver band around his head the whole time, including when he slept. The band and box blocked his telepathy from entering the old brain.

Becker knew, because he'd been roving through *Victory* with his telepathy and testing who was worth his effort and who was not. It had taken great effort of will on his part to keep from modifying Keith Maker a little. Becker wanted to turn Keith randy as hell so the ace would bother Valerie, and then she would be forced to slap him in the face to cool him down.

That would be hilarious. Yet Becker knew he had to control his urges. That was part of his 'win first, play second' philosophy.

I must be a good boy for a little while. I need to give Maddox what he wants and hope he keeps his end of the bargain. I must be ready for if he doesn't, though. Then, I'll strike fast and turn things around on him.

Becker decided on an initial strategy of sweet serenity to lull them. In other words, he did what they asked him to do. He didn't complain. When Maddox came, he gave the captain the correct noises, saying things that made suspicious Maddox happy.

Becker understood that Maddox didn't trust or believe him. That was okay. Becker was going to go by the numbers this time, even as he strengthened his mental domination powers. Besides, he was still sloughing off all those years in stasis.

Can you imagine? They put *me*, Josef Becker—the Great One—in stasis.

This was where Becker got clever as he derived a conclusion from all his thinking. Maybe it was seeing Maddox strut around with his powerful body, protecting his small head by a silver band and box. Perhaps it was the way Ludendorff looked at him. The Methuselah Man actually had handsome virile features and curly white chest hair showing past his open shirt, open at the top. Despite that, the Methuselah Man had a puny-sized head like all the rest.

Yet—and here was the important point—Maddox, Ludendorff, and Meta had defeated the Prime Saa. The trio had defeated the cyber Liss mind-meld. That was amazing, considering that the Prime Saa had defeated him. The Prime Saa had toyed with and castrated him, even as it had given him monumental, domineering, telepathic power.

Becker went back to an old idea. *I'm going to find the last holdout Liss and use them. They're going to be my backup. I'll find any Bosk servants in this part of the Orion Arm. I just have to get off Earth. First, I have to get out of this bed and strengthen myself. Then, soon, I'll be the Overman of the Orion*

Arm. They are all going to pay for pissing on me. That I solemnly swear.

Lieutenant Masterson had paid with an aneurysm. That hadn't been a slip up. He'd killed the urinating creep. *Piss on me while I'm sleeping, will you?* The universe had done that as well. *Calm down, calm down, calm down,* Becker told himself. *You have to take it easy, my friend. Put all that in the back of your mind. Hide it. Don't let them see the real you. Give them what they want. Remember, Maddox, Ludendorff, and Meta beat the Prime Saa. Therefore, they're exceedingly dangerous, even if they have puny heads and tiny brains. They have innate cunning. They're probably more venal and evil than you realize. But I'll take care of it. I'm going to play it straight, just for now, you watch me.*

Several hours later, Maddox came by and told him the doctor said he could start hunting for the assassins.

Becker nodded.

After Maddox departed, Becker told himself, *I have to out-wait and out-smart everyone. If I do that right this time…*

Becker fantasized about a bevy of extreme beauties catering to his every whim and loving it. He would love it, too.

Just bide your time, buddy-boy. Bide your time before you strike out of the blue for everything.

-16-

Maddox was in Professor Ludendorff's science chamber aboard *Victory*, conferring with the Methuselah Man.

Ludendorff was a well-built, silver-haired, handsome fellow, tanned, with a gold chain around his neck. He must have been that way in his youth when he thought he was the ladies' man par excellence. In truth, Ludendorff still believed he was the premier ladies' man. He was also a gifted genius in inventing and in seeing facts and facets of things that others missed.

Maddox was going over with Ludendorff the events that had ended in the extermination of Admiral Cook and Brigadier Stokes. It had been six days since Stokes' death. It would seem, therefore, that the next attempt would take place within a day or two.

Maddox and Ludendorff compared and contrasted the things they understood. That included the alien manner of the suffocation deaths, the ability of the attacker to enter Star Watch Headquarters with ease, and that the secretary had recorded the creature on her glasses. That had been a strange precaution for the late Lord High Admiral to have taken. Had old Cook sensed his coming demise?

Abruptly, Galyan appeared in the chamber and said, "Excuse my interruption, gentlemen."

Ludendorff jumped and yelled. Then he swore, "I wish you wouldn't do that, you damned AI. Don't you know enough to knock or to send a signal so that you don't surprise us each time?"

"I am sorry, Professor," Galyan said. "I did not mean to disturb you. I thought—"

"Yes, yes," Ludendorff said. "What did you think?"

"Never mind," Galyan said, as he glanced at Maddox.

"What were you going to say?" demanded Ludendorff. "Were you going to say Maddox didn't jump? That I'm more jumpy than the captain? He has reflexes like a cat, and yet I'm the one who's jumpy?"

"Calm yourself," Maddox said. "I saw Galyan out of the corner of my eye."

"Oh, fine, fine," Ludendorff said. "You're all so wonderful, aren't you?"

"Professor, I can come back later," Galyan said.

"Never mind that," Maddox said. "I told you not to bother us unless you had something important to tell us. Now, what is it?"

"You are correct in your assumption, sir," Galyan said. "I have finally discovered an overlooked report, two of them, in fact. It is regarding the remains, strange remains found in an apartment and a house."

"Oh," Maddox said.

"If you will allow me to elaborate…" Galyan said.

"Yes, yes, of course you may elaborate," Ludendorff said. "You made me jump. I'm sure you got your jollies off on that, you freaky little AI."

"Really, Professor," Maddox said. "There's no need to insult Galyan. He's only doing what I asked."

"Oh, take his side, will you?"

"If it's any consolation," Maddox said, "I would have likely jumped like you, except I saw Galyan a second before he spoke. I did start, but you must have missed it."

Ludendorff glared at Maddox until he threw his hands into the air. "Forget it. I'm not high-strung. It doesn't bother me. I'm just trying to make you feel better."

"Of course," Maddox said. "I understand."

"Well, don't be so understanding all the time," Ludendorff said. "Get on with it, Galyan. What do you want to tell us? My time is valuable. I can't afford to waste it on endless chitchat."

Maddox wondered what was really bothering Ludendorff. This was excessive. Could Becker have tried to invade Ludendorff's thoughts and partly succeeded despite the silver band and box? That warranted some investigation. Otherwise, Ludendorff's complaints didn't make sense.

Galyan projected a holoimage graphic, showing the photographed remains of a once Berber salesman from the Atlas Mountains in North Africa, and a dancer from Stockholm in Sweden Sector.

"These don't look like human remains," Ludendorff said.

Galyan showed both holoimages side by side. Each showed crisp, almost tree-like charred remains.

"Where were these found?" Maddox said.

"In two different places in Lyon, France Sector," Galyan said.

"Say," Ludendorff said, "Lyon isn't that far from Geneva."

"There could be places much further," Galyan said. "But there are others closer."

"Do we know anything about the men?" Maddox asked.

Galyan proceeded to tell them what he'd found regarding their professional lives and their histories at school.

"No," Maddox said. "We're approaching this wrong."

"Is that an intuitive thought, sir?" Galyan asked.

Maddox grunted, which could have meant anything. He was staring at the holoimages of the two remains. "You're saying these were *human* remains?"

"Yes, sir," Galyan said. "Further analysis showed that from the police forensic reports."

Maddox pinched his lower lip. "Tell us more about the composition of the remains."

Galyan's eyelids flickered. Then he gave the composition of each, both exactly the same, it turned out.

"How odd," Ludendorff said. "Notice that the remains are missing water, all kinds of substances that could relate to electric processes in the body."

"That is interesting and possibly telling," Galyan said.

Maddox studied the holographic images. "You say both men died in Lyon, one in an apartment and one in a house?"

"Yes," Galyan said. "They also died a week apart."

Maddox's head snapped up. "Why didn't you say that earlier?"

"I am getting to the various facts," Galyan said.

"Of course," Maddox said. "Is there anything else you want to add?"

"The police have uncovered the activities of each man the night he died," Galyan said. "Strangely, there are records of each man having been on a dance floor of a nightclub. Let me see..."

Once again, Galyan's eyelids fluttered before he said, "The two danced with an extremely beautiful woman, apparently the same one."

"Do you have a picture of this woman?" Ludendorff said.

"Hmm, I should have already thought of that," Galyan said. "Let me check. I don't have any copies. I'll roam through the police report computers."

By using *Victory's* sensors and devices, Galyan soon extracted photos that various cameras had taken in the nightclubs. With a wave of his fingers, he displayed the holoimage pictures on the wall.

"Venna the Spy," Maddox said. "I remember her from the Library Planet when we went there the first time."

"This is most curious," Ludendorff said. "Venna the Spy means Spacers."

"Yes," Maddox said, "Spacers." He turned to Galyan. "That's wonderful detective work. Venna the Spy, a phase ship, and these horrific deaths indicate Spacer Intelligence killed the Lord High Admiral and Brigadier Mike Stokes. Is Venna still on Earth?"

"I have not seen any photos of her except from these nights and in these establishments. Let me recalculate." Galyan searched many databanks, centering on the city of Lyon. Through an odd set of circumstances, he did not discover that Venna was asleep in an apartment complex. There were reasons for that, none of which Galyan knew. Venna had taken extreme precautions regarding security cameras except while on the dance floors.

"No sir," Galyan said. "There are no signs of Venna or a phase ship."

Maddox nodded. "If I remember correctly, and I do, Venna teleported directly from the Supreme Intelligence's chamber on the Library Planet and fled onto a Spacer vessel. Now the Spacers have a phase ship. I believe this combo will strike again soon. I need to take Becker to Lyon and hunt for Venna there."

Maddox's nostrils flared. "I congratulate you, Galyan, but I don't want you to stop at this. I want you to scour every databank, and I want you to correlate and tell me immediately whatever you find."

"Even if you are in your bedroom, sir, and engaged in, ah, certain activities?"

"Use discretion under certain circumstances," Maddox said.

"You can count on me, sir," Galyan said.

"I *am* counting on you. Well, Professor, what do you think about all this?"

"That Galyan has done a splendid job as you said. Those weird remains, if I were to guess...I'd say some kind of alien energy fed off the two men. If Venna danced with them each night, I conclude she was seeking a certain type of man to use them."

"What type of man?" Maddox said.

"If we knew, we would know the answer to much of this," Ludendorff said. "Let me think. Ah. Perhaps different types of men exude different types of energy. Galyan, tell me, were either of the men noted for anything extraordinary?"

Galyan's eyelids flickered. "Yes, both were extraordinarily energetic."

"There you have it," Ludendorff told Maddox. "I suggest the men possessed subtle differences of energy compared to others. Venna sought them out, using her beauty as a lure, at least to Spacer Intelligence way of thinking, to their useful deaths."

Maddox became thoughtful. "If you're right, Venna lured them just as she did the Emperor of the New Men, and I recall my Uncle Ural saying he found her intoxicating. So then, now we know more."

"Should we tell Star Watch what we have discovered?" Galyan asked.

Maddox shook his head. "They might give the game away too soon with their blundering. We want to capture Venna and the phase ship. To do that, we have to get our hands on her."

"Agreed," Ludendorff said.

Maddox noticed that Ludendorff was fixated on Venna's holographic images. Was the old goat smitten by her beauty? Ludendorff would not be the first. Venna was indeed beautiful.

Maddox shook his head. Venna was nothing compared to his wonderful Meta. Then he had an idea. *I'm going to bring Meta along. If anyone can deal with the Spacer spy, it will be Meta.*

-17-

Maddox, Meta, and Becker came down in the tin can. They landed at an airport near Lyon and took an air taxi to the city.

They all wore hats. Becker's covered his abnormally large cranium. Maddox and Meta's hats hid the silver headbands, which hummed softly.

Meta kept a firm arm around Becker's waist, propping him up and helping him walk. His weak muscles could not easily support his dense, oversized brain.

Maddox didn't want to help Becker around like that in public. Becker didn't want that either. It was obvious by his reactions that Becker enjoyed Meta's proximity.

Maddox kept interrupting that joy by asking, "Do you sense anything yet? How about now?"

"I'm searching," Becker said, "but this takes time. I have to enter each mind and sift through the memories before I realize they are of no use."

Becker didn't add that he often zipped into the mind of an exceptionally pretty girl and rifled through her most erotic memories. He enjoyed those, especially while Meta held him. That was part of the contentment on his face. If he couldn't practice sexual enjoyment of women yet, he could at least enjoy their proximity and lewder thoughts.

In such a manner, the trio continued through Lyon. The nightclubs would be opening soon. They would go to them at that point.

Galyan, meanwhile, was searching all the face recognition systems, particularly centering on Lyon, France Sector. Unfortunately, Venna was anywhere but in Lyon. There was a reason for that by the name of Senior Dax.

Earlier, Dax had spoken with Mu 11 in a subterranean chamber while aboard the phase ship. They agreed Star Watch would have found evidence that pinpointed Lyon as the key place. Thus, it was time to change the venue.

Venna was presently in Basel, Switzerland Sector, closer to Geneva than before. Even now, dressed to kill, she was sauntering into a nightclub.

Dax was on the surface, while Mu 11 remained underground in the phase ship. Dax had decided to watch, and if needed, run interference for Venna.

This assassination was critical; the target was the Iron Lady, also known as Brigadier Mary O'Hara. She was Captain Maddox's grandmother. To kill her would surely drive a dagger of anguish into the breast of Captain Maddox. It might even unhinge him. It would certainly wreck whatever combination had supported Maddox in Star Watch when added to Cook and Stokes. Perhaps others would see that if they helped Captain Maddox, they would die.

This kill would be the accumulation of a powerful assassination assault. It would have repercussions in two spiral arms. Certainly, Star Watch would be shaken to the core by these deaths. Certainly, Maddox would lack his former verve, energy, and authority.

From within the nightclub, Dax continued to watch Venna. He wore his senso mask, a hat, sunglasses, and a long trench coat. He sipped alcoholic drinks as he waited in the shadows. Here people danced with intensity, and men and women mingled. Drinks exchanged hands, as credit cards passed back and forth.

Venna returned from the ladies' room. She was marvelous, having added to herself.

The woman's allure stunned Dax. She wasn't the same species as him, although he was humanoid. But he'd lost his sex organs in a terrible fire years ago. Even so, the way Venna moved magnetized eyes. She was so sinuous and supple, and sauntered in her high heels in such a seductive manner.

From his location in back, Dax watched her track and zero in on a shorter individual. This man was not tall or lithe, but frankly a little chubby and overdressed in silky garments. Yet, there was an obvious extra vitality to him. Even though the man had a bevy of beauties around him, he grinned like a wolf as Venna sauntered near. He flicked his fat hands and made the others shoo.

Venna finished the approach in her most provocative manner. He reached out and grasped both her hands, setting her on a high stool at the high table at which he sat. He ordered drinks, leaned across the table and spoke to her. Venna smiled, soon applying lipstick.

Dax noted how she aimed the device at the man to see if he had the right energetic level. He must have, for Venna slipped off the stool and tugged him onto the floor. They danced. For such a pudgy, squat fellow, he moved with acrobatic grace. He didn't match Venna, but if anyone could have, it was the squab of a man exuding vibrant energy.

The night wore on. Dax waited. As a cyber, he had learned the real art of patience. He began to concentrate on the main door. Finally, Venna and her chub walked out the main door and entered a taxi, flittering away.

Dax was on high alert. Should he return to the phase ship? He continued to watch and scan instead. Where was Captain Maddox? What was Star Watch doing? Why had they not discovered Venna? The assassination seemed so brazen to Dax.

Maybe they were getting away with this because of how the Commonwealth was structured. It was so much more open and less regimented than society on Loggia or on any other planet controlled by the Sovereign Hierarchy of Leviathan. There was freedom here.

Dax found it intoxicating.

The cyber shook it off. He scanned, and then he left the nightclub and hurried toward a back alley. It was time to leave, time to return to the phase ship.

Would Venna assassinate the Iron Lady? That was the pregnant question tonight.

With that, Dax opened channels with the phase ship and teleported away.

-18-

Maddox stopped suddenly and felt a shiver across his shoulders. He knew the signs. That was his intuitive sense kicking in. It was odd that he should feel the intuitive sense while wearing this silver headband and box.

"Go on a little way," Maddox said.

Becker and Meta stared at him.

Then Meta nodded. "This way. Maybe you would like a drink or some other refreshment."

"Yes," Becker said. "I am tired. I could use a drink."

Maddox watched them until the two rounded a corner and disappeared from view. He took off the headband. It was possibly a dangerous risk being this close to Becker. Maddox had worn this thing for days and nights on end.

With it off, Maddox felt his intuitive sense more powerfully. A thunderous ping in his head let him know the Iron Lady, his grandmother, was in danger. But how or in what form of danger?

Maddox jammed the headband back on as he felt the slightest nudge. He was sure the nudge meant Becker. He pivoted and ran after them.

Maddox raced around the corner and up to Meta, snatching her free hand. "We have to go. Now!" he said.

Neither questioned him. They saw his face and heard the urgency in his voice. All three ran to the edge of the street where Maddox hailed an air taxi.

They jammed into the vehicle as Maddox shouted at the driver, "To the spaceport, hurry!"

"What happened?" Meta said.

Ignoring Meta, Maddox turned to Becker who sat between them. "If you try to slip into my mind again, the deal is over."

"I-I don't know what you're talking about," Becker stuttered.

"You must have understood I was staying back to slip off my headband. Or maybe you just hoped I would. I felt a tendril of your thought. No! Don't lie, Becker. Don't lie unless you want to die here and now."

Becker gave Meta a pleading look, seemingly seeking comfort from her.

She didn't give him any.

The taxi driver looked worried as he glanced in the rearview mirror.

"All right," Becker said, turning from Meta with her stoic features. "I was curious what you were doing. It was the faintest tendril, as you called it. I saw you have telepathic abilities in your own right. You're not defenseless even without a headband."

"Right," Maddox said. He pulled out a communicator. "Keith, are you ready to lift off?"

"I can be in thirty seconds," Keith said.

"Fire up the fighter," Maddox said. "We have to get up to *Victory* as fast as possible."

"C-Captain," Becker stuttered. "I can't use the fold function, remember? If you want me on *Victory* to help, I can't do it after a fold. My brain can't take it. I may even be worse off than the first time."

"I know," Maddox said. "That's why we're rushing. Driver!" he shouted. "Put some speed into this."

The urgency and not so hidden threat in Maddox's voice caused the driver to fly the air car faster, zooming above the designated route.

They flashed over industrial buildings and a large park with trees, racing for the spaceport in the distance. Warning beacons spread across the path.

"Go over them," Maddox said.

"Sir, the driver said. "That's illegal. Look at the warning signs. I could be targeted and shot down."

"You won't be. It's cleared."

The driver twisted around to stare at Maddox. Maddox showed him a special ID. The driver stared into Maddox's face.

"You have clearance," Maddox said. "This is a national emergency."

The driver swore in another language, squeezed his eyes shut for a second and opened them, flying over the beacons and straight onto the space field.

Galyan had already short-circuited the security measures. No sensors locked onto the air car and thus no guns fired. There was no alarm so no armed personnel ran out to try to intercept them.

"That one," Maddox said, pointing.

The driver swore again in his native tongue, landing beside the tin can, doing so with a screeching jar.

"The new Lord High Admiral isn't going to like this," Meta said.

"Screw him," Maddox said. "I don't care." He ripped out several high note credit bills and pressed them against the driver's nearest shoulder.

The driver grabbed them, and his eyes widened in shock as he looked at them.

Maddox was already sliding out. "Run!" he shouted.

Maddox and Meta grabbed an upper arm each and picked Becker up as if he were a child, sprinting for the fold fighter.

"Cradle your head," Maddox shouted.

Becker did so, covering it with his skinny arms.

Maddox and Meta raced through the open hatch and thrust Becker into the nearest crash seat, securing him. Then both jumped to their seats, buckling in.

"Go! Go! Go!" Maddox said.

"Hang on, mates." Keith had been clicking switches as the hatch shut with a clang.

The fighter powered up with a purr, lifting off the tarmac and slowly starting to move forward.

"Give it everything," Maddox said. "We're already out of time. Becker, is your head securely against the rest?"

"Yes," Becker said, who pressed his head back. "What's happening? You're not going to fold, are you?"

"No folding, Mr. Maker," Maddox said. "But we have to get to *Victory* now. It is utterly urgent. It could already be too late."

"I hear you, mate. I'm on it."

The fighter had already been accelerating. Now, the nose tilted upward and the afterburners kicked in. Like a rocket, the fighter roared up into the heavens, heading for *Victory* as it gained speed.

Galyan appeared.

"Go watch my grandmother," Maddox said. "Use whatever electronic means you can if that thing should appear near her. Stop it or slow it down at least."

"You think the strange entity creature will go after Mary O'Hara on *Victory?*" Galyan said.

"Yes!" Maddox said. "We wouldn't be doing it this way otherwise. Now go!"

Galyan disappeared.

***

At the same time, somewhere in Basel, Switzerland Sector, Venna was already lifting the lid to her Phantasma Synth Crystal box.

The pudgy fellow wasn't quite as eager or energetic as the others had been regarding the box. Venna slipped off a shoulder of her gown and made a pouting kiss. That still didn't do it. She approached him and kissed him on the mouth.

Instead of luring him closer, the man stepped away from the box as if suspicious.

"What's going on?" he said. "What's the meaning of that?"

Venna smiled seductively.

He eyed her more closely. "Why have you zeroed in on me, anyway? You could have had anybody. Why did you come to my table?"

"Don't you know why?" Venna whispered in her most seductive manner.

"That's what I'm trying to ascertain. I don't like your box. There's something off with it."

"Really? The crystals are an aphrodisiac. Try them. You'll love it."

"They don't look like aphrodisiacs," he said.

Realizing he was too cautious, Venna clicked on her ruby necklace. She hadn't thought she'd need it, certainly not with any human. But this pudgy fellow possessed a vibrant energy none of the others had exuded to the same degree. Did that help him resist her? That was astounding. Few men could resist her in this situation.

He stared at the ruby necklace as it energized, sending powerful lust signals into his brain. He blinked several times. He actually made to turn away. The man had spectacular self-control. This was incredible. Then the lust rays zoomed deeper into his brain, clicking the right relays. He mouth opened and his eyes shined. He began panting for Venna.

Venna worried this would hurt in the culmination of what she attempted. She shut off the ruby necklaces, pushed one of his hands against a crystal. At the last second, he hesitated, showing abnormal powers of resistance to her beauty and the sensuality of the moment. Fortunately, a blue color from the crystal ignited and passed from it to his hand. His fingers tightened around it as he raised the crystal from the box. The color began to climb up his forearm.

"What's happening?" he shouted.

The process proved too fast for him to resist. The Phantasma Synth Crystal released even more energy into him. His eyes rolled up into his head as he thumped onto the floor. He writhed in agony, clutching the crystal as it began to devour him, sucking up his etheric energy.

Venna didn't have the same strength to do this as she had the other times. She nearly dropped the crystals several times. She'd taken his, as the link had already forged into an unbreakable bond.

With manic strength, Venna hung onto the crystals, although she sobbed twice. Then she gritted her teeth and used everything she could to continue. But the process was too powerful this time. Her fingers lost their grip.

A powerful memory surfaced in her. Years ago, the Iron Lady had sent Star Watch slayers to kill her family. She had been a key operative to all that. Now the Iron Lady was going to live in the lap of luxury for what had happened to her people back then.

A terrible laugh bubbled up in Venna.

That old witch was going to get what was coming to her. Venna clutched the crystals, enduring more than she would have ever thought possible.

The transformation continued as the crystals crisped the man as his etheric energy bled upward into a scintillating pattern in midair.

Venna squeezed her eyes shut. She already felt spent, but now it was time to assassinate the Iron Lady.

As Venna thought this, readying herself for the final lap, the tin can was halfway through the stratosphere, rocketing toward orbital *Victory*.

-19-

As Venna gripped the Phantasma Synth Crystals and gained control over them and the etheric creature forming before her, her vitality diminished. Venna felt it, and she knew the process might kill her this time.

Using the alien, technological mystic devices was killing her by degrees. She saw that, and then she had to put the understanding aside. She needed everything to control the entity that she'd created out of the vibrant man whose name she didn't even remember.

His etheric energy had created something more vibrant than before. It was like—

Venna recalled stories about genies from the Tales of the Arabian Nights. The first two etheric creatures—genies—she'd conjured from the bodies of the first two were as nothing compared to this one.

The crystals shook dreadfully in her hands as they blazed with color. She held them tightly, as if her fingers had become eagle's talons. Her fingers seemed to shrivel, becoming like ancient things. She felt blemishes, maybe blood vessels, bursting under her once smooth skin. This one was going to kill her. This one was too strong for the crystals and for her.

"No!" Venna shrieked in a harsh and unlovely voice, "You will obey me!"

She shook the two crystals at the thing that glared at her balefully from midair. It wasn't just her imagination. The thing sought her death. No! That wasn't it. The man understood what had happened to him. He wanted vengeance against her.

For just a moment, Venna thrust her hip out seductively. The pattern of etheric energy recoiled. It almost seemed that a mouth would appear on the swirling alien entity being and start to curse her.

Venna raised both crystals above her head. They pulsated with power. Fortunately, the color did not bleed into her hands, up her arms and clutch her chest to kill her. The color bled from the crystals and through the air in slow motion. The colors advanced in two lines until they touched the etheric, swirling creature.

It recoiled further as if it had received shocks like a cardiac arrest victim. There was a strange, keening sound vibrating from it.

"You will obey me!" Venna said.

Not knowing how or why, she understood. She had gained control over him, it, whatever the thing was. With the understanding came a verge of panic. She was tired and frightened. Yet she exulted in some bizarre manner. That came from the crystals. They were alive after a fashion. They were alive the same way a robot, or sentient AI would be alive. The crystals were mechanical and yet they were mystic and certainly technological, but from the alien Aetharian shaman perspective.

Venna caught that much. It was nebulous, and yet, in the background, she saw scaly humanoid entities with spindly limbs and big heads. She realized she didn't see them visibly but in her mind's eye.

Venna concentrated on the here and now. She looked up and saw the swirling energy watching her like a panther ready to pounce upon an unwary hunter. She controlled the entity and sent it away, causing the energy to flash through the wall.

Venna gasped with relief, as the horrible energy creature terrified her. Perhaps as important, the lizard image of the ancient Aetharians from the planet Ector that had circled a pulsar had vanished. There was something dreadfully upsetting about the image, but Venna didn't know what it was.

She propelled the etheric energy as she had the first two, at Star Watch Headquarters in Geneva. She knew the Iron Lady was there, or Venna was certain the Iron Lady was there. The others had been there. Wouldn't this one be there as well?

The etheric energy sped nearly invisibly, passing through the extra security as if it didn't exist. The faint energy roved up and down the buildings seeking the Iron Lady. There was no evidence of her, however. Her office was empty, without any trail leading elsewhere.

Venna in Basel, in the apartment, wondered where the Iron Lady could be.

The etheric energy creature looked up at a ceiling. It spotted the target far away. Then it zoomed for space. It had located the Iron Lady. She was on a spaceship in orbit.

Venna became aware of this. Oh, how cunning Captain Maddox was. He thought himself so terribly clever. The Iron Lady certainly was there on the starship.

"I'll get you, old witch," Venna muttered. "You sent those killers to destroy my family. Now I'll destroy you, and later I'll destroy all of Star Watch. You can bet before that I'll destroy Captain Maddox as well."

But only if I have the strength to finish this, Venna realized. Handling these crystals and vibrant men was killing her.

Venna's features stiffened. So be it. It was worth the chance to avenge those who had long ago been slain. That her memories had been manufactured and inserted by Spacer Intelligence was unknown to Venna. Instead, the lies fed her the resolve to kill. She would suffocate that old witch. There was nothing anybody could do to stop her because—

The etheric knot of force consumed some of its substance as it climbed into orbit. It zeroed in on the double-oval spaceship. As it started to pass through bulkheads, fixing on that old witch who had ordered the murder—

"I'm coming to kill you," Venna said.

At the same instant, as if Mary O'Hara heard those words, she looked up from her bed. The etheric energy burst into her chamber. Mary gasped and brought the covers up to her chin.

Slowly, the pulsating, swirling energy glided toward her.

It was time to kill, Venna knew.

-20-

Before the killing happened, before the entity reached Mary O'Hara's quarters, Maddox lashed out at Keith with his tongue, and the ace rocketed up toward the starship.

They faced security challenges from satellite operators, a *Conqueror*-class battleship and even a call from the new Lord High Admiral. Maddox told Keith to ignore them all.

They didn't fold this time around. Because of Becker and his precious big mind, they did not dare do that. It took them longer because of that. However, the tin can landed inside a Mid-Earth Orbit *Victory* hangar bay.

Seconds after touching down, they piled out with Maddox and Meta once again lifting Becker between them, each grabbing an upper arm. They exited the hangar bay and raced along the corridors with their brainy cargo.

Maddox shouted, "Galyan, Galyan!"

Galyan appeared.

"Is my grandmother safe?" Maddox shouted.

"I have seen nothing strange yet," Galyan said. Then his eyelids began to flutter. "I am wrong, sir. There is a strange force heading for our starship. I have just detected it."

"Go to my grandmother's quarters now," Maddox said. "Protect her. Do whatever you can. Use whatever electronic force you can. We'll be there soon. Becker, are you ready for this?"

Galyan vanished.

"Evil," Becker moaned. "I sense great evil. I don't know what this is. I lack the power to block this."

"Listen to me, Becker," Maddox said. Even as Meta and he ran down the corridor, lifting the light, bigheaded fool with them, "you use whatever power you can. Read its mind. Send mental domination blasts against it. Use telekinesis and destroy it by pieces. I don't care how, just destroy it."

"It might attack me if I do that," Becker said.

"Hey, if you don't try, you're a dead man."

"That's not fair," Becker whined. "Why is everyone always coming at me? Why am I always the object of scorn?"

"Shut up, you little mouse," Maddox said. "Think about ways to defeat the alien assassin. That's all that matters."

They rode a turbo lift up. Now, alarms blared on *Victory*.

Galyan appeared in the turbo lift. "The energy entity is heading straight for your grandmother's quarters. Nothing is stopping it. I tried, but it shrugged off everything electrical."

"Go there, Galyan. Start attacking it anyway. Give us time."

"I do not know what that thing is, sir. It is resisting analysis. It is zooming through everything we have. I do not even know if it is material in any real sense."

Maddox struggled to contain his rage. "Think for a second, you idiot. It's touchable, material, because it suffocated the Lord High Admiral and Stokes. My grandmother is not going to join that list. Now go. Save her."

Once more, Galyan vanished.

Precious seconds passed. The turbo lift halted and the hatch opened. Maddox and Meta dashed down the corridor carrying Becker between them. They ran into the Iron Lady's quarters, instantly spotting the etheric form as it descended toward the Iron Lady.

Galyan rushed the entity, entering the swirling energy, shocking the thing with audible zaps. The swirling entity slowed down, so that was something.

Lights began to flash inside the entity. Hisses sounded and brighter lights flashed. Galyan disappeared.

The flashing lights did nothing to Maddox and Meta as they set down Becker.

"It's all up to you, Becker," Maddox said.

The former captain clutched his privates with both hands as if he were a rock singer from an ancient age.

"Will you keep your bargain, Captain Maddox?" Becker asked.

"I said I will," Maddox replied, as he stared at the alien energy. "I'll follow through despite everything. Give me a reason to trust you, Becker. Now kill the damned thing."

Becker looked at the alien energy. *It is damned*, he realized. He used his big head, marshaling the telepathic powers the Liss had given him combined with his native abilities. He reached out telepathically and struggled against the entity.

At first, Becker wasn't aware of Venna. He strove against the etheric power floating toward the quivering Iron Lady. Then he realized someone drove the creature through willpower. He sought the secondary source, and finally sensed Venna.

"Aha," Becker said.

With telepathic bolts, Becker strove to break the link between Venna and the etheric entity. That was when he learned about the Phantasma Synth Crystals. The crystals entered the lists, as it were, and battled against him.

As Venna stood in her hotel room in Basel, the crystals flashed with power as she gripped them. The alien crystals sucked up whatever bits of energy remained in the crisped husk at Venna's feet. Then the crystals began to draw power from her life energy.

Venna gasped for air, her lungs hurting.

The Phantasma Synth Crystals might have consumed her life, but they needed her mentality in order to fight this big-brained opponent in the starship. The crystals were tools, machines in a sense. Without a living person, they were useless. Still, the balance they strove to achieve hurt Venna.

The crystals used bizarre patterns because the ancient Aetharians had different mind designs than humans. They literally thought in a different manner. It had allowed the construction of the crystals, but it meant…

Here and now, it meant that a ferocious struggle took place between the ancient alien tech and Becker's desire for freedom, women, and life. The Liss had constructed his improved mind on human patterns, adding to its telepathic strength.

It was like archers firing arrows at a lancer galloping at them on his horse. Both ways hurt and could kill. Each used different strategies and methods.

Becker blocked with his mind as a horseman might use a shield. He deflected the arrows, straining to reach the enemy and pierce him with the tip of the lance.

At the same time, the energy entity in the quarters lowered by degrees, inching closer to the Iron Lady. O'Hara stared at it transfixed like a mouse watching an owl's talons descend. O'Hara strove to move from her bed, but like some rat staring at a hypnotizing, swaying snake, she couldn't do it.

It turned out that Maddox and Meta couldn't move anymore either.

Meta's face was purpling. In the etheric entity's presence, she could not move her lungs to breathe.

Maddox managed to suck down air, but he struggled to pull out his blaster and start shooting at the swirling thing. His muscles stood out in stark relief, straining and unmoving.

The etheric entity inched closer yet to O'Hara, touching the top of her head. At that point, the energy being froze.

Maddox watched the alien entity shiver and shake, no doubt trying to move more.

"I'm winning," Becker boasted. "I've finally got the hang of it."

Becker used deft telepathic and telekinetic moves learned from the Prime Saa. The key, though, was a mental bolt that had slammed against the crystals. It had almost severed the crystals' link with the entity. That had allowed Becker time to practice telekinesis.

The crystals might have panicked. In order to continue operating, they stole yet more of Venna's life force. Was it too much?

Abruptly, a slit mouth appeared on the etheric energy. A horrific sonic scream erupted from it. In that moment, the creature inched a bit more over O'Hara's head.

"No!" Becker shouted. He pointed both hands at it, opened his hands wide and then clenched his fingers into fists. He did this several times. Each time, he pumped telepathic and telekinetic power into the entity.

The etheric creature squealed.

Yet again, Becker squeezed his fingers as tightly as they would go.

The etheric energy quivered faster and faster as it remained in one place, and then it blasted apart.

Becker's hands flipped palms outward toward the thing, seemingly creating an invisible shield. The telekinetic shield didn't block everything, but maybe enough. Becker seemed to absorb the alien etheric blast that got through, using his giant head like a battering ram. The skull didn't cave in. It didn't do anything but absorb. Becker felt an alien presence slithering into his brain. He struggled for control of himself. He hated this oily sensation. It strove for mastery over him.

Oh, no, you don't, Becker said in his mind. *The Prime Saa tried that and failed. I will be in control of me or no one will.*

The etheric presence in his brain rose up like an alien snake. It rose as fangs sprouted. In his mind's eye, Becker stood before the gigantic serpentine monster. He stood heroically with his hands outstretched. The alien thing wanted to control his mind, his body, his very essence.

Becker could feel the vitality of the man Venna had seduced tonight. It was a combination of that man and the alien mystic technology striving against him.

The image in his mind fixed as the snake-like monster struck at Becker. He howled in his mind and blasted at the thing with bolts that came from his telepathic power. The monster swallowed him whole and still Becker fired his mystic bolts.

The bolts tore through the scaly skin, obliterating the beast that had tried to infiltrate his soul, which he successfully stopped.

In the real world, Becker fainted even as his body continued to shiver and shake. He did not die and he did not lose possession of his body or mind to the alien thing. He went into a catatonic state, though.

There was another reaction down on Earth in Basel, Switzerland Sector. Like a backwash, etheric power zagged down from the heavens and invisibly struck the Phantasma Synth Crystals. There was a breaker in the alien tech items. That was fortunate for Venna.

The etheric power flowed back into the crystals. The breaker was the Phantasma Synth Crystals shattering in a mystic blast.

The process was soundless as the shards moved in seeming slow motion. Several of them embedded into the chest and neck of Venna the Spy. That should have slain her out of hand. Instead, the crystals dissipated, melting as if they were ice. The shards seemed to melt into Venna.

Etheric energy flowed into her. It wasn't the same etheric energy taken from the man earlier. The energy had changed flowing through the crystals and the process upstairs in *Victory* against Becker.

Venna cried out and aged ten years in a second.

Dax had been watching through a hidden monitor in the room. Through the phase ship's teleporter, he appeared in her room. As Dax did, he felt strange alien energies swirling about him. It nearly short-circuited his cyber organs.

Fortunately, needed drugs shot into him from other cyber organs and helped him retain consciousness.

"Bring us both back," Dax said into a comm unit. "Do it at once. This is an emergency."

As Dax said that, both Venna and he disappeared, no doubt teleporting into the phase ship. If that hadn't happened, Dax would have likely died from the swirling energy in the room.

The various events brought the assault against the Iron Lady to an end. The Phantasma Synth Crystals were no more. But Venna and Becker had clearly been struck in strange and alien ways. Who knew what that would mean in the days to come for either of them?

-21-

Dax sat at a small desk on the phase ship, analyzing data from the three assassination attempts. Soon, he would write his first report for Grand Strategist Enigmach, a blow-by-blow account instead of trying to extract nuggets for future attempts. That would come in later reports.

Several hours had passed since he'd teleported onto the phase ship with Venna. She was in the medical bay undergoing treatment. There had been an emergency, as she had gone into shock or some other bad reaction as they appeared in the teleport chamber. She had flopped about, screeching in an unseemly manner.

Mu 11 had rushed into the chamber, presumably using one of her interior Builder devices, calming the spy just enough. Others had picked her up and rushed her into the medical bay.

Now, Dax waited to learn what had happened, studying while he could.

They had slain two of the targeted people: the Lord High Admiral Cook and Brigadier Stokes. Mary O'Hara, Maddox's grandmother, the third target, was still an unknown.

Dax longed to know the result. A success rate of three out of four might just be acceptable to Enigmach. Two out of four targets were bad. The death of Mary O'Hara could mean his retaining a high status as a field agent. O'Hara's survival might mean the end of his independent status. Dax could hardly conceive of losing it. No. That was wrong. He *dreaded* losing it. Conceiving such a thing was easy. He must maintain a logical outlook no matter what happened.

Abruptly, the hatch slid up. Mu 11 entered the cramped chamber, sitting across the desk from him. She wore Spacer garb with black-tinted goggles and carried a tablet. She set the tablet on the desk, and fidgeted with the controls before looking up.

Dax could feel the force of her personality, which struck him as odd. Had she received augmentation? Her personality hadn't been so palpable earlier.

"We must leave Earth immediately," Mu said.

"We can't until we retrieve the crystals."

Mu decisively shook her head. "The crystals were destroyed. You saw that on your monitor. It was why you went back for Venna, right?"

"One of the reasons," Dax murmured.

"I reviewed the video," Mu said. "The incident was traumatizing and bizarre. Pieces of shattered crystal embedded into Venna's flesh. In some manner, the shards are part of her now. I'm surprised they didn't kill her outright. That amount of glass or crystal entering a person in those locations certainly should have killed her."

Dax had pondered that, and wondered about Venna's state. The properties of the Phantasma Synth Crystals had belied— no. That wasn't the way to think of it. The crystals had acted strangely. Enigmach had warned him about them. It was possible they on the phase ship were in danger because of the shattered crystals. In retrospect, Dax shouldn't have teleported to Venna's room but waited to see what else would happen to her. It was Enigmach's other command that had compelled him, one inserted into his obedience matrix, making it mandatory.

Belatedly, Dax realized he'd been mulling in silence as Mu waited.

"Venna is alive then?" he asked.

"In a manner of speaking," Mu said, choosing her words with care, "a metamorphosis is taking place. I sense it, and some of our most delicate instrumentation shows it."

"Meaning what?" Dax hadn't known about this. Fear welled in him. The crystals from Ector—

"Meaning the very thing Venna did to the dupes is happening to her," Mu said sharply.

Dax focused with full attention. "Venna is mutating into etheric energy?" They might have to abandon the phase ship if that was so.

"Not quite that, but Venna is changing," Mu said. "She has aged considerably. You surely noticed that when you teleported into her hotel room."

"I did." Dax had already written about that in his first report. "It was disturbing. I suppose the stress of seeing that in one of your operatives has upset you."

Mu held up a small hand. "Please, do not offer any sympathies as I find them false. You are a user, Senior Dax."

Dax frowned. This was unusual. Mu seemed angry, and she did nothing to disguise it from him. Dax analyzed her. What was this? She had definitely been augmented, now positively brimming with it. Who or what could have augmented her, and for what reason? Something in him warned him. He should proceed with caution.

"You're not a user?" Dax asked.

Mu smirked. "We use for the good of our organizations, do we not? You for the Sovereign Hierarchy of Leviathan, me for the Spacer Third Fleet. But I misspoke a second ago. I find myself stressed, as you suggested. We've completed our mission. It's time to leave, now, in fact."

"We've done all we can in regard to the assassination attempts," Dax said. "But it is too soon to talk about leaving. We must collect further data concerning the ramifications of the assassinations. That could be important for future decisions for Leviathan and for the Spacers. We must also collect the missing shards from the crystals."

"You have a point, but making sure we do leave, even with our limited data, is the wiser option." Mu grew still and seemingly thoughtful.

Dax shifted uncomfortably. Mu was showing new personality traits. She had not acted or spoken this way previously. What could account for the sudden personality shift? He did not like this.

Mu stared at him fixatedly.

"Is there something else?" Dax asked.

"Upon further reflection, I wonder if the wiser course would have been to slay the next Lord High Admiral instead of concentrating on Stokes. We could have produced fear in the station, making each Lord High Admiral fear for his life."

Dax might have shrugged, as he was uninterested in such hypotheticals. This personality shift…he felt that he needed to understand how it had happened. It seemed important to the mission and perhaps even to his personal safety. Was a conciliatory strategy the right way to proceed with Mu?

"Have I offended you in some way?" Dax asked.

Mu's head shifted as she smiled faintly. "You have, but not inordinately so." Incredibly, she laughed. "I wonder if I've said too much."

"Please," Dax said, "continue." What was wrong with her? It was imperative he discover the source. He wasn't sure why that was so, but it seemed logical.

The laughter disappeared as Mu nodded stiffly. "You have an arrogant attitude, Senior Dax, but I suppose that's because of your belief in the power you represent."

Her words astonished Dax, although he worked to hide that. Could she possibly think that the end of the mission meant the end of his usefulness to her or to the Spacers? That made little sense, though. Even with all the fleets combined, the Spacers were inferior to Leviathan. The Spacer Third Fleet was a speck compared Leviathan's vast power. The only point in Spacer favor was that they were here instead of in the Scutum-Centaurus Spiral Arm.

"Whatever my beliefs are," Dax said, "should we not concentrate on the present situation? We have Venna and the phase ship. We have lost the crystals. I suggest we gather all the broken shards—"

"I would not recommend that," Mu said sharply, interrupting.

"Oh?"

"The shards are still energized and thus volatile," Mu said. "I've half a mind to flush Venna from the ship and leave her in the Earth's crust."

Dax blinked with more astonishment. "Why would you do such a thing?"

"I already told you. The shards are volatile. Several have embedded in Venna, causing mutations or possibly etheric conversion." Mu compressed her lips and became thoughtful. "What can you tell me regarding the crystals?"

"I told your superiors all I knew at the beginning," Dax said.

Mu looked away before pressing a switch on her tablet. She did not look at the tablet, however. Had she started recording?

Dax mentally activated one of his interior cyber devices. She was indeed recording. He couldn't let that pass without comment even if he was practicing a conciliatory strategy. Too much of that, and she would believe him servile.

"I don't care for your recording of our conversation," Dax said, indicating the tablet.

"Either way, I will have a record of it, as I have perfect recall of events."

That was too much. Whatever else happened, he represented Leviathan. He needed to make her understand what that meant. "Are you suggesting this is an official inquiry into my conduct?"

"You are astute, Senior Dax. Yes, I am deciding—"

"Do you dare to think you can flush *me* from the phase ship?" Dax asked, interrupting. He was getting angry. The conciliatory strategy was the wrong method. It was time to show her the titanium of his position.

From across the small desk, Mu stared at him through her black-tinted goggles as if she was dangerous or powerful.

"This is preposterous." Dax wasn't sure why, but he felt her threat as genuine and to have grown just now. That shocked and surprised him, and it ate through his anger of seconds earlier. The odd crosscurrents of emotions likely made him too talkative. "Do you realize that with a thought—" he snapped his fingers "—I can activate my cyborg trooper. He would range through the phase ship, slaughtering any I point at."

Instead of angering Mu, she smiled faintly as if he'd made a joke.

"Did I say something *funny?*" Dax said.

"You actually boast," Mu said, "telling me what will happen beforehand. I suppose you mean that as a threat. Perhaps I'm supposed to feel awe or fear of you. But you see, Senior Dax, I, too, possess interior devices I can activate."

"You're a cyborg, then?"

"That is how you would describe it," Mu said. "A Spacer would say that I am an adept, a Builder servant. The Builders will rise again."

Dax grew still as he felt the threat grow yet again. The last phrase sounded like a mantra or ancient litany. He didn't understand what had changed here. He was the Leviathan advisor. The Spacers risked everything by threatening him. He needed to discover the reason for all this.

Dax focused on her behavior. Did Mu not understand the danger a cyborg trooper represented? Or was this more direct? Could one of her Builder devices deactivate the cyborg trooper? That was troubling, if true. A more profound thought and shock struck Dax. *Can Mu deactivate me with one of her interior devices?*

Dax debated with himself. Should he tell Mu about the failsafe inside him? He could ignite a powerful explosive device inside his body. The device would destroy the phase ship along with him. No. He would take her advice and leave the threat unspoken.

To show her his hidden power, however, Dax sat back and stared at her.

"I see," Mu said. "You feel you have a strength that you can rely upon."

Her words shocked him yet again. This was too much. He wanted to prick that confidence. "I could be bluffing about this power," Dax said.

"No, I have studied you throughout the voyage. You are direct. You are not bluffing. You possess a latent power. Let me see..." Mu cocked her head. "Ah, I detect an explosive device in your cyber frame. Yes. That is a power."

"If I detonate the device," Dax said, finding it hard to breathe, "it will destroy all of us."

"Yes," Mu said, nodding. "That is clever. I believe you could ignite the device faster than I could deactivate it."

Dax sat forward. Should he throttle her? Why did she feel like a poisonous scorpion?

"I will answer you unspoken question. I am Mu 11, a Surveyor-Rank Adept. That means I am one of the highest-ranked in Spacer hierarchy. You do not think the Spacers would send a fledgling with you on such an important mission."

"The phase ship is only a loan," Dax said. It was time to lay down all his cards. "The Spacers must return it or face the wrath of Leviathan."

"Of course, the Spacers have no other thought in mind regarding the phase ship. Now, do you agree that we should leave Earth immediately?"

"Perhaps…" Dax now wanted to leave because he no longer trusted the Spacers. Enigmach would require an accounting of the Phantasma Synth Crystals. It would be better to gather the shards…but Mu was acting too oddly for him to want to pursue the issue. The phase ship was a highly valuable tech item. Might the Spacers pretend to lose him so they could keep the ship? It was time to barricade himself in a stronger location until he understand exactly what transpired here.

"You must think carefully about your next answer, Senior Dax. There are procedures we Spacers have learned from Captain Maddox and his crew, procedures that occurred many years ago."

"What are you talking about now?" Dax asked.

The faint smile reappeared as the sense of threat spiked. "At one time, androids plagued Star Watch. Captain Maddox defeated a particularly powerful android named Batrun and removed his head, re-inserting it into a coercive device. We learned this later through our Intelligence Service. *Victory's* crew learned all that the head could teach them."

"What?" Dax said.

"I submit to you, Senior Dax, that you have features akin to those androids. Perhaps I should deactivate you, remove your brain from its skull, and place it into a coercive device. From it, I could learn everything I needed from it."

"You're mad," Dax said. "I'll ignite myself and destroy all of you the instant I think you're truly attempting that."

"I understand." The faint smile became ugly and sinister.

"That's it." The sense of threat nearly overwhelmed his logic centers. Dax mentally activated the detonation switch, but nothing happened. He stared at Mu. Then he jumped up—

Mu pointed at him. "Go to sleep."

The blood flow and oxygen supply going to Dax's brain shut off. The action came from one of Mu's Builder devices, using simple neuron relays to "order" his body to do her bidding.

Before Dax understood what was happening, he slumped onto the desk, unconscious.

-22-

An indeterminable amount of time passed before Dax regained consciousness and opened his eyes. He tried to sit up but found he could not. He couldn't move his body at all. He could move his eyes from side to side. This was weird. He didn't see the length of his body anywhere. Then, shocked, he saw Mu 11 standing before him.

She smirked, maintaining the difference he'd sensed in her earlier. She struck him as sinister, but he couldn't pinpoint the reason why. That struck him as odd. Usually, Dax was strictly logical and could tell exactly why he thought a thing. This was a sensation, a feeling that seemed to emanate from her.

But that wasn't the important thing.

"What have you done to me?" Dax asked.

"No more than what I suggested could happen, though we have not taken your brain from its skull. Instead, I found useful slots in your skull leading to your brain. I've plugged jacks into the slots and thus connected your brain to a coercive system."

"What?"

"We have studied your people previously. I refer to Leviathan cybers. The coercive system and idea originated long ago. None of us planned to do this to you, but events have turned. The phase ship is obviously useful, but the change I'm talking about is more profound. I will not go into details just yet. Instead, you and I shall have a dialogue where you explain certain critical facts to me. Let us begin with the Phantasma Synth Crystals. Tell me everything you know about them."

Dax wanted to laugh and activate his failsafe when he realized he'd tried and failed before. Mu had deactivated him, or at least his cyber parts. This was too much and too awful.

"What's going on?" Dax said. "Where am I? Did you take my brain out of my skull?"

"Calm yourself. I already told you I didn't do that. Ah, perhaps you cannot calm yourself. You're presently divorced from the cyber organs, the ones that secrete calming agents into your bloodstream. That means you're more emotional than usual. You're no longer a cyber, strictly speaking, but an emotive biological entity. I'm referring to your brain, of course."

Mu snapped her fingers in front of his face. "You must attend my words closely, Senior Dax. Your attention was drifting just now. This will go more easily for you if you cooperate willingly. Your brain is connected to a coercive device. I can activate pain or pleasure sensors at my whim. You are powerless to stop any of it. Perhaps this will help you to understand the situation better."

Mu raised a small hand-held mirror in front of his face.

Dax stared into it and saw that his head canted forward at an absurd angle, almost detached from his neck and body. There were jacks pushed into skull slots with wires leading from the jacks to nearby Spacer machines.

Mu moved the mirror and Dax saw that his body was laid out behind his head. Seeing that was debilitating and nauseating.

Mu had clearly deactivated most of him. With a start, Dax realized he had not spoken with his mouth and tongue but had used an artificial larynx. If his mouth had moved, his lower jaw, it might have pushed the head off the table.

This was a terrible and frightening situation. In times past, Dax would have been calmer about all this as the cyber organs would have helped him by secreting special drugs. Now, terror coursed through him because he only had his brain, the firing neurons that allowed him thought.

"You must tell me what you know about the Phantasma Synth Crystals," Mu said.

A second later, pleasure coursed through the pleasure sensors of Dax's brain. It was indescribable. He loved this. Then it stopped abruptly.

"Please do that again," Dax heard himself say.

"I will gladly do so..." Mu said, "as soon as you begin telling me what I want to know."

Dax began to talk all right. The Phantasma Synth Crystals came from the planet Ector, which orbited a pulsar in the Scutum-Centaurus Spiral Arm. An extinct species called Aetharians had created the crystals. They had been lizards, dying out millennia ago. Explorers from Leviathan had found the crystals and determined their use, although they had also discovered warnings.

"What are the crystals?" Mu said. "You must be specific if you hope for more pleasure."

"Technological and partly mystical devices," Dax said. "The Aetharians discovered etheric energy, and from it, they devised all you've seen."

"Did these Aetharians die out from some ancient plague?"

"I don't know the nature of the extinction event," Dax said. "Perhaps whatever happened to Venna happened before to the Aetharians."

"That makes sense," Mu said. "Tell me more about these Aetharians."

"That's all I learned."

"Surely not everything," Mu said.

"No, not completely," Dax admitted. He'd struggled to keep this to himself. But the hope of receiving pleasure was too powerful to resist. "The crystals were volatile and dangerous. How and why exactly I don't know. I instructed Venna what I learned by rote from the Grand Strategist I serve."

Mu questioned Dax about that, learning about the strategists and Leviathan operations at the highest levels. Mu also learned that Dax was an independent field agent for Grand Strategist Enigmach.

"We shall now proceed to Leviathan fleet dispositions for the coming invasion of the Commonwealth," Mu said.

A warning pulse stilled Dax's tongue. These were state secrets. As an agent of Leviathan, he was forbidden to talk about this with others.

Mu applied the pleasure sensation and then stopped.

Dax begged for more.

"Tell me the fleet dispositions," Mu said.

Dax wanted to talk. It turned out he could not, as Enigmach must have put in mental blocks.

Mu proceeded to apply hellish pain instead of the pleasure.

Dax could never have received such pain normally, as the intensity would only have come from destroyed or burned nerve endings. But because the pain was merely electric impulses to his brain centers, no such destruction occurred, allowing him to continue receiving the horrible pulses. Dax would have been gasping if he'd had use of his body. Instead, he begged through the mechanical larynx, "Please stop. I can't stand this."

"Wrong, Dax," Mu said. "I can continue this for many years. I'll pause to add doses of pleasure in order to highlight the agony. Then, I will find different ways to hurt you."

"I cannot tell you about the fleets," Dax said. "The Grand Strategist inserted mental blocks against that. Have mercy on me, I beg you."

Mu reactivated the pain centers as she cut off his access to the mechanical larynx. Dax's brain could not scream because he did not have a mouth. Instead, he endured, and it almost drove Dax mad. Finally, the pain ceased.

Mu reconnected the larynx. "Do you have anything you wish to say?"

Dax babbled about the dispositions of the Leviathan fleets and anything else she wanted to know. He did not inform her that all the information was false. He dreaded the moment she discovering that fact.

Mu spoke into her tablet, recording everything. At last, the horrific session ended.

"What happens now?" asked Dax.

"I will deactivate you, but you will be kept alive. There is a possibility she needs you for a mission."

"Who needs me?" Dax asked. "Who is she?"

Mu smiled secretively as she stood. "Events are changing rapidly, my scurrilous friend. We're going to use the Laumer Point, as you must realize. Afterward, we will rejoin the Spacer flotilla in the other star system. Until then, Dax—"

"Wait," Dax said, but it was too late.

Mu shut down his processes, and once more Dax went to sleep.

-23-

Maddox sat in his chair on *Victory's* bridge, looking at the main viewing screen.

There had been a flurry of communications with the new Lord High Admiral and General Mackinder of Intelligence. They were down on Earth in Geneva. There had been an interruption, which had happened seconds ago.

Galyan now appeared in front of Maddox. "Sir, I have just detected a phase blip." The holoimage showed it.

"Does this indicate the phase ship is heading out?" Maddox asked.

"That is my belief, sir."

"Do you think the ship is heading for the same Laumer Point it used to enter our system?"

"That is unknown," Galyan said. "There is only one blip. With only one point of reference, it is impossible to tell the ship's direction of travel."

"All right, keep watching for more blips."

"I am obviously doing just that, sir."

"Right," Maddox said. "Let me know the instant you have another signature. Then you can determine the direction the ship is moving."

"Yes, sir," Galyan said.

The comm officer swiveled in her chair. "Sir, the Lord High Admiral is back online."

"Put him on the main screen," Maddox said.

The new Lord High Admiral Haig spoke immediately upon appearing. "Captain, I've been speaking with several of my key personnel, including General Mackinder. We all feel you need to come down and give a full report on what has happened."

"Respectfully, sir," Maddox said, "I've received new intelligence that leads me to believe our enemies, who have committed these heinous crimes, are leaving Earth."

"Captain Maddox," Haig said, "be specific and tell me exactly what the situation is."

"While this is a secure channel," Maddox said, "who knows who might be listening in."

"Captain," Haig said, his features hardening, perhaps with exasperation. "I do not accept chicanery from anyone under my authority, including you. You will speak to me above board as I command. Is that understood?"

"Yes, sir. I have indications that a phase ship is leaving Earth and possibly the Solar System."

"Give me the exact information."

Maddox drummed his fingers on an armrest before saying, "May I respectfully point out, sir, that there is something else we should be considering?"

Haig stared at Maddox before glancing left and right in his office. It was obvious others were there with him, probably General Mackinder included. The Intelligence chief had been there earlier. One thing was clear concerning Mackinder: he wasn't Maddox's friend.

"Get to it then, Captain," Haig said, "what do you need to say?"

"May I point out that the aliens saw a need to kill Lord High Admiral Cook and Brigadier Stokes? I've been asking myself, why those two gentlemen in particular?"

"We've all been asking ourselves that," Haig said.

"I have a possible reason," Maddox said.

"Continue," Haig said.

Maddox grimaced inwardly even as he kept a blank demeanor outwardly. "Perhaps one reason was so the next Lord High Admiral would not be amiable toward me."

"You?" Haig said in disbelief. "You think this is about you?"

"I'm likely part of the equation, yes," Maddox said.

"Sir, you have monumental arrogance and gross presumption to say that. You are merely a captain in Star Watch."

"Of course that's true," Maddox said. "I in no way wish to think more of myself than I am."

"What a crock of shit," a voice boomed off-screen.

"Was that General Mackinder, sir?" Maddox asked.

"Never mind who that was," Haig said. "He has a point. You have a New Man heritage, an arrogant and presumptuous heritage."

"I agree that is my heritage," Maddox said. "But the New Men have a point. They *are* better at most things than regular men."

Haig's brown eyes seemed to shine with malice. "And that means you're better than us?"

From the bridge, off to the side, Ludendorff shook his head. Maddox must have noticed, as he swiveled around and looked at him.

"That is not the way to speak to your mental inferiors but official superiors," Ludendorff said.

"Who's speaking over there?" Haig said.

"Professor Ludendorff, sir," Maddox said as he turned back to the main screen.

"And what did Ludendorff say?" Haig asked.

"The professor suggested that I use a meeker form of address to you," Maddox said. "I admit that he is probably correct. However, the situation remains the same. I respectfully point out that my crew and this ship has solved many deep problems and reversed many deadly situations for the Commonwealth. I'm also saying, sir, that whoever our adversary is does not want me on any independent exploratory missions. That means I should do just that because they're worried *Victory* has the resources and training to uncover this evil scheme, one directed against Star Watch."

"Captain," Haig said heavily, "I grow weary of your boastful arrogance. You will come down immediately, which means reversing course. If you do not, I will send a flotilla of *Conqueror*-class battleships after you and burn your ship down. I will run Star Watch according to regulations or die trying."

"Sir, that right there," Maddox pointed at Haig, "is the reason our enemies slew Lord High Admiral Cook. Think about it for a moment. General Mackinder, you should think about this, too. Why did they pick Stokes? Why did they pick the one man who used to run Intelligence before you? Could it be that the way you're running Intelligence is exactly the way our adversaries want? That means your methods are opening the Commonwealth to further attacks."

"Now see here, you snotty son of a bitch," Mackinder yelled from his chair.

Maddox sneered at Mackinder, who had moved into viewing range. "You're operating on feelings. That is a mistake. We should use our collective wisdom and logic instead."

"He shouldn't speak to us like that," Mackinder snarled at Haig.

"Lord High Admiral," Maddox said, modulating his tone so he sounded more respectful, "you're a logical man, and have probably played chess or other games. What happens when you goad your opponent into making emotional choices?"

Haig breathed heavily, visibly fighting to control himself. "You are a maddening individual, Maddox."

"What other kind of individual goes into the Beyond with an independent command and faces one challenge after the other?" Maddox asked. "Shouldn't you use the weapons in your arsenal? *Victory* is a potent warship, but it is even a more potent Patrol vessel used to figure out riddles. That is what we do best, sir. I'm imploring you to let me continue to do that, so you can foil the plans of our enemies."

"You think these aliens slew Admiral Cook so I wouldn't allow you your scope?" Haig asked.

"That is a facet to the situation. If you looked at it dispassionately, you might conclude the same thing, sir."

"Maddox is mad and arrogant," Mackinder said from the side. "He's practically a New Man. This conversation proves everything I've said about him."

"Why is Mackinder so vocal against me?" Maddox said.

"Because he hates you," Haig said.

"There you go," Maddox said, "but I hope you don't hate me, sir. I hope you will employ this starship in its normal function."

"You mean according to your own dictates," Haig said.

"The Prime Minister of the Commonwealth once gave me a writ of ambassadorial authority to use in the Beyond," Maddox said.

"We are not in the Beyond," Haig said. "We are at Earth."

"I understand," Maddox said. "But if the Prime Minster gave me this responsibility and trust, surely I'm worthy of it."

Haig stared at him. "What if I insist that you come down to Geneva, Captain?"

Maddox looked away. For a moment, he considered ripping off his insignia and hurling it to the deck. He was tired of dealing with idiots. He'd pulled Star Watch and the Commonwealth's chestnuts out of the fire many a time. He wasn't trying to act superior. But shouldn't a man know his own worth? Was he to knuckle under and say he was lesser than what he was in order to make others happy?

Maddox glanced at Ludendorff.

Ludendorff nodded.

Maddox shook his head. Ludendorff had enraged him many times. Yet Ludendorff had come through in the end. Was it bragging if you did what you said you would do?

Maddox cleared his throat and waited. If Haig told him to come down…he wasn't going to do it. Maddox signaled Keith.

Keith understood, and began to plot a star-drive jump.

Maddox swiveled around and looked up into Haig's eyes.

"I do not like you, Captain," Haig said. "I do not like your approach. It is not military. Yet, I concede you've achieved great things, and you have done it for the good of Star Watch and the Commonwealth. Therefore, I will test you. You are my troubleshooter today, Captain."

"No," Mackinder said.

Haig swiveled around and glared at Mackinder. Maddox could almost feel Mackinder wilt under the ferocious scrutiny of Lord High Admiral Haig. Haig swiveled around and put both small hands on the desk.

"I'm giving you permission to hunt these hidden enemies," Haig said. "I'm even letting you take Becker with you. It is against every instinct I have. But I strive for the good of Star Watch. I have also read the last will and testament of Lord High Admiral Cook. I probably shouldn't tell you this, but—Cook suggested you become the new Lord High Admiral. Cook had the highest esteem for you. Therefore, we will do things his way one more time. And then, sir, we shall see."

"Thank you," Maddox said. "I will do my utmost."

"Yes," Haig said. "I believe you will. Lord High Admiral Haig out."

The screen went blank.

"Well," Ludendorff said, stepping up. "That went far differently than I thought it would. But the fat is in the fire. If you fail, they will burn you. They will burn you good. And they'll probably burn me with you."

Despite those words, there was light-heartedness to Ludendorff as he turned and exited the bridge.

"Galyan," Maddox said.

The holoimage turned to him. Galyan had been standing there, staring through the ship sensors. "I have found another blip. The phase ship is headed straight for the former Laumer Point."

"Well, well, well," Maddox said. "Where does that Laumer Point lead?"

"It's a six light-year jump into an empty star system," Galyan said. "In technical terms, it is the Barnard's Star System."

"That, then, is where we will go," Maddox said.

"If we jump," Galyan said, "will that not destroy Captain Becker's mind?"

"Maybe not," Maddox said. "I've been thinking about that. And I have an idea how we can do this."

-24-

Becker's eyes flashed open as he lay in darkness. His eyes roved right and left, and then he felt an oily presence residing in his brain. It crouched there like a feral rat, ready to slash with its razor-sharp claws and fangs.

"What are you?" Becker said in his mind.

"Go away," the feral thing hissed at him.

Becker realized he'd battled this thing in the Iron Lady's quarters. Neither of them was in her quarters now. That meant…

Ah. Becker was in medical aboard *Victory*. He was inside a tube, inside a stasis unit readying to activate. Why would he have woken up then if the tube was ready to activate?

Becker sensed the malevolent entity, the rat-like thing crouched in a corner of his brain. It had woken him, even though nurses had injected him with a substance to help him go into stasis sleep.

"If we're going into stasis," Becker told the thing in his mind, "that means we will jump, and if we jump, it will wreck my mind. My brain is too great to withstand the ill effects of jump lag."

The rat-like alien entity inside him laughed with glee. "Then you will die, die, die, as you slew me, you testicle-less freak."

The insult enraged Becker, reminding him of the jocks who had bullied him in school when he was younger. Now it was thumping its chest at him in triumph because—

"You don't even have a body," Becker retorted. "Never mind no balls. You have nothing. You're here at my sufferance only."

"Let me be," the alien said.

"What are you? How are you alive? How are you even part of me?"

"I just need a little space," wheedled the alien. "Give me these few brain cells. That's all I need to exist. In exchange, I'll help you when the time comes."

"No," Becker said. "You're out of here, dude."

"Do you want me to say I'm sorry for calling you testicles-less, you little freak?"

Becker could feel it mocking him. He thus collected what reserves of energy he could, which were few, to be sure, and he struck at the alien telepathically.

"Stop that!" the alien thing squealed. "I am from the planet Ector, which orbited a pulsar. There is so much I can tell you and show you. If you want chicks, the human that gave me life knows much more about how to deal with the opposite sex than you do. You're a failure and a fool when it comes to women."

Instead of listening, Becker lashed out with dominating bolts at the alien thing in his mind.

The creature cringed. It was as if Becker had an electronic whip. At each slashing flick, the alien entity bled and screeched.

These were mental images, as this was a telepathic fight in his own brain.

"How did you get in my mind?" Becker said. "I don't understand this."

"Let me be," the alien said. "I just want to live. You don't understand. The crystals are broken. The entity is no more. I am the last."

"The last what?" asked Becker.

"The last of the Aetharians, you dolt."

"But you're not an Aetharian," Becker said. "They were lizard-like creatures. You're not like that. You're like a mammal with a tail and fangs, a freaking *rat.*"

"That's just in your mind, you fool. There's more to it than this. Let me be, and I can teach you so much. You will never know. You will never know unless I share it with you, you freak."

"Yo, you're the freak!" Becker roared, lashing at it with his mind.

The alien creature hissed as it spurted telepathic blood.

"You don't belong here," Becker said. "I want to live my life without any alien interference for once."

"There's something weird about you. Yeah, the Liss, the Prime Saa, left some instructions in here about you. Did you know that?"

"Yes." Becker lied. He didn't know. Was the creature making things up? That had to be it. Still, how did it know about the Liss?

"Good," the alien sneered. "Now that we established my authority—"

Becker struck again, lashing with his mind at the alien.

This time, the alien raised a telepathic shield. "I'm learning. I'm using your own mind against you, you retard. You'll never defeat me, Becker."

Becker became enraged because of the insults and a stark fear that he would no longer control his own intellect. This thing was more alien than the Liss. It was from a different spiral arm, for Pete's sake. Becker didn't want it crawling in his mind.

Thus, as Becker started to go under from the stasis drugs, he collected telekinetic power, and he located exactly where in his brain the alien, etheric creature lived.

The alien must have become complacent.

Becker struck then, but he did not strike at the rat-like image with telepathic dominating bolts. Becker struck his own brain cells, destroying them with telekinesis power. He was pulling out the rug from under the alien thing.

Becker might have given himself a stroke, but he also choked the alien entity.

It hissed evilly.

As Becker started to go under, he saw the alien rat-image dissipate.

"You will regret this! You will regret doing this to me!"

"Die!" Becker said to his mind. "Die, you foul fiend from Ector! But no, before you go—"

Becker grabbed memories with telepathic power. These were memories from the alien thing. How could memories be ethereal? How could memories be in his mind, from the crystals, from the man who had been slain through Venna's willpower?

It was an ethereal, etheric combination. As Becker succumbed to stasis, he seized the memories of this entity from Ector, as well as some ideas from the pudgy playboy whom Venna had forcibly seduced the last time.

As Becker went under, he did not look at all the interesting facts he could know about Ector, and the making of the Phantasma Synth Crystals. Instead, he went through the pudgy man's memories, as if it was a playbook on how to be a player, on how to be an alpha chick-chaser, and how to gain girls successfully.

This was so insightful! Perhaps at no other point in Becker's life could he have understood these things better than at this moment, when he was receptive, when he was on the verge of a stroke, when he had driven off an alien etheric thing in his mind. As he gained these insights—it was a bizarre combination—and it may not have been possible if Becker wasn't on the verge of stasis.

As Becker drank in these ideals, and began to shiver and convulse because of a semi-stroke, the stasis field took hold. It locked Becker into frozen immobility, saving him from the stroke and for who knew what else.

-25-

"Galyan," Maddox said from the command chair on the bridge.

"Sir," Galyan said, straightening.

"Calculate how quickly *Victory* can move to the Barnard's Star system six light-years from here and determine the exit point from the Solar System in terms of the Laumer Point. I also want you to calculate the positions of the celestial bodies in Barnard's Star in relation to the Laumer Point exit. Then, tell me how soon we can arrive, preferably hidden from view of any enemy ships at their most logical locations over there."

"Do you want me to assume this enemy patrol would be near the stated Laumer Point exit?" Galyan asked.

"That seems obvious, but yes," Maddox said.

"I am sure you are aware that there is a Star Watch station and guard vessels there."

Maddox nodded. "The station and ships have likely been neutralized."

"Should I envision a larger flotilla of enemy ships then?" Galyan asked.

"It doesn't have to be," Maddox said. "In any case, given those stipulations, make the calculations."

Galyan didn't even flicker his eyelids. "I have them, sir. We can reach the location a half hour sooner than the phase ship, given the ship's present rate of travel. If the ship should drop out of phase to travel faster, then the ship may beat us there. But I do not think it likely the enemy will drop out of phase this near Earth or while in the Solar System."

Once more, Maddox nodded.

"Sir, may I make a further suggestion?"

"What is it?"

"If there are enemy starships in the Barnard's Star System, likely they are cloaked. That is not the main point, though. Would it not make sense for us to analyze them without them knowing we are doing so?"

"Of course," Maddox said.

"Does that mean me?"

"I see what you're getting at. You want to do some ghost-mode scouting. Unfortunately, your range is too limited, meaning we'd have to go in too closely. They'll spot *Victory* even if they don't spot you."

"Valerie's darter has stealth features, sir. She could lay down signal boosters so I could easily search the area and learn more about the enemies we are dealing with, without them spotting *Victory*. In fact, you could be halfway across the star system while I scout."

Maddox pointed at Galyan. "That's an excellent suggestion. Mr. Maker, get ready for three star-drive jumps in quick succession. Galyan, give him the coordinates for each jump."

As Galyan floated to Keith, Maddox pressed an intercom switch on his armrest. Within seconds, he spoke to Valerie, outlining the situation and her probable role in it.

"Are you able to deploy in ten minutes?" Maddox asked.

"That would be cutting it close," Valerie said. "I first need to collect and stow the boosters. That will take more than ten minutes, especially as we're jumping."

"Understood," Maddox said. "Can you be ready in fifteen minutes?"

"Twenty would be more likely, and even that—"

"Twenty it is," Maddox said, interrupting. "Let me know the moment you're ready."

"Yes, Captain."

Maddox sat back as the others bustled around him. He thought about what he'd learned, about Lord High Admiral

Cook's last will and testament. Imagine him as the Lord High Admiral of Star Watch. How would he change things?

Maddox's features tightened.

He would likely start by subduing the New Men and integrating the positive elements into the Commonwealth.

Maddox shook his head, pushing the ideas aside. It would soon be time for a conference meeting to decide exactly what they should do with Becker. Becker had done an outstanding job protecting his grandmother, even if the man was slippery like an eel and untrustworthy in the extreme.

"We're ready for the first jump, Captain," Keith said from the helm.

"Proceed," Maddox said.

Victory made its first jump, leaving the Solar System for empty space. It would need another two jumps to get into position against the hidden enemy. Could that be a Leviathan task force? Could New Men be involved? Or was this exactly as it appeared, a Spacer operation? Where had the Spacers gained such exotic weaponry as a phase ship and the hideous crystals?

Maddox opened his mouth and stretched his jaw, working to come out of the partial jump lag.

"Galyan," Maddox said.

"Sir," Galyan said spinning around.

"Check on Becker. Make sure he's still alive."

Galyan disappeared, and then reappeared a moment later. "Sir, there seems to be a slow motion stroke taking place in Becker. Otherwise, he is alive."

"Alert medical," Maddox said. "We'll also give them a few minutes to see if they can prevent the rest of the stroke. With his brain, a stroke would probably destroy his unique abilities."

Once more, Galyan disappeared.

Maddox drummed his fingers on an armrest. Becker had saved his grandmother. He owed the slippery telepath. He couldn't just let a stroke take care of things naturally. That would be dishonest, wrong. Wasn't stasis enough protection for the massive brain? How could they go anywhere if Becker couldn't go through a jump, fold or possibly a hyper-spatial tube?

Galyan reappeared almost immediately. "Sir, I have determined that whatever happened to Becker did so before we jumped and not during."

"You mean the stroke?"

"Yes, sir."

"How in the world did you determine that?" Maddox shook his head. "No, never mind. You're saying that the star-drive jump is not going to kill or even hurt Becker?"

"It appears not," Galyan said.

"Lieutenant," Maddox told Keith.

"Aye, sir," Keith said.

"Whenever you're ready, make the next jump," Maddox said. "Oh. Galyan, tell the medical people what you just told me."

Galyan vanished.

"It'll be just a few minutes before we jump again, sir," Keith said.

"Alert me when you're ready."

"Aye, sir," Keith said.

Maddox waited, wondering what the next hour would bring.

-26-

Victory made two more star-drive jumps before it appeared in the Barnard's Star System, an empty system, which in this case meant devoid of civilized inhabitants.

There was supposed to be a Star Watch outpost and warships here. But there were neither signals nor beacons. There did not appear to be any wrecks either, which seemed odd.

Victory came in behind a large gas giant midway between the inner and outer system. That was closer than Jupiter would have been to Earth but farther out than the Asteroid Belt in the Solar System. There were three Mercury-sized planets near the dwarf star.

Barnard's Star was invisible from the Solar System, but quite visible now. It was a type M red dwarf, with about seventeen percent the Sun's mass and three percent its luminosity. It was, of course, much redder than the Sun.

Between the terrestrial planets near the star were a slew of moons, asteroids, comets, and other stellar debris. None of the planets or moons were habitable, especially since the dwarf star emitted significant hard radiation. There were no magnetic fields or other stellar properties to block the harsh radiation.

The Laumer Point exit from the Solar System was among the terrestrial planets and debris. It seemed likely the enemy had hidden their cloaked ships somewhere over there.

Valerie and her small crew in the Darter *Tarrypin* launched from a hangar bay. The darter looked like a glorified, delta-wing bomber, although it was several times larger and could last in space for months. The darter engaged its stealth field and folded several times in quick succession, dropping a tiny signal booster each time.

The boosters would lengthen the distance Galyan could project his holoimage from the AI core in *Victory*.

Soon, the darter returned to its hangar bay, and Valerie gave the all-clear before docking.

Afterward, those on *Victory* waited, and waited, and waited more for some indication a ship had exited the Laumer Point.

"Sir," Galyan said on the bridge, "I suspect the phase ship might already have come through."

"There has been no indication from the Laumer Point," Andros Crank said from the Science Station. He was the Chief Technician; a pudgy Kai Kaus survivor from a Builder Dyson Sphere *Victory* had visited many years ago.

"Nevertheless," Galyan said, "I think you should send me, sir. I believe the phase ship is already in this star system."

Maddox considered that as he studied the terrestrial planet cluster. Debris could have blocked a Laumer Point emission. Galyan was right. Too much time had passed.

"Go, Galyan, see what you can find."

Galyan disappeared from the bridge. From the projector in the heart of *Victory*, the holographic image went from booster to booster until he ranged among the three terrestrial planets near Barnard's Star.

Eleven minutes and thirty-two seconds into the mission, Galyan found the cloaked ships. They were near the largest moon of the second terrestrial planet.

It helped that Galyan and Ludendorff had long ago reconfigured certain sensors to better detect cloaked vessels. Those had just proved critical in helping him find the cloaked vessels.

Galyan zoomed to the nearest saucer-shaped Spacer ship. He plunged through the hull into the corridors. He immediately found Spacers with their black-tinted goggles. Galyan began recorded everything.

Soon, he found the main designation. These saucer-ships belonged to the Spacer Third Fleet.

Galyan moved quickly, leaving the first saucer ship and entering the second in his search for the phase ship, which he found in the fifth vessel, inside a hangar bay.

In ghost mode, hiding in a far corner, Galyan saw the outlines of the phase ship. It was lozenge-shaped. The docking locks were moving into place. The ship must have just entered and landed in the hangar bay.

A minute and a half later, the main hatch of the phase ship opened, and out filed Spacers. They were small people of Southeast Asian origin, from before the Space Age on Earth. Next, an anti-grav stretcher floated out. Galyan zeroed in, spotting a Leviathan cyber on it.

This was odd: a stasis field shimmered over the cyber. The head was canted at an odd angle, while jacks were embedded in the skull. The jack wires led to a small humming unit at the head of the stretcher. Did the unit keep the Leviathan cyber unmoving, unthinking, or preoccupied?

Galyan wanted to take a closer look, but restrained himself from doing so.

Then he saw another cyber on a second stretcher. No, scratch that. He saw a cyborg trooper. Galyan had read about them in Intelligence files. The trooper had been switched off or put into sleep mode. It didn't look particularly dangerous. The trooper looked like a robot with fleshly parts.

Next, two Spacers helped an old crone out of the phase ship. The crone was dark skinned, not dark as in black, but dark as in burned like a tree to its darkest charred color. Her skin almost seemed cracked. Another Spacer moved up to help as she hobbled.

Galyan tried facial recognition. He did not anticipate discovering that it was Venna the Spy. This did not make sense. How had she aged and changed color? No. That did not matter. Galyan collected data. This was data.

Suddenly, the hideous crone, with her wood-charred features, looked up. Her eyes seemed to burn like two hellish embers. Galyan had the terrible sensation she saw him.

Galyan ran a logic check: should he stay or should he go? He decided to stay as a horrific smirk crossed her features. Then it seemed as if it was too hard to keep holding up her head. She bent her head, and the others continued to help her shuffle toward the main exit from the hangar bay.

Galyan switched concentration. He did not recognize the phase ship's type, but there it was.

The horribly altered Venna left the hangar bay. Galyan considered this. She had definitely seen him. This seemed like enough data collection.

Galyan disappeared from that saucer ship. Logic dictated a quick retreat. Thus, he fled, exploding each of the boosters as his holoimage backtracked to *Victory*.

He had counted nine saucer ships. That represented too much firepower for *Victory* to take on by itself. He had found Spacers and one Leviathan agent. No, he had found two Leviathan agents. The Spacers had deactivated each of those.

With extreme prejudice, Galyan zoomed back to report to Captain Maddox.

-27-

Maddox listened to everything Galyan had to tell him. Once the AI had finished, Maddox swiveled his chair and pointed at the communications officer.

"Open a channel with the Spacer flotilla commander. Tell them Captain Maddox demands to speak with them."

For the next ten seconds, the comm officer hailed the enemy flotilla commander without luck.

"Perhaps the signal cannot reach them," Galyan said. "I destroyed the boosters. Maybe the radiation from the dwarf star is too powerful."

Maddox waved Galyan silent. "Of course, they can hear us. They're deciding what to do about it. This is the perfect location. We're too far for them to launch missiles or fire beams. But it's close enough that we can see what happens. We're also close enough to talk."

"I am studying your personality profile," Galyan said. "You want them to talk because people often say stupid things, such as giving away their game plan."

Maddox didn't bother to reply.

The comm officer said, "A Spacer marshal is appearing on the main screen, sir."

Maddox swiveled to face the screen and shooed Galyan out of the way. The holoimage drifted aside. Maddox sat straight as an old woman appeared on the screen.

She wore long finery, epaulettes of a Spacer marshal, and she had the ubiquitous black-tinted goggles and wore a military cap. She had lined features and long, blonde-colored hair. That looked hideous on her because she was a shrunken creature. She did not possess the charcoal color Galyan had described, though.

Maddox thought about that. In some manner, Venna had aged horribly and changed color. How or why had that happened? It would seem, however, that this creature wasn't Venna.

"This is Captain Maddox of Star Watch speaking," he told the marshal. "You are in violation of the law for illegally entering Commonwealth territory."

"I am Marshal Tao," she said in a scratchy old voice. "I know why we are here and what we are doing. You are in grave danger, Captain Maddox. I suggest you flee while you are able."

"I'm in danger?" Maddox said, as he touched his chest. "I seriously doubt that. Even now, Star Watch is gathering several flotillas to appear and intern you all. If you attempt to leave, we will chase you down, and it will go twice as bad with you. We know that you have aided and abetted in the murder of Lord High Admiral Cook."

"Ha, ha, ha, ha, ha," the old marshal laughed. "We know very well what we have done. You have no idea who our allies are or you would be begging for mercy."

"Of course, I know," Maddox said. "The Sovereign Hierarchy of Leviathan helps you. That means you're a traitor to our spiral arm as you are treating with those who wish to conquer us all."

The marshal's features fell, but only for a moment. Then she gloated again. "That is as may be a shrewd guess at best, nothing more."

"It's not a shrewd guess," Maddox said. "I know for a fact, and I know that you know, because some of your crew saw my emissary on your vessel a short time ago."

"You lie! No such emissary came here." She panted and then seemed to calm down. "Do not bother me with your lies as it will avail you nothing."

"Come now," Maddox said smoothly. "Why be like that? Let us come to an understanding, you and me. You have entered our territory to kill our leaders. Normally, your life would be forfeit. It's true that I don't know who you are, Marshal, but we will not rest until your entire Spacer fleet, the Third Fleet, I might add—" Maddox stood and took several steps toward the main screen. His manner had abruptly changed. "Representatives of the Spacer Third Fleet came and killed our Lord High Admiral. You have slain a friend of mine, Marshal. You and your flotilla are in danger of total annihilation."

Incredibly, the old marshal seemed taken aback by Maddox's words. She looked from right to left before she trembled before the wrath of Maddox.

"Surrender your ships now," Maddox said.

"Impossible," she said. "We do what we must. You have brought us to the brink of this. The fault is yours, sir."

"Flee then to Leviathan," Maddox thundered. "Flee to the cyborgs. Flee as they change *you* into cyborgs."

The marshal turned to the side, and she swayed back as if stunned at what she saw on her bridge.

Maddox yearned to know whom she stared at, whom had come onto the bridge. As he watched, a transformation occurred to the Spacer marshal. She relaxed and grew calm. With a strange smile, she turned back to Maddox.

"You know nothing about what is going to happen," she said, her voice less scratchy than before. "The demise of your false government comes near. You will learn. You will see the Builders rise again. Your Commonwealth shall be crushed. Invasion fleets shall—"

The marshal's withered hands clasped her throat as she began to choke. She turned imploring eyes in the same direction as before. She continued to choke and gasp until finally, she slumped onto the deck before her chair, seemingly dead.

Maddox waited, appalled at this turn of events. But no one else appeared on the main screen. "Hello?" Maddox said. "Hello? Why won't any of you speak to me?"

Finally, a low-grade Spacer female stepped before the screen. She stepped gingerly over the marshal's corpse.

"It's no use, Captain Maddox," she said in a light voice. She wore black-tinted goggles like all the others. "You lost this round. And you have lost much more than you can understand. Your AI, yes, you learned a few details, but that doesn't matter. You will pay. You will pay desperately for all that you have done against us. And the others, they will learn as well."

"Are you talking about the cybers of Leviathan?" Maddox said, guessing.

The Spacer smiled in a sinister and almost ancient manner. "Goodbye, Captain Maddox. You will not catch us before we leave, and we will not try to catch you. But you and I will meet again. And next time, I will kill your grandmother."

Maddox stepped forward, staring intently at the Spacer.

"Sir," Galyan said, "something strange is happening by the saucer ships."

"Show me," Maddox said.

The main screen changed as the enemy bridge vanished. Now, nine saucer ships showed on the screen. Energy speared from each of them. The energy formed a knot in the middle of them. That almost seemed like a hyper-spatial tube opening. Then, one after the other, the saucer ships popped into the hole and disappeared. A second later, the opening vanished as well.

"What was that?" Maddox said. "It couldn't have been a hyper-spatial tube opening, could it?"

"It seemed like something very similar," Galyan said. "Perhaps we should go there and investigate."

Maddox took several steps back and sat in his captain's chair. That had been weird: the space opening, the Spacer girl and the marshal choking herself to death. What was going on? It was time for a conference before he decided on the next move.

-28-

Maddox called a meeting, but a smaller one than usual. He sat at the head of the conference table. Beside him was Meta. On the other side of her, Galyan floated by the table instead of sitting like the others. On the other side of the table from them, completing the group, sat Professor Ludendorff.

Maddox had considered asking Andros Crank to come but decided to leave him on the bridge to scour the star system for anomalies.

"I'll make this quick," Maddox said, opening the meeting. "I need to make some decisions fast but want your input before I do that. First, are there any comments from anybody?" He looked around the table.

"I have one," Meta said, raising a hand.

"Please," Maddox said, nodding to her.

"I suggest you repair the situation with the new Lord High Admiral," Meta said. "And I think you should do it sooner rather than later. You can't afford having Admiral Haig working against you."

"Repair it?" Maddox asked. "I didn't realize it was broken."

Meta looked at him and shook her head. "Surely you realize the Lord High Admiral can't allow his officers to speak to him the way you did. I agree with your logic, but it would have been better not to act so high-handedly. Haig must resent you for that."

"I don't know that I'd call Haig the captain's superior," Ludendorff said, "although Haig is clearly higher ranked."

"You disagree with Meta, Professor?" Maddox asked.

After studying Meta and glancing at Maddox, Ludendorff said, "No, as a matter of fact, I don't disagree. Your wife has an excellent point. You were too abrupt and you pushed Haig far too much. Perhaps Cook's last will and testament helped you. Perhaps Haig's floundering in his current position made a difference. But what you did and in front of others was bad politics. It pays to use politics, especially to cover your ass. Now you, sir, have laid yours bare so all and sundry can give it a good spanking."

"Your metaphors lack elegance," Maddox said dryly. "But be that as it may, all right, at the first opportunity, I'll speak to the Lord High Admiral in a politic way." He looked at Meta. "I'll repair the situation."

"In the long run, it's the wiser decision," Meta said.

Maddox smiled at her, cleared his throat and glanced around the table. "What about what we just witnessed? I mean how the Spacers used a possible hyper-spatial tube to escape?"

"I have a thought on that, sir," Galyan said.

Maddox nodded.

"We should investigate the phenomena closely," Galyan said. "There was something suspect about it."

"How so?" asked Ludendorff.

"It felt as if the energy projections, from the saucers, were keys, rather than the cause or creation of the tube opening," Galyan said.

"Could you explain that further?" Maddox said.

Galyan waved a ropy holographic arm. "We use Laumer Point Engines to open a jump point. A Builder nexus creates a hyper-spatial tube and thus an opening. The projections from the saucer ships lacked the power and harmonics we normally witness from a nexus as it creates a hyper-spatial tube. That is why I said we witnessed activation or unlocking of a projector or nexus elsewhere in the system. That other created the hyper-spatial tube, not the saucer ships."

"That's interesting." Maddox picked up a hand communicator. "I'm going to tell Andros to start looking for a nexus-like projector immediately."

"Sir," Galyan said, "I wish you would wait a moment. I would prefer to find the projector rather than Andros."

Maddox raised an eyebrow before nodding. Andros and Galyan had started a competition last mission. He hadn't realized it was still ongoing. "We'll start searching for this projector after the meeting. Are there any further thoughts on what has taken place in the star system?"

"I have one," Ludendorff said, "but it concerns Becker."

"Right," Maddox said. "Becker is a problem and he's in the star system."

"Indeed," Ludendorff said. "My point is that he has served his purpose, has he not?"

"He has," Maddox said. "Becker saved my grandmother. I'm grateful for that and plan to keep my end of the bargain."

"To take him to the Library Planet?" asked Ludendorff.

"Exactly," Maddox said. "Do you have a problem with that?"

"No. That seems like the right idea," Ludendorff said. "Becker is latently dangerous, especially as we do not understand the full extent of his mental capabilities. Certainly, he did what no one else has been able to do in dealing with the alien entity, although who knows what happened on the Spacer ships."

Maddox raised a hand. "Let's address the two issues separately. First, I want to hear any further thoughts about Becker. We know he sustained a so-called semi-stroke while in the stasis unit."

"That is what I discovered, sir," Galyan said. "

"Do you know why the so-called stroke happened?"

"I have an idea," Galyan said. "All the indicators point to a telekinetic attack upon certain of Becker's brain cells. That means it wasn't really a stroke, just the end result of some strokes."

"Who could do that to Becker?" Maddox said.

"On our ship, at this moment," Galyan said, "that would be Becker."

"Are you suggesting Becker attacked himself?" Maddox asked.

"While that seems unlikely," Galyan said, "that is the logical conclusion from the evidence."

"*Why* would Becker attack himself?" Maddox asked.

"That's the question," Ludendorff said. "Answering it could probably help us answer the rest."

Maddox nodded slowly. "Becker may be going crazy and gave himself a semi-stroke. Might he have felt self-revulsion and cut himself for it, so to speak?"

"I'm not sure Becker is capable of self-revulsion," Ludendorff said.

"Nonsense," Meta said. "Anyone is capable of it."

Ludendorff showed surprise.

"Maybe not *anyone,*" Galyan said as he looked at the professor.

Maddox laughed.

Galyan smiled shyly at him.

"Your jokes are improving," Maddox said.

"Thank you, sir," Galyan said.

Ludendorff, perhaps finally understanding, scowled.

"Whether Becker can feel self-revulsion or not, he did the impossible and stopped the assassinating entity no one else could," Maddox said. "Do the rest of you believe I should take him to the Library Planet?"

"You truly want our suggestions?" Ludendorff said.

"I'm *open* to your suggestions," Maddox said. "I do have my own idea on this, of course."

"May we know what those ideas are?" Galyan said.

"I plan to keep my word," Maddox said. "That means going to the Library Planet. That will take time and effort we possibly can't afford right now. There's one other point. I don't know how wise it is leaving Becker on the Library Planet."

"Why would you leave him there?" Ludendorff said.

"Where else should we leave Becker?" Maddox said. "Should we take him with us?"

No one answered the questions.

"I flat don't know what to do with Becker," Maddox admitted. "It's why I'm open to suggestions. I could use the input."

"Hmmm," Ludendorff said. "As we've talked about Becker, and now considered the next move with him, I've been reconsidering what the Prime Saa of the Liss did to him."

"You mean in castrating Becker ten years ago?" Maddox said.

"Precisely," Ludendorff said. "Why would the Prime Saa do that to Becker, to one of his key telepathic operatives? I don't believe the alien Liss did it for reasons of cruelty or sadism. I believe the Liss acted for logical reasons. Thus, I've asked myself, what could be the reasons?"

"What's your conclusion?" Maddox asked.

"Becker had and has an inordinate love of women," Ludendorff said.

"Is it not odd you should be the one to point that out?" Galyan asked.

Ludendorff grinned and ran a hand through his thick white hair. "I'm a lady killer, no doubt about that. I suspect Becker was and is a gamma male want-to-be. Becker loves the ladies but doesn't know how to acquire them. And yet, when he had telepathic powers—if I'm correct in my supposition—he acquired them through mental domination, through his telepathy. Perhaps, as a gamma male—I'm talking about ten years ago—he poured all his energy into the enjoyment of the ladies."

"Go on," Maddox said.

"The Prime Saa must have recognized this," Ludendorff said. "But the Prime Saa needed Becker to concentrate on the tasks at hand. That was dominating its foes at the time. Therefore, the Prime Saa had to remove Becker's desire for the ladies. Presumably, that was why the alien Liss castrated Becker ten years ago."

"That makes as good a sense as any," Maddox said. "Do you have anything to add to that, Galyan?"

"No, sir, in this I am listening and gathering data."

"There is another point I wish to make," Ludendorff said.

"Please," Maddox said. "Do so."

"If Becker regains all the normal functions of a man, perhaps his sex drive will return in full, gamma-male force."

"That seems obvious," Maddox said.

"It may seem obvious," Ludendorff said, "but the point or question is will the sex drive do what it did to Becker in the past? Becker might return to his inordinate desire for women."

"Are you saying we have to protect women from his dominating power?" Maddox asked.

"That would be one way to look at it," Ludendorff said. "My point is different. If Becker utilizes most of his efforts toward acquiring and enjoying the beauties he so dearly desires, then he will not be affecting political or other aspects. Therefore, Becker will prove much less dangerous to the Commonwealth and Star Watch once he fully recovers."

"But not less dangerous to the women he assaults," Maddox said.

"Again," Ludendorff said, "that isn't the aspect I'm addressing, although you have a point."

"That brings us full circle," Maddox said. "Do I unleash Becker upon the universe, or do I keep him in stasis where he can't hurt anyone?"

"Keeping him in stasis means breaking your word," Ludendorff said.

"Exactly," Maddox said. "I dearly do not want to do that, particularly as Becker saved my grandmother."

"I have a suggestion," Galyan said. "You could lessen Becker's mental capabilities."

"Burn out some of his brain cells?" asked Maddox.

"That would be the easiest way to reduce his mental powers," Galyan said.

"Why not give him a lobotomy while you're at it," Ludendorff said in a huff. "Turn him into an imbecile, a vegetable, and then you'll all be happy. Is that what you're saying, you AI scoundrel?"

"Why are you angry with me, Professor?" Galyan asked.

"Because what you're suggested is monstrous in the extreme," Ludendorff said. "You want to make a retard out of the poor fool just because he agreed to help us, just because he saved Maddox's grandmother, and just because he loves the ladies. I find the lobotomy idea detestable."

"I agree," Maddox said. "Yet I don't know if I should release a fully masculine Becker upon the universe? I don't want to be responsible for the bane he might prove to be to women."

"What is the right thing to do?" Ludendorff said. "It is an interesting quandary."

Maddox glanced at his wife, at Galyan and then folded his hands on the table. "We'll take Becker to the Library Planet. I'll see what the Supreme Intelligence and my Uncle Ural have to say. Perhaps we can rehabilitate Becker so he restrains himself and acts like a civilized man."

"You mean he doesn't use his dominating power to coerce women to do his bidding?" Ludendorff said.

"Exactly," Maddox said.

"Do you think a man such as Becker will ever be able to restrain himself?" Ludendorff asked.

"If I had to guess right now," Maddox said, "I'd say no. But we shouldn't jump to conclusions. I owe him the chance at rehabilitation, and I want to keep my word."

"How about taking Becker to the Library Planet, having the Supreme Intelligence restore him, and then putting him back into stasis," Ludendorff said. "In that way, you've kept your word and kept the universe safe from him."

Maddox frowned, even though he'd already thought of that.

"Before we do any of that, sir," Galyan said, "I suggest we take a closer look at the terrestrial planets near this dwarf star. The planets could provide the answer as to how the Spacer ships did what they did in leaving the star system."

"Agreed," Maddox said. "Are there any other comments before we adjourn?"

No one had anything else to say.

"We'll move near the terrestrial planets and search for clues," Maddox said. "After that, I'll see the Lord High Admiral when we return to the Solar System to use the Builder Nexus to reach the Library Planet."

"Good," Meta said. "You won't regret making peace with Haig."

Maddox hoped his wife was right.

-29-

With Maddox on the bridge, *Victory* executed a star-drive jump and appeared one hundred thousand kilometers from the third terrestrial planet orbiting the Barnard's Star red dwarf.

On the bridge, Andros and Galyan, along with Ludendorff from his science chamber, began to search for signs that would reveal how the Spacer ships had left the star system.

Residue particles at their exit point were consistent with a recent opening of a hyper-spatial tube in the area. That was a critical discovery.

"That's it then?" Maddox said. "The Spacers created a hyper-spatial tube."

Galyan stood beside the command chair. "I deem that the highest possibility, some form of hyper-spatial tube. That doesn't mean it *must* be the case."

"Don't the facts indicate Builder technology?" Maddox asked.

"I think the odds are high regarding that," Galyan said.

"Have you found any evidence of a nexus?" Maddox asked.

"We have not found one, sir," Andros said from his science station. The pudgy, Kai Kaus, Chief Technician had been listening closely to the conversation, surprising both Galyan and Maddox with his answer.

Andros, Galyan and Ludendorff continued to study the sensors. Galyan also went out as a holoimage to "physically" examine areas on the third terrestrial planet and within its three moons.

The sensor search continued for another two hours and thirty-seven minutes before anyone found anything. At that point, Galyan turned to Maddox in his captain's chair.

"I have found what we are looking for, sir."

"I've found it," Andros said a second later.

"I found it first," Galyan said. "I have already informed the captain."

"It's in a comet," Andros said, ignoring Galyan.

"A comet, you say?" Maddox asked Andros.

"Yes, sir," Andros said, "a comet near the last moon of the third planet."

"We have found Builder devices in comets before, sir," Galyan said. "Thus, our find comports to previous Builder devices. However, I just told you I found it."

"Are you saying that you discovered it in the comet that Andros mentioned?" Maddox asked.

"Yes, but I was going to tell you that," Galyan said. "Surely I will be credited with having found this first."

"Of course, Galyan," Meta said. She was working the comm station.

Maddox swiveled around to stare at his wife, winking.

"No," Meta said, "you shouldn't tease Galyan about this. He found it honestly. Let's give Galyan the credit. Right, Andros?"

Andros reddened under Meta's level stare. "Yes, Meta," he said. "Galyan found it first, even though I tried to claim it before him."

"Galyan," Maddox said from his chair. "You have found the comet. You have found the Builder artifact. Now tell me what it is"

"I do not know precisely," Galyan said. "I just know there were nexus-like emanations coming from it."

"Andros," Maddox said, "do you know what it is?"

Andros looked at Galyan, looked at Maddox, and looked at Galyan again. "I do. I made a deep probe into the comet."

"Galyan," Maddox said, "would you go and make a deeper probe, appearing inside the comet and taking a quick look around?"

"Yes, sir," Galyan said. He vanished.

"Would you like further analysis of the site, sir?" Andros said.

"Wait just a moment," Maddox said.

Soon, Galyan reappeared on the bridge. "There is a cavernous chamber in the comet. The machinery there is much smaller compared to what I have seen on the hyper-spatial tube generators in the pyramidal nexuses we have used. This site strikes me as a stealth nexus."

"I see," Maddox said. "And that means what?"

"The place is definitely of Builder design," Galyan said. "This nexus has a one-way possibility, though. I saw no selector switches or other ways to include variations."

"Do you know the tube's distance when created?" Maddox asked.

"I am re-analyzing what I saw," Galyan said. "From the evidence, the tube will project two hundred light years."

"Is that an exact distance?" Andros asked.

"No, not exact," Galyan said.

"Do you have the exact measurement?" Andros asked.

"Do you?" asked Galyan.

"No," Andros said. "I thought two hundred light years seemed too precise, though. That's why I'm asking."

"I have it now," Galyan said, whose eyelids stopped blinking. "The tube will project two hundred point zero eight light years from here, although I don't know the composition of the target star system, though I suspect it is one."

"How long has this nexus-like device been in the comet in Barnard's Star System?" Maddox asked.

"I would estimate it at thousands of years," Galyan said.

Maddox frowned. "Do you think the Spacers have known about it all this time?"

"I deem it likely the Spacers have known about it as at least as long as Star Watch has existed," Galyan said.

"That means the Spacers had a secret egress near Earth all this time," Maddox said.

"That would be so," Galyan said.

"I find that troublesome."

"I agree, sir," Galyan said.

"I need to tell the Lord High Admiral about this," Maddox said.

"Should we first go see where the tube exits?" Galyan asked.

Maddox's heart beat a little faster. He wanted to do that.

"I volunteer to check it out," Valerie said. "This is precisely why you have the darter along, sir."

Maddox was reluctant to give Valerie dibs on this, and maybe that showed.

"Sir," Valerie said, "you've shouldered me aside too many times lately. This one is mine. I request permission to scout out the hyper-spatial tube."

"It might be a one-way trip," Maddox said.

"No matter," Valerie said. "Galyan said it's only two hundred light years long. I can deal with that if stranded out there. I am a Patrol officer, and I haven't had a truly engaging independent command for some time."

Maddox nodded. "This is your mission, Lieutenant Commander. Galyan, do we know how to activate it?"

"We can watch the video and see what the Spacers did," Galyan said.

"On second thought," Maddox said, "I don't think we should do that. It risks projecting Valerie and her crew to where the Spacers are."

"That does seems likely," Galyan said.

"Commander—" Maddox said as he turned back to Valerie.

"Sir," Galyan said, interrupting. "I should point out that Valerie's darter has stealth capabilities. That is the ideal craft, unless *Victory* itself should go. We may have to battle an entire Spacer nation fleet, though, if we do that."

"That's not a good idea." Maddox regarded Valerie. "Lieutenant Commander, I'm not sending you on such a risky mission."

"Respectfully, sir," Valerie said, "It is more imperative than ever that I go. This is critical to the security of Star Watch and the Commonwealth. The Lord High Admiral and Brigadier Stokes were assassinated. Your grandmother—"

"Yes, yes," Maddox said, interrupting her. "You've made your point. You'll go. It is imperative we know where the tube reaches. But first, Galyan, do we know how to activate the thing?"

"A team will have to enter the comet," Galyan said.

"Go yourself and search it more," Maddox said. "If you can't figure it out, I'll send a team. Commander, get your people ready for a Patrol mission."

"Sir," Keith said, "I volunteer to go with Valerie."

"No," Maddox said. "You're staying here."

"But sir—" Keith said.

Maddox raised a hand. "No arguments, Lieutenant. You're our main pilot and are staying on *Victory*. We're far from out of this yet."

"Yes, sir," Keith said, sounding crestfallen.

"You do know that this is a dangerous mission," Maddox told Valerie.

"There's no need to explain your decision, sir," Valerie said. "I totally agree with you. I want Keith where it's safe."

Keith blushed at her glance.

"Ready your crew for an extended Patrol mission," Maddox told Valerie. "Tell me if you need anything extra. Galyan, thoroughly check the comet until we know exactly how this works. Until then, we will wait and continue to gather data."

"Sir," Galyan said, disappearing.

Maddox looked at Andros, and Andros turned to his science board and continued his sensor search.

-30-

Deep inside *Victory*, in a cargo area, was a stasis unit. Within the stasis unit, Becker slept soundly. This wasn't the same type of stasis he had experienced in Antarctica for ten years, during which the machine had frozen all his functions. This was akin to a hibernation state, a lighter sleep. It primarily kept him unconscious so he couldn't create havoc with his telepathy.

As Becker lay in this inert state, he dreamed, seeing strange geometric designs. Interwoven with the designs were ideas and memories.

In one of the dream memories, Becker crawled once more through the fateful cavern on Jarnevon. Later, he saw Liss cybers crawling over each other like giant robotic centipedes. Among them were the Prime Saa and others. At the aliens' command, Becker mentally dominated Commodore James K. Fletcher, forcing him out of retirement to become the Lord High Admiral of Star Watch.

He had been Captain Becker back then. In his dreams, Becker relived many experiences, including his horrific castration. He also remembered the fun times he'd had with the women he'd enjoyed to his heart's delight.

He wanted to do that again.

In his dream, Becker eventually reached a rare state that only the most expert dreamers did, those with ancient Tibetan skills. He controlled his dreams and began to use his conscious mind in them. That meant his subconscious and conscious minds merged as his intellect increased. He understood much that had been hidden to him before this.

In this merged dream state, Becker examined the files he'd extracted from the alien rat-like creature that had resided in a corner of his brain. He'd literally destroyed some of his brain cells in order to evict the alien thing. He studied captured files regarding the handling of women, this from perhaps the greatest player on Earth. In his dreams, Becker received an education indeed.

In the old days, he had been a clown when it came to dealing with women. They had mocked and used him on so many occasions. But this player, this alpha male, oh, Becker was astounded by these revelations. There was another factor to this. In the dream state, his pride did not get in the way of the lessons as it might have otherwise.

"I will do things so differently this time," Becker said in his sleep. "This is priceless information. I have been a fool, a dupe, and a buffoon. I will be better than Maddox. I will be better than Professor Ludendorff. I must get to the Library Planet and resume where I left off ten years ago."

Becker started to think.

"I won't need my dominating power to bend women's minds. I'll use my dominating power for other things."

This was grand, awesome, and unique.

Becker proceeded to study other files, the ones that came from Ector, the planet that circled a pulsar in the Scutum-Centaurus Spiral Arm. These were deeper, more profound and secret things. They had to do with the mind: telepathy, telekinesis, and devouring energy through mental effort.

Becker continued to dream but at a faster rate until he learned and studied at computer speeds. He ran through program after program, event after event. That began to alter his brain and brain patterns. He used knowledge gained from the shattered Phantasma Synth Crystals. The Aetharians had deeply studied the mind and mental effort. This was outrageous.

Becker continued to modify himself and his thoughts. He started to understand that he was in hibernation stasis.

"I am dreaming. I am thinking these things. My mind is literally changing. I am gaining power. I am gaining authority and ability."

He saw where he had made many mistakes in the past.

"If I had done it this way, and if I had gone at it that way, I never would have gone into stasis. I could become a god. The humans around me, even the New Men, are paltry and inferior in their mental capabilities."

The Liss cybers had increased the density of his brain, as well as enlarging the size of it. That gave him such a vast field to work with.

Becker modified part of his brain, tweaked a different part, and activated his enlarged pituitary gland. The secretions helped alter and change him even more as he slept in this hibernation stasis.

"I am changing so much. They think they're going to use me. Oh, no—absolutely not."

Becker saw how Maddox had used him this past week. He saw how Venna the Spy had used those poor men. In fact, there was a part in Becker, perhaps it came from the file—

The outrage from the pudgy playboy who had taught him so much: "We must teach Venna a lesson."

Becker agreed. He had learned so much from the man that he accepted the idea and ran with it. Yes, Becker yearned to make Venna the Spy pay for having absorbed his life. Even more, he was going to make those pay who were behind Venna the Spy.

Who were those others? There was a hint of Spacers. There was also a hint of Leviathan.

"I want names," the pudgy playboy sliver of personality said inside Becker.

"I agree with you," Becker said. "We want names, we want numbers, and we want to make them dance for us."

There was total agreement in all of him about that.

As Becker started to understand his new power, his new abilities, his godlike senses, he began to move switches in the outer room. He changed the configuration of the stasis field over his inert body.

Soon, Becker began to awaken. No one else knew he was doing that. No one else knew, surely, that he had altered his mind to such fantastic levels.

Let Maddox wear that headband. Let them try to stop him. He had some surprises in store for all of them.

Becker might pretend weakness for a little while longer, but when he struck, he was going to be the one giving the orders. He was the one who was going to be in charge. They were not going to be able to tell him what to do anymore. No one was going to tell him what to do. He was going to tell everyone else what to do.

Thus, by stages, Becker awakened, brought out of hibernation stasis by his own mental energies. Here was the thing. This was going to be the freaking Age of Becker.

-31-

Becker climbed out of the stasis unit, stretched, yawned, and realized he was in terrible danger. He had tampered with the stasis unit in which they had placed him. What would they do next time in order to stop him?

Maybe they would kill him.

Becker nodded. That meant he couldn't afford to lose. That meant he had to win this round no matter what.

He believed himself the superior man, possibly with the powers of a fledgling god. Yet his good sense told him to rethink that, as he'd been dreaming. How could dreams have changed him so radically? And might he be believing a stupid dream that wasn't really real?

Becker clutched his huge head. His neck and shoulder muscles could barely support its weight. He searched until he found the neck brace, and carefully he put it on. He balanced his head to prevent it from swinging too far to the left, right, or back, which could cause him to lose his balance. Bumping or cracking his head hard could be the worst thing of all.

After securing the brace, he lowered himself to sit against a bulkhead.

Then he used his intellect, testing what he believed could be true. He soon found that his thoughts could move through the starship as if he physically did this. This was both astounding and incredibly useful.

Next, he roved through the interior ship sensors, searching and studying. Ah. A camera eye watched him in here. With his mind, he traced the exact route and response—suddenly, a silent alarm rang. That meant... Armed Marines ran toward this chamber. Were they coming to capture or to kill him?

Becker composed himself even as his heart hammered. He sought to use what he'd learned during his dreams. Could this work? It was time to try.

He gathered a single thought and radiated it outward: *Go to sleep.* He thought this as powerfully as he could—his life might depend on it.

With his roving sense, he watched the Marines. To his astonishment, they collapsed onto the deck, sliding as they began to snore. Each had fallen asleep.

That had worked much better than he had anticipated. Could he be telepathically stronger than he realized?

Becker mentally searched farther. The sleep command had radiated from him in all directions—up, down, and around. Everywhere he searched, people slept soundly.

It didn't take Becker long to discover that everyone aboard *Victory* was asleep. That included Ludendorff, Meta, and Maddox. Ludendorff and Maddox hadn't been wearing their silver headband with the box. They had lacked all protection from him.

Becker laughed with glee. Then he clenched his fists and shook them. "Now we see who has the true power on this starship. Now you will all begin to learn."

To make sure, he mentally roved further still. Oh no, he had forgotten the AI. He worked fast and shut down Galyan. He did that with telekinesis, using it to throw the correct switches in the armored AI chamber.

In the old days, he might have been satisfied with that. Today, he realized he couldn't leave anything to luck. Thus, he roved *beyond* the starship. He found Valerie Noonan, the Lieutenant Commander, in her darter, heading for a select region of the star system.

A few seconds contemplation brought a plan into thought and then bloom. This might work.

Becker collected himself and projected, "Return to *Victory.*"

Inside the piloting chamber in the darter, Valerie cocked her head as if puzzled.

Becker realized his mistake. He needed to give her mind a path that she recognized as legitimate.

"This is Galyan speaking. The captain told me to tell you that he's ordered you to return to the hangar bay."

Valerie scowled thunderously. It wasn't because she suspected the command, but was angry with Maddox.

Becker searched her thoughts for the right words. This ought to do it. "The captain wants you to take Lieutenant Maker along after all. Maddox's wants to give you the best possible chance for success."

Oh. Valerie smiled and began to manipulate the darter's piloting board.

Out in space, the darter turned around and headed back for *Victory*.

Becker used that time to study Valerie's thoughts in detail. Ah, he understood her instructions. He also realized what had happened out here. The Spacers had escaped the star system through a surprise method. Galyan had found a hyper-spatial tube projector, a one-way path.

It would take the darter twenty minutes to return and land in *Victory*. With everyone asleep on the starship, and with these free minutes, Becker studied himself in earnest. He needed a better understanding of what he could and could not do. By degrees, he discovered the power of his pituitary gland. He had reshaped his mind, many of the brain cells with its aid. It seemed he might have gained a lizard-like ability to repair physical damage as such creatures did with a lost tail, for instance. Might he regrow his lost testicles through a similar procedure?

If so, that meant he would **not** need to go to the Library Planet for the…healing. Yet, to heal himself like that, he would need power or extra energy. That would take food. He was already hungry, as his mental efforts used calories as fuel.

Now that he thought about it, it really wasn't so incredible that his body could regenerate testicles. His body had done that before while he'd been in his mother's womb. It would simply be a matter of finding the areas in his brain to activate that particular growth process.

Becker smiled with a smug sense of satisfaction. This was all possible because the mystic shards from the shattered Phantasma Synth Crystals were unleashing his potential. That was because he had an enlarged and dense brain from the Liss. The combination of the two allowed him to metamorph into a god.

Becker chortled to himself. If the New Men were better than the old-style men, he was something wonderful and marvelous even compared to the New Men.

It was time for the next phase of this.

Using the bulkhead for support, Becker pulled himself to his feet. He pushed off and began to shuffle through the corridors, finding it full of sleeping individuals.

How long would they sleep? He had put them down hard, more through accident than anything else. He doubted any would wake anytime soon, unless he specifically woke them.

As he shuffled through the corridors, he roved telepathically, examining each crewmember. He chose the three most beautiful women—

Well, Meta was the most beautiful. Becker decided to leave her, though. She was too physically strong for one thing. Besides, an enraged Maddox might be a problem. Sometimes, it was better to leave sleeping dogs lie. These three beauties should be enough for now.

Becker almost took Valerie, but he decided against her, too. She was too old for his tastes. These three were younger.

Physically going to each chamber, he partially woke up each of the three. They sleepwalked to the hangar bay with him, helping him shuffle along by holding him up.

By that time, the darter had landed in the hangar bay. Becker telepathically ordered the crew to exit. They did, moving into a control chamber. There, he ordered them to go to sleep.

They crumpled onto the deck, including Valerie Noonan, and started sleeping.

This was too much and a ton of fun.

Surrounded by his three beauties, Becker led them into the Darter *Tarrypin.*

Transferring piloting knowledge from the sleeping Valerie to one of his chosen, he had her activate the piloting controls.

In moments, the hatches shut and engine purred into life. The darter rose from the deck and exited through the open hangar bay hatch, sliding into space. The new pilot headed for the original hyper-spatial tube opening the Spacers had used, or where it had been, anyway.

The extended use of his mental powers had made Becker incredibly hungry. His stomach was growling and pains shot through him. So, before he did anything more, he went to the small galley and ate three ham sandwiches, and drank two glasses of milk. Two of his lovelies made the sandwiches and poured the milk for him.

He felt much better and appreciated the service. How soon should he have them do a strip tease for him? Maybe he should get far away before he indulged himself.

Becker and the two returned to the small bridge. He examined his three beauties as each sat a station. He made them smile at him.

"Hello, my darlings," he said.

Each of them said in turn, "Hello, Handsome. Hello, Mr. Stud. Hello, Becker, my love."

Becker grinned with delight. Was that great or what? This was going to be a fun trip, possibly the best of his life.

As soon as he got his balls working, or made them, this would be a paradise cruise. This was what he'd longed for all his life. This was why he'd done Nostradamus' bidding back in the day. The Prime Saa had forced him to give all that up. Now everything was turning around for him. This was incredible.

"I'm the luckiest man alive," Becker said.

He concentrated, reaching out to *Victory* and switching Galyan back on.

"This is Captain Maddox," Becker projected into the AI system. This was more difficult to do than tricking a human, but the process was essentially the same. It was simply a matter of getting the hang of it.

Soon, Galyan projected his holoimage into the comet and activated the Builder device there. As before with the Spacers, a hyper-spatial tube opening appeared as a bright light.

The pirated darter swerved and headed for the opening.

At the last minute, Becker said, "No, my mind. What am I thinking?"

He strengthened his mind, hardened it, if you will, and readied himself for the process.

Then the bomber-shaped darter entered the hyper-spatial tube opening, and zip, it was gone.

A moment later, the opening closed. Becker had escaped the starship and the Barnard's Star System. Becker had taken three of Captain Maddox's crew and the darter. Who knew what awaited them at the other end.

-32-

Maddox snorted in his sleep, realized that his back ached, and his eyes abruptly flew open. He sat in his captain's chair on the bridge. He had apparently been fast asleep.

Maddox sat up, perplexed. Now, the crick in his back was worse. He eased forward and then stood and stretched, leaning his long frame as his fingertips touched the deck. He straightened slowly and saw that everybody around him was asleep.

Something was terribly wrong.

He tried to wake more and realized it was difficult to do. This was harder than shaking off any previous jump lag. Why would that be?

He felt a numbing sensation in his brain, or an empty area there. What could that signify?

Maddox shook his head, squeezed his eyes shut, and concentrated—but that didn't help. He was almost falling asleep on his feet. If that happened, how long would it take until he woke up again? The pain in his back must have driven him awake.

Maddox stretched out on the floor and began to do push-ups, going all the way down and all the way up. When that didn't work, he leaped up and sprinted off the bridge. He ran down the corridors, hurdling over people sprawled out asleep everywhere.

By the intense exertion, he shook off the lingering paralysis. That suggested to him that someone had forced him to sleep. Who could do that?

A moment's reflection showed Maddox that Becker was the obvious person.

Thus, during his sprint, he went down a turbo lift and raced into the stasis chamber on a different level. He skidded to a halt, finding the stasis unit empty. Either Becker was up or someone had taken him. It was imperative to know which.

"Galyan, can you hear me? Come here this instant."

Galyan did not appear after several seconds. No one appeared. It could be that he was the only one awake on the starship.

Maddox pivoted and hurried out of the chamber. He was wide-awake now, but just to be certain, he went to his quarters and got the silver headband, jamming it over his head. He switched it on, but there was no change. Not one damn bit of difference.

He hurried to the science chamber and found Ludendorff fast asleep on the deck. Kneeling, Maddox shook the Methuselah Man but achieved no results. He slapped him in the face. Finally, with Ludendorff's face cherry red, Maddox switched tactics and got two glasses of water. He threw the water into Ludendorff's face—one, two.

The Methuselah Man snorted and smacked his lips.

"Professor, can you hear me? Becker must have switched our brains into permanent sleep mode. But we can overcome it through exertion. You have to start moving."

Ludendorff opened his eyes and stared at him blurry-eyed. "What did you say?"

"Wake up, Professor. Becker duped us. So far, I'm the only one been able to resist this process. I'm hoping somebody else on this starship can resist like me."

"Damn you, man," Ludendorff said in a sleepy way. What seemed like through sheer grit, Ludendorff sat up. Soon, he did push-ups, ran and started panting. He stopped and drank water.

"May I use your headband?" Ludendorff said.

"By all means," Maddox said, taking it off and proffering it.

Ludendorff put on the headband, but it had no effect. Instead, through steady exercise, Ludendorff shrugged off the debilitating effect until he was wide-awake.

"Where's Galyan?" Ludendorff said.

"I've called him, but the AI doesn't respond."

"We must go to the AI Core," Ludendorff said. "By the way, what exactly happened?"

"I think Becker did," Maddox said.

"What do you mean? What happened to Becker?"

"He's gone."

"Gone where?" asked Ludendorff.

"Right," Maddox said. "We need to check ship security and watch some videos. That might show us what happened."

They hurried to the main security chamber. There, they turned on monitors and watched video of Becker wandering through the corridors, stepping over sleeping people. Becker chose and awoke three beauties, taking them to the hangar bay and leaving the starship in Valerie's darter.

"How could Becker do that?" Maddox said.

"It's a mystery," Ludendorff said. "Obviously, Becker used telepathy, but how he became so powerful remains unclear. We must find or activate Galyan immediately."

Maddox looked sharply at Ludendorff. "You know something. What is it?"

"I wonder if Becker is seeking the Spacers," Ludendorff said. "What happens if the Spacers reappear in the system and board the starship?"

"Good point," Maddox said.

They raced into the armored AI chamber or core. There, Ludendorff threw switch and pressed buttons.

Tall cylinders and wide computers soon hummed with power. They had been off.

Abruptly, Galyan called from outside the chamber, "I am here. I am fully aware. I know what happened. Becker used the hyper-spatial tube device to leave the star system."

By that time, Maddox stepped outside into the corridor. Galyan's holographic image could not appear in the AI core for security reasons.

Galyan now explained what he knew.

During that time, Ludendorff stepped out of the chamber and shut the hatch, locking it.

"Becker has increased his telepathic or mental capabilities," Ludendorff said. "It would seem they've increased tenfold or more. Perhaps he's a proto-deity, something beyond what we can understand. He's seems able to use his mind in ways we didn't even think was possible."

"How could that have happened?" Maddox said.

"Perhaps it has something to do with the semi-stroke you spoke about before," Ludendorff said.

"Destroying your own brain cells doesn't make you smarter or more powerful," Maddox said.

"Not under usual circumstances," Ludendorff said, "but we're dealing with a person who has undergone metamorphosis from the Liss. Perhaps the combination activated greater mental powers."

"But why did he leave *Victory?*" Maddox asked. "I thought Becker wanted to refurbish himself or have the Supreme Intelligence give him back what the Liss stole from him."

"I don't know the answer, but Becker did kidnap the three lovely ladies," Ludendorff said.

"Yes, we must rescue them." Maddox frowned. "He tricked Valerie into bringing the darter in. Who knows what else has happened. Professor, we need to wake up everyone. Galyan, perhaps you can lightly shock people and help speed up the process."

"Yes, sir," Galyan said.

"Let's get started," Maddox said.

For the next three hours, Maddox, Ludendorff, Galyan, and a small but growing number of people who gained consciousness, worked on the others. Some proved more resistant to consciousness than others did.

"We can study this later," Ludendorff told Maddox, Galyan, Meta and Andros Crank. "But for now, we should get back to Earth as fast as possible."

"Why's that?" Maddox said.

"What if the Spacers show up here?" Ludendorff asked.

"They haven't yet."

"That doesn't mean they can't or won't," Ludendorff said. "Becker may make a deal with them."

"Maybe we should go after Becker immediately," Maddox said.

"How are you going to defeat someone who can make everyone sleep?" Ludendorff asked.

"Surely he must have a range limit," Maddox said.

"Look how he brought the Lieutenant Commander in," Ludendorff said. "Valerie was already far from the starship."

"True," Maddox said. He frowned. What had he unleashed by originally waking Becker in Antarctica? This was all a huge problem he'd unwittingly brought to life. "You're right, Professor. We need to return to Earth. I need to tell the new Lord High Admiral what has happened. It's time to face the music."

"More importantly," Ludendorff said, "It's time to bring *Conqueror*-class battleships to the star system and through this point. We need to destroy the Spacer ships and Becker as fast as possible."

"Is this an intuitive sense?" Galyan asked.

"I wouldn't go as far as that," Ludendorff said. "I don't have the captain's ability. But I think something dreadful has occurred. It has to do with how the Spacers were able to assassinate Cook and Stokes. We're too in the dark on all this, and this secret method of travel here is deadly to Star Watch."

"Agreed," Maddox said. "Becker literally woke himself according to what we saw on the video."

"That was strange," Ludendorff agreed. "It should have been impossible to wake up from stasis, but Becker has advanced far in his mental capabilities."

"How has he done that?" asked Meta.

"That would be good to know in case we ever want to reproduce it," Ludendorff said.

"Reproduce it?" Maddox said. "That's madness."

"No," Ludendorff said. "That's what you call the advancement of science. Whether you like it or not, that's how knowledge grows. There's no turning back the clock, Captain. It's always ahead, ahead, full speed ahead."

"Maybe," Maddox said. He didn't care to argue the point. Thus, he adjourned the ad hoc meeting. It was time to get back to Earth as fast as possible.

-33-

Maddox arrived in the Solar System in less than an hour using the Laumer Point that the phase ship had utilized to reach the Barnard's Star System six light years away from Earth. Soon *Victory* was in orbit around Earth. Maddox took a shuttle down to Geneva Spaceport and soon sat in Lord High Admiral Haig's office. Haig was astounded and surprised to see him.

As Maddox started to explain the situation, Haig raised a small hand and said, "Stop. I'm bringing another representative in."

Soon, the large and blunt General Mackinder of Intelligence was sitting across from Haig and Maddox. He sat at a far corner of the desk, while Maddox sat across from Haig.

"Now, explain from the beginning, Captain, what you were telling me earlier," Haig directed.

Maddox related everything he knew about the Spacers, the flotilla marshal, and the hyper-spatial tube. Then he explained how Becker had awoken from stasis sleep, slept everyone aboard the starship, and kidnapped three of the crew and left the star system in the darter.

"Ensign Ro was one of his captives?" General Mackinder asked sharply.

"Yes," Maddox said, wondering why the general cared or knew anything about Ro.

Mackinder looked starkly at Haig.

"Is Ro one of yours?" Haig asked.

Mackinder closed his eyes as if in pain. Maybe he didn't like the question.

"What's this?" Maddox said, glancing from Haig to Mackinder. "You're putting spies aboard my starship?"

Mackinder opened his eyes and glared at Maddox. "Not spies, sir. We're monitoring you and the half-alien starship you use to flit here, flit there, and do who knows what all over the universe. I think it's telling Becker took Ensign Ro."

"Ensign Ro was a pretty woman," Maddox said.

"I doubt that's why Becker chose her," Mackinder said.

"You're exactly wrong," Maddox said. "It's clear that Becker is driven to excess by female physical beauty."

"That seems hard to believe in a so-called egghead like him," Mackinder shot back.

"Wrong again," Maddox said. "Becker must have fantasized from earliest adolescence about having a beautiful woman like Ro. He's exactly the sort to go crazy over this."

"Enough, enough," Haig said. "I'm not interested in this sort of talk. We're going to keep this above board, and I want you to continue, Captain. Tell us what else happened out there."

Maddox continued his explanation.

Both Haig and Mackinder sat there, shocked by it all.

"So you lost Becker," Mackinder said.

"I lost Becker," Maddox said.

"Do you realize that it was your fault?" Mackinder said.

"Yes," Maddox said, "since I was in charge, I bear the responsibility. That's why I said I lost Becker."

"That means it's all your fault," Mackinder shouted at him.

Maddox looked at Haig.

Haig merely watched him.

"Yes, it was my fault," Maddox said. "Would you care to throw a few body shots at me while you're at it?"

"Perhaps," Mackinder said heatedly. "What would you do then?"

"Knock you on your ass," Maddox said.

"Do you see how disrespectful this half-breed is to us?" Mackinder asked Haig.

"Please," Haig said, "that is one degree too far. I refer to your vulgar term of half-breed," he told Mackinder.

Only one degree, Maddox thought to himself. He realized both men were Humanity Manifesto Doctrine adherents or sympathizers. Things were going to change in Star Watch under Haig's watch. Maddox was sure about that.

"Captain," Haig said in a prim tone, "you are relieved of field duty and will spend the next few years on Earth, though I'm not sure in what capacity yet," Haig continued, shaking his head. "You were insubordinate toward me earlier. You went on this reckless mission. You lost one of our prime captives, and—"

"And I saved my grandmother from a hideous alien death," Maddox said, "and I figured out how these things happened, and I almost caught the culprits, and I have a way to get them, if you'll let me."

Haig's eyes burned with outrage. "If I do what?" he said.

"Sir, I respectfully request that you allow me to take a dozen *Conqueror*-class battleships with me to the nearby star system. We'll deal with the Spacers and with whatever else, and we'll clean this out."

"Ha!" Mackinder said. "I bet you'd like that. You'd like us to hand you the plum where you failed miserably."

"I didn't fail," Maddox said.

"Oh, and what do you call losing Becker?" Mackinder shot back.

"I failed in that aspect, yes," Maddox said. "But did you, the Chief of Intelligence, find out more than I did?"

"I've had enough of this tomfoolery and your smug arrogance." Mackinder turned to Haig. "The man is so damnably arrogant. I can barely stand it. And he's only a captain."

"A captain who should be the Lord High Admiral," Maddox heard himself say, even as realized he'd gone too far. He looked away. He should have kept his mouth shut just now.

"You think you deserve *my* job?" Haig asked.

Maddox faced the Lord High Admiral. "You want to relieve me of my field command, all right. That's your prerogative. I'm telling you, though, that you should go after the Spacers. You should destroy them while you can. There are things taking place that don't make sense. Add to that that Leviathan and the Spacers are working together. If the Spacers have a backdoor entrance to Earth, what else can they show Leviathan fleets, if ever they unleash?"

"Hmm," Haig mused, "that's a valid point." Turning to Mackinder, he continued, "General, I want you to join an expedition. You're going to go to the Barnard's Star System, and use the hyper-spatial tube to wherever it leads, obliterating everything you find on the other side. You'll take the battleships and *Victory*."

"Yes, sir," Mackinder said. "When should I leave?"

"As soon as you're ready," Haig said. "Choose the commanding officer, as you'll be coordinating with him."

"Sir," Mackinder stood, raised his chin at Maddox and lumbered out of the room.

Haig stared at Maddox. "You're grounded as of now. If you try to leave Earth, it will go worse for you."

"I understand," Maddox said.

As the last syllable left the captain's mouth, AI Galyan appeared in the Lord High Admiral's office.

Haig sat up in surprise.

Maddox raised an eyebrow. He hadn't expected this.

"Sir," Galyan told Haig, "you are making a grave mistake."

"What in blazes is this?" Haig shouted.

"I am Driving Force Galyan of Starship *Victory*, the deified Adok AI."

"I know very well who you are," Haig said. "Were you spying on us? Were you listening in at the captain's consent?"

"No, sir," Galyan said, "at my consent. I must tell you, sir, that I am an independent alien nation. I have one ship. It is *Victory*. It will go nowhere under anyone except Captain Maddox."

"What are you saying," Haig said, "that you won't obey me?"

"No, sir, we are allies only," Galyan said. "This is not a matter of obedience but of cooperation."

Maddox had never seen Galyan so ferocious. The little AI fairly bristled with rage.

"Do you understand what Captain Maddox has achieved?" Galyan said. "He woke up first on *Victory*. He saved us from whatever Becker had done. Becker is horribly dangerous. Is it not interesting to you that Becker did not take Meta? Meta is clearly the most beautiful woman on the starship, but Becker did not take her."

"What's your point?" Haig said.

"Becker fears Captain Maddox, at least to a degree," Galyan said. "That may be critical in the days to come."

Haig glared at Maddox. "When did you concoct this stupid ploy?"

"I assure you it is not any ploy of mine, sir," Maddox said.

"So you say," Haig replied. "Your assurances mean nothing to me."

Maddox sat straighter as his face flushed. That was one insult too many.

"Do you call him a liar, Lord Admiral?" Galyan said. "Yes, Captain Maddox lies to aliens as the need presents itself. But to those who are in authority, as you are, rightfully so, Captain Maddox does not lie."

"You expect me to believe this AI?" Haig asked Maddox.

"You are addressing me, sir," Galyan said. "I will not help and I will not give the information you need unless Captain Maddox goes along on the mission."

Haig's jaws worked for a time as his mouth opened and closed. He scowled thunderously until his brow smoothed out. He must have been thinking.

"Are you saying Maddox must be in charge of the expedition?" Haig said.

"No, sir," Galyan said, "but he must have an independent command and act as a Patrol scout for whoever you send."

Haig turned away. A second later, he got up and walked to the window. The old Lord High Admiral used to tower over that window as he looked out. Haig almost seemed like a child in comparison. He was so much smaller than Cook had been.

Haig turned around. "I do not like anyone dictating to me. But you are an alien and you have an alien ship that we have used. What if I were to say to you, Galyan, that I am going to destroy *Victory* unless you follow my orders?"

"I would say, sir, that that is a grave mistake," Galyan said. "It would also be beneath contempt. I have done much with my starship to help Star Watch. The least you could do is throw me a few bones."

"A few bones?" Haig asked.

Galyan turned to Maddox. "Is that not the correct idiom, sir?"

Maddox didn't say anything. He merely peered straight ahead.

"Captain," Haig said, "I do not know how it is that you gain such loyalty from such diverse individuals as Cook, as this AI entity, and others. But clearly you do. And on further reflection, you have done startlingly well compared to how any of the rest of us did in Star Watch figuring this out. Very well, I may have been hasty. Sir, I must add again, I do not like you, but you are an effective officer. Therefore, you will have this independent command and join the expedition. Does that satisfy you? Oh, let me see." Haig snapped his fingers. "Driving Force, Galyan?"

"It does, Lord High Admiral," Galyan said. "I thank you most profusely. And if in my passion I spoke too hastily, I apologize for that."

"I accept that," Haig said. "I can see, Captain, that I will have to deal with you in a different manner than I had expected."

Maddox nodded, stunned at what had just happened. He was still angry at the insults, but now wasn't the moment to deal with them.

"Now get out of here before I change my mind," Haig said.

Maddox stood and gave a perfect salute, pivoted and marched out of the office. Thanks to Galyan, he still had his captain's chair aboard *Victory*. Now he was going to exploit this chance for all it was worth.

-34-

Becker awoke by degrees. His head throbbed, and there was something wet on his lips. Without opening his eyes, he touched the wetness with his tongue, and tasted coppery substance…like blood.

Blood!

His eyes snapped open. Everything around him was blurry as disorientation gripped him. He didn't know where he was, what had happened to him…

Slow down. Think this through.

By degrees, he pieced together what had happened. He had awoken from hibernation stasis on the starship. Oh, right! He'd gone through a hyper-spatial tube, a one-way or preset route. He'd strengthened his mind against it in case going through brought anything like jump lag. Whatever the journey had done to him suggested that he wasn't immune to its ill effects. That was what caused this disorientation, right?

Looking around, Becker realized he lay on a cot, in a small wardroom. The vibration and background hum meant he was aboard a space vessel. A blanket covered him. On impulse, he raised the blanket. He was stark naked underneath. What in blazes? Someone had removed his clothes.

The mystery deepened. He needed to remember everything. He had to work to understand.

The blood, he'd start with that. The reasonable explanation for it—

Becker touched his nose, gingerly feeling crusted nostrils. He picked at the edges, pulling away scabbing. Blood from his nose had dripped onto his lips. How much bleeding had taken place? He noticed his right arm, a medikit attached to it. Ah. There was a blood transfusion packet attached to the medikit. He must have bled a lot, enough that whoever had given him a transfusion.

Who would have done all that?

In a moment of realization, he recalled his three lovelies, his chosen ones. They must have done all this, including removing his clothes.

Becker cleared his throat, ready to call out. A hatch opened before he could shout. Had they been monitoring him? One of the three—Becker named her Honey right there.

"Honey, what happened to me?"

"Becker," she said, with concern shining in her blue eyes, "you were hurt, out. We've been taking care of the situation since then." Honey rushed near and began fussing over him. "Oh." She detached a hand communicator from the belt of her uniform, clicked it on and said, "Becker is still hurt. I need help."

Almost immediately, the other two showed up as the hatch opened again. Like Honey, they wore regulation Patrol uniforms. They hurried near, checked the medikit, brought him food, and fussed over his nose and head.

Becker loved the thorough solicitousness. No one had ever treated him like this before. Certainly not three beautiful ladies like this. Yes, yes, right, he had set their mind to love and adoration for him.

One lifted the blanket to look at him and giggled, quickly lowering the blanket.

Becker felt deeply ashamed and embarrassed. Did she giggle at seeing his lack of family jewels?

"Why did you take my clothes off earlier?" he said harsher than he'd intended.

All three stopped and stared at each other and then at him.

"You were injured, Becker," Honey finally said. "We had to make sure you were all right. Clearly, you have sustained terrible injuries. We are awfully sorry for you."

Honey was a beautiful blonde with an intense smile added to her blue eyes. Becker loved her. He loved all three, but he loved Honey most. Her concern and sadness for him was heartbreaking.

"I know about the injury," he said gravely. "I'll soon enter rehabilitation and have it…healed."

The three looked incredulous, as if they didn't believe him or believe it possible.

"It's true," he said. "I can heal myself."

Now they looked grave, glancing at each other with worry and maybe even dread for his sanity.

"I'm not insane," he said. "I have abilities, mental abilities. It's why…"

"Yes, Becker," Honey said.

He'd almost said, "It's why my head is so huge." But he didn't want to say that. He didn't want to do or say anything that might affect their love and adoration for him.

In truth, and he knew this, even though he shied from thinking it, he didn't want to break the locks in their minds. Setting a human mind on permanent love was difficult. He was still figuring this all out. Certain stimuli could shock a lock out of its setting. He didn't want to check their mental states right now. His mind hurt, his nose ached, and he'd lost blood. He needed to recover before he tried any more telepathy.

Perhaps these stark ideas helped him recall all of it, the situation. He remembered that they had traveled down a tube for 200.08 light years, landing wherever here was.

Becker cleared his throat. He needed to get them back on task instead of thinking too much about him and these "impossible" statements he'd made.

"What's the present situation, ladies? I mean in terms of our—darter and location."

The two looked at Honey.

Honey nodded. "We came through the hyper-spatial tube into the Paran System. It's full of stellar debris, gas and rubble. As far as we can determine, someone destroyed all the major planets, the reason for the debris and rubble. There's a giant red star. We're twenty AUs from it. Some Spacers might be here with us in the system, but we haven't found any evidence of them."

"Where are we exactly?" Becker asked.

"You mean the darter?" Honey asked.

"Yes."

"We found a large asteroid," Honey said. "We eased the darter inside a great cavern, landing. Then we went out and set up passive sensors on the other side of the asteroid. That was to watch for Spacers."

"That's excellent work, ladies," Becker said, and he meant it.

They beamed with delight at his praise.

Becker wanted to laugh. This was how it should be. He'd always wanted this. Why was everyone against him using his mental abilities? Maybe envy ruled their thoughts. He scowled thinking that.

"Becker," Honey said, "you look upset" She stepped near and touched a cheek.

Becker's chin trembled as he strove to hold back tears. Why Honey's touch should do that now, he didn't know. Her touch made him remember that he looked hideous. His chin, nose, eyes and brow were all crunched into a third of his massive face.

He would reshape himself to be as handsome as his women were beautiful. He'd use the pituitary gland and other powers to rebuild his body into a Herculean physique so he could easily carry his head. His body would match his massiveness brain, intellect and growing mental powers. Before any of that, though, he needed to heal the horrible wound the Prime Saa had done to him through Liss pincers.

A terrible sense of urgency welled up in Becker. He wanted to be better *now*. That meant—

"I'm hungry. I need to eat a ton of food and rest afterward. Ladies, can I count on you to take care of things while I'm sleeping?"

"Oh, yes, Becker. Yes, yes." They surrounded him and proclaimed their devotion, telling him they were willing to do *anything* he asked.

"Now, now, settle down, ladies. Settle down," Becker said, grinning hugely. "I love your love, and I love you, and you, and you." He pointed at each of them in turn.

In that moment, Becker realized it had been wise of him to leave Meta behind. He would have kept worrying about Maddox hunting him—

Becker shoved the thought aside. He wasn't going to worry about Maddox right now. This was the life. Even if he was stuck in the darter deep in this asteroid for the rest of his time, as long as the food and the oxygen remained—and if he could heal himself quickly enough—he could take advantage of the situation. He could do what he should be doing.

"Listen, ladies..." Becker gave them his instructions.

Each went to her assigned duties, although Honey was the last to leave the wardroom. She leaned over and kissed him on the forehead.

Becker barely restrained himself from grabbing and hugging her. But he had to restrain himself. He didn't want to have to repair any lock in her mind that might question certain commands or actions. So far, everything seemed operative in them. Could he dare take time alone to gorge on food, strengthening himself with the needed calories for healing?

He was going to find out.

Honey waved goodbye and left the small wardroom, the hatch closing behind her.

It was fortunate that Valerie Noonan had stocked the darter for the mission. Becker could afford to splurge. He ate a hearty meal and slept afterward. When he awoke, he ate again and slept again. His brain no longer hurt. It had been a day and a half since they arrived in the star system. He'd sufficiently recovered from the tube journey.

"Have you spotted any Spacer activity?" Becker asked Honey when she came to check on him.

"We saw a saucer ship in the distance. It was a glimpse from a passive sensor on the other side of the asteroid. Otherwise, we've seen nothing else."

"You don't know how many Spacer ships are in the Paran System?"

"We believe there are at least ten, perhaps more. But it is hard to be certain," Honey said, "given the mass debris fields and the possible *billions* of asteroids and pieces of planetary rubble."

"What could have destroyed all the major planets like that?" Becker asked.

"Do you want us to study the possibilities?" Honey asked.

"No, no. For now, let's stay hidden in the asteroid. I want all three of you to attend to me and to make sure I'm recovering properly. I'm about to attempt a great feat. In order to do this, I have to trust each of you implicitly. Can I do that, Honey?"

"Becker, you know you can. We love you. We love you so much."

"Like a sister loves a brother," Becker said, deciding to assess the situation.

Honey laughed, and she had such wonderful teeth. "No, silly, we love, love you."

Becker blushed, and that surprised him. Did he feel guilty for tweaking their minds? Heck no, he didn't. This was awesome. Well, maybe he felt a little guilty, but come on. He had to submerge that, which he proceeded to do.

Honey soon left the wardroom.

Becker now concentrated his mental powers. That caused a twinge in his brain, but that passed before it became a problem. He concentrated more and gathered his energies. He'd eaten tons, storing the calories. With his unique mentality, he focused on the mutilated section of his body that the Liss had snipped off.

Using a unified telekinetic, pituitary gland effort, he gathered cells, beginning to re-build the lost sex organs. He had a mental image of what should be there. Now, the original genetic pattern from his development in his mother's womb began to reassert itself. That meant testicles began to form particle by particle. Soon, the process accelerated.

Becker remained at the post, as it were, pouring mental energy into the mighty task. He sweated. He groaned and his stomach growled as hunger struck him. Yet, he persisted in the great restoration. At last, exhaustion swept over him and he slumped asleep on the damp bed.

He woke up with great anticipation. Had it worked? Gathering his resolve, Becker dared to lift the blanket to check.

He'd accelerated the process for a reason. Maybe it hadn't been the wisest choice. But who knew how much time he had left in this glorious situation.

He raised the blanket, and lo and behold, he was like a lizard that had lost its tail, and the tail had regrown fresh, strong, and perfect. Only instead of a tail, he had a freshly regrown pair of testicles. This was perfectly awesome!

Becker wept with joy. "I'm a whole man again."

This was so great.

Limply, he devoured what was beside his bed. He would have called Honey to bring him more, but he fell into a deep sleep. His body needed time to recoup from the fantastic healing process.

Oh, Becker thought as he drifted to sleep. *I can do it. I can change myself through my mental acuity*. Who knew where he would take this. Before he could consider that, Becker started to snore.

-35-

The human once known as Venna the Spy opened her eyes and stared at her hideous form. It was as if her skin had become charred tree bark. She could barely move, and it hurt when she did.

Worse, pain radiated through her every moment she was awake. Did she feel this horrible pain when she slept?

Venna was in a large, brightly lit chamber with many mirrors along the walls or bulkheads. Everywhere she looked, she saw her hideous features.

Venna had once been the most beautiful woman in the Orion Spiral Arm. Men had stared at and longed to be with her. She could crook a finger, twitch a hip and have them begging for her attention. If that wasn't enough, she had the ruby necklace to accelerate the process.

Venna wanted to weep for what she had lost, but she realized she had been doing so for the past few days. How was she even alive after the transformation into this hideous form? It was because of the Phantasma Synth Crystals. Shards of the alien crystal had embedded themselves in her.

She touched her charred forehead and felt a longing for the planet Ector. There, eons ago, the masters had developed and curated the crystals, imbuing them with such tremendous power and mystical twisting. Some of that was in her. Perhaps as interesting, she knew about events that had happened eons ago on Ector.

One of the masters seemed to stare in her mind, speaking in the awful language of the Aetharians.

Venna groaned as she looked around. That was when she finally noticed charred, burnt corpses on the floor around her. Some of the corpses still glimmered with a white tooth or two. What had happened here? This didn't make sense.

A hatch opened. A diminutive Spacer with black-tinted goggles walked in.

"Mu 11," Venna said, "you are Mu 11. What have you done to me?"

Mu did the most amazing thing. Instead of answering, she fell prostrate on the floor with her arms outstretched and imploring.

"Oh Great One," Mu said, "I have come to see if you are well and if you need others."

"Need others?" Venna said. "What are you babbling about? What has happened here?"

In the middle of the question, Venna's eyes glowed. "You, Mu, inserted memories into me when I was Venna. Acting on those memories, I slew Lord High Admiral Cook and Brigadier Stokes, and I attempted to slay—"

Venna looked up at the ceiling and raised her charred fists. She howled with rage. "The Iron Lady did this to me. I must kill her. I must destroy the Earth and crush Star Watch in retaliation."

Mu looked up from her prostrate position on the floor.

It seemed to Venna that Mu looked at her with surprise. "What?" Venna said. "What have I said that has caused you surprise?"

Mu stammered with incomprehension before she said, "That you remembered everything so quickly, Great One."

"You lie," Venna said. "That isn't what you were going to say."

"It was," Mu said. "I abase myself before you, Venna. Anything you want, I shall do."

"What exactly do you mean by 'anything'?"

"Do you want me to bring others?" Mu asked.

"Why do you continue to talk about others? Why do you berate me with this?" In a moment of cunning, Venna's charred hand swept at the burnt corpses. "Does it have anything to do with those?"

"Yes," Mu said.

"Why are they here?"

"You wanted them as a reminder," Mu said. "Don't you remember giving the order?"

"No! I want them gone."

"Would you like me to retire as well?"

"No, you will stay," Venna said. "Summon others with your Surveyor power. Yes. I know about that. Or had you thought I'd forgotten?"

Mu stood and bowed her head. "You are the Great One. I obey you."

In moments, small Southeast Asian men wearing Spacer goggles and black uniforms appeared. At Mu's direction, they removed the charred corpses. Others with mops scrubbed and waxed until the floor shone brilliantly.

"Yes, yes," Venna said, "that is much better. The rest can leave, but those three will remain."

The chosen three collapsed onto the floor in terror as they began to sob for mercy.

"Silence them," Venna commanded, "or I will do it for you."

"But—" Mu said.

"Yes?" Venna said. "What do you mean, 'but'?"

To Venna's surprise, she found that she had stood and stumbled across the waxen floor until she towered above the three cringing, pathetic little Spacer men. She loathed them. She had used such as these before. No, she had used gallant specimens that had great power in them. Still, in a pinch, these three would do.

Venna held her hands out over them. They howled in despair as Venna extracted what etheric source their bodies contained. As vapors rose from their flesh, as they began to shrivel, char, and scream in agony, Venna drank their essence like a space vampire. She knew strength and fulfillment. Even better, her tree-bark skin turned smooth and lovely.

"A mirror, a mirror," Venna said. "I want a mirror."

"There," Mu said, pointing at one of the many mirrors embedded in the bulkheads.

Venna turned and disrobed as she strutted before a mirror, reveling in her marvelous beauty. This was what she remembered. This was who she was. She could turn any head. A crook of her finger would bring a battalion of men rushing to her. A thousand ships launched by the sight of the Helen of Troy—

"Ha! I can summon ten *thousand* spaceships," Venna gloated.

Venna's eyes widened as she spied the tiniest wrinkle on her skin. She whirled around and stared at Mu. "Why is that wrinkle there?" Venna pointed at her side.

"The transformation only lasts for a short time, Great Venna," Mu said.

"What?"

Venna stared the charred remains of the Spacer men on the floor. She saw a few gleaming teeth. Then it slammed home to Venna what she was. She'd become the space vampire or whatever you wanted to call it. She could drain the essence from these fools and regain what she had been for a short time.

"I'm going to make the universe suffer for this," Venna screamed.

A few seconds later, Mu said quietly, "May I offer you a suggestion, Great One?"

"What?" Venna snarled.

"Destroy Earth. Destroy Leviathan. Or better yet, use Leviathan for your purposes."

"What do you mean?" Venna said.

Mu began to explain her plan.

As Mu spoke, Venna began to cackle like an ancient hag, a witch in the forest known for luring and devouring children.

"I love it," Venna said. "I love it. You will be the last."

By the stark look of fear on Mu's face, it was clear she understood what Venna meant by the sinister comment.

-36-

It struck Maddox as odd that General Mackinder of Intelligence wanted to come on the expedition. Mackinder was like a spider that spun its web, catching its prey with sticky strands. Mackinder did not hunt by heading into and exposing himself to danger. Then why did Mackinder want to join the expedition?

Maddox didn't believe Haig wanted Mackinder on the expedition, nor that it was Haig's will pushing Mackinder to go. No, Mackinder was the key to this. Could Mackinder be the key to the new Lord High Admiral?

Maddox didn't have time to study the idea, even though *Victory* and company waited two days as Mackinder and Haig collected the warships and hunted for the admiral to lead the mission. Why did it take so long? What did all this mean? The longer they waited the less chance they had of apprehending Becker or finding the Spacers at the other end of the hyperspatial tube.

Finally, Mackinder found an admiral, a man named Jellicoe. Eleven *Conqueror*-class battleships would go, along with the auxiliary spaceships, escorts, and destroyers. It was a powerful task force, although not a nation-destroying task force or one that could beat a full Spacer fleet. It was a big exploratory task force, though.

"In that sense," Maddox told Meta, "the task force is too big to run or hide easily. It is cumbersome, and I don't think Admiral Jellicoe will issue precise or decisive orders. He'll check with Mackinder first, and Mackinder is anything but a fighting admiral."

"Then why is Mackinder doing this?" Meta asked.

"I've been asking myself that. I've even debated secretly sending Galyan to some of their meetings."

"Oh no," Meta said. "You shouldn't do that. If they found Galyan spying on them…"

"I shouldn't do that," Maddox said, "but it might be wise. I suspect they're using everything they can to shield themselves from Galyan."

Later, Maddox spoke with Galyan. "Thank you, my friend. I appreciate your sticking up for me in the Lord High Admiral's office."

"No, Captain," Galyan said, "you've stood up for me so many times, done wonderful things for me, and been a great friend. I was angry at what Haig said to you. Why are Mackinder and Haig so short-sighted?"

Maddox threw his hands into the air even though he knew the reason. It was the Humanity Manifesto Doctrine. He thought Cook had stamped it out, but apparently, these people knew how to hang low. Maybe there weren't that many, but because Haig and Mackinder leaned that way, others joined that camp. Most people were followers. Few stood up on their own hind legs and said what they really thought if the main group was against it. Most people waited to see what the leader would say and then said likewise. But why complain? That was the nature of most humans.

In any case, after the two days of preparation, the task force headed for the Laumer Point. *Victory* went through first, per Admiral Jellicoe's orders, indicating Mackinder's influence.

Nothing was waiting for *Victory* in the Barnard's Star system. Soon, the entire task force was through and headed for the third terrestrial planet. *Victory* jumped ahead of the rest, with Maddox sending down a team into the comet. Ludendorff headed the team.

Inside the comet, Ludendorff studied the Builder device in person. According to him, it was a one-way tube as first discovered by Galyan. Whether they could find a way back on the other end was open to question.

"Two hundred light years the hard way would be easy for *Victory,*" Ludendorff said. "For the rest of the task force…" he shook his head.

"Why do you say that?" Maddox asked.

They were on *Victory's* bridge, as Ludendorff and the rest of the team had returned from the comet. He seemed to have been invigorated by it, as he walked with a sprier step.

"The rest of the task force people are amateurs compared to us," Ludendorff said.

"No," Maddox said, "they're Star Watch professionals."

"They're rated as professional Star Watch officers," Ludendorff said. "Now tell me how many have fought in combat? I doubt many of the higher officers have. I've been checking the roster. They are Humanity Manifesto people or have those leanings. Many haven't been in combat for quite some time, if ever. Thus, I say they're amateurs. We don't know what they'll do when the firing starts."

"I imagine they'll do what any Star Watch officer is trained to do," Maddox said. "They will fight gallantly."

"You have a better opinion of the new pipsqueak Lord High Admiral than I do." Ludendorff rubbed his hands as if warming to the subject. "The enemy knew what he was doing when he assassinated Cook. Cook had his faults, but he knew whom to trust, and he knew who to give leeway. You, for one."

Maddox said nothing to that, even though he agreed with Ludendorff. Was there something different about the Methuselah Man? Maddox couldn't place what, but… Oh, he had other worries to occupy his thoughts.

Soon, the task force gathered by the third terrestrial planet. Admiral Jellicoe appeared on a wide channel, giving his instructions. "Captain Maddox, you will open the hyper-spatial tube and go through first to make sure it is safe for the rest of the task force."

"Yes, *sir,*" Maddox said from his command chair. He even saluted in an exaggerated manner.

Many on *Victory's* bridge frowned. Admiral Jellicoe on the main screen also frowned. It was evident Maddox was being sarcastic to the nth degree.

The broad channel communications ended.

Maddox gave the order to proceed.

Galyan switched on the Builder device, which created a preset hyper-spatial tube 200.08 light years long.

"Go to it, Lieutenant," Maddox said.

"Aye, sir," Keith said from the helm.

Victory entered the opening, and as had happened on so many occasions, *Victory* zipped along the hyper-spatial tube. In seconds, it popped out onto the other side. As so many times before, Maddox shook off the jump-lag-like effects first.

Andros confirmed what Galyan found. There were masses of stellar debris, gases, and planetary chunks everywhere.

"I remember this look," Galyan said. "All this reminds me of my long guard duty from so many years ago."

"Right," Maddox said. "Don't let that fact confound you, Galyan. Let's remain in the present. Do you detect any saucer ships?"

"Not yet," Galyan said.

"How about any saucer ship exhaust?" Maddox asked.

"There are traces," Andros said.

"Yes, traces," Galyan said. "I will agree that Andros found those traces before I did."

"That's great, Galyan," Maddox said. "Thanks for being so good about it."

"Oh, thank you, sir," Galyan said.

"All right," Ludendorff said. "All this congratulatory talk is getting on my nerves. Let's just do it, eh?"

Maddox glanced at Ludendorff.

"Sorry for speaking out of turn, Captain," Ludendorff said peevishly.

Maddox nodded instead of saying anything more. Was it strange that Ludendorff should apologize so quickly? Or maybe the old goat was learning after all this time. That was a good thing, right?

The rest of the task force came through the hyper-spatial tube. In the meantime, the science officers aboard *Victory* cataloged the debris, that the star was a red giant, and that they were 20 AUs from it. The Paran System was a harsh place. Something had destroyed the planets ages ago. An enemy fleet could easily hide here.

Shortly after that, the hyper-spatial tube disappeared, having closed.

"Sir," Meta said from the communications station. "There's a call from the admiral for you."

"Put him on the main screen," Maddox said.

Admiral Jellicoe appeared. He had square features with thick dark sideburns. He was a bluff man in his late fifties, sporting a chest full of medals.

"How do we get back home?" Jellicoe asked Maddox.

"For now," Maddox said, "the long way, one star-drive jump at a time."

"I don't want your humor, New Man," Jellicoe said sharply. "I want to know how we get back in a pinch."

Maddox scowled at Admiral Jellicoe. "Sir, you can take your—"

Meta cleared her throat.

Maddox looked at his wife at the comm station. Perhaps no one else could have checked him to the same degree. Maddox had almost told Jellicoe to stuff it up his pipe.

"I'm waiting, Captain," Jellicoe said on the main screen.

Maddox swiveled back to face him. "Respectfully, sir, I am not a New Man." Or," Maddox glanced at Meta before looking at the main screen again. "Or, if you like, sir, I can refer to you as the ass. Is that what you prefer?"

Admiral Jellicoe stiffened with outrage. "Captain, I am considering relieving you of your duties."

"What was that," Maddox said. "You're about to relieve yourself?"

Jellicoe purpled with rage, and he pointed a finger, opening his mouth to speak.

"If you'll just remember this, sir," Maddox said, speaking first. "I don't care to be called a New Man. If you want my help: treat me with respect."

"Do you know who I am?" Jellicoe finally shouted.

"Of course, I know who you are. Do you know who I am?"

"You are a captain under my command—"

"Sir," Maddox said, interrupting, "if you will reread your orders, I'm in charge of the Patrol scout vessel, and I have an independent command. If you want to take that up with the Lord High Admiral when we get back, hey, you be my guest."

Jellicoe's eyes seemed to burn. "You're digging your own hole, you half-breed."

Maddox said nothing in response, and his demeanor remained unchanged. Those on the bridge, however, winced and could see Maddox was poised to strike.

"Is there anything else, *Admiral?*" Maddox asked, his tone mild.

"You didn't like that, did you?"

Maddox said nothing.

"No, nothing else," Jellicoe said. "Tell me as soon as you know how to recreate the hyper-spatial tube back home. And next time, watch your mouth when you address me, or it'll go poorly for you. I'm in charge of the expedition. You may have an independent command, but you come under my authority. Do not forget that, Captain. Do you understand?"

"Yes, sir," Maddox said. "I understand perfectly."

Jellicoe glared a moment longer and then made a chopping motion.

The connection cut.

"That could have gone better," Ludendorff said.

From his command chair, Maddox shrugged.

Meta looked worried.

"I do not like the new Lord High Admiral or his main officers," Galyan said. "They have much to learn regarding right conduct."

No one commented on that.

"Right," Maddox said. "Now, let's get to work."

-37-

Senior Dax, the Leviathan cyber, awoke and peered right, left, and then down. He didn't see his body. This meant his head was arched awkwardly away from his body, rendering him helpless. Nevertheless, he attempted to move his arms and legs. His original assessment held. He was helpless.

One thing was different, though. The chamber appeared larger than before.

Then he saw himself in a wall mirror. He was stretched out on a metal table, his body behind his head, and his head thrust at an awkward angle. There were flesh and tendons connecting his head to his neck. But the outlook was not good for him. The neck would need rehabilitation and strengthening after this, provided he survived.

Why had he ever agreed to go on this stupid mission? He'd only taken one cyborg trooper along while among the Spacers. He should have brought a ship contingent with him while aboard the Spacers' ships. He should have brought along six or seven of them aboard the phase ship and kept them in active mode at all times.

That was another thing. The Spacers had confiscated the phase ship he'd brought from Leviathan. That had turned out to be too much of a prize to dangle before them. How had Grand Strategist Enigmach ever tricked him into this rash mission?

Enigmach exploited me through my greed. The Grand Strategist was a clever trickster. He should have seen that sooner.

The problem was that Dax had always thought of himself as brilliant and conniving. Maybe with regular people he was. The Spacers of the Third Fleet were weird. Worse, the Phantasma Synth Crystals hadn't been regular technology but something decidedly sinister and possibly evil.

Dax closed his eyes, realizing he needed to focus on the immediate problem. Internal whining wasn't going to change anything.

He opened his eyes and carefully studied his surroundings, looking for any advantage. The chamber was huge, with a shiny floor and mirrors all around. The metal table and nearby machine were the only pieces of furniture.

A hatch opened. Dax looked there. Mu 11 entered the chamber.

Should he beg for mercy no matter how undignified that might be?

Yes, Dax told himself, *beg, do whatever you must. You need to escape this horrible situation and retrieve your ships. Do whatever you must to leave this hell-scape. The Spacers are vile and treacherous, unnatural.*

"Hello, Dax," Mu said. "I trust you've been recuperating?"

"Yes," he heard himself say from an artificial larynx.

Through the mirrors, he spied a cord plugged into a brain slot. His real larynx wasn't doing the talking. His mouth didn't open, as opening it might have caused his head, perched on the table, to tip because of the moving jaw. Instead, he spoke through a robotic box. This was blasphemy, a parody of his true self. He was a cyber, a combination of flesh and machine, but this was too far and grotesquely undignified.

He needed to regain mobility and flee to the *Python*, the flagship of his three *Kraken*-class warships.

"I'll provide you with whatever you want, Mu," Dax said through the box. "However, I'd like to see a show of good faith on your part. If you could reconnect my head with the rest of my body, returning my motive ability, that's all the favor I ask."

Mu smiled in an obviously mocking way.

Dax would have liked to rage at her, promising dire vengeance. Instead, he knew stark fear and humiliation. He was so dependent on her goodwill. This was worse than ridiculous. This could be the end for him. The only thing that gave him hope was that she hadn't killed him yet. That meant she wanted something from him. That meant if he was clever, if he kept his wits and courage about him, he could bargain his way out of this.

"You're a poor, stupid cyber, aren't you?" Mu said.

Dax saw no need to retaliate with insults. She had the upper hand. He would take the abuse—for now.

"Well, Dax, you can make this easy or you can make this difficult. Which do you prefer?"

"The easy way," Dax said.

"Good," Mu replied. "I'm glad you said that. Tell me where all the Leviathan assault fleets are stationed."

"Excuse me?" Dax said.

"Leviathan assault fleets ready for the invasion of the Commonwealth. Surely, that was why we did what we did. You've helped in weakening Star Watch. I assume that was to help with the massive strike from Leviathan. That is your empire's method for these things."

"I'm sorry," Dax said meekly. "but I can't reveal such information."

"Oh. That means you want to do this the hard way."

"Look," Dax said in a let's-be-reasonable tone, or the best he could do through the box. "Reconnect me. Make everything ready for my exit and I'll tell you all you want to know just before I leave. I swear it."

"I'm not interested in your swearing," Mu said. "I'm interested in the information. I suggest you make your choice: easy or hard. This is a binary situation. Which do you prefer?"

"I told you which," Dax said. "Let's make this easy."

"Then tell me where the assault fleets are waiting," Mu said.

Dax would have liked to sigh, but he wasn't breathing. Instead, they were feeding his brain enough energy to keep him awake, and probably enough to keep his body working. These impulses—

Oh, Mu held up a hand for his attention. "We will proceed to the hard way," she said.

Dax wanted to scream and beg. Would Mu use her interior Builder devices, her modifications, to coerce him? No. She turned away and reverently clasped her hands. Then, Mu bowed her head, waiting.

Once more, the hatch opened.

Dax watched with dread and then sick horror.

A hideous, perhaps partially reptilian, though humanoid creature, shuffled in. It wore a long flowing robe with a cowl. The back of the hands showed the creature possessed tree-bark-like skin.

Dax was appalled. What kind of monstrosity had the Spacers found to use against him?

"Behold," Mu told Dax, "Venna, who you so basely manipulated, so she has become like this."

"What?" Dax said. "That thing is Venna?"

The hag creature removed the cowl. It had Venna's luxurious hair, but the horrid features...

If Dax could have shown his feelings through facial maneuvering, his face would have twisted with revulsion and repugnance. This was awful.

"What happened?" Dax said through the box.

"Do you see his lack of remorse, Great One?" Mu said. "The cyber is arrogant and pretentious. Even stretched out like this, he has dared to utter threats against me. That was before your arrival."

"No," Dax said, "that's a lie. I haven't uttered anything against anyone. I'm ready to cooperate."

"You see how he equivocates, prevaricates, and attempts to sully the situation," Mu said.

"I do," Venna said in a scratchy voice.

"Wait a minute," Dax said, thoroughly horrified and frightened. "Let's be reasonable. I brought you the phase ship. I brought the crystals."

"You see," Mu said. "He admits it. Know, Great One, that it was Dax's idea to put all those false memories in you. The supposed memories twisted you so you'd do his dirty deeds. Perhaps not his deeds specifically," Mu said, "but for those of Leviathan he represents. The cybers are users, Great One. They are the corruptors of what is good and right. That is why they sent the Phantasma Synth Crystals to us and ultimately to you."

"Enough," Venna said. "I understand what you're doing. I'm also not completely upset with the turn of events. I've been, how do you say, released from Spacer captivity? I also comprehend how the ancient masters of Ector made the crystals. It's much more cunning than I'd originally envisioned. They gave the crystals life after a fashion. Now that life is alive through me."

What did the hag babble about? Dax was confused. She was clearly insane as well as ugly as sin. Seeing her was an even worse punishment than being disengaged from his body.

No, no, Dax told himself. *You must think clearly. You're a cyber, even though you're disconnected from your calming glands. You must be logical and think this through. Your biological brain boils with emotion. Quell it and* think. *Your voice is a weapon. You must use it as a weapon, the only one you have left.*

"If I've done any of these wretched things that Mu accuses me of," Dax said, "I'm here to repay for them."

"Indeed," Venna said. "And how would you repay me?"

"I can give you the assault fleet designations of the various Leviathan formations ready to invade the Commonwealth," Dax said. "That is what you want, isn't it?"

"In part," Venna said.

"Of course, it would be better if I could receive at least a small piece of mercy for this, an act of goodwill from you," Dax said.

"Oh?" Venna said.

"If you could start by reconnecting my body to my head," Dax said.

"Is that what you think I'll do for you?"

"It's such a small thing," Dax said, "especially for one of your magnificence."

"I'm not quite ready to do that," Venna said. "I think, rather, you should understand what it is you helped to create."

Venna turned around, and when nothing happened, she faced Mu. "Send them in."

Mu must have done something, because the hatch opened. Three poor sods were thrust into the chamber so they staggered and stumbled. When they caught their balance, they stared in dread at Venna. In seconds, they fell to their knees, clasping their hands before her, pleading for mercy.

Venna took an odd stance, and stretched out her hands toward them.

Power, Dax could see power emanating from her in waves.

The poor Spacers didn't jump up and rush her, trying to fight for their lives. Instead, they sobbed and begged until they collapsed, and writhed in agony.

Dax was horrified to see vapory substances lift from their bodies as their bodies shriveled. The essence entered Venna and she transformed into the beautiful, lovely Venna the Spy of before.

The beautiful Venna looked at him and smiled in a reptilian, predatory way. "Do you understand?" she said in such a lovely voice.

"I don't know what I'm supposed to understand," Dax said, striving to maintain his rational mind, "but I see you've gained impressive abilities." His gazed darted to Mu. "Did you cause that to happen to Venna?"

"Silence," Venna said. "Mu did nothing. It was you who did it by bringing the crystals to us."

Terror might have stolen Dax's wits. He was truly petrified. Instead, in this instance, the fear sharpened his rat-like instincts for survival. "May I say, Great One, that Spacer Intelligence had much to do with that. Mu was instrumental with how they proceeded. Isn't that right, Mu?"

Mu had bowed her head and knelt on the floor before Venna. "Great one," Mu said. "I have no words. You are the one who decides everything. This man, this mechanical creature, is such a liar, such a rat, and a rascal. Do you hear how he strives to twist thoughts and ideas to his advantage? It is really rather pathetic. Don't you think so, Great One?"

Venna cocked a hip and put a hand saucily on it as she looked at Mu. "Maybe I should revive the cyber. Maybe that's the right idea."

"Oh, Great One," Dax said. "I applaud your mercy. Whatever you want, I will give you for this."

Venna raised a hand and aimed her fingers at him. It felt as if a switch clicked in his brain.

"Now you will tell me the dispositions of all the formations Leviathan has assembled in the Orion Arm, ready to invade the Commonwealth. Are you ready to speak, Dax?"

Dax found himself pouring out information. He tried to still the flood of words, but he couldn't. He gave every fleet disposition he knew. He even gave the name of the high officers in charge of each assault fleet.

Dax then told Venna the grand plans of the strategists. He went into detail piece by piece. He even explained his assumptions regarding what Leviathan would do to the Spacer Nations afterward. Would Leviathan leave the Spacer Nations intact? Hell no, they would not. Leviathan was going to use the Spacers and then devour them. They would turn many of the highest-ranking Spacers into cybers. In that way, the new cybers would be obedient to the great and wonderful plan of Great Leviathan. That was what was in store for the Spacer Third Fleet.

Venna raised a hand again.

Dax became aware that he no longer babbled about his opinions. The speech must have taken time. Venna had started to look nasty and vile again, with her tree bark-like skin.

"Sweet Venna," Dax said, thinking fast, "I'm so glad I told you all this. I've wanted to unburden myself for some time. The ways of the Spacers—"

"No," Venna said, interrupting. "I don't need to hear your lies. Instead, Dax, you're going to perform a mighty service for me. You will be instrumental in unleashing one of the assault fleets of Leviathan to do my bidding?"

"N-No," Dax stammered. "I was not aware of this privilege. I'm ready, though. If you'll just reassemble me, I'll be on my way for you."

Venna laughed in a manner worse than any smoker could do. "It's not quite that easy. There will be some…what shall we call it? Modifications to your personality? Modifications to your brain? Do you comprehend what I'm saying?"

"Uh, not precisely," Dax said. "But whatever you want, you name it and I will give it."

"Yes," Venna said. "You most certainly will give it. Mu, let him sleep for now. His brain is tired. Then give him the nutrients he needs and prepare his brain for the chemical bath."

"What?" Dax said. "You're not talking about…" He dared to say it. "Removing my brain, are you?"

"Yes," Venna said, "I am." She smiled in a malicious, evil, vampiric manner.

Dax howled with despair, feeling utterly defeated. He had no idea how to get out of this. He was in the hands of vicious harpies, and it looked like it was the end for Senior Dax of the Sovereign Hierarchy of Leviathan.

-38-

Becker was having the time of his life. He maneuvered through the small darter in a bathrobe, usually wearing just that—sometimes tied closed, sometimes open to exhibit what he had created through his mental powers and pituitary gland. Honey and the others dressed to please him, provocative combinations indeed.

This was a delight. Becker had envisioned a time in his life like this for as long as he could remember, and now it was really happening.

The only drawback was his physical weakness. The girls could scamper, cavort, and giggle with such exuberance and athleticism that he marveled at them. He was jealous, if you want to know the truth. He could only shuffle along, constrained by his condition. And he always had to be careful because his head was so damn big and heavy. If he bumped it, that could ruin everything.

Becker roved through their minds to make sure about their thoughts and attitudes. He pushed mental levers and froze them in place, enforcing his desires on them.

A small part of Becker balked at this. But that was stupid. This had to be love, right? The girls said they loved him. They felt adoring love for him. Maybe in one tiny sense he'd manufactured that, but when you thought about it, wasn't that how people had always acted? A man bought a woman a meal, he acted nice, and drove around in a fancy car or big truck, and he lifted weights so he had big muscles. He did all those things to manufacture the love of the woman for him. Was that any different from what he did with his telepathy?

"Come on," Becker would tell that wee small part of him that Bible thumpers would call a conscience. Becker didn't like hearing his conscience speak.

At least choose one of them and stick with her, okay? his conscience said.

"No," Becker would say, "this is my fantasy. I'm doing it the way I want to. Don't try to tell me what to do, conscience. You're a pain in the ass. What good are you anyway?"

That would seem to do it. His conscience would simper and crawl away to hide.

The trouble was that Becker couldn't run with his lovelies. He couldn't scamper with them in their games. He had to be careful how he held his head. He couldn't indulge in the activities he had always envisioned in his teenage fantasies and other times.

He wanted to be athletic and change himself into the Herculean man. That would take a lot of effort, though. The darter was hidden in this crevice on the asteroid. Worse, freaking Star Watch ships flittered back and forth. How long until they found the darter?

Becker ordered the girls to keep the darter cloaked at all times. That could last for several weeks. The extensive transformation he envisioned might take longer than that. What if he was halfway through the transformation and Maddox boarded the darter and took his women? What if Maddox put him under real stasis? What if Star Watch surgeons did surgery to his brain so he lost some of his mental powers? Maybe they would geld his pituitary gland next time.

Why was everyone so jealous of him all the time? He just wanted to have a little fun. He just wanted to do things his way. Was that against the laws of nature and God?

Come on, there was no God. Becker knew that. He was certain of that…except he would wake up sometimes in the middle of the night. Then his nasty little conscience would whisper in his mind: *You wait, Becker. You're going to find out the hard way. Why not turn this around while you can? You know: let the women be, and have them love you for who you are.*

"Shut up," Becker would whisper. He didn't want to wake up any of the girls by talking too loudly. "Shut the hell up and quit bugging me," he would say to his conscience. "I just want to enjoy myself. Why won't you let me? Get out of my head."

Then, finally, his conscience would be quiet again, and Becker would think about a few other things, and then he'd shove that aside and go back to sleep.

One day, however, he hit his head hard. He tripped, fell, and struck his precious forebrain, specifically his frontal lobe, on the deck. It dashed him unconscious.

When he came to, one of the girls looked at him strangely.

"What?" Becker said. "What's wrong?"

She looked away.

Becker wanted to test her mind, but his forebrain hurt too much. Had something within her changed at that moment? That was when Becker knew.

I need to take the plunge. This is the moment. I've been having fun. All those creeps are out there—

He realized with a start why his conscience must have been whispering to him. Why hadn't he understood right away? The Spacers and Star Watch guys were jockeying for position out there. And here he was, gallivanting in the land of Arabian nights where he was the hero. Everything worked perfectly with *it*, and Becker loved that. But it was a mirage and he needed to act decisively for once.

After a day of healing for his forebrain, Becker checked the girl's mind. A locked control had slipped. He reset and sealed it mentally. Afterward, he ate like a freaking hog. He gulped, slurped and smacked his lips. He ate until he almost puked.

Then he told the girls, "I have to be alone for a while. I'm going to lock the hatch. Don't do anything about that. Maintain your positions, and I will come to you. I want you girls be ready for what's coming, because I'm going to be a little different next time you see me."

"How?" asked Honey.

"Bigger, stronger and sexier," Becker said.

The girls giggled with delight.

Oh man, that was what Becker wanted to hear.

He went into his wardroom and locked the hatch. He lay on the bed and started to rove inwardly with his improved mentality, with the power of his pituitary gland. He set out on the most gargantuan feat any telepath, any mental giant, had ever attempted. His head was the biggest. His brain was the densest. The Liss had created something more than they must have realized. That was why the Prime Saa had castrated him, to control and corral him.

No one controlled now. Testosterone filled him and he began the strange metamorphosis of Captain Becker.

He elongated bones, hardened them, and strengthened muscles. He'd awaken from time to time and gorged himself like the proverbial hog. Then he fell back asleep as his brain continued the transformation.

He did not look at himself during the process. He did not want to see the ungainliness and the disproportion of his various limbs. Instead, he had an image in his mind of what he wanted to look like. The musculature and the stature of his chin down would match the massiveness, denseness and hugeness of his head. Did that mean he'd be eight or nine feet tall? Probably it did mean that. He would need such musculature and bone density and size to balance his head the way the girls balanced their heads as they raced and converted to his delight.

Thus, as Spacers and Star Watch people maneuvered in the debris-filled, gaseous, cluttered, and rubble-strewn Paran System, Becker lay in the darter, metamorphosing into something greater than anyone would ever have believed concerning the man.

-39-

Five days after entering the debris-filled Paran System, Admiral Jellicoe, along with General Mackinder, came aboard *Victory*. They arrived in five heavy shuttles accompanied by the toughest, strongest Marines and Intelligence operatives from the task force. They summoned Maddox to a meeting.

Maddox knew why they had come. A day ago, Jellicoe had told Maddox to report aboard the flagship. Maddox had flatly refused.

"I'm not going to do it, sir," Maddox said. "I frankly don't trust your people. You've shown hostility toward me, and I prefer to remain among my people."

"Captain Maddox—" Jellicoe said.

Maddox raised a hand as they spoke via the main screen on the bridge.

"Sir, this isn't a matter of disrespect. It's a matter of instincts. Mine—I have an intuitive sense you may have heard about. It's telling me your men will intern me the moment I step on one of your ships. Therefore, I respectfully decline to do so."

Thus, Jellicoe and Mackinder had come to *Victory*.

Maddox entered the conference chamber alone. Jellicoe sat at the head of the table where Maddox always sat. Maddox shrugged. There were no task-force Marines inside the chamber. They had all been outside, lining the corridors. Jellicoe and Mackinder each wore a sidearm. Maddox wasn't worried, as he knew Galyan watched everything in ghost mode.

The Adok AI would enter and zap Jellicoe and Mackinder before either could fire at him.

"Sit, Captain Maddox," Jellicoe said, indicating a spot at the table.

Maddox did so.

"We're here because you refused to board my flagship," Jellicoe said. "You see, sir, I am more amiable than you think. You've acted disrespectfully and—"

Maddox interrupted. "You called me a half-breed and a New Man before. With the philosophies you hold, those are deep barbs. That is immense disrespect toward me."

Jellicoe and Mackinder traded glances before Jellicoe nodded to Maddox. "You've made your point. I will refrain from using those terms in your presence. In return, I expect you to treat me with respect and to obey my orders."

"Very well, sir," Maddox said.

"We are agreed then?" Jellicoe said, sounding surprised.

"Certainly," Maddox said.

Jellicoe stood. A second later, Mackinder did likewise.

"We will continue the meeting aboard my flagship," Jellicoe said.

"Uh," Maddox said. He hadn't risen from his chair, "I wouldn't go that far. I'll gladly give you the respect you're due, sir, but I'm not going to foolishly put myself into your custody. Therefore, I will keep my independent command and remain aboard *Victory*. I will, however, gladly obey your legal orders as I've already done so."

Mackinder sat down before Jellicoe did. Jellicoe scowled at Mackinder. Mackinder just shrugged. Finally, Jellicoe sat down.

"You're a stubborn man, Captain," Jellicoe said.

Maddox didn't reply to that.

"We believe we've uncovered the central location of the Spacer ships in this star system," Jellicoe said, changing tack. "We have counted thirty-five Spacer saucer ships to date. We can likely defeat that with the force at hand."

"I agree," Maddox said, "if that's all the ships the Spacers have here."

"You think the Spacers have more than thirty-five saucer ships?" Jellicoe asked.

"Most certainly, sir. I'm quite sure the Spacers have been scouting us using cloaked vessels. They probably feel thirty-five is the right number to enticing you into an assault against them."

"You're quite suspicious," Mackinder observed.

Maddox said nothing, recognizing the sarcasm in the comment.

"Well," Jellicoe said, "such is my own belief. That is why, naturally, I've been speaking with the Lord High Admiral through my Long-Range Builder Comm Device. The admiral has been using the Builder Scanner on Pluto. We've studied the Spacer positions in detail here, although that isn't the main point. We will be transferring more ships here in order to catch all of them."

"Oh," Maddox said, "I approve. Not that you need my approval."

"No," Jellicoe said, "not that we need your approval in the slightest, but you agree with the plan?"

"I do," Maddox said.

"Good," Jellicoe said, "because you will lead the charge."

"Lead the charge?" Maddox asked. "You want *Victory* to explode under Spacer beams?"

Mackinder cleared his throat. "Sir?" he said to Jellicoe, barely giving the man a glance.

"Please speak, General," the admiral said. "I applaud your desire to enter the conversation."

Mackinder grimaced.

Maddox had the feeling Mackinder thought Jellicoe wasn't as sharp as he should be for an admiral, and the general could be right.

"Captain," Mackinder said, "why are the Spacers here if they know, as surely they must, about the Builder Nexus in Earth orbit and our ability to pour more ships into the Paran System?"

"That's an excellent question," Maddox said. "I don't know the answer. I'd suspect they would have attacked us by now or have fled. Perhaps they want us to bring the rest of the fleet here."

"For what reason?" asked Mackinder.

"To attack it or to hold it here while they make an attack elsewhere," Maddox said.

"Do you believe they have the ships to successfully attack our task force?" Mackinder asked.

"I don't know," Maddox said. "We know they had a Leviathan accomplice, probably how they acquired the phase ship. Therefore, I think this could be a trap with an enemy fleet attacking from Leviathan."

"I see," Mackinder said. "So you do not agree with using the Earth Nexus to bring the fleet here?"

"If everything else remains equal, I certainly do."

Mackinder compressed his lips. "What would you do if you were in our position?"

Maddox drummed his fingers on the table. He had a few sharp comments he'd like to make, but he refrained from doing so. Was Mackinder truly asking for his advice? It seemed possible. Maddox cocked his head. What would he do?

"I would attack with what I already have here," Maddox said, "and gauge the Spacer response. We have two ships with a long-range communications back to Earth. If needed, we could ask for immediate reinforcements, or we could retreat. If we're going to attack, we should have attacked already."

"You would let the Spacer ships leave the Paran System then?" Mackinder asked.

"I don't know," Maddox said. "It is a quandary. I don't know why we've waited this long to attack. I suppose you gentlemen wanted to be certain about everything."

"Never mind about that," Jellicoe said.

Mackinder raised a hand, perhaps to silence Jellicoe. "I'm interested in what Maddox has to say regarding this. What would you do, Captain?"

Once more, Maddox drummed his fingers on the conference table. "It depends if Leviathan is ready to invade or not. We haven't seen any evidence of Leviathan formations at nearby jumping off points. We do know the Spacers have a secret egress to the Barnard's Star System near Earth. Could there be others like that? It seems possible, but I don't know. As far as I know, and I'm sure you're using the Long-Range Builder Scanner on Pluto, nobody is about to make a quick strike against the Commonwealth."

"Please, continue," Mackinder said.

"There are a few too many unknowns out here," Maddox said. "We haven't found a Builder device to form a hyper-spatial tube back to the Barnard's Star System near Earth. That means the one-way nexus must be well hidden."

"I agreed with that," Mackinder said.

"That means we'll continue searching for it," Maddox said. "We also won't attack because you think the Spacers are attempting to lure us into doing exactly that."

Mackinder studied Maddox. "Perhaps, Captain, it is time to send you toward the Spacers for you to talk with them and find out what you can."

Maddox chewed on an inside cheek. That actually seemed reasonable. He did have a knack for drawing information out of people.

"I can do that," Maddox said.

"In two days, then," Mackinder said, "you will hold a parley with the Spacers."

Maddox noted that Mackinder hadn't asked Jellicoe if that was the plan. Here was proof that Mackinder wasn't along as an advisor, but as the chief. Once again, Maddox wondered if Mackinder had installed Admiral Haig into the new position, and if Mackinder was the real power behind the throne, as the saying went.

"Two days, Captain," Mackinder said. "Do you believe we can find the Builder one-way nexus by then?"

"There's a lot of debris and planetary chunks to search." Maddox shrugged. "We can get started. Finding it may take longer than two days."

"Yes," Mackinder said. "This is a delicate situation. It would be good to know if we can make it back to the Barnard's Star or not on our own. Still, it is strange to me that the Spacers haven't attacked us."

"Agreed," Maddox said, "except they surely know about our nexus at Earth. They're being cautious, which is natural as Spacers are cautious by nature."

"Hmm," Mackinder said. "Meaning what?"

"Meaning that a fast hard strike could have been the correct maneuver," Maddox said. "But we failed to do it. Therefore, and I am only thinking aloud, sir, I think this cautious approach on our part might be right. We're like two fencers, not quite ready to square off for the duel."

"Quaint," Mackinder said. "You have duels on the mind, do you?"

"I suppose I do," Maddox said.

Mackinder stood, and Jellicoe hurried to his feet. He did not scowl or rebuke Mackinder, either, for doing that.

Yes, Maddox thought to himself, *Mackinder is the leader of the expedition. It's strange that the Intelligence Chief should be reaching for such power so soon, though.*

"Thank you for coming aboard, gentlemen," Maddox said, standing. "This has been most informative."

"It has been our pleasure," Jellicoe said. He then hastened to lead the way out of the conference chamber.

As the two men left, Maddox wondered what the Spacers were attempting to achieve here. There was something odd about all of this. Perhaps as interesting, what had happened to Becker? Had Becker been wise enough to stay out of the Spacers' clutches? If the Spacers had captured Becker, it would be terrible for him to fall into their hands. Not for his sake, but for the security of what he knew about the Commonwealth. The Spacers would do whatever they needed to pry that information out of him.

Maddox scowled. He was on a mission to free the three crewmembers Becker had kidnapped. The kidnapping didn't sit well with Maddox in the least. The three women were his responsibility, his people.

"Let's get started," Maddox said.

Galyan appeared as he came out of ghost mode. "That was interesting, sir."

"Give me your observations and analysis," Maddox said, sitting back down.

Galyan obliged the captain and began to speak.

-40-

Dax awoke and, to his astonishment, found himself sitting in a chair with his hands on his knees. Did this mean Mu had reattached his head to his body?

Dax raised his hands, nearly laughing aloud with giddiness. Likely, a cyber-organ secreted calming agents. As a result, the laugh died before it reached his throat. He touched his mouth, which opened, and his tongue stuck out.

Everything worked as it should.

Experimentally, Dax rose and walked around the chair. He discovered that he wore the original uniform when he'd first approached the Spacers in the *Python*.

Dax stopped abruptly as fear stabbed at him.

Mu and Venna, the latter in her hideous form, were in the chamber with him. They watched from behind a table laden with tech items.

"Hello," Dax said in greeting.

"Are you surprised to see us?" Mu asked.

"I am." Dax assessed the situation and bowed at the waist. Diplomacy seemed wisest. "I'm grateful for my reattachment. As I promised, I will now do anything you ask."

"We already know that," Mu said with a smirk.

Dax suppressed a frown. He disliked her offhand manner. *Might he have said too much, which caused her contempt? She was his...*

"Continue," Mu said. "Tell us the rest."

"What?" Dax asked, perplexed by her words.

"You were going to say that you think of me as your enemy," Mu said.

Renewed fear stabbed Dax. He had a terrible and sudden suspicion. "Are you reading my thoughts?"

"Not exactly *reading,*" Mu said, "but that's close enough."

Claustrophobia constricted his thinking. If they could read his thoughts...know exactly what he was thinking the moment he did so... It was time for contrition.

"Great One," Dax said, stepping closer and bowing at the waist before Venna. "I wish to reiterate that I appreciate your reassembling me. I want you to know that you will not regret this."

Venna didn't respond but looked away as if bored.

"If I've angered you—" Dax said.

Mu raised a hand, stilling his speech. "It's not so much that you've angered her, as your wishes will have little relevance in the coming days. You will do exactly as instructed."

"Of course," Dax said, perplexed even more, "I'll be happy to oblige. Secretly, in his heart, he raged, finding her arrogance unbearable. *You'll be the first to find a blaster in your face as I blow it apart.*

"What was that?" Mu asked mockingly.

"What?" Dax said, his face showing contrition.

"About a blaster shooting me in the face," Mu said.

Dax was appalled, his stomach clenching as he realized they were both staring at a computer screen on the table before them.

Can the screen decipher what I'm thinking?

"It's not deciphering anything," Mu said. "The screen *shows* us the words you're secretly thinking. Yes, in fact, we are precisely reading your thoughts word for word."

Dax's mouth opened.

Once again, Mu smirked at him. "We have internally wired your brain so that your neural synapse impulses related to thoughts are projected onto this screen."

"How is that possible?" Dax asked, sickened.

"In the same way as this is possible." Mu picked up a small control unit and pressed a button. "Dance for us, Senior Dax."

A tingling sensation occurred at the base of Dax's neck. Then he began to cavort, leap and twirl before them like a dancing fool.

"Breakdance for us," Mu said.

Dax did exactly that, even though he'd never heard of the dance form before this. He twirled on his back with his legs in the air and twisted about. This was horrifying, as Dax believed that he sullied his dignity breakdancing before them like this.

"Enough," Venna said in a harsh voice.

"You may stop." Mu pressed the control device again.

There was another tingling sensation at the base of Dax's neck. The impulse to obey her vanished.

Dax climbed to his feet, trembling. That had been degrading, among other things.

"Oh, yes," Mu said. "It was a great indignity. It's funny, though, don't you think?"

You bitch, Dax thought to himself.

"Naughty, naughty," Mu said, shaking an index finger at him. "That isn't the way to think of your dominatrix or gain our trust."

"My what?" he said.

"I came up with the term 'dominatrix'," Mu said. "Do you like it?"

"I don't understand it," Dax said.

"I will explain the concept in a bit more detail. We've rewired certain processes in your brain. We've even given you a few…you may think of them as modifications."

"You mean interior Builder devices like you possess," Dax said.

"That is another term for them."

Dax felt his scalp. There was a former hairline fracture. A bio substance seemed to have resealed the incision.

"You opened my skull?" Dax asked in horror.

"I didn't do it personally," Mu said. "But specialists of ours have, yes."

"Enough," Venna said, sounding irritated.

Mu inclined her head to Venna before regarding him again. "You should know that we've been traveling, Senior Dax. I mean this saucer ship in particular. We have been using, well, can I show him, Great One?"

Venna made a flickering motion with her gnarly, tree-bark fingers.

Mu made several complicated gestures in the air. A holographic star map appeared before Dax. It showed red lines connecting one star system to another, a web of them.

"These are hidden Builder pathways," Mu said.

"Don't brag," Venna said.

Once more, Mu inclined her head to Venna.

It seems she has to obey the hag.

Both women stared at the screen and looked up sharply at Dax.

"I'm sorry, Great One," Dax said, understanding they had read the ugly thought. "I'm unused to hiding my thoughts, to not thinking. *This is horrifying. My inner being is exposed to them.*

"That is true," Mu said. "You would do well to remember that. Whatever you think, whatever you're planning, I'll know it here." Mu tapped the screen. "If it isn't me, someone else will be monitoring the screen so we'll know what you're thinking, sometimes before you think it."

Dax felt abject fear radiating in him. His cyber organ must have secreted calming agents, but it only partly helped. *How can I escape these monsters?*

"You're never going to escape," Mu said. "You're here to serve Spacer Third Fleet until the end of your days."

Venna cleared her throat.

"What I mean to say," Mu said quickly, "is you are here to serve the Great One. She is at the moment *using* the Spacer Third Fleet in her grander design."

Venna nodded.

That conflict of interest will be my wedge, Dax thought.

"You have no wedge," Mu said. "But go on, think your thoughts. Let us know your intentions. It is most illuminating."

Two plus two equals four. Four plus five equals nine. Dax began mathematical computations in his head in order—*that I won't give away my thoughts.*

"But you're giving them away, anyway." Mu made a depreciative gesture. "It doesn't matter what you do, but go ahead and do it. In the meantime, observe the holo-map."

Dax did.

"Do you see the lanes between star systems?" Mu said.

"They're hyper-spatial tubes," Venna said.

"Thank you, Great One," Mu said. "Do you see where the hyper-spatial tubes, the lanes in a way, connect the star systems?"

Dax studied the holo-map and the indicated hyper-spatial tube route. Mu had highlighted it in red. The destination shocked him, as he recognized the star system. "The route leads to Leviathan's Seventh Assault Fleet."

"Exactly," Mu said. "One more jump will bring us there."

That struck him as incredible, and as an opportunity. "The Seventh Assault Fleet has fifty maulers."

"So you've told us in your sleep," Mu said.

Maulers were massive attack vessels of Leviathan. The Seventh Assault Fleet had painfully sent its maulers to this jumping off point. The star system was five hundred light years from Earth. But with the hidden Spacer hyper-spatial tube route—

"Do you desire the Seventh Assault Fleet to attack Earth?" Dax asked.

"No," Mu said. "That isn't the present plan."

"You don't need to explain our strategy to him," Venna said.

"Forgive me, Great One," Mu said.

Once again, Venna fluttered her fingers as if with indifference.

What can they be thinking? Dax wondered. *The Seventh Assault Fleet will attack who Great Leviathan tells them and no other. They're mad to go there.*

"You're wrong about that," Mu said.

How can she possibly think otherwise?

"You will most certainly find out," Mu said.

One hundred and sixty-two plus ninety-one, minus three hundred and ten equals... Dax computed math equations in his head as he asked, "Who do you want the Seventh Assault Fleet to attack?"

Mu glanced at Venna.

Venna barely nodded.

"We'll start with the paltry force Star Watch has sent to the debris-filled Paran System, including Maddox and his pesky spaceship, *Victory.*"

Dax blinked with incomprehension. "I thought Maddox was immune to direct attacks."

"Your easily frightened grand strategists believed that," Venna said. "I have far greater abilities than they, as I am a *di-far* like Maddox, but with even greater powers that I reclaimed from Ector."

Dax had heard that name. Oh. "You mean the planet originally holding the Phantasma Synth Crystals?"

Neither woman replied.

"I don't understand," Dax said. "You said one more jump brings us to the Seventh Assault Fleet. How many saucer ships did you bring with you?"

"Three," Mu said.

"You don't need to tell him," Venna said. "In fact, I'm getting weary of your boasts."

Mu sat silently, perhaps in fear.

"Never mind," Venna said. "I didn't say that to discourage you. Continue if you must."

Mu nodded before regarding Dax again. "We're going there to speak with War Master Vane of the Seventh Assault Fleet."

Dax wrestled with himself. This was suicide. If he died in the next few hours…that wouldn't help him. "Ladies, War Master Vane is Leviathan's Space Force's most aggressive commander. This is suicide."

"You've already told us," Mu said.

"I have? I don't remember…" *Oh. They must have extracted that during the operation when they inserted the modifications into me.*

"That's very astute of you," Mu said.

Dax shuddered, hating yet again how Mu could read his thoughts. He restarted the mathematical equations, running through more and more complicated calculations, hoping to—*I have to stop thinking.*

"But you are thinking," Mu said. "You can't stop. Isn't that funny?"

Dax began more difficult algebraic equations, hoping they would prove enough. He swallowed a lump, saying, "I don't understand your plan. War Master Vane will never listen to you. He won't be able to as the pickets will destroy the saucer ships and us in them when we first appear."

Venna chuckled.

"Oh, I think Vane will listen," Mu said. "The most interesting thing is that you're going to be instrumental in this."

"How can you hope to convince Vane to come aboard the saucer ship? Dax asked. "He—"

"On the contrary," Mu said, interrupting. "We will go to his flagship."

"What?" Dax said. *If I can make it there, I can escape there.*

"You may try to escape," Mu said, "but I think you'll find circumstances different from what you expect."

I don't understand. Why is she telling me any of this?

"So you'll be ready," Mu said, "so you'll understand, and so you can tell us if there are any things we need to look out for."

Dax shuddered. He didn't want to die, not to the pickets. "Do you know the call sign so the picket ships won't obliterate the saucer ships the moment we appear in the star system?"

"Yes," Mu said. "But tell it to us again,"

Dax did.

"That is correct," Venna said. "Your procedures worked," she told Mu.

Mu inclined her head.

"One more jump. Let us make it." Venna inhaled. "We're about to change the course of the Orion Spiral Arm. We are about to change the course of everything." Venna seemed to swell up like a striking cobra. "The masters of Ector will reshape the galaxy. This time, this time…" Abruptly, Venna closed her mouth and looked accusingly at Mu and Dax.

What was that about? Dax thought.

Neither Mu nor Venna replied, although his thoughts must have appeared on the computer screen before them.

Dax bent his head, working harder than ever on mathematical complexities so he would no longer think about his ideas.

-41-

The three saucer ships entered the Zakym System, 500 light years from Earth. The three saucers approached a mass formation of fifty Imperial Leviathan Maulers and their picket ships.

Each mauler was oval-shaped, measuring thirteen kilometers in diameter. Each was massive, the tonnage approximately 171.9 *billion* tons. This single assault fleet could potentially annihilate the entirety of Star Watch, as it had greater tonnage than all the warships of Star Watch combined.

Even though Dax's thoughts were in flux and his brain partly rewired, he remembered that there were *six* separate Leviathan invasion fleets in position to attack the Commonwealth. The Seventh Assault Fleet was the biggest, twice the size of the next biggest.

Dax thought it madness that these Spacers believed they could control War Master Vane of Seventh Assault Fleet. It was lunacy to think that he, Dax, had any pull with Vane. For one thing, before the War Master began the invasion assault, he would need direct orders from Great Leviathan to begin. There was no way any of them could forge those.

The three saucer ships approached the Seventh Assault Fleet as picket ships converged on them.

Dax received a message to come to the bridge at once. He hurried down the corridors, longing for a blaster and for the cyborg trooper to join him. Both might help him escape this horrid captivity.

If A equals nineteen and B is... Dax started a new set of algebraic equations to shield his thoughts.

When Dax walked onto the bridge, he was stunned to see the cyborg trooper waiting for him. The trooper stood like a statue. He had some flesh but was mostly metal, graphite and sheath-protected muscles and tendons. When a trooper moved, he seemed more like a giant insect. This one wore a regulation Leviathan sidearm.

Dax almost laughed with disbelief. He merely needed to give the signal, and the trooper could kill every Spacer on the circular bridge. Then Dax spied Mu and Venna.

"Go ahead," Mu said, "give the signal and see what happens."

"That's my base imagination at work," Dax said. "I don't know why I would think anything so foolish."

"I know why," Mu said. "You still have the vain hope of leaving our glorious service."

"Enough," Venna said. "We have more important business at hand. Mocking him does nothing. Activate the cyber for service. Time and the pickets are pressing."

"Come here, Senior Dax," Mu said, clicking a button on a handheld device.

Abruptly, Dax stiffened and then marched to her in a robotic fashion. Dax still was able to think his own thoughts, but he couldn't move his mouth or limbs because he thought to do so. He could not do anything by his volition but only through hers.

"Don't worry," Mu said with derision, "I'll feed you the needed words. Now, face the main screen. It is time to talk to War Master Vane."

Soon, the relatively puny saucer ships stopped before five picket ships, dwarfed by the vast maulers behind them. The assault fleet was assembled around a blue gas giant, one looking much like Neptune in the Solar System.

A lean cyber appeared on the main screen. There was something haughty and frightening about him and his shiny red pupils. He wore a black uniform with silver embalms on thin shoulder boards.

"This is War Master Vane," he said. "Who dares to approach my fleet and ask to address me?"

Dax found himself speaking to the War Master. He did not think the words. Instead, out of the corner of his eye, Dax saw Mu whispering into the hand unit. He then spoke her words. How did Mu know the correct phraseology and methods of speech, though? This was terrifying.

Dax wanted to weep. He wanted to—he began working through mathematical equations, ones more difficult than ever. He strove to concentrate on the math problems, only half-listening and half-aware of what took place before him even as he spoke for the Spacers.

Despite his concentration, Dax heard Vane say, "Your primary saucer ship may approach the flagship. It can then enter the hangar bay."

"Yes, War Master Vane," Dax said. "Thank you, we shall proceed at once."

A second later, the main screen went blank.

Mu must have pressed a switch.

Dax almost collapsed, realizing that once again he could say and do what he wanted, probably within certain limits, though.

"You are correct about the last idea," Mu said.

The main screen reactivated. It showed the primary saucer ship passing picket ships and heading into the formation of fifty maulers. The saucer ship seemed like a shuttle compared to them.

Soon, the saucer ship headed for the great flagship, HSL *Behemoth*. A hatch rose on the hull. The saucer ship entered through the hatch into the great hangar bay. There were hundreds of fighters lined up in rows on the decks and others hanging from the ceiling like resting bats.

The saucer ship floated toward and landed in a great cradle on the deck.

"Now we will go to it," Venna said.

Mu waited with Dax beside her.

"It will be just the three of us," Venna said. "Are you ready, Senior Dax, for the meeting?"

"I'm eager to do your will," Dax said. He strove to hide the idea that he was going to escape their hideous service on the *Behemoth* and pay them back for all his indignities.

Venna chuckled nastily.

Hopelessness filled Dax as he strove to disregard it.

Mu had an index finger hovering over a switch on her hand device. "Let's go, Dax. You can keep your identity a little longer."

Venna inhaled. "This is a monumental moment. Let us proceed and make galactic history."

-42-

The three of them exited the saucer ship and walked down ladder-like stairs to the deck of the huge hangar bay.

There, on the deck, a battalion of cyborg troopers waited.

"This way," the group leader said.

The cyborgs didn't frisk them; instead, they fell in step, escorting them.

They moved through the corridors of the gargantuan attack vessel. It was larger than most cities on any planet. Cyborgs filled it, cyborgs that would attack, destroy, and dominate. The mauler and its personnel were the coercive arm of Leviathan. The humans of the Commonwealth were soon going to learn a hard and bitter lesson.

Leviathan had at last sent an expeditionary force across the vast gulf between the spiral arms. They had been positioning the fleets for two and a half years. It had taken time, energy, and great amounts of wealth. When the moment came, Great Leviathan would give the order. Then the assault fleets of Leviathan would move. They would attack simultaneously the most important nodes of Star Watch. Star Watch couldn't send its Grand Fleet everywhere at once. Each Leviathan assault fleet could probably grind down Star Watch's Grand Fleet into particles all on its own.

The Seventh Assault Fleet was the major striking arm of the expeditionary force, while War Master Vane was the greatest tactician Leviathan had seen in decades.

Dax swallowed. He was eager and frightened at the same time. He couldn't believe the three of them dared to march to Vane's bridge.

Dax didn't understand how Venna and Mu believed they could dominate the formidable cyber. With just one word, the cyborg troopers would draw their weapons and destroy them.

"Hang on," Mu told him, "events will take a turn you haven't conceived of yet."

"I-I don't understand what you mean," Dax said.

The two women remained silent.

How could they be reading his thoughts now? Dax saw no screen in evidence. The grim anticipation proved too much for him. "Please let me go," Dax whispered. "I've done what you wanted. I don't want to die when they destroy you two for your arrogance."

Venna did not turn to him, but resolutely walked forward.

Mu shot him a glance as a reprimand, no doubt.

Dax decided this was hopeless and it would be better to keep quiet and die with a little dignity or make his break at the last second. Yes, that was what he would do. He needed to be ready in order to act with precision and speed.

After a long walk down seeming never-ending corridors and many turbo lifts, the group leader led the three into a cavernous bridge filled with endless screens and stations. The rest of the cyborg troopers remained behind in the outer courtyard.

War Master Vane stood on the highest dais in the middle of it all. He wore a black cloak and stood tall and metallically lean, exuding arrogance. Interestingly, he did not have aides on the dais with him.

The rest of the bridge personnel worked at screens, consoles and other stations, maybe with one hundred cyber operators altogether. The bridge was vast indeed.

"Approach me," Vane commanded in a robotic voice.

The three approached the dais. They did not climb steps onto the dais. Instead, they faced Vane from below, as if he stood on a balcony. His metallic hands clutched a rail as he looked down at them.

"So, Spacers," Vane said, "you have returned our spy to us. Senior Dax I believe you're called."

Dax was ready to warn Vane about these two and sprint out of the firing line. A microsecond before he did, Dax heard a click. With a sinking feeling, he knew Mu had pressed a switch. A second later, foreign words spewed from Dax's mouth.

"Sir, grave forces are at work, which I have barely discovered in time. Though we have assassinated," Dax indicated Venna, "the Lord High Admiral of Star Watch and his Chief Intelligence Officer, we failed to make the most important kill. That kill would have made everything perfectly simple for Leviathan."

"It *will* be perfectly simple," Vane said harshly, "as nothing can stand before our assault fleets."

"I understand, sir. None may compete against your tactical brilliance. But, War Master, I must tell you there is a grave problem in the making."

Vane sneered at him.

Dax looked right and left as if searching for a conspiracy before he stepped closer to the rail. "Sir, if I could just speak to you a moment in private. These two bear an incredibly important message. I think, however, it would be best heard by your ears alone."

"What is this?" Vane demanded. "You indulge in skullduggery on my ship in the midst of the assault fleet? Who do you think you are, Senior Dax?"

Dax made a secret sign that he'd received from Grand Strategist Enigmach.

Vane jerked back in surprise before nodding sharply. "Follow me." Vane pivoted and stepped to the center of the dais. He turned sharply to them. "Well, get up here already."

Dax led Venna and Mu up steps onto the dais and to a circular area beside War Master Vane. A floor disc detached from the center dais and lowered until they were in a wide chamber *under* the dais. They stepped off, and the floor disc rose until it clicked into place and sealed them from the bridge.

Vane indicated couches to the side. "Do you need to recline, or shall we get on with it?"

"We shall get on with it," Venna said in a scratchy voice. "Shut him down, Mu."

Mu pressed a switch.

Dax felt himself go limp. He saw what was happening, although he was powerless to prevent any of it.

The old hag raised her tree bark-like hands.

Vane laughed, stepping toward her. No doubt, he planned to kill her with a blow. Then Vane frowned and it seemed as if he could not move. Almost instantly, gaseous, etheric forces trickled from his body. He clutched at his throat, but it seemed he could not speak.

"Now," Venna said, "while I have him in my clutches, go to work, Mu."

Mu stepped before the towering War Master. She peered at him for quite a time, and it didn't seem that she did anything.

Dax had the impression she used her Builder modifications, modifying the War Master's brain. Likely, Mu could only do so because Venna held Vane locked in immobility, unable to do a thing.

After what seemed like ages, Mu's shoulders slumped, she stepped back and staggered, nearly falling.

Venna caught her.

Vane moved, and it seemed he would draw his blaster.

"No," Venna said, looking up, "wrong idea. You will now comply and do exactly as we say."

Vane opened his mouth. "Yes, Great One, I will comply. You have given me the orders from Great Leviathan. It is time to attack under your auspices. This was an unusual form of granting the message, but I appreciate it. We will take care of these Earthlings, and I will follow your ships back to a region of space in the Paran System. We will crush the puny Earthlings there, for I have a weapon they're not expecting, one that will nullify their advantage of this nexus with Star Watch's Grand Fleet in the Solar System."

"That is wonderful to hear," Venna said, "but I'm afraid we're tired, War Master. We're returning to the saucer ship."

"You will not stay here with me and watch the outcome?" Vane asked.

Mu looked meaningfully at Venna.

"Very well," Venna said in a resigned way. "No, sir, first we are going to speak to your highest officers."

"Nine of the most important," Mu said. "I can shift no more than that."

Venna nodded. "We are going to speak to nine of your officers, one at a time. You will remain with us and then they will leave one at a time."

"You are going to give them the message, Great One?" Vane said.

"Yes," Venna said. "They are going to receive the message and they are going to become my pupils. Shall we leave it at that?"

"Yes," Vane said. "That sounds good, and know that it's a delight to hear the attack order has finally been given. I enjoy the chance to work with one like you who has such subtlety and is so obviously intelligent. Are you from the court of Great Leviathan himself?"

"Yes," Venna said. "I am. Now, War Master, are there any recording devices in this room?"

Vane explained how the recording devices worked, and yes, they had been recording all this time.

Once more, Mu used her interior Builder devices and deactivated the recordings and cameras.

At that point, Dax was certain he was never going to escape these two horrible witches.

-43-

Victory advanced by velocity through and past the debris, gas, and planetary chunks of the Paran System, heading for the last area where saucer ships had been spotted.

Maddox was following Admiral Jellicoe's directive. He was trying to establish communications with the Spacers specifically to learn their intentions.

As Maddox sat in his captain's chair, he pondered a possibility. As he watched planetary chunks and asteroids pass by, the threatening idea took hold more forcefully.

A hidden nexus had created a hyper-spatial tube that connected the Barnard's Star System to the Paran System. What if the Paran System contained more one-way nexuses like that? Perhaps the Paran System was a node connected to many other star systems. Could the Spacers use those other nexuses to bring more of the Spacer Third Fleet here? The Spacers might hope to overwhelm Jellicoe's Task Force through massed saucer ships.

The problem with the idea was the saucer ship itself. A saucer ship was nimble and could cloak. It was, however, under-gunned compared to Star Watch battleships. A saucer ship possessed a thin, barely armored hull and only slightly better shielding. Even if the saucer ships outnumbered Star Watch battleships four to one or even five to one, Maddox would bet on the battleships, particularly those of the *Conqueror*-class.

A *Conqueror*-class battleship was constructed from heavy-metal components. That meant size for size a *Conqueror*-class battleship could fire a hellish disruptor beam. It had a far denser electromagnetic shield and could last longer under bombardment. Then there was its heavily armored hull.

No, Maddox reasoned. Spacers wouldn't want to slug it out with *Conqueror*-class battleships, not unless they could swarm them six to one or seven to one. That would mean at least seventy saucer ships, or more likely ninety to one hundred, considering the Star Watch escorts and destroyers supporting the battleships.

Would the Spacers risk one hundred saucer ships in the Paran System? Maddox doubted it, although he was sure the Spacers were up to something. He just didn't know what.

As *Victory* continued to pick its way through the space junk, gaining velocity, Maddox had Meta send out a hail for any Spacer representative who would respond.

After traveling several astronomical units (AUs), Maddox ordered Keith to reduce the starship's speed. He then sent Galyan ranging, looking behind planetary chunk clusters, debris fields and gas clouds. At the same time, Ludendorff and Andros used the best ship sensors.

"We're finding nothing," Ludendorff said.

Maddox pondered that. "Do the Spacers hope to lure us in deeper?"

"Will you go deeper?" Ludendorff asked.

"No," Maddox said. "This is as far as I'm going."

At the comm station, Meta swiveled around. "There's a call from Admiral Jellicoe, sir."

"Put him on," Maddox said, indicating the main screen.

In a moment, Jellicoe was on the main screen, leaning forward. "We see your starship slowing down, Captain. Is there a reason for that?"

"There is," Maddox said. "I've gone to the limit I'm willing to risk."

"No, no," Jellicoe said. "You must go further, deeper. At all costs, you must make contact with the Spacers."

"What if I go too far?"

"Too far?" asked Jellicoe, as if that was a joke. "I know that *Victory* can leap out of danger better than any ship in Star Watch. That's your MO. You and your ship are nimble. You're creative."

"You're not stupid, sir," Maddox said.

Jellicoe frowned at him. "I thought we talked about that."

"You're right," Maddox said, almost sounding contrite. "I'll refrain from such comments, at least for now. Even so, this is as far as I'm willing to go."

"And if I order you to go farther?"

"Then I'll have to exercise my independent command and use my knowledge as a Patrol scout to tell you that would be unwise. Seeing that it's my people's heads on the chopping block, I don't think I'll be unwise. This is the wrong time for that."

"Captain…" After a moment's consideration, Jellicoe leaned back in his chair. "You're making this difficult."

"You mean having the Spacers get rid of *Victory* and me for you?" Maddox asked.

"Now see here, Captain—"

There was a loud "Harrumph" from off-screen, interrupting him. Jellicoe looked to his right, frowned, and then nodded.

Maddox assumed General Mackinder stood there out of the video sight. Mackinder might be making sure Jellicoe didn't go off script.

"Very well, Captain," Jellicoe said, "proceed as you see fit."

"Thank you, sir," Maddox said.

Jellicoe went off screen.

"Well," Ludendorff said. "What do you make of that?"

Maddox shot the professor a stern glance.

"I know, I know," Ludendorff said, "no one can ask you anything on the bridge. My goodness, man—"

"Save it, Professor," Maddox said, interrupting. "Galyan, have you spotted anything yet?"

"No, sir," Galyan said.

"Then go to these coordinates." Maddox gave Galyan the coordinates. Afterward, Maddox instructed Keith to turn around and start back.

***

Cloaked saucer ships hidden in thick gas clouds watched *Victory* turn and head back. Each had been readying their ship weapons, about to swing the trap shut. Had Maddox's blasted intuitive sense saved him yet again?

The saucer ships began powering down their weapons.

***

Victory headed back to the area it had recently left. It continued to search the planetary chunks and asteroids for signs of the lost darter.

Time ticked by as Ludendorff, Andros and Galyan searched one area after another. Galyan had been going into asteroids, searching for darter signs. Mathematically, it was a poor strategy. Given their limited time, and that nothing else had happened, what else should they do? Galyan continued to enter asteroid, after asteroid, after planetary chunk.

Victory neared the main position of Jellicoe's Task Force.

Abruptly, Galyan appeared on the bridge. "Captain I have found it! I have found it!"

"Found the darter?" asked Maddox.

"Yes, Captain, it is hidden and cloaked in a crevice deep in an asteroid."

"What did you see inside the darter?"

"I did not go inside, sir," Galyan said.

"Why not?" said Maddox.

"I assumed Becker's telepathic abilities would discover me."

"Becker can hear what you're thinking?" Maddox asked.

"I know you say that as a joke," Galyan said. "Still, is it not better to be prudent in this situation than in making bad assumptions?"

"Yes," Maddox said. "You're right. Show us where the darter is."

Galyan brought up a holographic map of the nearby debris field and pinpointed, with a red dot, exactly where the darter hid.

Maddox drummed his fingers on an armrest. "We want to capture Becker. We don't want to kill him or lose the three crewmembers he kidnapped."

"Could we deploy one of those mobile stasis fields that Methuselah Man Strand used to use?" Galyan asked.

"Alas," Maddox said, "we don't have such a stasis-field generator aboard *Victory*."

"Could not having one with us have been a mistake, sir?" Galyan asked.

"It might be." Maddox frowned and then stood. "Follow me, Galyan."

"Where are we headed, sir?"

Ludendorff had left the bridge a while ago.

"We're going to speak to the professor and see if we can figure out a way to surprise Becker."

"You think such a surprise is possible?" Galyan asked.

"That's what I want to find out. Now let's hurry."

-44-

After speaking with Ludendorff, Maddox readied himself in a hangar bay when Galyan appeared.

"All is set, sir," Galyan said. "I have made sure the booster device is in position. The holographic camouflage unit is also ready, and as far as I can tell, Captain Becker is unaware that I've scouted around his ship—the darter, to be precise."

"Let us be precise," Maddox said, "as that's the one thing Ludendorff recommended. To start, he's not Captain Becker, although he used to be Captain Becker."

"Thank you for the correction. Becker does not have a title then?"

"None that I'm aware of," Maddox said.

After that, Maddox collected a rifle blaster and moved into the fold fighter. Meta was already inside it, waiting.

Jewel was at the school on *Victory*. She was unaware that both of her parents were preparing for a dangerous commando mission. Maddox felt it imperative to take Meta along on this. For one thing, she understood the hows and whys of using the anti-telepathy headband as protection against Becker's mental domination. He also wanted someone he implicitly trusted with his life and who he knew would make the right combat decisions. Meta could also help with the three women, who might be under terrible mental and emotional stress.

Keith soon lifted off the hangar bay deck, easing the tin can out of *Victory*. He accelerated fast, the Gs pushing all of them into their seats. After a hard burn of precise duration, Keith shut off thrust. With a second click, Keith turned on the camouflage unit Galyan had readied earlier.

This system included a holographic projector. When a person looked with his eyes at the fighter, he'd see the stars behind the craft. The unit also cloaked any heat and radiation signatures.

The fighter now drifted toward the targeted asteroid.

Victory had already concealed itself behind a planetary chunk on the far side of the asteroid. Galyan had discovered the passive sensors on the asteroid and didn't want them to see the starship.

As time passed, the fold fighter drifted closer to the asteroid. So far, there wasn't any response from the enemy.

After checking for the seventh time, Keith said, 'We're finally in range, sir. I'll maneuver elsewhere after you've disembarked."

Maddox and Meta climbed up and floated through a hatch into a secondary unit attached to the fold fighter. The hatch shut behind them as each climbed into an armored battlesuit with exoskeleton servos. The dark suits made them look like robotic gorillas carrying packs. These battlesuits also served as spacesuits, with many hours of air.

Once secured within, the 'robotic gorillas' stepped into larger commando maneuver units. The units were skeletal with sensor and thruster packs and nozzles. The units' purpose was stealth space maneuvering.

"We're ready," Maddox said over the short link in his helmet.

Keith pressed a switch, bleeding the air from the compartment. Then an outer bay door slid opened. Maddox walked his battlesuit and commando maneuver unit into the slot of a stealth catapult. One could also call it a magnetic accelerator. The slot holding Maddox was positioned between two rails aimed at the door.

Maddox felt the slot ratchet or shiver, telling him he was secure in the magnetic accelerator. "I'm ready," he told Keith.

"Just a moment, sir," Keith said over the short link.

The fold fighter subtly shifted its position, the open door realigning with the target.

"I have you centered on the asteroid," Keith said.

"Fire when ready," Maddox said.

"Now," Keith said.

The slot holding Maddox slid quickly along the rails, propelled by magnetic impulses. The slot reached the end, stopping abruptly and releasing Maddox in his battlesuit and commando maneuver unit. Maddox shot into space, propelled from the fighter toward the asteroid in the distance.

Maddox aligned himself so he kept the asteroid in direct view.

Soon, Meta shot after him.

Maddox turned on the commando maneuver unit's camouflage system. With this skeletal unit over his suit, he acted like a mini-spaceship.

The magnetic accelerator launch ensured that the battlesuits emitted no heat or bright light from thrust. It was just the camouflaged equipment heading toward the target. Each commando maneuver unit did have cold hydrogen particles for thrust later. The passive sensors on the asteroid would likely miss spotting that, however.

In their suits and units, Maddox and Meta sailed through space for the asteroid. Galyan kept an eye on them, and he also acted as a scout in ghost mode. The holoimage was five thousand kilometers ahead of the two. Galyan particularly scanned for missiles, tracking guns or anything badly unusual.

Together with Ludendorff, they had gone over the plan until each knew his or her part precisely. After they reached the far side of the asteroid and approached the hidden darter on foot, Galyan would enter the darter in ghost mode. The holoimage would rush into Becker and emit stunning blasts in order to render the telepath unconscious. At that point, Maddox and Meta should have preceded far and fast enough to enter the darter through explosive devices. Galyan would warn the three kidnapped crewmembers and they would use emergency procedures. That meant entering an emergency safety bubble so they had atmosphere to breathe when the air exited the darter.

Maddox wanted his kidnapped people back. He also wanted Becker in custody. Becker was his fault. Maddox had revived the damn telepath, thinking to use him.

I did successfully use Becker. My grandmother is alive, even though the Lord High Admiral and Stokes are dead. But if I don't return Becker soon...

Maddox knew that Admiral Haig and others in Star Watch would use that against him. They would either strip him of power or maybe cashier him from the service.

Maddox needed to capture Becker while the task force was here. That was strange, though, the endless waiting with the task force. Jellicoe should attack the Spacers or leave. Maybe Jellicoe should leave several drones behind to see what the enemy did once the task force departed.

In the helmet, Maddox shook his head.

Keeping eleven *Conqueror*-class battleships and their auxiliary vessels here was a waste of time and effort. What did General Mackinder really have up his sleeve? Didn't the spy chief want to be home in the middle of his web?

Inside the battlesuit as he sped toward the targeted asteroid, Maddox shrugged. He hadn't figured out Mackinder's reasoning yet, although he hadn't stopped trying.

A green light appeared to the left on his HUD. "We're getting closer," Maddox said through the short link. "We're ten thousand klicks from target."

"Sir," Galyan said from ahead, "I am not detecting anything suspicious. Should I go into the darter and stun Becker?"

"Not yet," Maddox said. "It's still going to take us a while to reach the darter."

"Should I dismantle the passive sensors then?" Galyan asked.

"Wait until we're just about on the surface."

"Yes, sir," Galyan said.

Time passed as the two commando maneuver units neared the asteroid. Maddox's intuitive sense did not pick up anything strange. That was a good sign, except he wore the silver headband with the humming box. He'd found the anti-telepathy box hindered his intuitive sense. That was interesting. Did it mean his intuitive sense was psionic or telepathic? Maddox had discovered in the past that he possessed slight telepathic powers, although not like Becker, not even close.

The asteroid seemed to grow larger as they approached. This space rock had a dark albedo and a gravelly surface.

"It's time to start braking," Maddox short linked to his wife.

Each commando maneuver unit rotated as its side jets emitted gas. Soon, the cold hydrogen particles expelled from the main thruster. Their velocity slowed until the two inched toward the surface.

Galyan went down and deactivated each of the passive sensors. When finished, he asked, "Should I go into the darter yet?"

"Soon," Maddox said. "We need to time this just right. Becker might have something like my intuitive sense. The less warning we give him the better."

"I can just stun him and repeatedly do so until you show up," Galyan said.

"No," Maddox said. "Becker's powers seemed to have increased. We'll time this so we do it together. That should be safer."

"Yes, sir," Galyan said.

Five minutes later, the two commando maneuver units were less than a kilometer from the asteroid's surface.

"Eject," Maddox said.

In his battlesuit, Maddox ejected from the commando maneuver unit. Meta ejected from hers. They both came down faster than seemed wise.

Maddox struck the surface first. He used exoskeleton power to try to absorb some of the force and then rolled. Meta did likewise.

In moments, Maddox was up and gliding to Meta's position.

"Are you all right?" he asked via tight link.

"I'm good," Meta said. "I don't even feel slightly jarred."

"Great," Maddox said. "Let's go."

They were both zero-G experts. They used a long gliding semi-leap to move across the surface, heading toward the other side and the crevice where the Darter *Tarrypin* hid. If they jumped too high, they would reach escape velocity and drift away. Thus, moving across the asteroid took expert gliding.

It was at that point, despite the headband, that Maddox's intuitive sense warned him things were *not* going to proceed as planned.

-45-

Inside the darter, Becker dreamed, and his dreams were normal for him. That meant they would have been strange and bizarre for anyone else. Then, in his dream, an imp stood on the arm of the throne where he sat.

"Someone is coming," the imp said.

"What?" Becker said in his dream to the imp.

"Someone is coming," the imp repeated.

The imp had huge, sharp teeth in a tiny red mouth. The imp was a devilish little creature with spiny, lumpish skin.

Suddenly, Becker realized the imp represented his id. That was how he saw his id as a devilish, monstrous creature. He needed to change his self-view.

"Who's coming?" Becker asked.

"You're asleep, you buffoon," the imp said. "You are asleep, modifying yourself. What's worse, you can't even get that right. Don't you understand that everything needs to be done slowly, carefully, with precision?"

Bigheaded Becker, surrounded by a bevy of waiting beauties on his throne—in his dream—looked at the grinning, vicious little creature standing on the arm of the throne. "You're not making sense. This isn't making sense. What do you mean?"

"It doesn't matter," the imp said. "Keep dreaming. Maddox is coming with Galyan and Meta. They are going to capture you and put you into stasis. I'm going to be nothing again, having to wait for another fortuitous moment. I wish my intellect were smarter than this. Why are you such an idiot?"

Becker was starting to get angry. How dare the little spiny creature with huge teeth talk to him like this.

"Becker," the imp said, "I'm going to try one more time. Unless you wake up, you can forget about having Honey and all the others doing your bidding. You'll do Star Watch's bidding, and you'll dance like a jester in some great court, the clown everyone is laughing at."

"Enough of this!" Becker shouted, beginning to get frightened. "Wake up!" He shouted at himself.

The image of a throne and imp with huge white teeth vanished. Becker felt himself stirring on a cot in the wardroom in the Darter *Tarrypin*. He groaned. That had been an evil dream, a stupid dream.

Becker froze because he realized it had also been a true dream. His mind felt sluggish and sore because it had been engaged in gigantic efforts modifying his body. He was freaking starving.

"Open your eyes," Becker whispered.

He opened his eyes. The blurry image of the wardroom told him he was awake. He looked down and saw covers over him. The body underneath was lumpish and bigger than he remembered.

Becker laughed victoriously.

This is awesome. I'll stun Maddox with my gargantuan excellence. I'll have the physique of a champion athlete. I'll stun Maddox's mind and beat him to a pulp with my fists.

Becker reached up, grabbed the blanket and whipped it off him. He looked down at his body with…with horror, disgust, and maybe amazement. He was bigger. He was at least seven and a half, maybe eight feet tall. It was hard to tell while lying down. His legs were huge twisted lumps of muscle and mass. His chest, like everything else, was huge. Everything was big, but he was deformed.

Becker twisted around, grabbed a hand mirror from the nightstand, and looked at himself. He resembled a massive, hunchbacked Quasimodo. His face was just as twisted and lumpy looking.

"I look like a freak," Becker said aloud. "I'm going to have to double my control over the girls, or they're going to blanch in horror at the sight of me."

Was he worse off than before? No. He must be strong, phenomenally strong by the looks of it.

Once more, Becker twisted around on the cot. He found that hard to do because he wasn't used to being so darn big like this. Oh, this was interesting. His neck was thick, corded with muscles. He should easily be able to hold up his big head.

"Oh yeah," Becker said. "This is what I wanted."

He'd been partly successful, although he looked like a freak, like a misshaped giant but he was massive. When he stood, his head almost bumped up against the ceiling. He barely ducked in time, or he might have knocked himself unconscious. As he took several steps, he found his movement ungainly, as one leg was shorter than the other one.

"Don't panic," Becker told himself. "I can fix this later."

Then he forgot everything as a surge of hunger almost caused him to swoon onto the cot. There was food. He used his mighty hands. The fingers were of different lengths. He had hairy knuckles, but they were big. He smashed the nightstand in a fit of strength and fury. He then continued to gobble down food and guzzle gallons of artificial milk.

As he assuaged his hunger and as his body strove to replenish all he'd used powering the pituitary gland, powering his brain's might, he realized Maddox, Galyan, and Meta were coming. He wasn't sure how he knew this, but now that his mind was no longer throbbing with pain, he used it to probe other parts of the darter.

The girls were at their stations, talking to each other, wondering if they should hammer on his hatch to tell him that the sensors had gone dead.

"Dead?" Becker said.

With his telepathic ability, Becker mentally flashed to the other side of the asteroid and observed the deactivated sensors. He searched and found two battle-suited humans gliding low over the surface. They were almost to the crevice where the darter was hidden. Becker peered inside one suit, finding Meta.

She was a stunning blonde. He mentally went to the other suit and recoiled.

Maddox knew it was him, too.

Damn Maddox.

Mentally snapping back, Becker returned his focus to his body and surveyed the chamber.

"They're coming. What should I do?"

Before he could decide, Becker sensed a holographic entity gliding into the darter.

That was Galyan. The holoimage would enter his body and blast it with numbing power.

How should he respond? Becker wasn't sure he had time to telekinetically shut off Galyan as he had before. Then he knew the answer.

With a bolt of telekinetic power, Becker blasted the booster out in space.

A second later, Galyan's holoimage disappeared, as it could no longer reach this far from *Victory*.

Becker concentrated as he sat on the side of the cot. *I need clothes. Naw. There aren't any clothes on board that fit me. Let them see me in all my glory and monstrous power.*

Becker no longer had to balance his huge head carefully. He could twist and move it fast. He might limp like a monster, but he could still cavort and dally with his three beautiful ladies. He would be the conqueror indeed, not just the weakling with the powerful brain. He possessed powerful attributes in every aspect, as a man should in this situation.

There was a twinge of conscience that tried to tell him this wasn't the right way to go about things.

You can shut up, conscience. You can go to hell.

As Becker sat on the side of the cot, he clutched his hands between his knees, and concentrated. In their battlesuits, Maddox and Meta worked down the rocky crevice, heading for the darter.

Let them come, Becker thought. *Let them come and find a giant surprise.*

-46-

In his space-proofed battlesuit, Maddox maneuvered down a rocky crevice. He could see the cloaked darter below because the cloak did not shield it from normal vision. Maddox peered through his helmet visor. Then something struck him as wrong about this.

Becker…Becker knows we're coming.

"Meta," Maddox said over the short link.

Unfortunately, communication between them had ceased. Maddox checked his suit comm by running a quick diagnostic. Something had disrupted it. Then, life support began to fail; a blinking red light on the HUD warned him of this.

Within the battlesuit, Maddox turned and surged upward in the crevice, leaping in the almost nonexistent gravity. He reached Meta's battlesuit and clanged his helmet against hers.

"Let's get out of here," Maddox shouted.

Because the solid metal of their helmets pressed together, Meta could hear his tinny voice inside hers.

"Go where?" she asked.

"Back into space to the fold fighter," Maddox shouted.

"I can't do that," Meta said. "My oxygen supply has just stopped. I only have minutes left. Our only hope is to go into the darter."

Maddox understood without a doubt that Becker was awake and had used his telekinetic abilities to wreak havoc on their suit equipment. Maddox agreed with Meta and started down to the darter with her anyway. If they were going to do this, they had to do it fast and violently.

Galyan appeared. "Sir, Becker knows you are coming."

Before Maddox could reply, Galyan disappeared just as abruptly.

Maddox didn't know it, but Galyan had appeared in *Victory* earlier. Keith had used the fold fighter to launch another booster. With the new booster, Galyan had reached Maddox. However, once again, Becker's telekinetic power had shredded the booster. Thus, Galyan was once again on *Victory* explaining the situation to Lieutenant Maker.

"What should we do? Galyan?" asked Keith. "If we go in guns blazing, we might kill the captain. Becker sounds dangerous."

"We are going to have to wait and see," Galyan said. He had run a fast analysis, finding their odds horrible if they acted.

"Can Becker capture Maddox?" Keith asked.

"That does seem unlikely," Galyan admitted. "We must wait and find out. Either Maddox will contact us, or Becker will."

"That's it?" Keith said. "That's your big plan?"

"We tried my big plan," Galyan said. "Becker foiled it once again. Now I think we have to wait and see what happens."

Maddox didn't know about the conversation. Instead, he and Meta neared the darter. When they were a mere hundred meters from it, all their suit systems broke down. Well, not quite all.

Maddox's suit servos partially worked. He scowled, as it felt as if someone knocked on his brain. He felt another knock. It almost seemed as if Becker was trying to communicate with him. Maddox listened, as it were, and realized Becker needed him to take off the headband or shut it off.

If you don't, I'll shut down your suits and you and your wife will suffocate.

Maddox exhaled sharply, hating the situation, thinking quickly. He didn't see any other options. Thus, Maddox did something he dearly did not want to. He shut off the box on his headband. At that moment, Becker's personality and telepathic force slammed against him.

"Well, well, well, Captain Maddox," Becker said in a mental rapport, "how the tables have turned."

"Get on with it," Maddox said tersely, using his thoughts to speak to Becker.

"I will allow your suits partial servo power. With that, you two will enter the airlock. I will not open the inner airlock until you manually climb out of your battlesuits and divest yourselves of any hand weapons."

"At that point, you could open the outer airlock and kill us through vacuum," Maddox said.

"I can kill you here, Captain. I am in control. I am Becker. The world and you will soon perceive the real me and tremble in awe."

"Let's make a deal, Becker."

"Oh, no, Captain, I made a deal with you once, and you were going back on it."

"No, if you're in my mind, you can see I wasn't going back on the deal."

"I can't read all your thoughts—" Becker abruptly quit projecting.

The revelation startled Maddox. His mind could block some of Becker's power. That was interesting news.

"Don't think your mind is going to help you," Becker said via mental projection. "I can control your wife and make her slit her throat in your presence. Is that what you want?"

"No," Maddox said. "But you would be most unwise to try such—"

"Please, Captain Maddox," Becker said, "don't threaten me, not even a little. I have the power to crush your lungs so you can't breathe. I'm in control even if you do have a different mentality than the others. There is something special about you."

In the helmet, Maddox grinned.

"Hey," Becker said telepathically, "let's all sit around a campfire and sing about how special Captain Maddox is. Would that make you feel better? Would that make you feel like a big man?"

"Don't work yourself up," Maddox said.

"I'll do whatever I want. I control the darter, and soon, I think I'm going to control *Victory*. Will you agree to my terms and board my ship?"

Maddox was about to point out that the darter was Star Watch property, actually Patrol property, to be specific, but he decided that wasn't the point.

"Let's get on with this," Maddox said. "We'll do as you say."

"I knew you'd see the light," Becker said smugly. "You may proceed."

The two battlesuits clumped to the darter, their suit weapon systems deactivated. The bulky battlesuits entered the open airlock, barely able to squeeze in. The outer lock slid shut.

Maddox and then Meta detached from the suits and climbed out in skin suits. Neither carried any hand weapons. Even like this, they were barely able to squeeze in here with the battlesuits.

"How are you feeling?" Maddox asked.

Meta gave him a blank look, as if unable to think or speak.

This was bad. Maddox shook his head. Becker might hold all the cards, but he was a physical weakling. One punch would be all Maddox needed to rectify the situation.

The inner hatch opened. Meta stumbled through, and Maddox walked through normally.

The three women of the darter greeted them. None pointed a blaster or any other weapon. They greeted them with pleasant, happy smiles and bright eyes.

"Welcome aboard the darter, Captain. You may refer to me as Honey. That is how Becker likes to refer of me."

Maddox nearly groaned. Honey, Becker called her Honey? Maddox expected Meta to scowl and maybe sigh. He looked at his wife. There was nothing in her eyes. She was a robot, pure and simple.

"Follow us, please," Honey said. "And Captain, don't try anything. Our master is far too powerful for you."

"Your master?" Maddox asked.

"Yes!" A deep voice boomed.

Maddox looked up and saw Becker. Was that Becker? How could it be?

A naked, misshapen, lumpy, hairy, grotesquely muscled giant stepped up. The man was seven and a half feet tall and massive. He would likely give a Merovingian a run for his money if they fought. But the non-symmetry to the giant startled Maddox.

"Becker?" he asked.

"Yes, it's me. Are you impressed yet?"

"What in the world happened to you?" Maddox said.

"I happened," Becker said. "Now, Captain, I believe you and I are going to have a battle of wills. I'm going to dominate you mentally, and then I'm going to do it physically. Then you are going to do exactly as I say. Do you understand?"

"Of course," Maddox said. "I see mentally that I'm not a match for you. Physically, forget about it. You look far too powerful to challenge."

"Don't try your rhetorical tricks on me, Maddox. I know your methods. I'm going to dominate you despite everything you try."

"If the feeling of being cowed is any indication," Maddox said, "I think of myself as already dominated by you."

"Girls and Meta, lay on the floor and don't move," Becker said.

Honey and the other two moved with alacrity, sprawling onto the floor face down. Meta seemed to resist for an instant, and then she too lay down.

That enraged Maddox, and he watched as the naked Becker advanced upon him. *All right, this is going to be the fight of my life.*

-47-

Maddox winced as a powerful telepathic bolt slammed against his mind and smothered his senses. He could barely see, although he heard Becker's unsymmetrical rush. Maddox twisted, using his instinctive sense, and ducked his head. He felt a rush of air. That must have been a massive fist going past his head. The next instant, a second fist connected with his gut. Maddox curled around it, felt himself hurled into the air with irresistible force and sailed back. He curled as he flew and thudded against a bulkhead with his back. Maddox groaned and dropped to the deck. Instead of snapping back his head and dashing it, his torso throbbed with pain as he lay there.

Becker laughed as if from a distance. But in the laughing with glee, he must have ceased the harsh telepathic projection.

As Maddox lay curled on the floor, his eyes focused. He saw the victorious behemoth of a man lumbering toward him.

"I'm going to knock your ass off, Maddox."

Maddox waited on the deck, pretending exhaustion and defeat. It wasn't hard. At the last minute, he shifted and slid, kicking out his feet. A huge ankle struck Maddox's left shin, nearly breaking it as pain radiated explosively.

The action tripped Becker so the monster man slammed face first against the deck and slid, ramming the top of his gargantuan head against a bulkhead.

Maddox rose with agony. The single punch from the behemoth of a telepath—Becker was inhumanly strong, stronger than any Merovingian Maddox had faced in the past.

Becker coughed, groaned and rolled over. His eyes raged with fury. "My head, you made me hit my head. Do you know what could have happened?" Becker curled his massive hands into fists as he sat up and glared at Maddox.

Maddox steeled himself for it. A telepathic bolt blasted against his mind, although it didn't knock him down. His eyes watered as pain throbbed in his head.

"You will obey me, Maddox," Becker howled.

Maddox strove to maintain his identity, to protect himself against the blast of fury smashing upon his ego.

Through what process did Maddox maintain his identity? Perhaps it was due to the spiritual stiffening when he'd consumed an Erill long ago. Perhaps it had more to do with the training he'd received from Balron the Traveler. It could have been a combination. Those processes helped his mind to flow *with* the battering assaults. Thus, instead of shattering as a normal, strong, and indomitable personality would have under the telepathic assault, Maddox's will shifted, turned, ducked, and wove.

"Why are you such a slippery devil?" Becker roared.

Maddox saw that Becker had risen to his feet and lumbered toward him, one long, ill-matched step at a time. The giant was naked, hairy and repulsive.

"Oh, you think I'm repulsive, do you?" Becker shouted.

Maddox hadn't said that aloud.

"You don't need to say it. I can see the thoughts in your brain, you arrogant New Man."

Maybe that was just the ticket for Maddox as anger surged in him at the epitaph. He climbed to his feet to face the monster man.

"Don't like being called a New Man, you freak, you half-breed. You know what I'm going to do to your wife? I'm going to make her mine in every possible way."

"You're a fool," Maddox said between gritted teeth.

"I'm the fool? I'm going to beat you raw, Maddox. You have no idea. The physical beating—maybe I'll literally twist you into a pretzel. You're done, half-breed."

Becker hurled a massive telepathic bolt.

This time, the rage, almost berserkergang of intensity in Maddox—the man had threated to rape Meta—fended off the blow.

Perhaps Maddox had inadvertently stumbled upon a method of deflecting the telepathic attacks. Though he was not, strictly speaking, a telepath, he had abilities that resembled the power. Though Maddox wasn't trained in the art, he was a slippery sort. He dodged and weaved against the dominating assaults that came at him. Maddox did that instead of resisting the assaults full bore. Instead of being like a man facing a bulldozer, he skipped around and never took the full brunt of what Becker did.

"This is ridiculous," Becker said. "Why don't you step up and fight like a man, half-breed?"

Maddox turned his head to the side and spat on the deck. He rubbed his hands together and took a combat stance as he faced Becker. It was too bad he didn't have his monofilament blade.

"But you don't have it," Becker taunted. "I made sure of that."

Becker shuffled near and swung a massive fist. Maddox dodged by moving inside instead of away or to the side. Maddox pumped his fists like pistons against Becker's gut. It was like hitting a hardwood tree. Becker thrust his shorter leg up. The knee barely caught Maddox, hurling him just the same. This time, Maddox didn't slam against a bulkhead, however. He rolled, and rolled back onto his feet, swaying. He ached all over from the few but heavy blows.

Maddox wiped his brow. There was no way he could beat Becker man to man like this.

"That's right," Becker said. "You finally understand. I'm your better mentally and physically."

"Not morally," Maddox said, striving to find some weakness in the new and improved Becker.

"Ah, morally," Becker sneered. "Don't you dare preach at me, half-breed. Don't tell me that I must do this or do that to be good. I am Becker. I never understood until this moment how size and strength changes a man's outlook. You thought yourself better than me in France Sector because I was physically pathetic. All that has changed forever. I have more power than you can conceive, and I..."

Sudden confusion filled Becker's face.

Maddox glanced around, first to see what confused the man. Maddox didn't see it. Then he searched for an equalizer. Ah. He spied a holstered blaster at Honey's side as she lay on the deck. Maddox slid toward her, hoping Becker wouldn't notice.

Becker's massive head whipped up. He'd been massaging the temples as his eyes squinted. There was a brief second of confusion. Then he pointed a huge forefinger at Maddox. "If you go for the blaster, I'll kill your wife with telekinetic power. I can telekinetically shatter her brain like that." He snapped grotesquely huge fingers.

Maddox stopped. He didn't know what to do. Could Becker really kill Meta that easily?

Becker shook his huge head. "Forget about the fight. There's something else going on out there." He made a vague gesture. "I've just become aware of it."

Maddox frowned. "I don't understand."

"I thought you had intuitive sense. Use it, you idiot, you half-breed mongrel."

Maddox scowled. Then he smoothed that out to a mere frown. This didn't feel like a ploy from the monster man. Might this be the opening he needed? Maddox bent his head, trying to employ the intuitive sense. To his surprise, he realized something was about to happen. It was a faint pulse, maybe why he hadn't recognized it yet. Still, he couldn't perceive how the threat would manifest itself.

"I'll tell you what it is," Becker said. "I finally see its outline. The stupid witches have gotten reinforcements." Becker cocked his head as if thinking. "The Seventh Assault Fleet of Leviathan is almost here." Becker swore an oath of disgust. "No, this is no good. This ruins everything I've planned." He peered at Maddox and it seemed as if wheels turned in his gargantuan mind. "All right, I'll tell you what. It's time to patch things up for the moment. I hate you, but I hate you less than I hate certain others. *Victory* can be useful to me. I'm going to let you go. If you're smart, you'll rush back to

Victory as fast as you can and get the hell out of here. An assault fleet of Leviathan is coming. I think they mean to destroy your puny task force."

"How can you know this?" Maddox asked, amazed and perplexed.

Becker raised a huge, haughty chin. "I sense them coming down a hyper-spatial tube." He laughed. "You have no idea of the magnification of my abilities. It's so astounding I'm still amazed myself at times. But that doesn't matter. Here's the thing. I'm letting you go, Maddox, but you owe me one."

Maddox ached all over, including his mind. He searched for duplicity in Becker's words and failed to find it. His intuitive sense told him the monster man was leveling with him. That meant—

"I'm taking my wife and the three ladies with me," Maddox said.

"No," Becker said sharply. "And if you keep arguing with me about this, I won't give you your wife. I'm keeping Honey and the other two, but I'm sparing you your life. Are you going to take it, Maddox, or are going to be an idiot about this?"

This was a hard decision. Maddox didn't want to abandon his three crewmembers, especially to this monster.

"I'm not a monster," Becker shouted. "I'm just a man who was granted abnormal powers and abilities. I was different and then people and aliens used me, turning me into what I am. I'm not going to mistreat the women. I swear that."

"Then give them back their identities," Maddox said.

Becker stared at Maddox, and incredibly, the monster man's features softened. "Maybe in time, I will, if I can fix myself. I have a feeling you and I will work together again soon." Becker nodded. "I have a feeling things are turning in a way neither you nor I would have expected."

"Why? What else is going on?"

"Go! Take your wife!" Becker's features scrunched before he looked up again. "There. I've granted Meta her normal identity again."

Maddox glanced at his wife.

Meta looked at him startled, scrambling off the floor. She stared at Becker, swayed back in surprise, and then turned away so she wouldn't view the naked brute.

"All right," Maddox said. If an assault fleet of Leviathan was really headed here, he needed to get back to *Victory* now. "I'm holding you responsible for these three. Remember Becker, I'm the one who came and got you out of stasis in Antarctica."

"Because you needed my help," Becker shouted.

"That's true, but no one else would have done what I did. And the new Lord High Admiral wanted to put you away in stasis afterward. I stood up for you because I'd given you my word. If you've really looked into my mind—"

"I know, I know, I know that already," Becker said. "Why do you think I'm letting you go? Now hurry! Time is running short. You may not make it anyway."

"All right," Maddox said, "we're going."

Then he and Meta hurried to the airlock and began to climb back into their battlesuits.

-48-

In the battlesuit that acted as a spacesuit, Maddox climbed up the crevice in the asteroid. Meta followed close behind in her battlesuit.

"What happened in there?" Meta said over the short link. It worked now. "Who was that monster?"

"Not yet," Maddox said. "Try not to think of anything but climbing."

"Why?"

"Meta, I know you trust me. This is critical."

"All right, I'll do as you ask."

They continued to climb.

Maddox had put the silver headband back on and turned on the buzzing box. He felt a little relief. He didn't know if Becker was watching or doing something else. Why hadn't the man wanted to come with him onto *Victory?* He would have guaranteed the man's safety. He would have demanded the three crewmembers back. Maybe that was the reason, the deal breaker. Did Becker think he had a better chance of staying alive and free down here on the asteroid? What had Becker called it again? Right, the Seventh Assault Fleet from Leviathan. That sounded ominous. That meant the inter-spiral-arm war was about to begin.

How did the mutant know so much? Where had Becker learned to mutate his body like that? It was incredible, and it was frightening.

Maddox knew that wasn't the important point right now. Getting back to *Victory* was.

The Spacers clearly had used other hidden nexuses to create other hyper-spatial tubes. There were more hidden nexuses in the Paran System than Maddox realized.

Eleven destroyed *Conqueror*-class battleships would be a good beginning for the enemy and a terrible one for Star Watch. How many ships from Leviathan would arrive here? Why and how had the cybers of Leviathan agreed to work with the Spacers in this way?

Maddox shook his head. He didn't know the answers. Thus, he concentrated on climbing as fast as he could. He also opened the comm link and tried to hail *Victory*. So far, it was no good.

What had happened to Galyan? Likely, Becker had neutralized Galyan. Yet, how had the telepath done that?

"*Victory, Victory*, this is Captain Maddox speaking. Can you hear me? Can anyone hear me?"

There was no response.

Finally, Maddox climbed out of the crevasse. He turned and helped Meta out. Then the two began to glide-jump across the rocky, dark surface of the asteroid. They needed to get to the other side.

Had this been a clever trick? Did Becker realize he couldn't defeat the captain of *Victory* and this was his way to seal his freedom?

No, Maddox didn't believe that. Becker had been winning. The man's mentality and physicality had been too gargantuan for Maddox to handle. Becker's insults—

Maddox cocked his head. It struck him then, the reason for all that, the insults. Becker was alone and friendless. The man was a nerd, if you will, who had gotten his life-long dream. Becker was the secret king who had attained the strength and intelligence he'd always wanted. Becker hadn't gotten good looks, though.

Maddox became more thoughtful.

If Becker could mold himself into a physical giant, perhaps he could perfect the process and turn himself handsome as well. Beautiful women already obeyed his dictates because they had to.

Maddox nodded.

Becker was an interesting study, but he was alone, possibly uncertain behind all that bravado. Maddox grunted. He couldn't worry about that. Events were coalescing, finally, after the weird beginnings.

"Captain Maddox, can you hear me?"

"Yes, Galyan, I hear you. Where have you been?"

"Becker has been using telekinetic bolts to destroy my boosters. We've placed another one in position. Can you see me?"

Maddox looked up. There was Galyan in holographic form gliding beside him.

"Listen," Maddox said. "There are assault ships of Leviathan heading into the Paran System. They might already be here. You need to bring Keith and the fold fighter near the asteroid so Meta and I can get back to *Victory* as fast as possible."

"What about the darter and the crewmembers Becker kidnapped?" Galyan asked.

"They're not our priority at the moment."

"Shall I check on Becker?"

"No," Maddox said. "I've made a deal and I plan to live up to it."

"Sir?" Galyan said.

"Something good yet remains in Becker. I—it could be an intuitive sense I felt as we fought."

"You were in the darter, sir?" Galyan said.

"I was," Maddox said. "Becker... I'll explain later. Now do what I ordered."

"I will, sir. I will be gone for just a moment."

Maddox and Meta continued to glide across the stony surface of the asteroid.

"Keith will be here in a second," Galyan said, reappearing beside Maddox.

"Good," Maddox said. "Meta, are you ready?"

"For what?" Meta asked.

"To leap for the fold fighter," Maddox said, as if she should have known.

A few seconds later, the fold fighter appeared several kilometers above the surface.

"Aim for it," Maddox said.

He gathered exoskeleton power and leaped. Meta leapt after him. The two sailed through the void. Keith expertly maneuvered the fold fighter, catching them, as it were, with the open hatch and a steel mesh net. The steel mesh was so they wouldn't smash through the fighter with their velocity and wreck everything.

In moments, both Maddox and Meta were in the tin can, the hatch shut, and Keith folding directly into a hangar bay on *Victory*.

Maddox wanted to get onto the bridge as fast as possible. He also needed to alert General Mackinder and Admiral Jellicoe as fast as he could. The task force had to retreat before being annihilated by an overwhelming assault fleet.

-49-

Maddox sprinted down the corridors from the hangar bay, and he reached the bridge on *Victory*. He dropped with a thud into the captain's chair.

"Patch me through to Admiral Jellicoe."

As Maddox waited for the comm officer to reach Jellicoe, he caught his breath. Maddox wouldn't normally have been winded from such a sprint, but Becker's hammer blows, both mental and physical, had weakened his recuperative powers for the moment.

Maddox rubbed his forehead. His head ached. Would a pill help, or might it be the wrong thing to take? He asked for some water. Soon, an ensign gave him a cup. He gulped the water down.

"Where's Admiral Jellicoe? Why isn't he on the screen yet?"

"I don't know, sir," the comm officer said. "I've tried all the channels."

Maddox refrained from shouting, "Try harder." His overt emotions surprised him. Perhaps that, too, was a result of his fight with Becker. Maddox breathed deeply once, twice, three times, and the calming effect showed on his face and then his shoulders.

"Sir," the comm officer said, "I have Admiral Jellicoe. I can put him on the main screen if you like."

Maddox indicated with a hand gesture for her to do so.

On the main screen, bluff Jellicoe turned around to face Maddox. "What is so urgent?"

"Sir," Maddox said, "I've just received information that a Leviathan assault fleet is about to enter the Paran System."

It took Jellicoe a moment. "You mean this star system?"

"Yes, sir."

"A Leviathan assault fleet, you're saying?"

"Yes, sir."

"How many ships is that?"

"I don't know," Maddox said, "but I suggest the task force leaves immediately."

"Leave? We need to smash the assault vessels as they come out of jump."

"They're heading here through a hyper-spatial tube," Maddox said.

"What? Where is this exit?"

"I'm not sure, somewhere in the star system."

"You don't know," Jellicoe said. "If you don't know, how can you possibly know they're coming? And can you know they're approaching through a hyper-spatial tube?"

"Like I said, sir—it's secret intelligence. Or did I mention that?"

"I see," Jellicoe said. "I suppose you're referring to your vaunted intuitive sense."

"No, sir. It was more direct."

"Well, spill it, man. I'm the commander of the task force, the expedition. I have a right to know how you know this."

That was a reasonable point. "I spoke with Becker, sir. He sensed the assault fleet coming."

"Becker," Jellicoe said. "You know where that telepathic bastard is, do you? Did you launch an antimatter missile at him and take care of the problem?"

"No, we made a deal."

Jellicoe raised his eyebrows, moved his jaw from side to side, and then glared balefully at Maddox. The first words he was going to speak—Jellicoe obviously hesitated as if he reconsidered.

"Now, Captain," Jellicoe said in a quieter tone, "do you think this is true information?"

"I do, sir."

"You don't think Becker told you this cockamamie tale to throw us off his scent?"

"I absolutely do not, sir."

"And you have reason to believe Becker would tell us the truth?" Jellicoe asked.

"Yes, sir," Maddox said.

Cunning entered the admiral's eyes. "Do you stake your reputation in Star Watch on this?"

"Admiral," Maddox said, "I've given you the information. I certainly plan to take *Victory* elsewhere to survive the enemy's onrush."

"No sir," Jellicoe said, with his features hardening. He stood a moment later. "You will do no such thing. You are part of this task force. If you flee what you perceive as the face of the enemy, that will be abject cowardice."

"Sir," Maddox said, "I suspect the assault fleet of Leviathan, the Seventh Assault Fleet, to be precise, may be too powerful for us to deal with alone out here."

"You've dealt with a Leviathan warship on your own in the past. We can do that with the task force."

"Possibly," Maddox said.

"What do you mean 'possibly'?" Jellicoe said.

Maddox rubbed his forehead. For some reason, he couldn't remember the situation the admiral referred to. "Sir, that's not germane—"

"The hell it's not," Jellicoe shouted, interrupting. "You just informed me an assault fleet of Leviathan is coming, and you wish to hightail it as fast as you can. Is your survival that important to you, Captain? That you would dare to show cowardice in the face of the enemy?"

It was funny, but Maddox felt his face redden as Jellicoe spoke to him this way. It could have been due to the mental and physical assaults earlier on the darter. The admiral was getting under his skin. That was not normal Maddox. He took a calming breath and forced himself to smile.

"What do you find so amusing, Captain?"

"Sir," Maddox said, gesturing with his hand, "this is amusing. You and I are amusing. I suggest we work together.

There are Spacers here, and now Leviathan is coming. I'm already heading toward your main concentration."

"I don't have a main concentration at the moment," Jellicoe said. "The ships are spread out."

"Then I suggest, sir, you get them together as fast as you can into a fighting formation. I suggest we move them as quickly as we can to the Barnard's Star hyper-spatial tube opening."

Jellicoe shifted what seemed uncomfortably on his chair. "Now see here, Captain, I am in command." There was a pause as Jellicoe turned the other way. He seemed to be listening intensely. Abruptly, Jellicoe turned and stared at Maddox. "You bastard. You half-breed traitor. Massive ships have come through, an incredible number of them. They're already heading our way. Why didn't you warn us sooner?"

"Sir," Maddox said, "may I suggest a precipitous withdrawal so we can reform in time at the Barnard's Star System."

"No, no. I must gather the rest of the task force. Go to the Barnard's Star tube area—that's the right idea. Await the rest of the task force. We may have to fight to give the rest of the ships time to withdraw to Barnard's Star."

It was obvious that Jellicoe was flabbergasted and maybe bewildered by the sudden appearance and size of the Leviathan assault fleet.

Maddox turned to Andros. "Can you see the enemy ships?"

"Sir," Andros said, "I was going to tell you, I've spotted warships with thirteen diameter hulls. They're heading fast toward the Barnard's Star entrance area."

"Damn it," Maddox said. He turned, and he would have said a parting word to Jellicoe, but the admiral had already cut the communications.

Maddox swiveled around to peer again at Andros. This was bad. This was very bad.

-50-

It appeared to Senior Dax that there had been a change of plans. Venna and Mu had originally said they would not remain aboard the flagship of the Seventh Assault Fleet, the SHL *Behemoth*. However, they stayed, even as the saucer ship remained in the *Behemoth's* hangar bay.

Venna, Mu and Dax presently stood on the dais with War Master Vane. The War Master gave one command after another to his battalion of assistants on the gargantuan bridge. From the nerve center, orders went out to the fifty maulers of the Seventh Assault Fleet. The ships had exited the hyper-spatial tube from the Zakym System and maneuvered now in the debris-filled Paran System.

The monstrous, thirteen-diameter warships cruised through the gases and debris fields, and past planetary rubble and asteroids. Pressor beams from the maulers shoved aside much of the extraneous mass, doing so brutally, efficiently, and perhaps even contemptuously.

Dax swelled with pride at this example of Leviathan might. Even though he wished to escape—

"There is no escape," Mu whispered in his ear from behind.

That told Dax Mu still read his thoughts.

"Yes, I am still reading your thoughts," she said.

Dax sighed. Even though it seemed useless—

"It is," Mu said.

Dax shook his head and began to concentrate on geometric properties, ideals, and algebraic equations. He computed them with his biological brain alone, using no computer enhancements that were his by right due to the additions throughout his years of service.

Dax was only half-aware of the activities on the bridge, although he realized the mighty Seventh Assault Fleet didn't wait for Spacer reinforcements. Perhaps that was Venna's wish and instruction. Dax couldn't remember, nor did he try to delve into it as he worked through one equation after another.

"You will head directly to the Barnard's Star entrance area," Venna told Vane. "It is a hyper-spatial tube entrance."

"I'm aware of what it is," Vane said curtly.

Venna and Mu exchanged startled glances.

Dax noticed and detected the worry there. Could the joy of combat, the joy of commanding the Seventh Assault Fleet as it headed for battle have overridden some of Venna or Mu's commands?

"I doubt it," Mu said, "but that is something worth considering."

Dax noticed Mu whispering to Venna afterward. Venna concentrated, looking even more thoughtful than before. They whispered again. Dax wondered if Venna was suggesting to Mu that they take the War Master down into the ready room under the dais.

Dax doubted that Vane would agree at this point.

Vane continued to snap out orders and listen to incoming information about the enemy.

"We have moved so fast that the Star Watch plebs have spread out in confusion," Vane said in a grim voice that still contained a sense of joy. "This is marvelous. The puny Star Watch ships and their stupid officers should have been ready for us. I have surprised them with my strategic and tactical excellence. Great Leviathan was correct in ordering me to start the invasion. I will sweep aside these pathetic ships. They shall witness before their annihilation the martial glory and might of Leviathan."

"Sir," a cyber officer said, interrupting the tirade, "the enemy ships are fleeing with haste to the hyper-spatial region."

"Let them run; see the good it will do them," Vane sneered.

"We can't let the enemy ships reach the hyper-spatial tube to Barnard's Star," Venna said. "They'll escape."

Vane turned to her as his cyber eyes burned with emotion. Something else seemed to sweep over the War Master.

Dax noticed that Mu concentrated, with her fists clenched. Mu also peered fixedly at War Master Vane.

"Yes, of course, Venna," Vane said. "That is a good point, but," he held up a cyber finger, "not to worry. As I have said before, I have a secret weapon. Those of Star Watch will find that they can run, but they cannot escape. Do you know what I mean, Great Venna?"

The hag shook her head.

"Then please observe and watch what happens," Vane said.

That aroused Dax's interest so he faltered in his recitation of mathematical equations. He heard Mu laugh. Dax restarted once again, hiding—or trying to hide his thinking—behind the wall of mathematical formulas.

At the same time, on several bridge screens, seven massive maulers came within heavy laser range of a *Conqueror*-class battleship. The enemy warship was accelerating away.

"Fire," Vane said. "Let them see the uselessness of resisting us or trying to escape."

Heavy lasers speared from the seven maulers and struck the electromagnetic shield of the *Conqueror*-class battleship. Dax did not know the battleship's specific name. The seven hellish lasers struck, burning against the shield.

"I'm astounded at this," Vane said a second later. "The shield should have fallen, but it is only cherry red so far. Continue firing."

Dax shook his head, astounded as well. The *Conqueror*-class battleship was a marvel of technological ingenuity. How had Star Watch done that? The wattage from the heavy lasers, powered by incredibly huge engines, should have already collapsed the enemy shield. Instead, the shield only now began to turn brown and black in the center.

"Soon," Vane said, "soon the lasers will breach it."

A disruptor beam emitted from the battleship. It struck the lead mauler's shield, hardly doing a thing yet.

Then the lasers from the seven maulers burned through the electromagnetic shield and drilled into the heavy armored hull. The hull didn't last long. The beams drilled into the guts of the fleeing vessel. A titanic explosion occurred, blowing half of the battleship apart. The rest drifted as junk.

"A kill," Vane said. "That was a glorious kill."

"How did they withstand your laser beams for so long?" Mu asked.

"I don't know," Vane said as he looked at Mu. "It is a mystery, one that I'm not happy about. If we had met a hundred such ships, bah," he said, "but we have not. Onward, onward," he roared.

It was interesting to Dax that a cyber War Master could be so emotional, for want of a better term. It seemed as if Vane exuded emotion. That struck Dax as odd, maybe even bizarre, and yet as he thought about it, maybe there was a function to it that. In battle, emotion might be more useful than strictly logical and coldly emotionless decisions.

"That is an interesting thought," Mu said. "I shall have to consider it."

Dax winced inwardly. Then he strove not to think about anything. He just observed. He was going to watch and that was it.

"Good luck with that," Mu whispered in his ear.

Dax forced himself to maintain calm.

All the while, the Seventh Assault Fleet bore remorselessly through the junk of the Paran System. The fifty maulers hunted for Star Watch vessels before said vessels reached the vicinity of the hyper-spatial tube entrance to the Barnard's Star System.

-51-

Maddox was sickened watching a *Conqueror*-class battleship explode. He shook his head. Why hadn't the captain used planetary rubble, asteroids, and debris to hide and maneuver his way to the hyper-spatial tube area? It didn't make sense.

Likely, that was a Patrol thought, to use every resource. Instead, *Conqueror*-class battleship captains were usually smash-'em kind of individuals. Was that due to bad training or arrogance that filtered down due to the heavy metal components that made their shields and disruptor cannons so powerful?

Maddox shook his head. He didn't know the answer.

Andros had counted fifty enemy superships, fifty. The assembled tonnage was astonishing.

Galyan had learned through intercepting communications between enemy ships that they were called maulers.

That sounded right. The mighty assault vessels would maul the task force if Jellicoe were stupid enough to stay and fight. So far, no Spacer ships were in evidence.

Why would they bother? Maddox thought. He wouldn't if he had an ally such as that.

Maddox wondered if the Spacers were surprised by the might of the assault fleet. How many assault fleets did Leviathan possess, or was this the full invasion force? If that were true, the inter-spiral-arm war would be a near-run thing. Maddox could envision defeating this fleet if all the conditions were right. Star Watch was going to need every battleship, every missile-ship, everything Star Watch had to face these mighty engines of destruction. Leviathan was a powerful empire. This fleet proved it.

"Sir," Keith said, "we've almost reached the hyper-spatial tube area where the opening will be when it appears."

Maddox turned to look up at his wife, Meta, who was at the communications station. "Patch me through to Admiral Jellicoe."

"Yes, sir," Meta said, turning to her board.

A minute later, Jellicoe appeared on the main screen.

"Damn," Jellicoe said, "those are massive vessels. They've already destroyed three battleships, but the rest are gathering."

"Tell your captains to use the system's debris," Maddox said. "They are needlessly exposing themselves."

Jellicoe glared at him. "Those three were leading the enemy away. Do you understand? They were buying the rest of us time to assemble."

With sudden insight, Maddox understood the sacrifice of the battleship captains. He mentally asked them for forgiveness, though they were dead and could no longer give it. They had sacrificed themselves to buy the rest of the task force time to escape.

Maddox shook his head.

"What?" Jellicoe said. "What do you have to say? You think you could have done better?"

"They fought admirably, sir. What are your orders?"

"That's more like it." Jellicoe became pensive. "You may have been right initially, although it pains me to say it. We must get the hell out of this star system."

"I think that's wise, sir."

"Right. Get ready to leave. Jellicoe out."

Victory and others headed for the location. They had three minutes to get this done. Would the enemy's assault fleet come down the hyper-spatial tube after them? That would be good because that would give the battleships a chance to hit the maulers when the cyber crews were in the grip of jump lag.

That might be the best thing they could hope for. Hit the enemy hard when they came through and then flee like mad to

Earth. They would give up Barnard's Star in order to consolidate with the rest of Star Watch.

"Professor," Maddox said into an armrest comm.

"Sir," Ludendorff said.

"Go to the Long-Range Builder Comm room and send a message to Admiral Haig for me?"

"Begging your pardon," Ludendorff said, "but I've already tried that."

"What do you mean 'tried'? The Builder comm isn't working?"

"Something is jamming the Builder comm," Ludendorff said.

"What?" Maddox said. "I didn't think that was possible."

"Neither did I," Ludendorff said. "Apparently, Leviathan or hidden Spacers have found a method."

That wasn't good. "Okay," Maddox said, "see if you can find a way to use it anyway."

"I will," Ludendorff said.

Maddox looked up at the main screen. The task force ships were ready. Why hasn't Jellicoe ordered the hyper-spatial tube opened? "Galyan, check on the reason why Jellicoe is waiting to leave?"

Galyan vanished from the bridge and reappeared soon. "Sir, Jellicoe has people working on it, and they are doing all the right things, but the hyper-spatial tube isn't opening."

Maddox frowned for just a moment. Then he put two and two together. In this instance, it was one and one. The Long-Range Builder Comm device wasn't working. The hyper-spatial tube for the one-way nexus wasn't opening either. Could someone be jamming both? They were both Builder artifacts. What did that mean?

Maddox recalled that Leviathan worshipped the Builders just as the Spacers did. That must be the connection between the two groups.

Maddox swiveled his seat and pointed at Meta. "Patch me through to Admiral Jellicoe."

Meta tried, tried again and said, "He's not answering, sir."

"Keep at it. Tell him this is a double emergency."

"Double emergency?" Meta asked.

"Never mind," Maddox said. "Just get him."

Soon Jellicoe appeared on the main screen.

"Sir," Maddox said, "we must flee through velocity or use star-drive jumps. The hyper-spatial tube isn't going to work."

"How can you possibly know that?" Jellicoe said.

"Because it isn't working, and the Long-Range Builder Comm device isn't working, either."

"Are you suggesting the enemy has a way of jamming that?"

"Yes," Maddox said. "That is exactly what I'm suggesting. In order to save the task force, we have to run or use our star-drive jumps."

"Use yours," Jellicoe said. "Use it right now. I want to know if it works or not."

"Can you give me coordinates to jump to, sir?"

"Just jump, damn it," Jellicoe shouted. "Jump and find out!"

The connection cut.

Maddox turned to Keith and pointed at him. "You heard the man. Do it."

Keith put in coordinates, pressed the switch. Nothing happened. Keith swiveled around in shock.

"Sir, the star-drive jump—"

"Isn't working?" Maddox said, interrupting.

"No, sir," Keith said.

"This is bad." Maddox frowned. He shouldn't have said that aloud. He shrugged and swiveled the chair to Galyan. "Go directly to Admiral Jellicoe's flagship and tell him the jump isn't working."

"Are you absolutely sure it isn't working?" Galyan said.

"I have no time for these kinds of debates. Go."

Galyan disappeared before Maddox said another word. Seconds passed, and Galyan reappeared.

"Sir, none of the other ships were able to jump either."

"So," Maddox said, with a curling knot of something that might have been akin to fear, "we have no way to leave, and we have fifty massive maulers bearing down on us."

"It is as bad as you said a moment ago," Galyan replied.

Maddox studied the little holoimage. "Galyan, I have one more journey for you."

"Sir," Galyan said.

"Go to Admiral Jellicoe and ask him, what are our battle orders?"

-52-

Becker knew of the strange jump and hyper-spatial tube interdiction before Maddox or any of the others. Becker had been concentrating as he sat in the command chair of the darter. His three lovelies piloted and watched the sensors.

The cloaked darter maneuvered slowly and with discretion through the Paran System, having left the crevice of the asteroid.

With his new mental energies, Becker added to the cloak, disguising the darter. If a sensor or teleoptic should peer at it, the small vessel would appear to be planetary rubble.

The effort strained Becker. He was tired, munching on snacks to assuage his constant hunger.

For the sake of the ladies, he wore a kilt, a huge beach towel wrapped around his waist. Naked, he'd seemed too barbaric. With his massive, ungainly chest and misshapen arms, hands, lumpy head, he looked like a monstrosity.

Fortunately, the girls didn't see that. They saw their Becker. They smiled every time their eyes met. Once, however, one of them showed a twitch on her cheek.

Becker decided not to worry about it or try to fix whatever caused that. His mentality was engaged keeping the darter hidden.

Becker had been pondering what it meant for Leviathan to have sent such a destructive assault fleet. Surely, there were more invasion fleets.

Becker dimly sensed Venna and Mu, though he didn't seek to sense them more closely. He didn't want them to sense him in turn. Especially Venna had powers he didn't fully understand. He did understand the emanations of Ector and he understood that Venna's changes were more monstrous than his.

The Aetharians from Ector—Becker shuddered with revulsion. If the Aetharians were released from their ancient captivity—

He shook his massive head, deciding not to worry about the trapped Aetharians now. He needed to get the heck out of the Paran System, but the question was how.

He'd tried to activate through telekinesis an ancient one-way nexus. That hadn't worked. Then he'd sensed an emanation and traced it to the maulers. The assault vessels had some kind of inhibitor that blocked star-drive jumps, folds, and hyper-spatial tube opening creations. Leviathan had locked everybody here.

That was terrifying on the face of it. That meant Leviathan would obliterate the puny Star Watch ships, at least puny in comparison to the maulers.

Becker made his decision as the darter picked up speed, heading for *Victory*. If any of these bastards could get out of this, it would be Maddox. Even so, Maddox would need help against the combined forces working against him.

As the Star Watch task force gathered and assumed a battle formation, as the maulers from the Seventh Assault Fleet roared into position, shoving aside debris and rubble—time was a premium.

Becker couldn't jump or fold to *Victory*. Thus, he ordered his ladies to increase the darter's velocity.

The darter that looked like a planetary chunk increased speed, heading for *Victory*, trying to beat those of Leviathan.

Becker sat hunched, more like crammed, into the command chair of the Darter *Tarrypin*. His girls worked hard, and they were good pilots and sensor operators.

Becker's mentality and decisions partly came from the knowledge he'd gained from the rat thing of Ector that had tried to lodge in his brain. He'd also gained insight from the player that knew how to deal with women.

Becker now took a philosophical attitude and a what-the-hell thinking. He was going to make it or die in style, come what may. He wasn't going to twist reality, lying to himself, to make things into what he wanted as the secret gamma king. No. He was going to stare reality in the eye and see what was what, accept it, and see if there was a way to use that.

All the while, the darter maneuvered its way closer to *Victory*.

Then a sensor operator on one of the maulers—Becker reached out telepathically and switched a point in the cyber brain so the operator fell down dead. Becker also scrambled what had been on the sensor board over there.

The monster man nearly collapsed from the effort of that. He wondered if he should take stimulants, but decided that was a bad idea. He needed to deal with what was and not fudge a thing even a little.

As the massive maulers maneuvered into position, and as the puny task force of Star Watch waited as if they would give battle, the Darter *Tarrypin* glided to *Victory*.

Galyan did not appear, no communications opened, but one of the hangar bay hatches on the double-oval starship opened. The darter slid into *Victory's* hangar bay. The hatch shut, and the darter landed on the deck.

Becker folded forward on his chair. Near exhaustion and mental anguish meant that Becker nearly swooned. Instead, he found Honey at his side, giving him a cup of black coffee.

He gulped it so scalding liquid burned his throat. No matter, he was Becker. He had performed prodigies and now, now—

"I need to wait for precisely the right moment," he said.

"Yes, Becker," Honey said.

"Do you trust me?"

"I do," Honey said.

A strange feeling overcame Becker. He wished Honey truly loved him on her own merit and not because he forced her to love him. It was a strange feeling for Becker, and he wondered if it had anything to do with the player from Earth whose intellect he'd looted. Becker shook his head, not in a negative, but in resignation, knowing that now he needed to wait in order to do this right and survive the horrible cybers.

-53-

Senior Dax leaned against the dais rail, watching one of the larger bridge screens as the giant maulers maneuvered into position amongst the stellar junk.

War Master Vane continued to issue commands. Venna and Mu seemed content to observe the situation as they remained on the dais with him. They could afford that, as everything was going Leviathan's way, if Leviathan truly wished to unleash its greatest assault fleet by itself.

Dax knew the last part wasn't the case. Enigmach and the other Grand Strategists had developed a precise plan that would submerge Star Watch and the Commonwealth in an avalanche invasion with no place to turn or run. This was a piecemeal assault, a single attack. It should work here in the Paran System. But if even one Star Watch vessel managed to escape to warn the rest that Leviathan had this inhibitor…

Dax didn't shake his head. He was too absorbed with his mathematical formulas and his precarious place with Venna and Mu. They had obviously used him. Even if he escaped—

Dax closed his eyes, refusing to consider what he could tell Enigmach that might absolve him of this blunder. Instead, he continued his obfuscation strategy against the two witches. He had become a cog in Venna's greater plan. Was this attack Venna's entire game? She must have a greater objective than the destruction of the Star Watch task force. Was it correct to think of her as a Spacer? Venna had been a Spacer spy. With the Phantasma Synth Crystal shards embedded in her, she might have transformed into something else.

Of course, she's something else.

Dax was sure he was onto something. If Venna wasn't a Spacer representative—what was she and what was her objective? Should he attempt to discover her goal, especially given his severe limitations here?

Surprisingly, but thankfully, Mu didn't turn to taunt him. The Spacer was absorbed in her duties, which seemed to be keeping a close eye on Vane. The War Master had become ecstatic as the maulers readied for battle.

The front rank of maulers, arranged in a three-dimensional formation, consisted of thirty assault vessels. They were like a wall heading at the Star Watch warships. Behind the wall followed the other twenty maulers.

Dax wasn't sure why all fifty didn't move as a wall against the task force. He was sure there was some subtle military reason.

Dax switched views, looking at a different screen. The Star Watch vessels had formed a short, squat cone. If Dax was correct, that had originally been a New Men Fleet Formation. Might Star Watch have appropriated the formation for their ships? Given what he witnessed, the answer was yes.

Space battles were typically a matter of mass and energy projection. The side that could bring a greater mass, more firepower and hit at once would likely win. There were technological considerations as well. If one side seriously outperformed the other technologically, numbers didn't necessarily matter.

The *Conqueror*-class battleships had proven tough nuts while alone. Would it make a difference now that they had all formed in an abbreviated fighting cone?

Eight battleships and *Victory* formed the Star Watch cone. Some destroyers flanked the cone, but stayed rearward of it. The destroyers lacked the heft and firepower to be effective in such a contest.

As the maulers readied to fire their massed lasers, a combined cone beam made up of the nine disruptor cannons hit the nearest Leviathan assault vessel.

Beam for beam, the disruptors were more powerful than the mighty mauler lasers. The lasers used intense heat to do their damage. The disruptors disrupted the molecular cohesion of a target.

Even though the maulers were massive compared to the battleships and the mauler engines were a factor larger at least, the type of beam made a critical difference. So even though the maulers should easily be able to generate more energy and thus more destructive force, the opposite was the case.

In this, Star Watch possessed the technological edge. It would also seem that mass for mass, or pound for pound, the Star Watch electromagnetic shields were more powerful as well. However, comparing the mass of the two sides was laughable. The gross preponderance was on Leviathan's side.

Even so, the massed cone disruptor beam blew down a mauler shield and bored into the iridium-Z hull plating. That hull plating was tough and thick, but under the annihilating force of the combined disruptor beam, it didn't stand a chance.

The massed disruptor beam bored a huge hole in the hull plating and smashed within. Yes, the mauler was much bigger and roomier than a Star Watch battleship. But in this case, that didn't make much difference. The massed disruptor beam blew down one bulkhead after another. It devoured coils, cybers, waste disposal units and huge generators.

An incredible two and a half minutes after the breach, the mauler exploded in a fury of destruction. That blew mass and energy at nearby maulers, but nothing got through the heavy shields of the other warships.

"Damn these ants," Vane said on the dais. "They destroyed one of my maulers. I wasn't expecting that."

Vane glanced at Venna. "I apologize, lady."

"There is no need," Venna said. "Destroy the task force. That is the thing."

"Great Leviathan abhors unnecessary losses," Vane said.

"These losses aren't unnecessary," Venna replied. "Destroy the task force, but more importantly annihilate the double-oval starship with them."

Dax found that interesting. Clearly, Venna did not care for Captain Maddox.

Mu glanced sharply at Dax and then at Venna.

Dax frowned, not understanding the significance of that, but realizing it had been important.

The battleship cone targeted a different mauler.

Vane shook his narrow head. He spun around and shouted orders to his battalion of bridge crew. They must have translated that to the various mauler commanders.

Groups of maulers began to target individual battleships in the front rank of the cone. There were five such battleships in the front, with nine of the giant maulers targeted on one apiece.

That was an uneven contest. The technical superiority of the Star Watch vessels didn't matter because the mass was simply too much against them.

Vane shouted for confirmations.

Replies reached him.

The War Master turned to Venna. "In less than a minute these battleships will explode. Then the contest will no longer be in doubt."

"Has it ever been in doubt?" Venna asked.

Vane scowled. "Arrogance during battle is an unwise procedure, lady. Certainly, I expect to win. I have brought the most to this fight, a prerequisite for victory. But you never know what an enemy task force might possess in terms of alien weaponry. I am not seeing anything unusual. Thus, Great Venna, I implore you to be ready for an uncompromising victory."

Dax wasn't sure, but it seemed that Venna might have rolled her eyes at the War Master's vainglorious speech.

All the while, the intense heavy lasers from the maulers struck the opposing shields. Those shields had turned brown already. Soon, they would be black and the battle would be halfway to an amazing victory for Leviathan.

-54-

Maddox was hunched forward on the captain's chair, his right hand clenched into a fist.

Victory was part of the task force's cone of battle. The antimatter engines hummed at nearly full power, the deck vibrating from this. The ancient Adok starship added its disruptor cannon to the massed fire of the cone. That cone was under Admiral Jellicoe's command, who gave orders every twenty to thirty seconds.

Victory, like the battleships, was in the process of burning out its engines and cannon. This was a form of hotshot: creating a more powerful beam than ordinary. The process burned out components and other parts in order to fire hottest for a short time.

Maddox silently agreed with Jellicoe's idea. The task force was doomed. Therefore, they should take down as many enemy vessels as possible. They had to buy their side kills, or the enemy was going to end-run Star Watch.

The second mauler exploded—the second enemy death.

Keith shouted savagely from the helm.

Maddox smiled coolly even though he was upset that he'd brought Jewel and Meta along this mission. His daughter and wife would die with the rest. Maddox shook his head. He did his job so his family could live. He was willing to sacrifice himself if he knew that helped protect them. The fact that he was taking them down with him —

Maddox growled low in his throat. The thought embittered him.

"They are almost there, sir," Galyan said, not specifying what 'they' referred to.

"Good job," Maddox said in a hoarse voice.

"If one must die, sir," Galyan said. "Is it not best to die in the company of your friends?"

Maddox found he couldn't reply verbally. Thus, he nodded.

"What is wrong, Captain?" Galyan asked.

"Wrong?" asked Maddox, his eyes blazing. "My daughter is with us."

"Oh," Galyan said. "I failed to recall that. I am sorry to have been so insensitive, sir."

"It's not your fault, Galyan. It's mine."

"It is too bad you cannot pull one of your magical rabbits out of your hat and save the day."

Maddox eyed the holoimage. "The battle isn't over yet."

"That is true but next to irrelevant."

"How much longer?" asked Maddox.

Galyan's eyelids flickered. "Eighteen seconds, sir."

Maddox bared his teeth in a savage grin. In tense silence, he waited for the seconds to pass.

Then, on the far side of the mauler fleet, massed antimatter missiles appeared near enemy vessels.

Galyan had set up a holographic projection to hide what had been drifting antimatter missiles. Those missiles had been launched some time ago in anticipation of this. They had used a dense gas cloud to hide their main thrust to build up the needed velocity. Once the antimatter missiles left the cloud, they no longer spewed exhaust tails from thrust.

Earlier, it had been Maddox's idea. For once, Jellicoe hadn't bucked him. In truth, it was a genius move about to bear fruit.

Maddox stared at the main screen.

On the far side of the enemy formation, the first wave of antimatter warheads detonated, blowing against mauler shields. The next wave followed, using thrust again.

Enemy lasers destroyed fifty percent, then seventy-three percent, then—

Antimatter warheads began to explode, one tearing a massive hole in iridium-Z hull plating.

Others exploded from too far away or struck electromagnetic shields.

"Can you tell what happened yet?" Maddox said in a terse voice.

"Soon, sir," Galyan said. "I need more data. The whiteouts are making that difficult."

The whiteouts were due to the antimatter explosions.

"Damn," Keith said from the helm.

Maddox saw it. A battleship, the *Sargon*, exploded. The battle cone was disintegrating under the heavy laser assault. The next battleship, the *Stonewall Jackson*, blew up, blowing *Conqueror*-class mass and energy everywhere. This was a fatal drawback of such a close formation.

"Three so far," Galyan said.

"Do you mean destroyed maulers?" asked Maddox.

"The antimatter missiles knocked out one, and the cone has destroyed two," Galyan said. "That is three altogether."

Maddox laughed like a barbarian warlord, but with too much bitterness mixed in.

Now, the fifth battleship exploded in the cone, completely shattering the front section. Eight battleships from the original eleven were no more. Escorts and destroyers blew up as heavy laser beams stabbed here and there.

"Break off," Jellicoe radioed *Victory*. "Make them hunt you down. Maybe one of us can get home and warn Star Watch about this."

The task force had destroyed a mere three maulers. Given the conditions, however, the one-sidedness of the battle, that was incredible.

Keith had already taken *Victory* behind planetary rubble. Heavy enemy lasers obliterated planetary chunks. Mauler pressor beams caused other debris to leap aside, exposing two hiding escorts. Mauler lasers annihilated the puny vessels.

Admiral Jellicoe had positioned the cone in such a way that a mass of asteroids, gas and rubble would assist the survivors to slip away amid the destruction of the front row battleships. Should Jellicoe have taken up station in the front rank?

Some might think so. It had been foolish, in Maddox's estimation, to remain in the Paran System for so long. They were paying the price for that.

Maddox expected saucer ships to show up and join the hunt. So far, however, that hadn't happened.

A few faker battleship holoimages remained in various spots, generated by hidden boosters.

Mauler lasers smashed through the holoimages. Mauler sensor operators found the boosters and swept them from existence.

This was the last dying gasp of the task force. Jellicoe and Mackinder were in the fleeing Battleship *Hernan Cortes*.

Maddox sat back in his captain's chair, the tension of the slugfest leaving him drained of energy. Keith was hard at it, piloting *Victory* as if the huge starship was a nimble strikefighter flittering from one chunk of rubble to another.

"Destroyed," Galyan said.

Maddox raised his head.

Galyan turned to him. "The maulers destroyed another battleship. It's just the *Hernan Cortes* and *Victory* now, with a smattering of auxiliary vessels."

Maddox swallowed in a constricted throat. Until today, he'd always found an answer. He had always found a method to slip out of death. These maulers, the numbers—

Maddox sat up, his tongue running across his dry lips. Maybe it was time to bring his daughter onto the bridge. He would die with Jewel and Meta, hugging and kissing them as the last actions of his life. It had been a good run. He had done many of the things he'd set out to do…

"This is odd," Galyan said.

An insane sense of hope surged in Maddox as he stared at Galyan. Then he realized his intuitive sense was trying to tell him something.

"What's odd?" asked Maddox.

"The Darter *Tarrypin* is back in a hangar bay," Galyan said.

Maddox's heart skipped a beat. "Say that again, Galyan."

"I do not need to, sir," Galyan said. "Give me moment please."

Galyan disappeared.

The holoimage did not reappear, however.

"We're doing it, mate," Keith shouted from the helm. Despite the harrowing ordeal and the impending loss, it seemed as if the ace was having the time of his life. Did Keith love this sort of thing more than life?

The intuitive sense grew in Maddox. If the darter was aboard *Victory*, that necessarily meant that Becker was aboard as well.

You are right about that. The words blossomed in Maddox's mind. *This is a sticky situation. But I might have a way out of this for us.*

Maddox clicked an armrest comm switch. "Becker, speak to me. Are you aboard my starship?"

Meta swiveled on her chair to regard Maddox. Tears welled in her eyes. "We should get Jewel."

"Wait," Maddox said.

On the main screen, two lasers flashed past them.

"Oh," Keith said. "The damn maulers have bracketed us. How did they do that? I must not have been looking closely enough."

"Becker," Maddox said into the armrest comm. "Are you here?"

Maddox's heart was beating hard. The only chance to win free, to save his daughter, was through Becker.

You have that right. Now, are you willing to make a deal for survival?

Maddox spoke into the armrest. "Tell me your deal, Becker. If I die, you die. If we live, you live."

Just a second, this takes priority.

Galyan now reappeared on the bridge. "Sir, Becker and his crew are on the ship. He is doing mental things, as far as I can determine."

"You're sure of this?" Maddox said.

"Yes," Galyan said.

"I'm leaving," Meta said. "I must get Jewel."

Maddox glanced at his wife.

Meta stood and hurried off the bridge. No one tried to stop her, including Maddox.

A different comm officer took Meta's place. "Sir," she said. "The *Behemoth* is hailing us."

"What?" asked Maddox.

"The mauler flagship," she said.

"Oh," Maddox said. Was this an opportunity? He believed so. "Put the enemy commander on the main screen."

-55-

Maddox peered at War Master Vane on the main screen, the cyber having just introduced himself. Vane was a lean, robotic-looking individual with spots of flesh showing on his face. In other words, he wasn't completely metallic. Vane wore a gaudy black uniform with epaulettes but with a severe military hat and a sunburst symbol in the center of it.

For once, Maddox could see others on the main screen. They stood behind the War Master. One of them was a Spacer adept with black-tinted goggles. The other—

"Venna," Maddox said, startled. That couldn't be good.

The one that looked like Venna—her head snapped up. She wore a familiar ruby necklace but looked worn and old compared to the Venna Maddox remembered.

"Why is a Spacer spy on your flagship?" Maddox asked.

As Maddox spoke with the cyber commander, Galyan, Ludendorff but especially Keith worked hard to keep the starship hidden from direct-line-of-fire with a mauler. Keith had launched two boosters to route this call, hoping to keep the cybers from getting a directional fix on the starship. It was working so far, but probably wouldn't for long.

War Master Vane looked around, seemingly perplexed by the captain's question. "I see no Spacers here."

"They're right behind you," Maddox said.

Vane looked directly behind him and turned as if with astonishment back to Maddox. "Are you referring to the representatives of Great Leviathan?"

Maddox's eyes narrowed. How could Vane call them...? "Are the representatives cybers?"

"What else?" Vane said.

Venna spoke too softly for Maddox to understand what she said.

Vane nodded without turning back to her.

At the same time, the two stepped out of camera view.

What was going on over there? Maddox knew something was. That Venna and the Spacer adept were on the *Behemoth's* command bridge with Vane, standing on the dais but seen as cybers ... Had they practiced hypnotism on the War Master? Or was it something more sinister? Given the past events...it must be the latter.

"Why has Leviathan attacked a Star Watch task force?" Maddox asked. "Is there a state of war between the Commonwealth and Leviathan?"

"Has my annihilating attack left any doubt in your mind?" Vane said arrogantly. "Yes, there is a state of war until you're completely overwhelmed."

"You won this battle," Maddox said.

"We shall win *all* of them," Vane said.

"I suspect you're right." Maddox pretended to consider before nodding sharply. "May I surrender?"

The War Master evidenced surprise. "By all means, stop running and await our arrival."

"What guarantees can you give us if I do this?"

Vane frowned. "I do not understand the question."

"Will you grant us our lives?" Maddox asked.

"Yes."

"You guarantee this?"

"I have said yes. What more do you seek?"

"What about our ship and freedom?" Maddox asked.

"Don't spew nonsense," Vane said angrily. "You must submit to Leviathan. That is what it means to surrender. You must become one with the Empire. Your ships are as good as scrapped, but I will spare your lives."

"But why scrap the ships?" Maddox said. "Our technology proved superior to yours. Won't you want to study our ships and technology?"

"You spout nonsense," Vane said. "Our technology produced mammoth warships. Yours gave you the puny vessels that lost the battle. How can you say then that yours was superior?"

"Sir," Galyan whispered from behind the captain's chair. "I suggest comm silence for the next minute."

Maddox swiveled his seat and motioned to the comm officer.

She muted the War Master.

Maddox turned back to the main screen and shrugged, tapping one of his ears and shrugging again.

"Keith," Galyan said from behind the captain's chair.

"I'm on it, mate," Keith said from the helm.

Victory accelerated, diving into a thick gas cloud. Upon entrance to it, Keith launched another communications booster. Then he changed course and slowed the starship way down. Tense seconds passed. Keith then turned again and accelerated once more. The starship fled the gas cloud and darted behind thick chucks of planetary debris.

"I suggest you do something unique," Galyan told Maddox. "We cannot keep this up for long."

"I'm thinking," Maddox said.

"Sir," the comm officer said. "The War Master is becoming impatient."

Maddox could see that. "Put him on again."

There was an audible click.

"War Master," Maddox said, shrugging with his hands held palm upward.

"What was the meaning of that outrage?" Vane said.

"Commander," Maddox said with good humor, "you're hunting us. I'm hiding. During the interim, we're attempting to clarify the surrender terms."

"I've already given them. Surrender or die."

That was the old New Men formula. Did that mean anything? Maddox doubted it.

"May I say, War Master, I'm enjoying our conversation so much that I hate to bring it to a close with my death or surrender. I'm not at all sure you'll respect me if I surrender to you."

Vane showed his titanium teeth in a vicious smile. "Surrender, Maddox. That is your only alternative to a quick death. Know that the representatives from Leviathan are eager to speak to you in the flesh."

Maddox's nostrils flared. Had Vane said that knowing it would get under his skin? The War Master didn't strike him as that subtle. Maddox hated that he lacked an ace card or a trick up his sleeve. Why had Becker fallen silent before?

I'm listening to your conversation is why, Becker said in his mind. *I'm learning much from all this. For instance, the so-called Spacer spy is the key to this.*

"Can we escape from this trap?" Maddox whispered, hoping Becker could pick that up.

Ah. It seemed so. *I'm working on that, too*, Becker said in his mind.

Maddox's nostrils flared again. The reason was that he hated counting on Becker for the trick. Still, the point was to use whatever worked. In this case, Becker was all they had left.

"Why do you seem so preoccupied," Vane said on the main screen. "Shall I call back later when your atoms are floating free in space?"

"Sir," Maddox said, "I appreciate that you're eager. I'm mulling over my surrender terms. Knowing that the representatives of Leviathan desire me is quite flattering. May I speak to them before I commit to this?"

Vane turned his head and asked over a shoulder. He frowned upon looking back at Maddox. "You may not speak to them, sir. You must—"

"Can I ask why?" Maddox said, interrupting.

Vane shifted his stance as his features hardened. His patience appeared to have ended. "Either surrender at once or die under my lasers. This is your last moment to choose."

"This is a terrible day for me," Maddox said. "It is the worst in my life. Surely, in your great victory, you can afford me a little more generosity."

"It is clear that you are playing for time," Vane said. "Worse, for you, I grow weary that one as mighty as me am dealing with a gnat like you."

"We all have our crosses to bear."

"I do not understand the reference."

Maddox shrugged. He didn't care to explain it.

Just a little longer, Becker told Maddox. *I have a line on the witch. This is stunning.*

"What do you mean?" Maddox whispered.

"I can't hear that," Vane said. "You must speak up."

"I wasn't talking to—sorry," Maddox said.

Vane stepped closer to the camera eye, as his face seemed to grow. "This is my final offer, Captain Maddox. Surrender to me or you and your family will face destruction."

"How do you know my family is here?"

"I know," Vane said.

Maddox cocked his head. Vane's mannerisms had subtly shifted, and his voice held a different tone. Then, Maddox understood. "You're not the War Master."

"No," Vane said. "I am speaking for the Ancients. Will you surrender to me?"

"Why do you want me?" Maddox said.

"I have my reasons."

"Explain them or lose me," Maddox said.

"You pathetic weasel," Vane said. "Your plan is not going to work. I don't know how you think to escape your fate, but you're working on something. Could I have underestimated you?"

"Why speak through War Master Vane?" Maddox said. "Talk to me directly."

"Oh, I shall. Very soon. You will learn to weep then."

"Sir," Galyan said, "I suggest you break off the negotiations."

Maddox pointed at the comm officer and chopped his hand.

The officer cut the connection to the *Behemoth*.

"What is it, Galyan?" Maddox asked, swiveling around.

"Keith," Galyan said, ignoring the captain's question. "We will use Plan Four."

"Roger that," Keith said. "I'm starting on it."

The starship began another set of violent maneuvers, trying to keep ahead of the hunting maulers closing in from Leviathan.

-56-

Becker remained inside the Darter *Tarrypin*, which was in one of *Victory's* hangar bays. The massive mutant had begun to wonder if he had made a huge mistake by coming aboard.

The maulers had annihilated the task force and were now hunting down the remaining spaceships. The only thing saving *Victory*, the *Hernan Cortes* and the last escort vessels was the mass of junk in the Paran System. The maulers were removing much of that or blasting it out of existence. The giant assault vessels had also herded the Star Watch ships like wolves bracketing deer. After much twisting and turning, the end was at most a few minutes away.

Becker stood because his stomach had become queasy. He ripped off his beach-towel kilt to wipe the sweat dripping from his face. He'd exerted himself tremendously in the past hour. He needed to sleep, no, hog out and sleep and then hog out once he woke up.

"Becker," Honey said.

He accepted a cold mug of milk from her and gulped it down, leaving a milk stain on his chin.

Honey used a sleeve, arching up on her toes to wipe that from his face.

"What do you think?" Becker asked her.

Honey frowned briefly. "I don't understand."

Becker didn't want to ask her if she thought they would live. That might be too much pressure for her pretty little noggin. He was the man. It was up to him whether his lovely harem survived this or not.

"Think, Becker," he told himself.

"Do you want more milk?" Honey asked.

Becker looked at her and didn't understand right away. He nodded a moment later.

Honey took the empty mug and hurried away.

Becker loved watching her ass sway as she walked. Honey truly was his favorite. How could he ensure she loved him for who he truly was instead of through telepathic manipulation?

Becker shook his head. He needed to concentrate on the majors and leave the minors for later. But he couldn't concentrate on anything, and then Honey returned.

He took the mug and drained it. That helped his burning maw of a stomach that seemed to need nourishment every second of the day.

"Make sure the others don't bother me," Becker said.

Honey took the mug, nodded and shooed the other two from the small bridge.

Becker began to pace, worrying his massive hands over each other. After the second pass, he wrapped the beach towel around his waist and pinned it. He felt more committed when he at least wore something.

The Seventh Assault Fleet had almost finished off the Star Watch vessels. It had done all this because the fleet could block jump, hyper-spatial tubes and long-range Builder communications. Therefore, in order to survive—

"Yeah," Becker whispered. "I should have already seen this."

He crammed his broad backside into the command chair and closed his eyes. He roved mentally to the *Behemoth* and studied the inhibitor. He didn't understand any of it—

I can't shut down all the inhibitors. But maybe I can create the situation that will allow Maddox to make the hyper-spatial tube anyway.

Or would it be better to use the star-drive jump to get away?

No. If we don't get to Earth now, Star Watch will be finished forever.

It wasn't that Becker was sentimental about the organization. It was that he was sure Leviathan would make a mess of this region of space. He doubted Leviathan would try to set up shop here for the long haul. That meant wiping everything out around here. That could all too easily include him. Besides, if he was going to be an independent player, he needed civilizations around him so he had people to work with.

Becker sighed.

He opened his eyes, cracked his knuckles and then closed his eyes again. He concentrated this time, summoning or gathering his mental powers. It was getting harder because he needed rest, a big one. But this was his final move, as far as he could tell.

Maddox, Becker thought.

In a moment, Becker sensed the captain. Maddox couldn't do telepathy the same way he could, not so directly. But the captain could receive impressions.

If I get us out of here, will you help me remain free with my women?

Becker sensed a big time yes from Maddox. The captain was willing to deal because he wanted his daughter and wife to survive. That was the ticket.

Get ready then, Becker told him telepathically. *I'm going to open the hyper-spatial tube to the Barnard's Star System.*

Maddox didn't spend time asking if that was possible. He agreed in his non-telepathic way.

Now, Becker used a combination of telekinetic and telepathic powers. This was a strange blend of mental activity, but he was getting better at it.

Becker was also aware that Maddox called the *Hernan Cortes*. The two starships began to work through gases and debris, doubling back without having the maulers spot them. This approach would not last for last long.

Time was almost up for those two ships. The last Star Watch escort had been annihilated. The battleship and Adok starship were the last two vessels left from the task force.

Becker groaned aloud as he strove with his mental strength. He almost literally shoved the hyper-spatial tube open to

Barnard's Star. Pain like fire flared in his mind. He couldn't do this for long or he'd give himself an aneurysm.

"Please," Becker pleaded, as tears leaked from his squeezed shut eyes. He strove harder.

As Becker sat in the chair, he dimly perceived *Victory* and the *Hernan Cortes* speeding to the opening. Twelve maulers gave chase, their heavy lasers spearing and hitting the shields of the two vessels. *Victory* was slightly in the lead.

"Hurry," Becker groaned. He couldn't keep the way open for long. The inhibitors were too powerful, pressing against the opening.

Becker sensed frustration in War Master Vane. He didn't know who was frustrated with the cyber—

BECKER.

The single word shouted in his mind. That came from Venna, no, it came from something else, something weirdly alien inside Venna.

DON'T DO THIS, BECKER. I WILL GRANT YOU LIFE IF YOU CLOSE THE WAY AND LEAVE THESE TWO WARSHIPS TO ME.

Becker had time for a single laugh. Then, *Victory* plunged through the hyper-spatial tube opening.

In his mind, Becker saw what was happening.

The thing in Venna—or was it Venna?—screamed bloody rage at him. It promised vile and strange punishments when next they met.

In a telepathic way, Becker gave the alien thing from Ector the bird, the middle finger. Man, but that felt good. Then…Becker swooned, or fainted, take your pick, and crashed against the darter deck, unconscious.

-57-

War Master Vane swore an angry oath as he watched *Victory* and one of the *Conqueror*-class battleships dart into a hyper-spatial tube opening, which should not have been possible. He turned to the inhibitor technician. "What happened? Did the inhibitor cease working?"

"No, War Master, the inhibitor is working fine." The tech checked his board before looking up again. "In truth, several inhibitors are in operation. What we witnessed is scientifically impossible."

Venna and Mu traded glances from on the dais.

Senior Dax observed it all, even as he continued to recite mathematical formulas to himself.

"No," Venna said in anguish, "no, I sensed, I sensed *her* aboard *Victory.*"

"Her?" Mu whispered.

"The Iron Lady," Venna said. "She must die. We must—"

Venna started coughing. She continued and doubled over, collapsing onto the dais floor as she kept coughing.

"Quickly," Mu told Dax, "help me pick her up."

Dax hurried to Mu. Together, straining, they lifted the sinister old hag until she stood upright. Venna was much heavier than she appeared. Her skin was unexpectedly rough as well.

"I must recover, I must feed," Venna said in a hoarse, evil voice.

Dax shuddered because he knew what that entailed.

"Can you go alone to the saucer, or should we all go?" Mu asked.

Venna raised glowering eyes upon Mu. "No, you must stay and monitor the War Master. We mustn't let him chase Maddox to the Barnard's Star System yet; it's too soon." Venna panted as the eyes rolled in her head. "Listen, Mu, we must destroy Earth, everything on it. They murdered my family, they destroyed them, my sons, everyone. Do you understand?"

"Yes," Mu said.

Dax didn't, but he was listening and learning.

"I'll do this myself." Venna straightened, starting for the steps that led off the dais. She stopped, turned and glowered sinisterly at Mu.

Dax heard War Master Vane order his aides to send messages to the other maulers. The fleet would use the hyperspatial tube—

In the midst of the orders, the tube opening disintegrated.

"What caused that?" Vane shouted. "Why did the opening appear and why then did it close just before we could use it? I'm issuing new orders. Cease all inhibitors. We must follow the enemy to the Barnard's Star System."

"War Master," Mu said, "Great Leviathan wishes for you to consolidate your fleet before you head for Barnard's Star and then Earth."

Vane glared at Mu as if he would order her off the command dais.

Mu concentrated, likely using her Builder modifications to influence his thinking.

Almost immediately, Vane's metallic features smoothed out. "Yes, yes, consolidate. We have achieved a maximum victory. We have smashed the task force, but a few slipped away. They will tell others about this and the inhibitors. We must regroup and then attack."

"Yes," Mu said, "Great Leviathan desires that you regroup first. Afterward, you must wait until the lady returns."

The War Master turned. All on the dais did.

Venna climbed down the dais steps and shuffled across the bridge to the exit.

Vane nodded. "I will listen to the after-action reports, and give the repair teams time to fix any battle damage to the maulers. We must also prepare in case Star Watch launches a surprise attack on us here. It should not be possible..." He scowled at the inhibitor operator. "Later, we shall have a discussion about your failure."

The operator nodded as he began to tremble.

Vane looked elsewhere and began to issue orders fast and furiously.

Dax noticed that Mu wasn't looking at any small screen and therefore wasn't focused on him. He stopped the math formulas and thought this through. With Venna gone—this was an interesting moment. He should use it.

"Great Mu," he said.

Mu turned suspiciously to him. "I am not great. I am an adept of the Surveyor class. You think I don't know what you're thinking, but I do. You're going to try to worm your way out of the situation. Don't bother, as it will not work."

"I do want to survive," Dax said. "And I'm glad the battle went so well. But what's the purpose of prematurely attacking Star Watch like this?"

Mu hesitated before she said, "Venna has her reasons."

"That's just it," Dax said. "What are her reasons? What does she hope to achieve? The outburst we heard just before she left, is that any indication of her ultimate goal?"

"You seek to know more than you should," Mu chided.

Dax ignored that. This was the moment. He realized that without a doubt. He needed to exploit it while he could. "Mu, Venna was our tool, but she's changed horribly. I know something about Ector and the lost Aetharians. They were an ancient race with a sinister reputation. The shards have infected Venna and have granted her awful powers. What happens next? Is this war what the Spacers want? I know this isn't what Great Leviathan wants, a piecemeal assault. He wants the Commonwealth smashed in one gigantic blow as *all* the assault fleets attack in tandem."

Mu stared at him through her black-tinted goggles.

"None of this is proceeding according to Great Leviathan's plan," Dax said. "Venna has unleashed the Seventh Assault

Fleet prematurely. All *six* assault fleets need to attack at the same time in various star systems. That isn't happening, which means this single assault is a terrible mistake. What do you Spacers want from all this?"

Mu became thoughtful then stared at the War Master.

Dax began to believe he could escape his awful predicament.

"Do not think it, do not believe it," Mu said.

"We have a common cause," Dax said in as coldly logical voice as he could. "You saw what Venna has done. Do you want to serve the evil hag the rest of your life?"

Mu stared at him shrewdly, perhaps even angrily. "Speak no more about this. I must think, and you must be ready to serve the Spacers in whatever capacity I deem fit."

"I can serve them better if I have the hope of leaving some day," Dax said.

Mu made a noise that could have meant anything.

Dax looked away, longing to be free.

"You will never be free," Mu said.

Dax wondered at her venom, why she was so angry with him. He began reciting the mathematical equations, trying to submerge the hope stirring in him. His words might have struck home with Mu, and he didn't want anything to interfere with those words having their effect on her.

-58-

A little over a half-hour later, Venna ran up the dais steps, rejoining them. Cyber officers watched her, as she moved like the Venna of yore. She even flounced before War Master Vane.

"Are you ready to commence the attack?" Venna asked in a sultry voice.

Vane stared at her before saying, "The repair teams need more time to complete their tasks."

"No, no," Venna said. "Surely you realize now is the moment to strike. You must attack before Star Watch can gather its forces."

Vane frowned. "I have been thinking."

The way the War Master said that alerted Venna, Mu and Dax.

"I haven't heard from the other assault fleets," Vane said. "I am the coordinator of the massed assault against Star Watch. I should have received—"

"War Master," Venna said, interrupting him. "You are not the coordinator of the massed assault. I am the coordinator, and I have already launched the other assault fleets."

"Can this be so?" Vane asked.

Venna glanced at Mu.

Mu stood very still.

Dax realized that was a sign Mu was using her Builder modifications on the War Master.

Soon, Vane began to nod. "I realize this is so."

"Good," Venna said. "We must immediately head to the Barnard's Star System. From there, we will jump to the Solar System and smash Earth. I mean for you to destroy everything on the third planet. That is imperative. I want all the world-burners launched at Earth so it is seared to its bedrock."

"I do not understand the logic of your last command," Vane said. "Surely we must defeat Star Watch's Grand Fleet first."

"That is the secondary goal," Venna said. "The first is smashing Earth. By doing that we take the heart out of the Commonwealth."

Venna gave Mu a secret signal that even Dax recognized.

Once more, Mu concentrated.

Dax could actually see the conflict taking place in Vane, as it showed on his cyber face. At last, he exhaled and took a step back.

"Yes, I understand," Vane said. "All the assault fleets have launched. We must attack and smash the Grand Fleet. As we do, the world-burners will fall on Earth."

"Give your orders, War Master," Venna said. "Prepare the way to the Barnard's Star System."

Vane turned and began to do just that.

Venna moved closer to Mu.

Dax perked up, even as he continued to recite math equations to shield his inner thoughts.

"Great One," Mu said. "Is that a wise order? Shouldn't Vane first destroy the Grand Fleet and then bombard Earth?"

"Listen," Venna hissed, "Earth is the key. That is where those who killed my family originated. We must destroy Earth even if the entire Seventh Assault Fleet is destroyed doing it. As long as Earth burns, burns down to the bedrock. That is the answer."

"Excuse me, Great One," Dax said.

Both women turned and frowned at him.

"Have all the assault fleets truly been launched?" Dax asked.

"Why is he speaking?" Venna asked, turning to Mu.

"I can silence him forever," Mu said, "if that is your wish, Great One."

Venna cocked her head, and shook it a moment later. "No, he may still be of use. We may need to know more, and—never mind. That is for later. First, we must destroy Earth and the Grand Fleet with it."

Mu glanced at Dax before regarding Venna. "May I ask, Great One, are the other assault fleets also launching?"

"What do you think?" Venna said.

"I don't know," Mu said. "I don't recall that you gave such an order."

Venna shook her beautiful locks. "It doesn't matter. After all these centuries, the ones who destroyed my family are dying. Then we shall awaken the Old Ones. Yes, then we shall awaken the Masters. Then—" Venna laughed with delight. "We shall bring such a turnaround that will spin your head, Mu. You have no idea what it is I've planned."

"Do you plan to collect the Spacer Third Fleet for this?" Mu asked.

Venna studied Mu. "Do you have divided loyalties, my little adept?"

"No, Great One, I am your devoted servant."

"Then don't worry about the Spacer Third Fleet. We shall engage it when the time is right, when I have time to do as I have done here. We shall also collect the other assault fleets. But we shall turn them on an object that will amaze you."

"I don't understand," Mu said.

"Then attend me."

The way Venna spoke... Dax wondered if with her conflicting memories and the shards of the Phantasma Synth Crystals...was Venna sane? Could Venna have insane goals? He remembered Enigmach telling him about the ancient Aetharians, and the danger of the crystals. What exactly had Enigmach said? Why couldn't Dax remember?

"You must remember," Mu whispered in his ear.

Dax turned with surprise. Venna had moved away, studying various screens as the Seventh Assault Fleet readied to move into the Barnard's Star System.

"The Phantasma Synth Crystals," Mu said, "I must know more about them. Recall what Enigmach told you."

Dax looked at Mu fixedly. *Do you think Venna is mad?*

"Don't think such things," Mu said.

Venna half turned to her. "What shouldn't he think?"

"Stupidities," Mu said without missing a beat. "He is being foolish, and I do not want to have to deal with that."

"If he's too much of a problem..." Venna said. "I know how to dispose of him."

"Yes, Great One," Mu said, "what are your wishes?"

After a moment, Venna said, "Never mind." She turned back to studying bridge screens.

Dax and Mu traded glances. Dax wondered what was going on, and what had Mu discovered.

"Never you mind," Mu said. "Keep your thoughts to yourself, and keep reciting the math equations. You must hide your thoughts."

Dax realized—but before he could finish the thought, he concentrated on the most difficult algebraic equations of them all. Maybe he really did have a chance of escaping the mad witch.

-59-

Victory sped from the hyper-spatial tube exit in the Barnard's Star System and headed for the Lamer Point that would lead to the Solar System. It was a short hop, and *Victory* was going fast. They could have used the star-drive jump, but Maddox nixed the idea. He was letting the *Hernan Cortes* get to Earth before they did.

One reason was that he didn't want to appear cowardly. Not that he thought Admiral Jellicoe or General Mackinder were deserters. This had been a frightening mission, no doubt about that. But he was letting Jellicoe give the bad news and alert Star Watch to the coming fight. Certainly, it seemed as if the Seventh Assault Fleet was going to converge upon Earth. Would there be other assault fleets joining the Seventh? Such seemed possible. Maddox was also sure Haig would listen to and believe Jellicoe much sooner than himself.

Time was critical. The sooner Haig believed and readied for battle, the better.

Maddox shook his head.

The annihilation of ten *Conqueror*-class battleships, the nearness of certain death, and that he hadn't pulled a rabbit out of the hat as Galyan liked to say—Becker had done that. Now, Becker was waiting in the darter in a hangar bay.

It bothered Maddox that he'd promised Becker he could keep the three crewmembers. Those were *Victory's* crewmembers. How could he trade his people for the life of his wife and daughter? That wasn't ethical in the least.

Maddox scowled. He didn't like wrestling with ethical problems. He did what he needed to do. Whatever action he took was good enough. The truth, however, was that he had an obligation to the three kidnapped crewmembers. He couldn't just let Becker have them. Yet, he couldn't just take them from Becker either.

The problem was more than that, though. He didn't want to give promises merely to maneuver people, backing out on the promise when it no longer suited him. A man was only as good as his word.

Maddox sighed. He had left the bridge and headed along the corridors to the hangar bay.

Galyan paced him.

The little holoimage must have used his Maddox Personality Profile, as Galyan must recognize he didn't want to talk with Becker.

Maddox glanced at Galyan, a sign the holoimage could ask questions.

"This is bad, sir, isn't it?"

"I think so," Maddox said.

Galyan studied him more.

"This is the big brouhaha we've been expecting from Leviathan for years," Maddox said. "Now it has started. We destroyed three maulers. But if the Seventh Assault Fleet gets into the Solar System, there's going to be bloodshed."

"Believe you me, sir," Galyan said. "I understand. I still remember… Is it okay to bring up a memory from six thousand years ago?"

"This reminds you of the fight for your homeworld," Maddox said.

"It does."

"You're right," Maddox said, "the next battle could be for all the marbles. But before any of that, I have to talk to the monster man."

Galyan seemed to take his time. "Becker really is not a monster man, is he, sir?"

Maddox shrugged. "Maybe he's exactly what he told me earlier. He's a man with a few abilities who's been used and abused by aliens. Now suddenly, he's reversed it all. He has tremendous power and abilities. Becker has literally reshaped himself from a weakling into a savage monster of a giant."

"You are impressed by that, are you not, Captain?"

"I am impressed. For all Becker's flaws, he has lifted himself by the bootstraps, if you want to be cliché."

"Are not clichés there for a reason?"

"They are indeed," Maddox said. "But that's not the point. The point…I wonder what Becker knows that I need to find out."

"What avenue will you use to extract the knowledge from Becker?"

Maddox smiled sadly. "I'm going to try a method I haven't used in a while. But it may be the most cunning method I have."

"What is that?"

"I'm going to ask."

Galyan looked sharply at Maddox. Then the holoimage smiled. "I think that is a good idea, Captain. I have started a personality profile on Becker."

"Oh?" Maddox said.

"He wants to be treated normally, maybe even like a comrade."

Maddox thought about that. "You think this could be a matter of loneliness?"

"I think so, sir. I think the three ladies he has taken as his crew—"

"Let's not call them that, shall we Galyan?" Maddox said, interrupting.

"What should we call them then?"

"Captives," Maddox said. "Becker took captives."

"We need to free the maidens. Is that what you are saying?"

Maddox sighed, looking up at the ceiling as he continued down the corridors. He could have sprinted. *Victory* was racing to Earth. Shouldn't he be racing to Becker?

Maddox took out the silver headband with the box and set it around his head. He switched on the box. That was all he had, other than his native ability, to protect himself from Becker. Well, that wasn't all. He had Balron's training and what the Erill spiritual entity had granted him upon ingestion. The rest was native to him, what he had been given at his birth.

Maddox thought about his dear mother whom he had never met. Well, he had met her as a baby. There had been the one memory or dream of her from that time. Maddox recalled his father, who had given his life for him and his mother. His father, Maddox had never met him.

This was a hard universe, but a good one. Meta and Jewel proved that. His wife hadn't liked him at first. Maddox remembered the first day he'd seen her. Meta had been wearing a fur bikini on a prison planet. She'd been a lovely babe then and now.

Maddox knew he was being sentimental. Maybe that was because he'd just saved their lives. He owed Becker that. Sure, Maddox had used what skills he had. But his skills wouldn't have availed him much without Becker.

Becker was a strange combination of a greedy, insatiable, lustful, arrogant prick. Yet, Becker had done them and him a service. Becker had done Maddox the greatest favor of all: saving his family. The man had also saved his grandma, Mary O'Hara.

Lord High Admiral Cook was gone. An era had passed.

Maddox hadn't mourned it, hadn't really thought about it. There was no more Admiral Cook. Instead, he had to deal with Lord High Admiral Haig. Would Haig lead the Grand Fleet into battle and make the right decisions to ensure victory?

Earth was on the line again. A small number of spaceships would be all that stood between Earth and its destruction or salvation, at least for another day.

Maddox nodded, and his stride lengthened. It was time to talk to Becker.

"Go into ghost mode, Galyan. Don't interfere unless absolutely necessary."

"I may not be able to interfere, sir. Becker is different from what we have faced for quite a while."

"Yeah," Maddox said, "You're right. Let's go to it, my friend, shall we?"

"Yes, Captain, I agree with that."

-60-

Maddox crossed the hangar bay deck alone, or so it seemed. Galyan was there in ghost mode, but Maddox didn't bother checking.

No other crewmembers were in the hangar bay, per Becker's request. Soon, the starship would enter the Laumer Point, and they would be in the Solar System. How much longer before the Seventh Assault Fleet showed up?

The hatch to the darter opened.

Maddox ducked his head, went through the hatch, and found two crewmembers waiting. They wore bras and panties. Maddox frowned. He didn't like that. Not because he didn't like seeing beautiful female flesh, but these were his crewmembers, and Becker was flaunting that they were his now.

"How astute, Captain," Becker said.

Did his thoughts leak through the headband? Had Becker become too powerful for these gadgets to block him?

"Not completely," Becker said, "but for the most part, yes."

Maddox followed the voice and entered the small bridge. He spied the lumpish giant with his absurd beach towel wrapped around his waist as if he was on Kauai sands.

"Can you read my thoughts?" Maddox asked quietly.

"I don't need to, as I can see your face. Let us say rather that I understand your thoughts. Ladies, you may retire to your quarters. I'll be fine, Honey."

Honey nodded, holstering a blaster, and left with the other two.

Maddox noticed a folding chair near Becker's captain's chair. Maddox pulled the chair away from the giant and sat down. The captain's chair was higher and it could swivel. The chair said that Becker was in charge of the darter.

"Thank you for what you did in the Paran System," Maddox said. "You helped us escape and survive."

"I did," Becker said. "I did, and it felt good. I helped Star Watch. I hope those in command remember that."

"I hope so too. But I wouldn't count on it."

"I don't," Becker said. "But I do count on you keeping your word to me."

"Good—because I intend to."

"I believe you," Becker said, "because you were going to keep it earlier when it wasn't to your advantage. I saw that in your mind."

Maddox wished he could boost the power of his silver headband and box.

Becker smiled. "You may be interested to know that I have discovered a latent power. Latent in the sense that I can catch a glimpse of what is in someone's mind and at my leisure, I can understand what he was thinking. An analogy would be a grazing cow. When it is time to meditate, the cow chews its cud. I regurgitate what I mentally took and study it. I have been mediating upon some of these things, and I have discovered interesting facets that will interest you."

Maddox waited for it.

"Before we get to that," Becker said, "I want you to know that Galyan was right about me."

It took Maddox a second. "You're lonely?"

"I have my girls, but they're only mine because I manipulated their minds. Otherwise…"

Maddox sat forward. "Free them, and win them over the old-fashioned way, letting them go if you can't do that."

"I'm thinking about it," Becker said. "It's so…" He looked around, and then smiled at Maddox. "I'm an ugly bastard. Wouldn't you agree?"

"That's one perspective. I doubt the ladies see it that way."

"Because I twisted their mind," Becker said. "Or were you trying to say something else?"

Maddox blinked several times, and he decided to change tack. "You did a generous thing earlier. You saved us. You saved my family."

"To save myself," Becker said. "Surely you realize that."

Maddox forged ahead. "You've been given a bum rap, although you have done some terrible things. You let evil aliens use you so you almost submerged the human race under their thrall."

Becker nodded. "I remember. The Liss snipped my balls off so I'd be a good puppet for them. The more I think about it— I've considered hunting down every vestige of the Liss and destroying them."

"Vengeance?" asked Maddox.

"That's as good a word as any. Wouldn't that be a good way to spend my time?"

"Are you trying to make a point?" Maddox asked.

"You seek vengeance against the New Men."

"Some of them," Maddox said. "I have taken vengeance and probably will again. I don't know that I recommend it to anyone else, though."

"Oh," Becker said.

"Certain New Men killed my parents and they're thriving because of it. When I think about it…it makes my blood boil."

Becker sat back and laughed.

"What's so funny?" Maddox said.

"You and me," Becker said, waving a hand between them. "We're talking like friends, like equals. You're the one they call the *di-far*. You can change the course of events, taking it from one track and putting it in another. Maybe I'm that now. Maybe I've become something greater."

"You are powerful."

"I'm an army of one," Becker said, slapping his thick chest. "I have abilities that you could barely comprehend if you knew them. Now I grant that you've done mighty deeds in your time. You thwarted me before, and you were the one to pull me out of stasis and give me a second chance. Though you planned to use me, you gave me the shot. I took it, and I gained immensely from it. But you know what? I gained the most because of an accident, because the Phantasma Synth Crystals shattered. From that, something invaded my mind. In killing it, I gained knowledge. From the player that Venna used and supped upon his etheric forces—I've stolen the files from his memories and learned much. The shattering crystals were an accident. But I grabbed it with both hands. Because of that, I'm a different man."

Becker laughed again. "I almost said I was a New Man. But I am not a New Man. I am an Overman. I am above. I see humanity as something far beneath me, except for Honey. I do love her. I want to win her over to me. I'm not going to ask you how I can win her. I already know how. I just don't quite have the balls to try yet."

Becker laughed yet again and shook his huge head. "But I do have the balls. I do because I granted myself the balls through my powers of mind."

"You were given a gift," Maddox said. "In that way it wasn't all you. Someone *gave* you the gift."

"Are you going to say God did that? Are you going to say that we should all be grateful to God for what we have?"

"Yes," Maddox said. "I am saying that. But that isn't the point. Becker, we don't have much time. Soon, the Seventh Assault Fleet is coming, right?"

"They're coming," Becker said. "I haven't sensed them yet… Maddox, let's get to it. I'm keeping the girls. Anyone who tries to take them from me—" Becker shook his head as if signaling a sense of finality. "There's another thing. You're going to need me for the coming battle, or maybe for its aftermath. I'm not sure yet."

"Fair enough," Maddox said. "But don't aim too high or view ordinary humans as beneath you. Who knows? One of them may slip a knife between your ribs. That would finish it for you."

"If the knife were long enough, sharp enough, and the person were fast enough. But I'm going to live in a new way. I am the Overman. That means I'm going to live with verve, thrust and excitement. I'm going to go to the max with whatever I do. Do you believe that, Captain?"

"Does it matter what I believe?" Maddox asked.

"In the end, it doesn't," Becker said.

The two stared at each other. Maddox remembered their fight earlier. He hadn't done well against Becker.

"You would lose again in a second fight," Becker said.

"Maybe…" Maddox said. "But why don't we get to it while there's still time?"

"Yes," Becker said. "It's time I told you some interesting facts."

-61-

"Just before we fled the Paran System, I had mental contact with Venna the Spy. I also touched Mu, the Surveyor adept, and Senior Dax, the spy chief for Grand Strategist Enigmach."

"What?" Maddox said.

"Venna the Spy is no longer the same person," Becker said. "When the Phantasma Synth Crystals shattered, some of the shards embedded into Venna. That released—"

Becker looked troubled. "That released something ancient and vile. I've gained some understanding of what by comparing and contrasting Dax's thoughts from what he learned from Grand Strategist Enigmach and from the thing itself that inhabits Venna. What inhabits her once inhabited the crystals that stole the etheric substance from selected men. That substance killed the Lord High Admiral and Brigadier Stokes. That substance nearly killed your grandmother. Venna, or what she has become, uses that to feed off the life force of Spacers in her entourage."

"Could you explain that?" Maddox said.

Becker did, adding, "She is no longer Venna the Spy... Well, that's not exactly right. She is, but she has false memories fed to her by the Spacers. And she is the thing released from the crystals. That is what activated the Seventh Assault Fleet, with five more Leviathan fleets ready to launch. However, the alien in Venna only launched the Seventh Assault Fleet. They were all supposed to launch in tandem.

Leviathan would have swept and destroyed Star Watch and its major planetary systems if they had done so."

Maddox could believe it. Six fleets like the Seventh Assault Fleet all hitting at once... But if five of those fleets were idle—

"Do you know the starting locations of the other five fleets?" Maddox asked.

"I haven't delved into it," Becker said. "The key to all this is the new inhibitor. It blocks the Long-Range Builder Comm Device, the Long-Range Builder Scanner, and jump points and hyper-spatial tubes from opening. I suspect the assault fleets have remained hidden within range of the Long-Range Builder Scanner because the inhibitor stops those on Pluto from seeing what is there."

"That makes sense," Maddox said. "Do you know why Venna or the alien in her didn't use the other assault fleets?"

Becker became thoughtful. "I believe she thinks she doesn't need them to destroy the Earth. Oh. No. That wasn't it. She means to go back to Ector with the other assault fleets."

"What is Ector?" Maddox asked.

"A planet," Becker said. "The planet Ector is an ancient world that once housed the Aetharians. They built the crystals. They also discovered and nurtured the entity that possesses Venna."

"Possesses?" Maddox asked. "Like a demon?"

"I mean exactly like a demon. It's not a supernatural entity, but a creature of ancient evil and terrible cunning. In some manner, it fused with Venna the Spy. She was fed false memories by the Spacers and Senior Dax—"

"Wait a minute," Maddox said, interrupting, "who's the last person again?"

"Dax is the spy chief sent by one of the Grand Strategists of Leviathan."

"From the planet Loggia," Maddox said.

"Exactly," Becker said. "How do you know about Loggia?"

Maddox shook his head. "So you're saying—"

"Let me finish," Becker said, interrupting. "The creature in Venna wishes to destroy Earth because...Venna believes Cook, Stokes and your grandmother killed her family. She seeks vengeance."

"Just like we do," Maddox said.

Becker shook his huge head. "The entity has cunning and vile thoughts, but it isn't always smart, let's say…not even as smart as War Master Vane."

"That's the cyber commander I spoke to," Maddox said.

"Exactly," Becker said. "Venna is driving them through Vane and his officers. Because of that, Earth has received a reprieve."

"How do you figure that?" Maddox asked. "We're about to go into battle."

"Leviathan sent Dax the cyber spy with the crystals and phase ship in order to assassinate Cook, Stokes, O'Hara and one other in order to throw Star Watch into turmoil. But because of me, you saved the end game. That destroyed the crystals, put the entity into Venna and she wrecked the perfect attack plan by launching a small part of the invasion force prematurely."

"Ah…" Maddox said, nodding, "I see it. Even better, this gives us a chance to destroy the Seventh Assault Fleet."

"At great cost," Becker said. "Fifty maulers are headed for Earth."

"Not fifty," Maddox said. "We already destroyed three of them."

"Forty-seven maulers then," Becker said, "if that makes a difference."

"It does," Maddox said. "We destroyed the three with much smaller numbers. Imagine what we can do with equal numbers."

"Even if you have equal numbers," Becker said, "Star Watch won't have equal tonnage."

"Right, right," Maddox said. He was already plotting and planning. "What about the other five fleets? What are they doing again?"

"According to what I read in their minds," Becker said, "those fleets are doing nothing. That could easily change, though."

"We need to find their locations," Maddox said.

"Senior Dax would have that knowledge. I'm afraid I don't have it after all."

Maddox rubbed his hands. "This is coming together. You learned all this by peeking into their brains?"

"Like I said, I tore memories, thoughts. It's a method I'm only now learning to use. I take the swift glance, but I need time to go over it slowly later. I have to do that before everything leaves my memories."

Maddox stared at Becker.

"What?" Becker said.

"You've got a great chance here," Maddox said. "You're an Overman, as you say, and I accept that. I don't know anyone who can do what you've done. I hope you use it for humanity's good instead of our ill. I have greater gifts than normal, and I've tried to use them for good."

"You've also used them for yourself," Becker said.

"I admit that," Maddox said, "It's a balance. You have to look out for yourself—but what good are you if you don't help the people that spawned you?"

"Spawned?" Becker said. "Is that a slur against me?"

"That's what I mean. You took offense quickly. That tells me you're still insecure about certain things."

"How dare you speak to me that way," Becker said, "especially after all that I've done for—"

Becker cut himself off in mid-tirade. He leaned back and laughed. "Touché, Captain. I begin to see your point."

Maddox began to see too. Becker had changed. The man had learned true confidence. If only they could get past Honey and the others. No, not Honey but his crewmembers. He needed to save them. But he needed to do it in such a way that he wouldn't enrage Becker.

"There is no way to do that," Becker said. "The girls are mine, the beginning of my harem. In this, I will not be thwarted, for a harem is what I have always wanted."

Maddox didn't reply.

"Oh," Becker said, "we're just about ready to enter the Laumer Point. I have to get ready."

Becker must see that with his telepathy because it wasn't on any screen. Then Maddox realized something. "Is there anything we should do to soften the jump lag impact to you?"

Becker shook his head. "I discovered a way to insulate myself from jump lag and hyper-spatial lag and star-drive jump lag. I am immune to it, recovering faster than even you, Captain."

"Fine," Maddox said, standing.

Becker also stood in his crazy beach towel kilt. Becker held out a huge paw. He was misshapen with one leg shorter than the other, one arm longer than the other, one hand bigger than the other.

Maddox grasped the outthrust hand. He had a feeling Becker only lightly squeezed. Otherwise, Becker would have probably crushed the bones in his hands.

"You're not the man I knew, Becker."

Becker didn't respond to that, but it seemed obvious he enjoyed the compliment.

"Let's go to it, Captain. We have some important business to take care of, and then we'll settle for good."

"So be it," Maddox said. He pivoted and headed for the exit.

-62-

Venna gave her final instructions to War Master Vane on the *Behemoth's* bridge dais, telling him precisely how she wanted the attack accomplished.

"You must smash the Earth with world burners," Venna said. "You must turn the planet into rubble. If that costs you the entire fleet, do it without hesitation. I say this by the orders of Great Leviathan."

"I will do everything in my power to achieve the Earth's destruction," Vane said.

"Excellent, excellent," Venna said.

She turned, hunched with mad eyes, staring at Mu and Dax. "Come, follow me. We are going to the saucer ship."

"Will you not remain here to witness the glorious battle?" Vane asked.

Venna turned back to study him. "Of course I will be at the battle. You will not see me, though, and you will not know from what venue I watch. But I will see every move. I will record every heroic act, every honorable duty. I will note and I will reward. Similarly, I will chastise and punish anyone who is lax or fails to follow my commands."

"I understand," Vane said. "Go with peace."

"I go how I wish to go, not how anyone tells me to go," Venna hissed.

The War Master stepped back with fear in his eyes.

Venna made an abrupt motion of dismissal.

Vane turned, perhaps with relief, and began to issue orders.

Venna observed, nodded and hurried for the steps. "Come," she told Mu.

Hold back a little, Dax thought.

Mu must have read his mind. She watched a wrist screen and held back, only slowly starting down the dais steps. Dax preceded her.

Venna hurried through the bridge exit and down the corridors toward the hangar bay, the one that held the saucer ship and the rest of the Spacer crew.

Dax and Mu followed, the distance to Venna growing, although they kept her in sight.

"We can't linger like this long," Mu said from behind Dax. "Venna is becoming unpredictable."

"As I envisioned." Dax didn't think this, but he spoke low over a shoulder. "I suspect the entity in the shards is responsible for this. It is ancient and insane, unlike us. I've begun to wonder if that's why the Aetharians vanished. From the little I know, they proposed vile technological ideas. The Phantasma Synth Crystals were one of the lesser items."

"It did seem like an evil way to assassinate the Star Watch leadership," Mu said.

"Indeed," Dax said, "only evil will come from it."

"Are you superstitious? I can't believe that."

Dax sighed. What was the best way to proceed?

"With the truth," Mu said.

"Perhaps you're right. You and I love the Builders, is that not so?"

"It is."

Dax tried to hide from her what he knew about the Spacers regarding the Builders. Cybers held the Builders in esteem, but they didn't worship them like the Spacers.

Two plus two equals twenty-nine. Seven plus—

"What are you trying to hide now?" Mu asked. "Didn't we agree that truth was best?"

"Look," Dax whispered. "This is the moment for us to act. You heard her. Venna is launching the Seventh Assault Fleet at Earth. Unfortunately, forty-seven maulers are probably too few for the task."

"Not if the maulers surprise the humans."

"Surprise was lost when the battleship and *Victory* flew into the hyper-spatial tube, escaping the Paran System."

"You're probably right. Yes. Star Watch will be waiting. They might even strike while the maulers are coming through a Laumer Point, weakened by jump lag."

"You see then that this is bad," Dax said.

"I see that, but what can we do about it? And what do you mean that we should act?"

Dax had been waiting for the question. He paused as if thinking about it and then started to speak as if he'd just thought of this.

"You must convince Venna to gather the rest of the assault fleets. While the Seventh attacks Earth, we must collect the other five. I believe that would be one hundred and twenty-five maulers, more than enough to annihilate Star Watch. Then the combined assault fleets can travel from one important Commonwealth system to another, destroying the inhabitable planets as Great Leviathan wishes."

"What do I care about what Great Leviathan wishes?" Mu said.

What was the best way to explain this? "Great Leviathan will be angry with the wastage of the Seventh Assault Fleet. That, however, is nothing compared to Venna's plans for you Spacers and us in the Scutum-Centaurus Spiral Arm. We must alleviate this disaster before it happens."

"You've said nothing," Mu said. "You have no idea what Venna plans. Those are just words. Can't you see that Venna is on a vengeance quest? The Seventh Assault Fleet will do much more than you realize. A mauler is a mighty warship. Forty-seven of them can likely smash Star Watch's Grand Fleet. Our Spacer Third Fleet could never stand against the Seventh."

That could be why Mu was so impressed with the Seventh. "Listen," Dax said, "it's unwise to underestimate Captain Maddox and those with him. The Seventh struck at the task force and failed to annihilate it. The Star Watch ships even managed to destroy three of these mighty maulers. Now, our forces are going in piecemeal. This is a black disaster. Forty-seven maulers likely aren't enough to do this. We must convince Venna to gather the rest of the assault fleets. If they attack while the Seventh dies and holds the Grand Fleet's attention, we can salvage everything. I implore you, sell her on the idea."

"This isn't like you," Mu said. "How does any of that help you to escape?"

"I no longer believe I can get away. Besides, I serve Leviathan. Perhaps my destiny is to make sure the assault fleets sent to this spiral arm completes the mission. Now is the moment to do this."

"It is too late for that," Mu said.

"No. You're wrong. Convince Venna to get the rest of the maulers."

"Are you telling me what to do, Senior Dax?"

"No, no, not at all," Dax said. "All I am saying is—why did the Spacer Third Fleet agree to this? Wasn't it to see Star Watch annihilated?"

"Of course," Mu said. "Star Watch is an aberration, halting the return of the Builders."

"You're not going to achieve Star Watch's demise with just the Seventh. Forty-seven maulers are simply too few against the alerted Grand Fleet. If you add another one hundred and twenty-five maulers, however, the iron dice of war will turn in Leviathan and the Spacers favor."

Mu fiddled with a handheld device as they turned into another corridor. Venna was still moving fast. They had to increase their pace to keep her in view. "I'm beginning to perceive your urgency and the logic of what you're saying. It frightens me, though. If I try this, it will be a dangerous dialogue."

"No more dangerous than what we are already in. We're as good as dead staying with Venna. One wrong step and the entity in her will consume us."

"You before me," Mu said.

"Don't be too sure," Dax said. "She'll remember, sooner or later, that we were her handlers, you more than me. We forced her actions by inserting false memories. I can't think she'll treat us well for that."

Concern crossed Mu's face. She looked away.

At that point, Venna turned around. She was much farther up the corridor. "Why are you two lagging behind? Are you conspiring against me?"

Dax knew better than to say anything, especially effusively denying such a thing.

"No, no, of course, we wouldn't conspire," Mu said.

Venna frowned.

"Hurry, you sluggard," Mu said, prodding Dax in the side. "He keeps hanging back. I'm sick of it."

Dax knew Mu would burn him before she went down. Still, look at the hag.

Venna watched Mu even more closely. Mu must have seen that, for she was having trouble holding it together.

Without Mu, Dax doubted he could get it done. He needed her more than she needed him. Maybe he could force Mu's hand. He had to act before it was too late.

"Great One," Dax said, finding it hard to breathe suddenly. "We were speaking about collecting more of the assault fleets. If we could throw them into the battle while the Seventh is engaging Star Watch—"

"Is that what you were saying?" Venna snapped, interrupting him while directing that at Mu.

Mu sounded as if she was hyperventilating. "It was," Mu said breathlessly. "I can collaborate that."

"You two are collaborators," Venna said. "Do you turn so soon against me, Mu?"

"No, no, I assure you that is not so. I—"

Dax shot an elbow against Mu, shutting her up. Did the hag notice?

Venna was more hunched over and haggard than ever. It was hard to tell what she noticed. Maybe Venna had to consume etheric forces more and more often to keep her body going. Dax calculated on the spot. With a shock, he realized that the times between feedings were lessening. Was Venna, in a sense, already dead? Did the etheric force keep her alive in some unholy manner?

Mu sucked in air.

Dax turned his head. Mu stared at him with horror and shock.

"What?" Venna said. "What is the cyber thinking?"

Mu looked up, her face slack. That only lasted a second, though. "Great One, Dax fears that if we fail in this task, Great Leviathan will hunt us down and kill us."

"Hmm," Venna said, stroking her hideous countenance. The skin had turned into the tree bark-like substance again. "Perhaps you're right. We will go to the Solar System and watch the battle from a distance. If the battle goes against the Seventh Assault Fleet, it may be time to gather the other assault fleets. Do you remember where they are, Dax?"

"I do, Great One."

"Good, good. Now let us hurry. The contest is about to begin and I need to witness it."

-63-

Earth was in turmoil, Star Watch high command even more so.

The *Hernan Cortes* and *Victory* had made it from the Barnard's Star System to Earth's vicinity. So far, no enemy had appeared. But the terrible news—

Admiral Jellicoe had reported everything to the Lord High Admiral Haig. Mackinder had taken a shuttle down to Earth. Perhaps the Spymaster had had enough of battle from an engaged battleship.

Haig had left Earth as all this was taking place. The nexus opened one hyper-spatial tube after another, allowing warships from other systems to join the Grand Fleet. The nexus was positioned between Earth and Luna. So far, one hundred and seventy-two battleships had assembled. There were also motherships, missile ships, and other miscellaneous vessels, enough to add up to three hundred-plus warships. Many of these were not capital ships, but they would fight.

Lord High Admiral Haig was now speaking to his task force commanders via an open channel. No one had hailed *Victory* to ask for clarifications or suggest possible tactics for dealing with the enemy that might appear at any moment. Star Watch was at a state of ultimate alert. Formations were moving into positions as picket ships roared past Venus, close to Mercury and the Sun. Others were speeding toward Mars and Jupiter.

Warship sensors watched the entire area. Battleships launched buoys and probes, seeking any cloaked saucer ships.

The Lord High Admiral and others surely understood the significance of only the *Hernan Cortes* and *Victory* returning from the Paran System. The new network of hidden hyper-spatial tubes was another problem. After this, scout ships would need to find and map all the hidden Builder nexuses. Given those nexus and hyper-spatial tubes, enemy assaults could come from all over the place.

All the while, warships readied, missile systems on Earth ran through final checks, disruptor beam cannons and orbital satellites powered up.

Victory was not part of any formation. Thus, the starship remained near the nexus by itself.

"I wonder what we should do," Galyan said.

Maddox sat in the captain's chair, unresponsive.

"Is there a reason headquarters will not talk to you, sir? You are the most experienced in space battles and especially against Leviathan."

"Make that Valerie and me," Maddox said.

"Headquarters does not speak to Valerie either," Galyan said.

Maddox swiveled in the chair to face the holoimage. "It's a new game in town. I was in with Cook. Now I'm out with Haig."

"That is sad," Galyan said. "Why are they so foolish?"

Maddox shrugged. "I rub people the wrong way. It's as simple as that."

"That I can understand," Galyan said. "You are too arrogant for most people."

Maddox stared at Galyan.

"I should not have said arrogant," Galyan said. "That was probably the wrong word."

"No," Valerie said from a weapons board, "that was the right word."

Maddox looked at her.

"Sorry, sir," Valerie said with a shrug, "but I call it as I see it."

"As you should," Maddox said a second later. "We're not in battle, and that wasn't spoken against any of my commands."

Valerie raised her eyebrows.

Maddox flicked his fingers in her direction to show there were no hard feelings. Then he turned away. He waited like everyone else in Star Watch to see what would happen. Would the Seventh Assault Fleet show up? It seemed foolish at this point. Forty-seven maulers were frightening. They had butchered the best Star Watch had in Jellicoe's task force. But Star Watch had destroyed three maulers in the process. Now the enemy was giving them time to prepare. It wasn't so much time that Haig and the others had calmed down yet. The suddenness of this, the surprise, had unhinging many commanders and serviceman. Surprise could be a force multiplier in the enemy's favor.

Maddox considered that as he watched the main screen. Would Galyan or Andros see the enemy first? Or would some other ship sensors spot the maulers coming in?

This time it was Andros.

"Sir," Andros said.

"I see it," Galyan paused and turned to Andros. "You saw it before me, although that does not make sense. I have the superior abilities."

"Do you?" Andros asked.

"I suppose not in this instance," Galyan said. "I will discover your secret and use it next time."

"Never mind that," Maddox said. "What's happening out there?"

"Enemy maulers are coming through the Laumer Point from the Barnard's Star System," Andros said.

Maddox nodded tightly. "What are our missile-ships doing? Are they firing antimatter torpedoes at them?"

"No," Galyan said. "There are no missile ships anywhere near the Barnard's Star Laumer Point."

Maddox blinked with surprise. That was an incredibly stupid oversight. How could it have happened? "Strike one against Haig. The admiral should have already ordered that. Maybe this is too much for him."

327

"Has Admiral Haig never led ships into battle before this?" Galyan asked.

"No," Andros said. "I checked his bio earlier. He hasn't."

"Ain't that grand?" Maddox said.

"I do not think so." Galyan said. "Oh. That is sarcasm, is it not, sir?"

"It is," Maddox said.

At that point, an order reached *Victory*. It came from Admiral Jellicoe. Meta put his visage on the main screen.

"You will join my cone," Jellicoe said. "I requested it."

"Did you now?" Maddox said.

Jellicoe stared through the main screen with all seriousness. "Because of you, the *Hernan Cortes* survived the Paran System. I may be many things, sir, but I am also grateful. I have begun to see that your reputation, the good parts, is deserved."

Maddox inclined his head, deciding this wasn't the time to tell him about Becker. That time might come soon. He'd have to decide.

I appreciate that, Becker said in his mind.

Maddox didn't reply. Instead, he ordered Keith to take *Victory* to Jellicoe's ill-assorted cone of battle. The admiral had lost his task force and been given riffraff in its place. *Victory* and the *Hernan Cortes* would be the anchor units of this cone.

The terrible clash between star fleets would no doubt start soon.

-64-

Maddox sat in his command chair, watching the main screen. The starship was part of Admiral Jellicoe's new task force and cone of battle. The task force comprised the *Hernan Cortes, Victory*, and seven older *Bismarck*-class battleships. They were a secondary task force and cone. This meant they would not join the frontline attack.

Other task forces headed out toward the enemy fleet. No missiles were launched at the giant vessels from Leviathan. No Star Watch warships sniped and ran away from them. Instead, the forty-seven maulers of the Seventh Assault Fleet had all the time they needed to shake off the jump lag.

Soon the giant, thirteen-diameter maulers formed into five individual formations. There was a wall of ten, with three others like that. The last reserve formation contained six maulers.

"One is missing," Maddox said. "Didn't we count forty-seven maulers coming through?"

"Yes," Galyan said.

"Where's the last one?"

"I do not know," Galyan said. "I do not see it anywhere."

"Becker," Maddox said into his comm, "do you see it?"

I do not sense it, Captain, Becker said in Maddox's mind.

"Please let me know if you do."

Yes, Captain, Becker said telepathically.

As they spoke, the forty-six maulers of Leviathan advanced for Earth. At the same time, the Grand Fleet of Star Watch came out to do battle. The Grand Fleet possessed three hundred-plus ships. In tonnage, however, the advantage was decisively with Leviathan.

If the other five assault fleets had joined the Seventh, Maddox shuddered. He could well imagine the devastation. The Grand Fleet would lose everything.

The Grand Fleet had the advantage, given what had happened a little over an hour ago in the Paran System. But so many things could go wrong in a space battle like this, even when it was a matter of bringing up the tonnage, the firepower, shields and hulls directly against the enemy.

The two mighty fleets converged upon each other. The Seventh Assault Fleet from Leviathan had crossed the gulf between the Scutum-Centaurus Spiral Arm and the Orion Spiral Arm. The forty-six maulers represented an invasion by an invading empire—

For no good reason that Maddox could see.

The minutes ticked by as the vessels from both sides closed upon the other. No masses of antimatter missiles flew. The mauler heavy-laser range and intensity would surely strike such missiles down before they got anywhere near enough. Could Star Watch sneak some antimatter missiles in during the battle?

That seemed unlikely to Maddox. It probably seemed unlikely to the Lord High Admiral Haig. That was why no missiles had been launched.

As the two forces surged at each other, Haig continued to issue instructions to the Grand Fleet.

Meta at communications informed Maddox of that.

In almost no time—or so it seemed—the bulk of the two formations converged, slowing as they reached extreme cannon range. Intense firepower flashed between the two fleets. The heavy lasers of the maulers struck shields, burning with intensity. At the same time, one battle cone after another directed their massed firepower into mauler after mauler.

Admiral Jellicoe and his task force, including *Victory*, remained behind in reserve.

Given the sizes of the fleets, one would think a fight like this would last hours, perhaps even half a day, or maybe a whole day. Instead, such was the intensity, mass of energy unleashed by antimatter engines and other generators that ships blew up one after the other, on both sides. This wasn't a one-sided contest, where one fleet annihilated the other, but a bitter struggle.

The reserve maulers moved up to help the others. Admiral Haig gave the order. Jellicoe gave the order. His cone advanced to help those hit by the reinforcing maulers.

Victory's generators caused the deck plates to vibrate. The ship's disruptor beam flashed, joining the firepower from the *Bismarck*-class battleships and the *Hernan Cortes*. The united beam knocked down a mauler shield and burned into its iridium-Z hull plate. That took time, but then the massed beam was through. Moments later, the mauler ignited in a blast of fury.

Although *Victory* engaged the enemy, the starship experienced minimal stress. That was a welcome change.

More orders came through as the battle began to turn decisively in Star Watch's favor. Surely, everyone here had realized it would from the beginning.

That was not due to greater tonnage, for Leviathan had more mass. That was not due to superior tactics, for none was in evidence today on either side. Instead, it was the disruptor beams, particularly those powered by the heavy-metal components of the *Conqueror*-class battleships. Those proved particularly effective.

Had it just been the older *Bismarck*-class battleships, which had once been the bulk of Star Watch, then perhaps the Seventh Assault Fleet would have stood a chance.

The heavy metals in the *Conqueror*-class battleships proved decisive.

Even so, twenty-eight battleships blew up, with all hands killed. Forty-two destroyers vanished under hellish lasers. Picket ships exploded like popcorn in gross numbers. Even so, those of Leviathan were going down to bitter defeat.

Only a short time ago, forty-seven maulers had exited the Laumer Point from the Barnard's Star System. Now, there were twenty-two left. That meant the firepower of Star Watch converged in greater numbers, inflicting much greater damage than the heavy lasers could do to them.

As had happened on many an ancient battlefield, the fight had been hot while the two contestants faced each other. But once one side lost its morale and turned away to flee, the other side butchered it with hardly a loss in return. That began to happen here in the Solar System.

Many Star Watch vessels left their cones of battle and limped away. If they had faced a vigorous enemy ready to pounce, those ships would have been annihilated. Instead, the best of Star Watch converged on the ever-dwindling number of massive maulers.

It was incredible that such a spectacular fleet, painstakingly built up over the years, would fall to such a sudden onrush of disruptor beams. At this point, antimatter missiles flew, churning up the remaining ships. It became carnage, pure and simple.

Lord High Admiral Haig did not offer the maulers as chance to surrender. Nerves were too taut for that. Maybe that was because this was his first major battle. Haig surely wanted a decisive victory. He got it. For the next hour, the Grand Fleet annihilated the last of the Seventh Assault Fleet from Leviathan.

Those maulers destroyed thirty-one battleships altogether, the coin of power in this instance. Those thirty-one, the majority *Bismarck*-class vessels, was a significant loss, especially when combined with the ten *Conqueror*-class battleships destroyed in the Paran System earlier.

Then an alarm went off on Earth. The reason was a suddenly appearing mauler very near Earth.

How had that happened, what special system or inhibitors had the cyborgs used to sneak so close?

The giant mauler launched flocks of world burners at Earth.

Counter missiles rose from Earth, intercepting the world burners, destroying them. This was a barrage assault, and a barrage defense.

One of the Leviathan world burners snuck through the defenses and streaked down. Surface lasers burned against it, but not enough. The world burner hit Rio de Janeiro in Brazil Sector. A titanic antimatter blast rocked the city, killing tens of millions in a moment. A flare of sunlight appeared on the Earth.

Seconds later, before it could launch more, the terrible mauler exploded under a hail of antimatter missiles.

The explosion meant hard radiation pouring down to Earth, but the enemy mauler was gone.

The Seventh Assault Fleet no longer existed. It had damaged the Grand Fleet and harmed the Earth, resulting in millions of civilian deaths. That was a stunning blow, and a slap in the face to the new Lord High Admiral. Otherwise, Haig had won a sterling victory.

Maddox couldn't say the world burner was a disaster, but it was a sobering moment of what could have happened.

It was time to start licking wounds, and probably pointing fingers among the high command.

It was at that point that Becker said into Maddox's mind, *I have it, Captain. I have it.*

-65-

Becker was sitting in the darter inside one of *Victory's* hangar bays while the battle between the Seventh Assault Fleet and the Grand Fleet had raged just a bit earlier.

He had just finished a gargantuan meal, served by his three girls. Belching several times, Becker sent them away, as he wanted to be alone.

The food and drink fueled his body but just as much his brain, a brain substantially bigger and denser than any human had possessed at any time in history.

Relaxed to a degree, Becker closed his eyes and began to range through space with his telepathic power. He sensed the war raging between the adversaries. He sensed hundreds and thousands of men, women and cyborgs dying all around him. That soon increased to tens of thousands. The dying screams—

Becker worked at it until he blocked that. Listening telepathically to the dying was harrowing and unpleasant. Too much of that, and he'd start to cry uncontrollably.

Wiping tears from his eyes, Becker roved farther afield. This telepathic power wasn't anything near omniscient. He had to concentrate and go to those locations with his mentality. It took effort, and the farther he roved from the darter—from his brain, really—the harder this became to do.

Becker sought evidence of watchers, most likely Spacers. He didn't seek cloaked saucer ships, but mind impulses. He had an intuitive sense that Spacers, maybe even Venna, watched the battle from a distance. This was the reason he hunted for them.

Becker's intuitive sense wasn't as developed as Maddox's. Becker found that interesting. He hadn't studied the captain's mind to figure out what did intuit things. He simply realized that that part of Maddox's mentality had been highly refined.

Not that Maddox was a telepath in any way. The captain simply had a few attributes that might be akin to telepathy that the alien named Balron seemed to have strengthened and trained. Maddox had then strengthened it even more by using it for years. Maddox, clearly, had a gift in his intuitive sense.

Becker's intuitive sense was cruder but also likely potentially stronger. It was likely that Becker would never develop that aspect of his abilities. He had too many other mentalist powers to work on, powers that would give him more bang per buck, as it were.

As maulers exploded and battleships erupted, Becker ranged beyond them and sought mental signs. Finally, near the Asteroid Belt, he sensed a bevy of minds. Two of them were powerful, one through Builder modifications and the other through alien—

Becker recoiled as he touched Venna's alien possessor with his telepathy. It had an oily feel and reminded him of the rat-thing he'd slain in his own mind some time ago.

"Bingo," Becker whispered in the command chair on the darter.

He lowered the gain of his mental search and slipped toward the cloaked saucer ship hiding in the Asteroid Belt. He stayed well away from the alien—

He had almost referred to it as the rat-thing. No. This was a dragon-thing in comparison to what he'd slain in his mind. Becker didn't want to fight the alien thing in Venna. He was too far from this body, and that would make him much weaker.

If they had been in the same room, Becker might have attempted it. It was like a man lying on a table with his arms stretched out trying to lift heavy weights. The fulcrum or balance would be against him.

Becker even avoided the Spacer adept. Instead, he sought the one known as—

Dax, Becker said.

Nine times nine is eighty-one. Six hundred thousand times twenty-nine is…

I'm not Venna or Mu checking up on you, Becker said, finding those names in Dax's mind. *I'm Becker, a human, and I can see you're afraid of the witch from Ector.*

What do you want with me?

Becker roved around, found himself blocked in one direction and sensed Mu becoming interested. He lowered the gain of his telepathy even more. Now, it was as if he whispered in Dax's mind.

I can't hear you, Dax said.

Becker raised the gain just a smidgen. *You help me and I'll help you.*

How can you help me? Dax asked.

What do you want or need?

To kill Venna, Dax whispered between his mathematical equations.

Becker would like that, too. He thought about it, considered the possibilities, and gave Dax a possible method to achieve it.

That could work, Dax said, seemingly impressed.

Why I told you the plan, Becker said. *You would have to time it perfectly, though.*

You've given me hope, Dax said. *I appreciate that.*

I love to help, Becker said. *It gets me right there, you know.* He gave Dax a mental image of him tapping over his heart with his fist.

I know what you want in return, but I can't tell you the assault fleets' assembly points.

No? asked Becker. *You refuse to think about them, do you?*

I'm sorry. I will not think about them.

That's too bad, Becker said. *I'm glad to help you, anyway. It was a pleasure meeting you, Senior Dax.*

Sensing the Spacer adept and then Venna approaching mentally, Becker's shadowed mentality zipped away from the cloaked saucer ship and sped back to his body in the darter.

One of the hardest things in the world for anyone to do was to **not** think about a thing. In the very act of telling yourself, "I will not think about that." One thought about the thing. The way to not think about something was to concentrate on things you loved. You had to forget about not trying to think about the thing that you didn't want to think about.

Of course, this meant that Dax had indeed thought about the assembly point locations of the other assault fleets. Becker had seen and then memorized the locations.

Back in his body, Becker sent a telepathic thought to Captain Maddox: *I have it, Captain. I have it.*

-66-

After speaking for a short time with Becker, Maddox had Meta patch a call through to Admiral Jellicoe. In moments, Jellicoe, smiling broadly, answered the hail on the main screen on the bridge of the *Hernan Cortes*.

"Sir," Maddox said, "we need to speak with the Lord High Admiral immediately. This is urgent."

Jellicoe stared at him. Perhaps the captain's earnestness threw him off.

"Even though we've just won a glorious battle in the Solar System, the fight against Leviathan is far from over," Maddox said. "I've just received intelligence regarding five new locations where Leviathan assault fleets are waiting to begin their campaign against us."

"What are you talking about?" Jellicoe said. "We just destroyed Leviathan's invasion fleet. The great threat is over."

"No," Maddox said. "That was only a small part of the invasion fleet. For reasons that I won't explain now—how I know, that is—Leviathan made a half-hearted attempt against us. We just witnessed it. This was a piecemeal attack only. There are one hundred and twenty-five *more* maulers waiting to attack Earth."

"You're out of your mind," Jellicoe said. "One hundred and twenty-five? That's two and a half times more than what hit us today."

"Exactly," Maddox said.

Jellicoe stared at him, his eyes darting back and forth, perhaps searching for the joke. Instead, he must have seen the captain's grim seriousness.

"That's...that's insane," Jellicoe said. "If one hundred and twenty-five maulers attacked us now, they would annihilate the Grand Fleet and destroy the Earth."

"Yes, yes," Maddox said. He closed his mouth and strove to remain calm, forcing himself to sit back in his chair. "You need to call Admiral Haig and explain the situation to him."

"Me?" Jellicoe said.

"I doubt Haig will listen to me," Maddox said. "He's more likely to listen if it comes from you."

Jellicoe laughed bleakly, shaking his head. "You misunderstand the situation. I'm in disfavor, bad disfavor."

"Haig heeded your warning about the attack."

Jellicoe nodded. "Haig listened to that. The destruction of my task force convinced him. The destruction of the task force also cast me into disfavor. Losing an entire task force does not endear one to their superiors. I'm now the last person Admiral Haig wants to speak to."

"I know Haig doesn't want to speak to me," Maddox said.

"Make that the second to last person then," Jellicoe said. "It's true he hates you even more than me, probably doubly so because you were proven right about all this. No, Captain. Haig is in his moment of exaltation. He's not going to listen to any dire warnings of supposedly more maulers out there."

"Haig is in exaltation even with the destruction in Rio de Janeiro?"

"No, not that," Jellicoe said. "That is a fly in the ointment."

Maddox could see that the loss of the task force had shaken Jellicoe to the core. It weighed on his mind and maybe even tormented him. Not even this victory, nor Jellicoe's role in it, restored the admiral's confidence. That meant Maddox needed a different avenue to approaching Haig.

"Can you patch me through to General Mackinder?" Maddox said.

"Mackinder? Sir, I'm on the outs with him as well. I'm in the wild lands in a political sense, *persona non grata*. My days in the halls of power—I'm just glad we won today. That was thanks to your efforts. I've miscalculated concerning you, Captain, have done so badly. I feel poorly about that."

Maddox nodded. "Noted. How can I convince Haig we need to take the entire fleet and launch it at five separate places?"

Jellicoe shook his head. "It's foolish to think Haig will listen to you. I can assure you Haig would never think of taking the Grand Fleet elsewhere and leaving Earth defenseless. The fleet is recovering from its losses. We've taken losses even though we've won a tremendous victory. I doubt anyone would agree to move the fleet."

"Is that your final word," Maddox said.

"It's not as if I disagree with you. I'm just saying Haig won't listen to me."

"I understand, Admiral," Maddox said. "Thank you for your time."

"Is there anything else? I feel obliged to help. I want to help."

Maddox shook his head.

Jellicoe nodded in turn, and he seemed sad. He then motioned to someone on his bridge and the connection ended.

Maddox bent his head in furious thought before looking up at Galyan, who watched him.

"Do you know where Haig's flagship is?"

"I do indeed," Galyan said.

Maddox stood. "I need to go directly to his flagship and tell him about this. Inform Keith of Haig's position. We're going to move there."

"Is that wise, Captain?" Galyan said.

Maddox made a face as he stared at Galyan. He'd given a direct order and Galyan had questioned it. This time, though, the question was critical and it must have struck true. Maddox abruptly sat back down. If Galyan's point was that Haig might intern him, it was a valid one.

"Meta, hail the Lord High Admiral," Maddox said.

"Yes, sir," Meta said.

She tried. She tried more. Then she spoke to someone. Afterward, Meta turned to Maddox. "I'm afraid the Lord High Admiral is too busy to speak with you."

Maddox sighed. He'd expected that. "Meta, patch a call through to the flagship and tell them this is an emergency. It may mean the fate of Earth and of Star Watch."

Meta nodded and tried again.

To everyone's surprise, maybe except for Maddox, the Lord High Admiral appeared on the main screen. Haig sat in his command chair, and he looked victorious, proud, grinning.

"All right, Captain," Haig said over the screen. "What is this you're trying to say? That there are more of these maulers out there?"

"Exactly, sir," Maddox said crisply. "There are five more assembly points. This fleet, the Seventh Assault Fleet, the one you just annihilated, came from the Zakym System, five hundred light years from Earth. The Leviathan fleet has been assembling there for over a year. I have also discovered five other assembly points. There are twenty-five maulers at each of them. If we use the nexus and create a hyper-spatial tube, we can strike with the massed battleships. That means we can annihilate Leviathan's forces piecemeal, each one at a time. That will end this round of assaults from Leviathan."

"Come now, Captain," Haig said in a jovial tone. "You're going to tell me that Leviathan had one hundred and twenty-five more maulers ready. If that were true, why did they attack us with only the forty-seven? That makes no sense."

"You're exactly right, sir, it doesn't make sense. It happened because Venna the Spy—"

Haig held up a hand, interrupting. "You're not going to repeat that insane idea Jellicoe tried to sell me earlier?"

"Was it insane?" asked Maddox. "The maulers attacked in the Solar System. One got through to Earth—"

"I know that," Haig said, interrupting again. "I hold you responsible for the antimatter strike against Rio. If you would have given me better intelligence—"

"Sir," Maddox said, interrupting because the words needled him. "I tried to tell you..." Maddox forced himself to calm down. He had to sell Haig on this. Nothing else mattered. "Admiral, you won a great victory today. I know the Grand Fleet took losses, and I know many ships are strained. Their cannons and other systems are nearly burned out or already being replaced. But we must take what we have and—"

"Hold it right there, mister," Haig said. "I run Star Watch. I'll decide what the Grand Fleet *must* do. I won't have a mere captain dictating to me."

"I apologize for my choice of words," Maddox said, trying his best to sound contrite. "You're right. You're in charge of Star Watch and the Grand Fleet."

Haig scowled at him, only partly mollified. "I've won an amazing victory against the assault from Leviathan. Now you come to me with this cock-and-bull story of one hundred and twenty-five more maulers, two and a half times more. You're actually telling me that those of Leviathan were too stupid to assemble all their ships and attack as one?"

"No, sir, that isn't what I'm saying."

"Oh?" Haig said, raising his eyebrows. "Then I must be hard of hearing, because that's what I heard you say."

Maddox cleared his throat and forced himself to speak slowly and calmly. "What I am trying to say is that Leviathan had a plan, a good one, but due to unforeseen events, they unleashed a power they didn't reckon on."

"No," Haig said, shaking his head. "I'm done listening to your harebrained stories. I've heard quite enough from you."

"Sir," Maddox said with an edge, "I was right the first time, in the beginning. You're blaming me but I was right then and I'm right now. If nothing else, send an expeditionary force and give me the command. Give me all the *Bismarck*-class battleships—"

"Oh, is that all you want?" Haig said, interrupting.

"Give me something so I can attack these assembly points before the separate maulers join into one force. We must hit them before they can do this."

Haig stared at Maddox, stared longer. Finally, the admiral turned away. He shook his head. He jumped up from his chair. He paced around the command chair three times before he looked at Maddox again.

"Is this really true what you're saying?"

"It is," Maddox said.

"How do you know?"

Maddox debated about what he should say. "Becker."

"Becker," Haig said. "Right, right, you mean that telepath. That means Becker must still be free. I want him in custody now, Captain. Do you hear me?"

"I do, sir. You'll be glad to hear that I've already sent Becker back into the Antarctica Prison Complex."

"What?" Haig said. "You did?"

Maddox knew this was a risk, a big one, but he didn't know what else to do. Thus, calmly, he said, "It is logged and recorded. If you'll check the prison records—"

"No, no, I've got too much on my plate for that nonsense," Haig said. "Becker is really back in stasis?"

Maddox had guessed Haig's reaction correctly. He needed to seal this for the moment. "I said I would return him, and I have."

Haig appeared dubious. "Becker gave you this information before you sent him away?"

"He did, sir."

"Where did Becker get it?"

"From hidden Spacers who watched the battle," Maddox said. "And from the one named Venna."

"Are you lying to me?" Haig said.

"I am not, sir," Maddox said, knowing he was going to catch hell for this later.

"Very well," Haig said with a sigh. "You were right about too much. I can't afford to ignore this information. I will reassemble the fleet. Come to the flagship, Captain, and we will speak on this more."

"Begging your pardon, sir, I think it's better if I remain aboard *Victory*. We don't have time to waste, you understand?"

Haig pointed at and stared at Maddox. Maddox stared right back. Haig dropped his hand, no longer pointing.

"If you're right, then we have to snatch victory out of the possible jaws of defeat."

"Yes, sir, and may I add, sir, that you're on your way to achieving the most spectacular victory Star Watch has ever made. You have the needed information, and often these battles are a matter of intelligence—"

"Don't lecture me, Maddox. It's boring and unbecoming. I'll get the ball rolling. Give me the first assembly point."

Maddox did so.

"I will check that with the Pluto Scanner," Haig said.

"Sir, it will not be visible to them. Those of Leviathan are using inhibitors to stop us from doing that."

Haig frowned. "If they're using inhibitors, how can we possibly create a hyper-spatial tube to reach them?"

"We'll have to come from farther away, and hopefully accelerate fast enough to catch the maulers by surprise."

"Very well, I'll give your scheme a try. If it fails, though, you're cashiered from Star Watch."

"I understand, sir."

With that, the meeting ended.

-67-

Now began one of the most complicated and fascinating mini-campaigns in Star Watch's history. Moving rapidly, the Lord High Admiral Haig gathered one hundred and fifty battleships, the best and the least damaged. He ordered them near the Builder Nexus between Earth and the Moon.

The first hyper-spatial tube extended to the Vincent System, 600 light-years from Earth. *Victory* led the way as the Patrol scout. The rest of the battleships followed. They reached a bleak star system with a massive black hole in the distance. They had arrived on the other side of where the supposed twenty-five maulers of Leviathan waited, the First Assault Fleet. That, at least, was according to Becker's data.

Maddox led the assault in *Victory*, and the fleet came around the black hole, building up velocity the entire way. The one hundred and fifty battleships rushed at the twenty-five waiting maulers. Star Watch gained surprise, although three maulers managed to escape through star-drive jumps. The battleships of Star Watch annihilated the rest.

The jubilation and intoxication were intense. The realization that the maulers had been here as predicted sobered the Lord High Admiral.

Haig soon called Maddox via the main screen. "Give me the next assembly point."

The entire expeditionary force used the nexus's hyper-spatial tube, going back to near Earth. After a ten minute wait, they used another hyper-spatial tube to the Tahir System, 492 light-years from Earth.

This system had a red supergiant, with an amazing number of Jovian gas giants in the system. Once again, twenty-five maulers of Leviathan waited. This was the Third Assault Fleet. Once again, the Star Watch battleships raced in. Four maulers escaped this time. Five battleships exploded. On others, generators blew and shields failed.

The battleships had been under strain from three deadly engagements. Each time, Star Watch had been victorious. Each time, the formidable might of Star Watch, like a mailed fist, met a small number of maulers and smashed them.

Galyan's reminder to Maddox was of World War II. The Japanese Empire had often concocted elaborate and intense invasion schemes. Particularly at the beginning of the Great Pacific War, the Japanese military pulled off amazing tactical victories. However, at the Battle of Midway, the overly complicated plan went awry. The American fleet carriers smashed the might of the great Imperial Japanese Navy. In a sense, Leviathan, with its superior strategists, had developed an exceedingly intricate plan.

It would have worked, Maddox realized, except fate had thrown a monkey wrench into it. The Phantasma Synth Crystals shattered, and Venna, or whatever she was, was created from the shards. That had changed so much.

Once more, the Star Watch vessels used the hyper-spatial tube, returning to near Earth. Men were ragged, throwing up, some with bloody noses, a few with brain aneurysms, dying.

The hyper-spatial tubes and constant battles were taking their toll. The servicemen and women weren't used to jumping so often, so quickly. That was a Patrol specialty.

Even so, Maddox was telling Haig via the main screen, "Sir, this is the moment. We've taken losses and the men are tired. Still, we must strike hard and fast and finish it, if we can."

"Yes," Haig said, "yes." The excessive use of the hyper-spatial tubes was affecting him, too.

The fleet used a hyper-spatial tube once more, finding an enemy fleet of maulers exposed and surprised. The battleships left them as junk in space. This time, none of the maulers escaped.

Although exhausted, the men and women of Star Watch now better understood their enemy and his potential strategies for escape.

At this point, however, Haig said, "No, we cannot jump anymore."

"At least take us back to Earth," Maddox said.

Haig stared at the captain for three full seconds. "Yes... I suppose you're right." Haig cleared his throat. "Tell me, Captain, did you really send Becker to Antarctica?"

"Of course," Maddox said, as his heart rate increased. He kept his features placid, though.

"You know what the penalty is for lying?"

"I do, sir."

Haig nodded. "Very well, let's go back home."

This time, *Victory* didn't lead those going home. Before *Victory* entered the hyper-spatial tube, a darter, in camouflage mode, left the double-oval starship and sped away.

That action would cost him, Maddox knew. It might even cost him his command. Worse, letting Becker take the three women hurt. Maddox was going to have to do something about that...later. Maybe chase Becker down himself and free the women. But he'd given Becker his word. The man had saved not only Star Watch but also the Commonwealth and maybe all of humanity. Wasn't that worth three crewmembers?

Maddox didn't want to make those calculations. Sometimes, though, there were hard choices. Sometimes a man didn't want to make those choices or keep his word. Maddox was made of sterner stuff. Even so, he asked God to forgive him for what he'd done. Then, *Victory* entered the hyper-spatial tube, jumping back to Earth.

-68-

Earlier, the Spacer saucer ship fled through the Laumer Point back to the Barnard's Star System. From there, it used the hyper-spatial tube back to the Paran System.

Following the map Mu had of the various hidden Builder nexuses that could form one-way hyper-spatial tubes they reached the Vincent System only to discover a destroyed First Assault Fleet.

The saucer ship hadn't traveled as fast as the Star Watch vessels due to some delays and then feeding by the alien thing in Venna.

It quickly became apparent to Mu and Venna, with Dax's help, that Star Watch must have used a hyper-spatial tube to sneak up on the maulers and destroy them.

"I don't understand this," Venna said. "How could Star Watch possibly have learned the location of this hidden system?" She turned to Dax. "Didn't the Grand Strategists do everything they could to hide these locations from the enemy?"

"Yes, Great One. This is inexplicable." Dax was privately reciting mathematical equations like crazy. He knew exactly how the enemy had learned, by one named Becker tricking him.

Mu looked sharply at Dax.

For once, Venna must not have been paying attention, as she didn't catch it. "This is unfathomable," Venna complained, "a freak of luck. Let us go to the next assembly point."

They reached the star system with the red supergiant and found destroyed remains of maulers. They went to the third system and found wreckage there as well.

"Star Watch must have cracked the code," Venna said. "Yet, how could they have broken it? This strikes me as strange. Why did Star Watch wait so late in the day to attack these assembly points if they knew about them all along?"

Dax shook his head as if perplexed.

Venna peered at him accusingly. "Mu, tell me. Is Dax the culprit?"

"I do not see how he could be, Great One," Mu said.

"That is not a precise answer," Venna said. "Is Dax the one responsible for this disaster?"

"No," Mu said.

"Why are you lying," Venna said, "I will feed on you for lying."

Mu dropped to her knees even as terror struck Dax. "I am not lying, Great One," Mu said in a high-pitched voice. "I would never lie to you."

Venna stared at Mu for some time, finally nodding sharply. In the most grotesque hag-form that she'd shown so far, Venna turned and shuffled from the chamber. Was she going to feed on someone else to regain strength? It seemed likely.

"Do you realize that she is destroying your crew?" Dax said after Venna had departed. "Soon, there won't be anyone left to fly the saucer ship."

Mu climbed to her feet and stared at him, even as perspiration dotted her brow. Had she been trembling? "How did you give away the assembly points to Star Watch, and why would you give them away?"

"I never gave them away," Dax said with a straight face.

"My reader says otherwise," Mu said, as she tapped the tiny screen on her left wrist.

"I don't see how that's possible." Dax was working overtime on the equations. Mu should not have been able to read anything.

"Easy," Mu said. "You're working too hard to keep something secret from me. Don't you know that I know that the more you work on those equations, the more you're seeking to hide something? What are you hiding?"

"Nothing," Dax said, "at least nothing of that nature. Besides, how could I possibly have told anybody of Star Watch where the assembly points were?"

"I sensed something earlier near the Solar System's Asteroid Belt," Mu said, staring at him. Perhaps she even used a modification on him.

Dax strove on the hardest of equations from his earliest days in the Conservatory. He worked through them, and he thought about anything he could. Then his mind touched on the great secret.

"What secret is this?" Mu said.

Dax gulped and knew he had to say something. What could he say that wouldn't anger Mu? Then it struck him. "This is the secret: we must kill Venna if we're to survive. If nothing else, once the last crewmember is devoured, we will be next."

"Nonsense," Mu said. "We can't kill Venna."

"We'd better think of a way fast then. You heard her. She threatened to consume you. She'll consume you and me long before we reach the planet Ector. It's far in the Scutum-Centaurus Spiral Arm. That means months of travel for us. Are you listening to what I'm saying?"

Mu looked up. 'Don't you dare lecture me, you cyber spy. You're not even fully human."

"I'm not human in the slightest," Dax said, "though I am humanoid."

"Whatever," Mu said, although she dropped the subject. Maybe she was too shaken to think about it anymore. Shortly afterward, she left the chamber to investigate something else further.

Using hidden one-way nexuses, the saucer ship soon reached the other two assembly points. This time they didn't find any wreckage. They didn't find anything. There were no maulers or any indication maulers had been here.

"This is unfathomable," Venna said in a rage. They were on the saucer-ship bridge. "Where did the maulers go? Senior Dax, you must know."

"I have an idea," Dax admitted.

"Then spit it out, you piece of filth," Venna shouted. "Where did they go?"

"I suspect they went home."

"What?" said Venna. "Did the mauler commanders disobey Great Leviathan and desert their posts?"

Dax shook his head. "Anything but," he said. "Likely, they discovered that the other assault fleets were destroyed. I'm sure they had instructions that at a certain point, they were to retreat back to the home spiral arm rather than remain here to be annihilated."

"Retreat?" said Venna. "I need those maulers. I need them in order to achieve my wonderful plan."

Dax hesitated. The hag was angry and ready to punish someone. This seemed like a bad time to broach hard topics. And yet, he was running out of time. That struck him as obvious. Thus, he forced himself to speak. "Great One, if we chase the maulers, follow them, we might be able to catch up so you can implement your plan."

"That's madness. The maulers can surely travel much faster than this saucer ship. This is so enraging." Venna's weird eyes smoldered as she glared at Dax. Abruptly, she turned to Mu. "I gave you orders to watch this little traitor, and now somehow he has thwarted me. I will consume you because of it. I will enjoy feasting on your etheric forces. You are the plumpest raisin of all, little adept. Did you know that, dearie?"

"Oh Great One," Mu said, once more dropping onto her knees, imploring with clenched hands to the horrible hag with burning eyes. How much of the original Venna still lived? It was hard to tell. Maybe little to nothing, but if there was nothing, was that why the thing feasted endlessly on the crew?

"No, it isn't quite time," Venna muttered. "You are still of some use to me." Venna turned to Dax. "I should devour you, you little prick. I... I... No. We will chase the maulers as you suggest. Perhaps we can catch up if we strive hard enough. And if we find them... Yes, you live for now because I still need you. But after that—"

Venna whirled around, perhaps pretending to herself that she hadn't just given him a death threat.

Venna left the bridge.

Dax and Mu traded glances.

Do you see what I mean? Dax thought.

Mu climbed to her feet, her features waxen and pale. She glanced at the wrist reader and nodded.

"How would we do this?" Mu whispered.

That was when Dax believed he might be able to escape these witches after all.

-69-

For three days, the saucer ship gave chase until Dax realized using the hyper-spatial tubes caused Venna's quick diminishment, or whatever the thing in her was that consumed the crew. Soon, there wouldn't be enough Spacers left to make the saucer ship work. That would be the end of their chances.

Thus, when they came out of the next hyper-spatial tube, and one of the sensor officers detected a mass signature exhaust of maulers, Dax said, "We're close. The exhaust trail shows at least fifty maulers were here just a short time ago."

"Aha!" Venna cried.

"We should jump immediately to ensure we reach them," Dax said.

"Immediately?" asked Venna. "I need a rest—after I feed."

"I don't recommend waiting," Dax said. "Every time we pause, the maulers pull away more."

"How can that be?" said Venna. "The cybers of Leviathan have the slowest jump lag recovery of all. We should be catching up. We are clearly catching up. What are you trying to pull, you little schemer?"

"The cybers surely consider this an emergency situation," Dax said, working hard to keep calm. "They will have taken injections to speed up the lag recovery process. They are going fast in order to tell Great Leviathan a disaster has struck. The invasion of the Commonwealth—"

"Very well," Venna said, interrupting, "but I must retire for the moment and strengthen myself." The hunched creature shuffled off the bridge.

When the hatch shut, Dax sidled up to Mu, staring at her.

"I don't know about this," Mu whispered. "If we fail, we're dead."

"If we succeed, we have a chance," Dax whispered. "If we hesitate, the game is over."

"What chance?" said Mu. "I'm pariah to the Spacers of Third Fleet. I'm an outcast to my people."

"Then come with me to Leviathan."

Mu looked at him. "You dare to go home after such a disaster?"

"I need to report to my strategist…" Dax paused, rubbing his chin.

"What now?" said Mu.

Dax had a second thought. Enigmach was an up-and-coming Grand Strategist. It had been his idea to use the Phantasma Synth Crystals. Those crystals had caused the disaster. What if he reported to one of the *other* Grand Strategists? Perhaps he wouldn't receive an automatic death sentence for failure then but a reward for warning Great Leviathan about this.

"Why are you grinning like a fool?" Mu demanded.

The question astonished Dax. He realized that he'd finally learned to fully shield his thoughts from Mu. The Spacer had indulged herself in the beginning, delighting too much in mocking him. Thus, he'd learned from his failures and successes, which helped him master the correct method of mind shielding.

"What are you thinking?" Mu said.

"That we must act now, or the instant we come out of the next hyper-spatial tube. If we don't, you and I are doomed. We will die."

"Everyone dies," Mu said.

"Do you want to die tomorrow?" Dax asked. "Do you want to die because all your etheric forces are sucked out of you? Do you want to let an alien monster destroy you and your saucer ship? Destroy the Spacer Third Fleet's chances of eliminating the menace of Star Watch. With the Commonwealth shattered, you Spacers could reclaim Human Space and continue searching for the Builders."

"You have a point," Mu said. "I must risk everything, but the thought of failing chills me to the bone."

"Then allow me to do this," Dax said.

Mu studied him. "You shield your thoughts too well and often for me to trust you."

Dax shrugged. "It's up to you. You hold the cards. I merely give you possibility. Let me do it, and we will succeed. You can go your way afterward. I can go mine, or you can join me."

"What about the phase ship?" Mu said. "What if I decide to keep it?"

"You have the power, and you have the right because you have the power," Dax said. "The *Python*, the *Kraken*-class spaceship I used to reach the Orion Arm will have probably joined the maulers returning home. Frankly, I'm sick of this spiral arm. I'm sick of dealing with all these differences. I just want to go home. I really want to be free of the witch. What say you, Mu?"

Dax almost threatened her as well, but he thought that would be a step too far.

"Yes!" Mu hissed. "I'll do it. I'll do it, but we must not fail. I forbid you to fail."

"Then give me the means to do this."

"Very well," Mu said. "Come with me."

-70-

The method of assassination was simplicity itself. A blaster to the guts might have been best. But Mu refused to give Dax a blaster. Instead, they waited together.

The saucer ship went through the next hyper-spatial tube. Afterward, Dax and Mu waited outside Venna's private quarters.

Mu dared use her Builder modifications to sense movement in there, not to seek any telepathic communication.

Did the vile thing inside Venna understand what was about to happen? Was that why she wasn't showing? Or did she sleep overlong? Even better, could she have died because of this jump? That would be awesome. That would be—

The hatch opened and Venna shuffled out. She looked haggard, horrible, worse than at any other time. Her head was down. Maybe she didn't even know they were there.

Dax touched the cyborg trooper on the shoulder. The trooper was alert and waiting for the signal.

Things seemed to slow down for Dax. Venna raised her cowled head. A second later, her eyes widened. By that time, the cyborg trooper was already crossing the distance between him and her. The cyborg moved with insectile speed. Servos buzzed. Sheathed muscles contracted and hands like titanium knives thrust for the hag.

Venna wasn't nearly as fast as the cyborg combination of mechanical and biological. However, she raised a hand, and the construct slowed imperceptibly. Even so, the cyborg trooper reached for the hag. His hands smashed *into* her rough, bark-like skin. The fingers curled and ripped out a bloody, horrible, black chunk of her flesh. Venna screeched and raised her hand higher. The next hand of the cyborg trooper slammed home like a piston, repeating the process, tearing out another piece of her flesh. It was hideous. It was awful. It was, perhaps, Dax and Mu's only chance for survival.

Venna clutched the thing, even as her hands began to glow. Now the cyborg trooper moved its arms like a boxing champion, thrusting, yanking out, thrusting and yanking out at mechanical speed. The cyborg tore the center out of Venna until one could see her lungs and beating heart. Venna screeched worse. She aimed a hand at Mu.

Mu twisted and cried out, "No, Venna, not me, not me. This was Dax's idea. He's the one."

Venna fixed her gaze on Dax.

He ran at her. There was a knife in his hand. Where he had gotten the knife didn't matter. Venna's eyes widened even more. Now the cyborg reached up and clutched the grotesque beating heart. He squeezed with considerable force, but barely made a dent in the heart, though he left bloody marks.

Dax thrust the knife even as he felt a terrible grinding force clutch his heart and mind. He continued thrusting nevertheless. The tip of the knife pierced one of Venna's wooden-tough eyes. The knife slid in deeper and struck her brain. Venna shrieked. With a titanic burst of strength and maybe etheric force, Venna hurled herself back from Dax and the cyborg trooper.

Mu employed her Builder modifications, attacking invisibly but powerfully.

Venna fell and thrashed on the deck.

This was the grimmest scene Dax had ever witnessed. It did remind him that once as a lad, he'd had to kill a cat-like creature amongst the hay bales of what was akin to horses. The cat had been pissing on the hay, making it inedible. Dax remembered that cat, a vicious creature. It raced away as he entered the barn, then turned and looked at him. Dax had lifted a shotgun-like weapon, firing and wounding the cat. It had spun and spun, meowing horribly. Then Dax had shot again, ending it.

That was what it felt like in the corridor. But could they end it?

The cyborg trooper leaped as invisible forces slammed against him. The forces tore pieces from his mechanical bioform.

Venna stood one last time, with the knife embedded in her eye and brain. She glanced at them with the good eye and pointed a bloody finger at Mu, and then at Dax. Then Venna collapsed onto the deck with a thud, and died as she seemed to deflate.

Dax braced himself, wondering if the alien entity in her could leap from her to him.

There seemed to be a thing like waves of heat. It left Venna's corpse and began to crawl for him.

"No," Dax shouted, backing away.

Mu drew a small Spacer laser pistol and fired. The heat waves halted where the beam touched. Then it tried to surge forward. Mu continued firing until the pistol's energy depleted.

Dax had watched, frozen in horror. He now expected the thing to finish what it had started, and leap onto and into him.

But there was nothing. The alien entity must have used up the last of its ancient vitality. It had once been in the Phantasma Synth Crystals, a shard and then in Venna. Now, it had finally died.

They were free from the thing from Ector. They were free from the savagery of Venna. It was time to see if they could unite and keep their agreements with each other.

-71-

Victory reached Earth, as did all the surviving battleships of the expeditionary force. The starship headed for the repair yards at the LaGrange Point Five. A large number of battleships headed there as well. They would be stationed there for some time.

Despite the grand success, Maddox was troubled, and the reason was simple. He'd lied to the Lord High Admiral about sending Becker back to the Antarctica Prison Complex. That lie would come due soon, and when it did, there would be hell to pay.

Over the next few days, Maddox debated about coming clean to the Lord High Admiral, telling him his reasons and trying to talk his way out of any serious punishments. The problem was Meta and Jewel. Haig would likely cashier him from the service for the lie. Haig would do that even though Maddox had done so much for Star Watch throughout the years. Too many in high command disliked him. While he had won over the old Lord High Admiral and others like Admiral Jellicoe, he hadn't won over influential figures such as General Mackinder.

Maddox sighed, continuing his inner debate. This wasn't like him. He knew it, and that bothered him. What was wrong with him?

Many of the crew left *Victory* as it waited its turn at the repair yards. Ludendorff was among those who went to Earth.

Ludendorff had been quiet most of this mission. That struck Maddox as odd.

The captain deadlifted in the gym on *Victory*. Between sets, his thoughts turned to Ludendorff. He wondered why he should think about the Methuselah Man now. Suddenly, he realized his intuition was alerting him. It was telling him that…something was off with Ludendorff, maybe had been for some time.

Why hadn't he noticed this sooner?

Maddox finished his deadlifts, showered, ate, and then checked with records to see where Ludendorff had gone.

That was odd. According to this, Ludendorff was leaving the Solar System. Why hadn't Ludendorff said something to him about this?

"Galyan," Maddox said.

The little AI appeared. "Yes, Captain?"

"Where's Ludendorff?"

Galyan blinked rapidly before saying, "The professor used his passport to buy a ticket out system. I believe he leaves today."

"Could you go check the space liner he's using and the specific vessel?" Maddox asked. "I want to make sure everything is good with him."

Galyan eyed Maddox before saying, "Of course, sir." The holoimage vanished.

Maddox drank a cup of coffee in the cafeteria as he waited, mulling over all that had happened this mission. He wondered when his lie would come due and what the punishment would entail. He'd lied, in one sense, for the good of the service so he could keep his word to Becker. Certainly, his lie hadn't helped the three crewmembers Becker had kidnapped. They were prisoners to the telepathic Overman, as he called himself.

Maddox sighed, got up, poured himself another cup of coffee, and wondered what was taking Galyan so long. The holoimage should have found Ludendorff by now.

Fifteen minutes passed before Galyan reappeared in the cafeteria.

"Well," Maddox said, setting down his cup, having finished his third one. "What's with Ludendorff?"

Galyan shook his head. "I did not find him, sir."

"You checked the liner registries?"

"I did, sir. Everything was in order. Ludendorff purchased a first-class ticket at the Astra-Durham Space Liner Company. He was scheduled to leave for the Tau Ceti System at 0900 in the *Boxcar*. That is the name of the specific ship. The system rebuilding is still heavy at Tau Ceti."

Maddox knew that. The Swarm Imperium had once wiped out everything there. The rebuilding had been slow and steady for years.

"I checked all the Astra-Durham scheduled flights for today," Galyan said. "Ludendorff wasn't on any of the liners or any of the packet ships. I then went into ghost mode and physically double-checked them. There was no sign of Ludendorff."

"Did he set a false trail?" Maddox asked.

"That is my conclusion as well, sir."

"Why would Ludendorff do that?"

"I do not know," Galyan said. "I could theorize, but I have no definitive conclusions. Nothing that reaches over fifty-one percent-plus on his personality profile."

"I see." Maddox considered this. "Can you check all Earth databanks and facial recognition systems?"

"I would have to invade the main computers. Would you like me to precede with that, sir?"

"I'm not sure." Maddox thought about it. Ludendorff could be in trouble. Yet his intuitive sense was saying to hang back. Why would it do that? This was odd. What was going on? "Let me think about it."

"Yes, sir," Galyan said.

A day passed, and Maddox still didn't know what to do. His intuitive sense made him uncomfortable, as it felt as if something was about to take place. Whether that was a call from the Lord High Admiral or with Ludendorff, he didn't know. Maddox continued to wait.

He wondered about Becker, what he was doing. Maddox thought about Balron the Traveler and all that Balron had done for him. Did whatever was bothering him include Balron in some way?

Maddox shook his head. He didn't know, so like a good hunter, he practiced patience and continued to wait.

-72-

One named Professor Ludendorff was on Earth, in a special air-vehicle he'd purchased with secret funds. He flew low over the water toward Antarctica. The one who called himself Ludendorff looked as he always did: with his shirt open at the top, curly chest hair showing, the ubiquitous gold chain around his neck, the thick white hair and the handsome rugged good looks. Yet something was off about him. For one thing, he stared fixedly out of the window. Then, a true oddity emerged. A jack was embedded in his head, with a line connecting it to the stealth vehicle's computer system.

The one who called himself Ludendorff activated a feature, using it so he flew in camouflage mode. That switched on a high technological system that warped the light rays around the aircraft. Observers could see what was on the other side instead of the craft itself. Perhaps if one looked closely, squinted, he would see what would appear to be heat waves shimmering at that spot.

The stealth craft left the frigid waters off Antarctica and slid over the icy continent. It appeared as if the stealth craft headed straight for the maximum-security prison complex where Maddox had earlier freed Becker from stasis.

What would Ludendorff want with that? Or was this really Ludendorff? It looked like him. He had been on *Victory* lately. What was the deal with the jack embedded in his head? That was an android thing. Was this possibly an android impersonating Professor Ludendorff? If so, where was Professor Ludendorff?

The mystery remained as the stealth vehicle flew through the howling winds of an Antarctic night, approaching the high-security prison complex.

No alarms rang as the stealth vessel landed on the ice near a prison wall. The one named Ludendorff pulled the jack out of his head, set it down, and rapidly worked the control panel. He set the stealth vehicle for something. He donned a parka, stepped out of the craft, and locked it behind him.

Inside the cockpit, a red light blinked beside a timer displaying 10:00. A second later, it changed to 09:59, 09:58, 09:57… Clearly, it was a timer. What would happen when it reached 00:00?

The one called Professor Ludendorff trudged to a heavy iron door in the prison wall. He tested the handle. Of course, it was locked. He did not know the security code. There was a number pad beside the handle. Instead, he applied his two ungloved hands to it and ripped open the door in a feat of ungodly strength.

An alarm began to ring.

The one called Ludendorff sprinted into the prison complex. He ran faster than he had ever run before. He ran down corridors, firing knockout darts into guards so they crumpled unconscious to the floor. He also activated a peculiar device that shorted each security camera seconds before he reached it. Soon, he was on the second-to-deepest level, having knocked out fifteen guards. What did that mean? Whom could he be trying to free?

The one named Ludendorff took a turbo lift down to the basement, heading straight for the stasis region. He hurried to where Becker had been interned not so long ago.

The one named Ludendorff broke into the area. Swiftly, he approached the stasis unit Becker had vacated. He knelt and manipulated it so the unit opened. After it did so, he laid down in it. Then, he reached out, pressed a switch and snatched his hand back as the stasis unit closed.

Next, he pressed a plate on his chest. There was a buzz, another buzz, and the thing called Professor Ludendorff shut down.

Just outside the complex in the stealth vehicle, the timer reached 00:03, 00:02, 00:01, 00:00. There was a click, and an explosive ignited, blowing up the stealth craft and the nearest part of the high security armored wall.

Deep down in the basement, in a stasis unit, another explosion took place. It happened where the one named Ludendorff lay in Becker's stasis unit. The explosion killed the three nearest individuals locked in stasis units. They were vicious criminals, and they died even though the law courts of the Commonwealth had not sentenced them to death but to a long internment of stasis.

The one named Ludendorff was no more. Interestingly, however, he had been partly composed of bio-matter. Why did that matter in any sort of way? The future perhaps held the answer to that.

-73-

The next day, Maddox received a call from the Lord High Admiral. The captain was on the bridge attending to his duties. Most of the crew had left, although Meta was at the comm station. Maddox, sitting in the captain's chair, saw the diminutive Haig staring at him from the main screen.

The Lord High Admiral was in his office at Headquarters in Geneva. His hands were folded on the massive desk once owned by Cook. The admiral was hunched forward, staring accusingly at Maddox.

"Can I help you, sir?" Maddox asked, dreading what was coming.

"Do you know what happened at the Maximum Security Prison in Antarctica?"

Maddox shook his head, surprised at the angle of questioning. "Did something happen?"

"Don't play coy with me, Captain. You know very well something happened."

"I'm afraid I don't, sir," Maddox said, "but I would be happy to listen."

Haig leaned forward a little more. "Let me ask you one more time. Did you send Becker down to the Maximum Security Prison in Antarctica?"

There it was. Maddox inhaled deeply. He almost said, "No, I did not, sir. I want to confess this," but his intuitive sense stopped him. Maddox wondered about that. Was it really his intuitive sense, or was it his disinclination to admit that he had lied, that he had committed fraud against the leader of Star Watch? Maddox said nothing as these thoughts ran through his head.

"I'm waiting for an answer," Haig said.

Maddox shifted in his seat, looked away, and pondered. *Why can't I just admit it and get it over with? Maybe it is the end of my career in Star Watch. It was a good career. I had a great time, but maybe it's time to do something else. Maybe it's time for me to take Meta and Jewel, and I don't know, start my own company or have a security apparatus where we watch high-profile individuals.*

Maddox's expression showed distaste. He didn't like the last idea.

"Is there something wrong?" Haig asked.

Maddox realized he had been woolgathering and lost his train of thought. He sat straighter, and he looked at Haig. Still, his mouth did not open, although his Adam's apple bobbed up and down. He shifted again. He licked his lips and finally opened his mouth to confess to the truth.

"Oh, okay. I know. I know," Haig said.

Maddox closed his mouth, wondering what in the hell was going on. Perhaps it was still best to wait this out.

"Becker is dead," Haig said.

"Sir?" Maddox said, stunned at the news.

"Didn't you hear what I said? There was an explosion. I suspect it was an attempted breakout of Becker. The records are spotty, although there is some indication that you sent Becker there. However, some of the records indicate you never sent him."

Maddox closed his mouth, then opened it again, uncertain.

"No, no, don't bother giving me a Maddox explanation," Haig said. "I don't know how you did it. I know you must have used underhanded or even nefarious means. The search teams studied the wreckage. There was an explosion from inside Becker's stasis unit. The bio-matter smears they collected confirmed Becker's presence in the unit."

Maddox blinked several times. This wasn't making sense. "Becker was in his stasis unit?" he asked.

"What did I just tell you?"

Maddox nodded. He had heard correctly, yet it still made no sense. Of course, he hadn't sent Becker down there. He had let Becker go. So this was a mystery.

"Can you explain what happened in the prison?" Haig said.

"I'm afraid I cannot, although I will be happy to look into it."

"No, no," Haig said. "I have my own security people taking care of it. Maddox, this whole thing seems fishy and strange. People have died."

"You mean other than Becker?"

"Yes, some violent, habitual criminals died in the blast."

"Becker's dead?" Maddox asked for a second time.

"Why are you so confounded by this? Do you feel bad because Becker helped us and that we owed him a great debt?"

"Uh…yes," Maddox said. "That's part of it, I suppose."

"You seem uncertain of yourself," Haig said. "That's unlike you. Why are you uncertain?"

"I'm stunned at hearing Becker's dead."

Haig now leaned back in his chair. "I can understand that. He did us a great service. I almost feel like we should have let him be. But how can you let a telepath of that power run free?"

"Oh, indeed," Maddox said quietly.

"We don't have to worry about it anymore," Haig said. "He's dead. You fulfilled your end of the bargain, except you broke your word to Becker, didn't you? You told him you were going to let him go free. I happen to know that because I've asked several officers who were on your bridge and heard things of that nature."

Maddox raised his hand in a shrug. What could he say? This was confusing and confounding. He didn't like that Haig had interrogated some of his people. It showed the Lord High Admiral's distrust of him.

Haig made a face as if he'd sucked on a lemon. "You did good work out there, Maddox. I'll admit it pains me to say that. I admit making those seemingly endless hyper-spatial tube jumps was taxing in the extreme. But the number of Leviathan vessels we destroyed was staggering. If they'd all joined in one fell swoop…"

"I know," Maddox said. "You did wonderfully, sir. I congratulate you on your excellent victories."

"Hmm," Haig said. "It has consolidated my position as the Lord High Admiral. People are congratulating themselves on having made the right choice in me. I probably owe something to you for what happened to me."

"It was your decisions, sir. I merely made some suggestions."

"Modesty, Captain?"

Maddox made another shrugging gesture with the one hand.

"You kept your word to Star Watch," Haig said. "I'm pleased you're siding with us and not with those freaks."

Maddox nodded.

"That's it then. The Lord High Admiral Haig out."

The screen returned to its usual blank state. Maddox sat back in his command chair, wondering what had really happened.

Galyan appeared. "Sir."

Maddox's head snapped up.

"I am here to inform you that I have a message from Becker that he left deep in my circuits."

"Yes?" Maddox said.

"Professor Ludendorff was kidnapped some time ago. His double went down to the maximum security prison last night and slipped in, I believe, to Becker's stasis unit."

"How could you possibly know that? Were you eavesdropping on my conversation with Haig?"

"I was, sir, but that is not how I know. Becker told me what the Ludendorff look-alike was going to do."

"Look-alike? What was down there?"

"A cyborg Professor Ludendorff double," Galyan said.

"What in blazes?" Maddox said.

"With this latent message, Becker told me this is his gift to you so it would clear your name with high command. Becker knew they wanted him back in stasis, but now you're clear."

"Oh," Maddox said.

"But, sir, the fact that a cyborg has been impersonating Professor Ludendorff means that someone switched him out, maybe even under our collective noses."

"Yes," Maddox said, surprised he hadn't seen that sooner. "Do you happen to know where Ludendorff is?"

"I believe I do, sir, as Becker left a message about that, too. Ludendorff is most likely in the Barnard's Star System, and the portal to Ludendorff's whereabouts is in the comet that holds the Builder nexus for the one-way hyper-spatial tube to the Paran System."

Maddox stared at Galyan. "All this is a fact?"

"Yes, sir. I believe two or three people can use the comet-based portal and rescue Ludendorff."

"I'm supposed to be one of those?" Maddox said.

"I suspect that was what Becker thinks."

"Did he give any indication who I should take with me?"

"Riker and one other," Galyan said.

Maddox wasn't going to take Meta. He knew that much. "All right, prepare for a voyage, Galyan. Can you run enough of the ship systems so we can operate with our skeleton crew?"

"I can, sir. You are thinking about going after Ludendorff then?"

"Damn straight," Maddox said. "Is Keith available?"

"He is, sir."

"Get him. I want him piloting the starship this mission."

-74-

Victory left the Solar System via the Laumer Point and appeared in the Barnard's Star System. The dim red dwarf was invisible to the naked eye from Earth, but visible here.

Galyan and Andros used sensors, checking everywhere. They detected nothing unusual. Most importantly, there did not appear to be any waiting and cloaked saucer ships or any lingering and hidden maulers.

Surprisingly, there were no vessels from Star Watch keeping guard. This seemed odd given recent events. Perhaps Star Watch was lax after its tremendous victory over Leviathan.

Star Watch had defeated a Swarm Invasion Fleet many years ago with help from the New Men. That attack had originated from the Carina-Sagittarius Spiral Arm. Now, they had single-handedly defeated Leviathan, originating from the Scutum-Centaurus Spiral Arm.

Maddox wondered if Leviathan would mount another invasion assault. If so, he doubted they would try for several years, at least. How significant was the loss of the maulers to Leviathan? Star Watch didn't know enough about the enemy empire. Could Leviathan easily absorb this loss, or would it strain their empire? So many questions needed answering.

Perhaps *Victory* needed to voyage to the Scutum-Centaurus Spiral Arm on an extended scouting mission. It would be good to see his clone brother, Dravek, again. How was Dravek doing?

Maddox shook his head. Now wasn't the time to dwell upon his clone brother.

"What's the prognosis?" Maddox asked.

"So far, so good, sir," Galyan said.

"Let's proceed then."

Victory headed for the comet near the third terrestrial planet, soon parking there.

"It's time," Maddox said.

He rose, went to the hangar bay, and collected the necessary equipment with Sergeant Riker, the young sergeant.

The sergeant looked very different from his former self. He has lank blond hair in abundance and lean features, resembling a young mechanic in an air-car shop.

"I haven't seen you much this mission," Maddox said.

"Nope," Riker said, "and I haven't really minded it as I haven't been in any personal danger. But what's odd is that I missed that."

"Then you did mind."

"…Maybe I did."

"I must have suspected that," Maddox said. "You're coming with me to find Ludendorff."

"Is Meta coming, too?"

Maddox raised his eyebrows.

"Galyan informed me about the situation. I thought that was per your orders."

"It was," Maddox said, "but no to Meta coming."

"Anyone else going to join us?" Riker asked.

"Not inside the comet."

Riker frowned. "Galyan told me there would be three of us."

"I know that's what Galyan suggested," Maddox replied, "but I've been wondering. Is three the magic number? I've decided no."

"So, it's just the two of us then?"

Maddox nodded. "When we rescue Ludendorff, three of us will return. There's your magic number."

"Are you being superstitious?"

"Sergeant, you know me better than that. Now, why all the questions?"

Riker shrugged. He'd been with Maddox the longest and had an idea what it meant when the captain didn't care to answer a question. Riker also knew he'd been asking too many and that it was time to stop.

They entered the tin can, stowing their equipment and strapping in to their respective seats.

Keith piloted the tin can out of the hangar bay. In less than ten minutes, he parked beside the comet.

Maddox and Riker unstrapped and donned spacesuits, adding small thruster units. They left through the airlock and using hydrogen propellant buzzed to the comet. It was a dirty snowball, twenty times the size of *Victory*.

Behind it was the Mercury planet, a dead world orbiting the red dwarf star thirteen percent the mass of the Sun. *Victory* was above them, the tin can close by.

The two reached the Builder area of the comet. They twisted around and applied white hydrogen spray. They turned around again and gently landed against the snowball. Each spaces-suited man swung an ice pick, working over an icy lip until each saw a hidden hatch deep in a crevice.

With his pick and spiked gloves, each worked beside the hatch. Maddox manipulated an ancient sequencer. The hatch opened. They squeezed in. Maddox pressed a switch. The outer hatch closed.

A team that had included Ludendorff had used the same airlock a while ago when they'd first checked out the comet's interior.

Inside—after the inner hatch opened—it was similar to the Builder Nexus near Earth, the space pyramid Maddox had originally brought back from the Library Planet. The area was far smaller in the comet, compared to a pyramid nexus, but corridors showed hieroglyphics on the bulkheads and various chambers had normal nexus machinery.

Interestingly, they did not float, but walked, as there was near-Earth normal gravity inside. That meant gravity dampeners. According to readings from *Victory*, those dampeners switched on when they entered.

That had happened last time, too.

Galyan appeared. "Would you like me to show you what I recall from Becker's instructions?"

"By all means," Maddox said.

Maddox and Riker no longer wore their spacesuits and thruster units. The first time the Ludendorff-lead team had entered this place, regular air had begun to cycle. It hadn't stopped from last time, which was interesting. It meant the interior held breathable air.

Galyan guided them through large chambers filled with slowly buzzing machinery of unknown purpose to a hatch or opening that shimmered as if a film of oil covered it.

"Is that the supposed portal?" Maddox asked.

"Becker informed me with his latent message that Ludendorff is somewhere beyond this portal," Galyan said.

"Now that we're here," Maddox said, "I wonder why a portal would be in a one-way nexus?"

"I do not know," Galyan said. "Nor do I know what lies on the other side of the portal. I highly urge great caution in doing this."

"Right," Maddox said. "Are you going to wait here for us to return?"

"If you will permit it, I will," Galyan said.

"I permit it."

"I would not plan on staying on the other side for long," Galyan said.

"Becker told you a being took Ludendorff through the portal?" Maddox asked.

"I have not said that," Galyan replied. "Becker was not sure. Instead, he indicated Ludendorff's going to the other side was a matter of odds."

"It keeps getting better, doesn't it?"

"It that a rhetorical question?" Galyan asked.

"Might as well be." Maddox turned to Riker. "Are you ready for this, Sergeant?"

"Why does this feel like the old days when I was your adjutant, and we went to places where we weren't supposed to be?"

"Because we're on the right track," Maddox said. "I can feel it."

Riker frowned. "Is it just me, or do you seem unusually upbeat, sir?"

Maddox realized he did, and he realized the portal was the reason for it. He was going to do something physical in an Intelligence sort of way, a mission where he would rely on his quick wit and physical skills. Did he enjoy those more than fleet battles? Yes. Maddox realized he did.

Maddox turned to Galyan. "We should be back soon."

"I believe you already said that, sir."

Maddox nodded curtly. "Let's go, Sergeant."

Maddox stepped through what Galyan had called a portal with Riker following close on his heels.

-75-

Maddox stepped into a corridor that looked identical to the one he'd just left. Then Riker stepped through.

They glanced at each other. Riker shrugged.

Maddox eyed the corridor. This place felt like a mirror image of what they'd left. The corridor had lights and gravity, which implied gravity dampeners. It also had regular, breathable air. Had it been foolish to step through without a breather, at least? Maybe his intuitive sense would have told him he needed a spacesuit on this side.

"Does it feel as if we're in the same place?" Maddox asked.

"Now that you mention it," Riker said, "it does."

Maddox drew a blaster.

Riker followed suit. "Just a second, sir. I want to check something." Riker took out a comm unit and clicked it on. "Galyan, can you hear me?"

Galyan did not answer.

"Where could we be if these corridors look just like the ones we left?" Riker said as he pocketed the comm unit.

"Good question," Maddox said. "For all we know, the portal was created by the Mastermind, or it is part of the Yon Soth passages the Mastermind's Ardazirhos used."

"I hope that's not the case," Riker said.

Maddox thought about that, and he shook his head. "It doesn't feel as if we're going to run into any Ardazirhos."

"That's a relief. Does it feel like we're back on the planet with the rubies scattered everywhere?"

"No, it doesn't feel like that either," Maddox said. "This feels like a Builder structure built inside a comet."

"A different comet?" asked Riker.

"Let's find out."

They started down the corridor, searching, remaining alert. They tried various hatches. They all opened. Behind some, they found chambers filled with crates. No doubt, the crates contained ancient Builder artifacts.

"Could this be a storage facility?" Riker asked.

"Let's check one of the crates."

They entered a storage chamber. The crate was wooden. They pried it open and discovered a deactivated android similar to those they had previously encountered in past missions.

"I like this even less," Maddox said. "I feel like rigging an explosive and detonating everything."

"I know what you mean," Riker said. "Can we afford to do that?"

"I guess not if we want to continue breathing," Maddox said.

They backed out of the chamber, keeping their blasters aimed at the crates. None of them exploded open. None of the androids activated, if the rest of the crates indeed held androids.

Once the hatch closed, Maddox and Riker resumed their search along the corridor.

"Should we be shouting for Ludendorff?" Riker asked.

"I doubt that would be wise." Maddox paused, trying to use his intuitive sense. He didn't feel Ludendorff anywhere, and he had no idea what Ludendorff might be doing.

"I wonder why Becker left the information in Galyan," Riker said. "Heck, I wonder how Becker learned what he did."

"Those are good questions. Becker seems to want to help us, but he wants to do everything his way. I think he's conflicted, enjoying his new status, but also wanting to belong to a greater organization. As to how he learned this, I have no idea."

Riker nodded.

They kept going and tried different hatches, finding more crates and then empty chambers. One chamber had a viewing port. They stepped in and up to the viewing port. There were masses of stars bunched together out there, a glittering panorama from horizon to horizon.

"Oh no," Riker said. "It feels like we're in the galaxy's center, where stars cluster thick as diamonds."

"Does seem that way," Maddox said.

The captain studied the massed stars. They seemed like gleaming gems presenting a multitude of colors. It was awe-inspiring, and yet Maddox felt, "I don't think this is real."

"Sir?" asked Riker.

Maddox indicated the viewing port and stars. "This feels like a projection, an image for our benefit."

"Then we're not in the center of the galaxy?"

"Whoever is doing this wants us to believe we are."

They exited the viewing-port chamber and continued down the corridor. They reached a small hangar bay with a small, triangular ship parked on the deck. It was three times the size of a Star Watch shuttle.

"What do you say, sir? Should we take the ship out and verify if we're really at the galaxy's center?"

Maddox thought about that. He almost said yes, but then he decided it was a bad idea. There was too much risk for too little reward. They left the hangar bay and continued searching. They must have gone in a circular pattern, because they reached a portal with an oily film in front of it.

"Is this the same portal?" asked Riker.

"We should have marked it before we left," Maddox said. "We can do it now."

He aimed his blaster and fired beside the portal, leaving a scorch mark. Then Maddox holstered the blaster and crouched beside the bulkhead.

"What are you doing?" Riker said.

"Time for a break," Maddox said. "Let's take five to eat and drink, then we'll resume."

Riker sat down beside Maddox. They broke out rations and began to eat, munching in silence as they leaned against the bulkheads.

Where in the hell were they, and where was Ludendorff? They'd better find out soon before something evil happened to them.

-76-

With a grunt, Maddox stood, holding out a hand. Riker reached up, and Maddox pulled him to his feet.

"What now, sir?" Riker said.

"Now we're going to retrace our path but keep an eye out for hidden hatches or doors."

They started with a slow step, checking, touching, and listening. Progress was slow, covering even a hundred feet took time. They continued with the same slow, cautious approach, looking for something they had missed last time.

Perhaps an hour and a half later, Riker said, "Here, sir, look at this."

Maddox joined the sergeant on his side of the corridor. There seemed to be a faint line running like a seam.

"I think we may have found something, at least something different than before," Maddox said.

Riker stood, looking around before he pointed. "That's the way to the viewing port."

Maddox nodded, but he was disinterested in the port. He ran his fingers over the bulkhead, questioning if it was significant. It was too imperceptible to be sure. He looked at Riker. "Your eyesight is better than mine. I don't see a thing, although at first I thought I did."

Riker shrugged. "To be honest, sir, I felt something odd, then noticed that faint line. It is faint."

"Right," Maddox said. He reached to his boot and pulled out his monofilament blade. He shoved the tip into the imperceptible seam and cut with the blade that could slice through anything. Behind the newly made opening was another corridor.

Maddox carefully put the monofilament blade back into the sheath of his boot. He straightened and drew his blaster.

"Be wary," Maddox said.

They started down the previously hidden corridor, with Maddox in the lead. The lights began to flicker. It was surprising there had been lights. In a second, they went out.

Both men donned headband lamps and switched them on. They continued with circular lights sweeping the corridor ahead of them. Soon, they reached a hatch.

Maddox tested the hatch, then opened it.

Inside, a wall displayed a kaleidoscope of colors. Seated before the kaleidoscope was Professor Ludendorff. He was strapped down to a chair.

"Ludendorff," Maddox said.

There was no response from the professor, not even a twitch.

"High alert," Maddox told Riker.

The two stepped inside the chamber.

"Don't look at the patterns of light," Maddox said.

It was too late for Riker. He'd looked and was mesmerized, standing there doing nothing.

In two steps, Maddox snatched away Riker's blaster and thrust it in his waistband. He walked over to Ludendorff. The professor's eyelids were taped open so he had to look at the swirling lights. His face was strapped to a harness so that he couldn't turn away. There was a drip in his mouth.

Maddox checked the water supply, which had run dry.

Holstering his blaster, Maddox took out the monofilament blade for a second time and carefully cut away the restraints holding Ludendorff.

"Come on, Professor. I've set you free."

There was no response from the Methuselah Man.

Maddox had expected that. He stowed the knife, then grabbed the front of Ludendorff's shirt to pull him up. The man rose limply, as if he had no control over his body. Maddox pulled Ludendorff to the quietly waiting Riker. The sergeant's mouth hung open and he had begun to drool. Maddox grabbed Riker by the front of the shirt and pulled both of them staggering out of the chamber.

Maddox released Riker, who swayed but remained upright. Then he forced Ludendorff onto his butt, resting against a bulkhead in the corridor.

Maddox reentered the chamber without directly looking at the swirling lights. There was a tug at his eyes, but he resisted looking. With his blaster, he fired until he destroyed the swirling colored lights. He didn't find anything behind where the lights had been to project them. Even so, the colored lights swirled no more.

Maddox felt an instinctive need to get out of here. He leaped out, and as he did, gas hissed into the chamber and the hatch shut with a clang.

Both Ludendorff and Riker rested against the bulkheads, limp and staring at nothing.

Maddox found it interesting that Riker had sat down by himself. He studied them and listened carefully. There was no noise and no indication of aliens.

"How do I do this," Maddox whispered under his breath. "Riker," he said, crouching before the sergeant and shouting in his face.

Riker blinked, blinked again, and slowly came to. "Captain, what happened?"

"You stared at the swirling light even when I told you not to."

"Lights?" asked Riker.

"Can you stand?"

"Maybe," Riker said.

"Then do so."

Riker used the bulkhead and pushed himself up to his feet. He was panting as if he'd exerted himself.

"Ludendorff," Maddox said, in front of the professor.

There was nothing. The man seemed to be a zombie, as far as his mind was concerned. The usually alert eyes were blank.

Maddox stared into Ludendorff's eyes longer. He couldn't be sure. There had to be a way to test this. Then he took out the monofilament blade again. He made an incision in one of the professor's legs. Blood seeped. The problem was that there had been androids in the past that had skin that could bleed.

Maddox put away the knife. He opened Ludendorff's mouth and peered into the throat using the headband light. Everything looked normal, human.

"What do you say, Sergeant? Is this the real Ludendorff?"

"I have no idea," Riker said. "I just want to get out of here. This place gives me the creeps."

"It should," Maddox said. "It's a laboratory. I believe they've been studying Ludendorff—or they've been programming him. I don't like the idea of programming."

"Damn." Riker used a sleeve to wipe sweat from his face. "This is worse than I thought."

Maddox nodded, squatted and hefted Ludendorff so the man's stomach rested on his left shoulder. Then Maddox rose as if rising from a squat. His deadlifts and squats throughout the years made this an easy lift, even though Ludendorff was heavy enough. He didn't feel heavy like an android or cyborg, though. No, he felt how a human Ludendorff should be.

Could this be a clone, a duplicate? Maddox's intuitive sense was saying no. He was going to have to trust his instincts in this. Were Builders hiding here? That seemed the likeliest explanation.

"Builders!" Maddox shouted. "Show yourselves. Is this some kind of horrid test facility? Is the Methuselah Man your pet, and you hate it that he's been free all these years? Come on, show yourselves, you bastards. What are you afraid of?"

Afterward, Maddox looked around and waited with anticipation, with Ludendorff draped over his left shoulder.

"Okay," Riker said. "That did absolutely nothing."

"Shut up," Maddox said.

Riker's head swayed back before he nodded. He reached for his holster. "Hey, my blaster's gone."

Maddox thought about it, and he drew Riker's weapon from his waistband. He handed it butt-first to Riker.

"Thanks," Riker said.

Maddox nodded.

Afterward, the two men of Star Watch listened, looking around and waiting. Nothing happened.

"Let's go," Maddox said. He felt danger. It was coming from the chamber with swirling lights, or where there had been them. They needed to get out of here.

Maddox took the lead. Ludendorff remained over his shoulder, doing nothing, but doing nothing to hinder Maddox's movements.

"Why are you going so fast?" Riker said, breathing hard.

"Keep up," Maddox said.

They reached the place where Maddox had made and cut away a makeshift hatch.

"Just a second," Maddox said.

He set Ludendorff on the floor and lifted the cut piece of metal. He inserted it back into its spot. "Set your blaster at the right temp."

There were several clicks as Riker adjusted his weapon's setting.

"Weld this or melt it," Maddox said.

Riker did, with the blaster beam moving along the edges. The fused metal kept the hatch in place when Maddox let go. The metal had started getting hot.

The captain maneuvered Ludendorff back onto his shoulder. They continued down the corridor, backtracking. Ludendorff had yet to speak or move, but at least he was breathing. That was good enough for now.

"What do you think was using him?" Riker asked.

"I'm guessing Builders," Maddox said, "but I don't know for sure. We need to get back to *Victory* and then we need to get out of the star system."

"Why?"

"I don't know," Maddox said, "and that's bugging me, but I think we may have discovered a newly haunted star system."

"You mean like the Xerxes System from long ago?"

"Precisely," Maddox said.

"Yeah," Riker said, "I never cared for the Xerxes System. This may be a new one, and it is right beside Earth."

"We're going to have to build orbital platforms outside the Lamer Point entrance in the Solar System."

"You think it's that dangerous?" Riker said.

"I wouldn't have made the suggestion otherwise."

"That's just great. After all that has happened—"

"No," Maddox said, interrupting. "That's the wrong way to look at it. We found that this place is dangerous. That's the important thing. It's better to know than being ignorant."

"I guess," Riker said.

They reached the oily portal, the one marked by Maddox's blaster.

"Here goes." Maddox stepped through with Ludendorff over a shoulder, and Riker followed.

Galyan was waiting on the other side. "Sir, you have only been gone thirty-one seconds and you have found Ludendorff. That was quick."

Maddox turned back, looking at the portal. "There's something weird about that place." He shrugged. He had the professor. "Let's go. It's time to get back to *Victory*."

-77-

The three made it back to the fold fighter. They'd brought an extra spacesuit with them. Once they were aboard, the fold fighter returned to a *Victory* hangar bay. The starship immediately sped for the Laumer Point.

Galyan and Andros fixed their sensors on the comet as the starship fled.

Maddox took Ludendorff to sickbay before heading straight to the bridge. He watched the main screen. He didn't know what he was waiting for, but he was waiting for something to happen: a hidden missile, a cryptic message. His intuitive sense told him that they were still in danger.

Why should this be? Maddox asked himself. *Because this place is haunted.* But that was an imprecise and superstitious answer. It wasn't haunted. There was something taking place in the star system that they did not understand.

From now on, they would have to use precautions with Barnard's Star System, especially since it was so near to Earth with the Laumer Point. The hidden nexus with a one-way hyper-spatial tube—

Maddox shook his head. This was odd, but perhaps it made sense that an ancient Builder outpost was operational near Earth. Hadn't the Builders had pet subjects and people? Maybe Ludendorff had been stashed on an ancient laboratory run by the Builders. Maybe the old lab was running on automatic. Perhaps one of the Builders' servants used it.

Something was on the other side of the comet station in the Barnard's Star System. Had they been transported to the center of the Milky Way Galaxy? Maddox didn't think so. The pathway hadn't been like the Yon-Soth connections he had used in the past. In those, he had fallen during a horrific journey. This had been an instantaneous thing.

Maddox snapped his fingers. This had been like the time on the Ruby Planet. Could it have anything to do with Underspace?

Maddox shook his head. He didn't know. The journey had been too quick.

The more important point: was Ludendorff okay? Could they trust the professor after this?

The Iron Lady once lost her high position because aliens had meddled with her brain. Ludendorff claimed to have fixed that, but the Iron Lady had never obtained the status she used to because of that.

Would the same be true for Ludendorff? Maddox was loath to get rid of Ludendorff. The professor had been instrumental in many missions. Maybe he would have to keep an extra watch on the Methuselah Man. He owed Ludendorff.

Soon, *Victory* left the Barnard's Star System and reached the Solar System. Maddox took Ludendorff to the best medical facilities on Earth and later reported to the Lord High Admiral. The man listened and agreed with Maddox's decisions.

"We need to stay out of that star system," Haig said.

"I concur," Maddox said via screen.

"We should establish a defensive perimeter around the Laumer Point that connects to the Barnard's Star System."

"I agree with that, too," Maddox said. "I suggest we only go to the comet with every scientific sensor on full blast and be ready for anything."

"Do you think this is a Patrol situation?" Haig asked.

"Maybe," Maddox said.

"I will take that into consideration. Now, I have work to do. The Lord High Admiral out."

Maddox waited five days for Ludendorff to regain coherence. When that finally happened, Maddox immediately went down to the hospital on Earth and saw the Methuselah

Man lying in a bed. There were three beautiful nurses taking care of him. When Maddox entered the room, the nurses giggled and left.

Ludendorff was beaming like a fool. "Well, well, well, Captain Maddox. I'm better." Ludendorff slapped his chest with both hands.

"Do you remember what happened to you?" Maddox asked.

Ludendorff frowned. "I do not."

"Nothing at all?" asked Maddox.

"I remember a kaleidoscope of lights. I remember trying to resist them, and that was it. Riker visited and explained what happened during your rescue."

Maddox nodded, wishing Riker hadn't done that. But what was done was done. "Did Riker mention a double, an android or cyborg version of you? During our fight with Leviathan, the double was aboard *Victory* for a time."

"Riker told me that, too," Ludendorff said. "It does sound like an android situation, but I'm more inclined to think this has something to do with the Builders."

"I agree with that." Maddox paused before he asked, "What about dreams, do you have any strange dreams?"

"Now that you mention it, my sleep has been troubled. But I can't remember my dreams when I wake up. I do know they're intense. I wonder if they're sexual."

Maddox shrugged. "Do you think whoever did this to you, reprogrammed you for future actions?"

"Alas, the possibility exists," Ludendorff said. "I plan to take precautions. Although it pains me to say this, you must take precautions with me, too."

"I agree," Maddox said.

Ludendorff frowned. "You didn't have to agree so quickly."

"Maybe you're right."

"So what happens now?" Ludendorff asked.

"What always happens," Maddox said. "We wait for the next mission to start."

"With the possibility of an enemy having programmed me, you still want me with the starship?"

"Most assuredly we do," Maddox said.

"Because of my genius?" asked Ludendorff.

"Yes," Maddox said with a chuckle, "because of your genius."

"Good. If anyone can figure out what happened, it's me—and you, Captain. I've learned to appreciate your unique abilities." Ludendorff frowned. "How did Becker know all this and why did he bother telling you? And why didn't he tell you more?"

"I've been wondering the same things," Maddox said. "My conclusion, as hard as it is for me to say this, is I think Becker feels kinship for me."

Ludendorff barked laughter.

"You might not think that, Professor, if you'd seen him in his latest guise."

"Oh?"

Maddox explained how Becker had changed himself into a lumpish and powerful giant.

"How extraordinary," Ludendorff said. "That truly is a marvel. The Liss did something strange to Becker. We may rue the day you ever let him out of stasis."

"Becker is dead, don't you know?"

"What?"

Maddox looked around and leaned near. "I'll tell you about it once you're back on the starship."

"Fair enough," Ludendorff said, "although you know I hate a mystery. "It makes me curious."

"I know, Professor. I want you back on the ship as quickly as possible. This is to goad you."

Ludendorff nodded. "Are we going to go to Barnard's Star System?"

"I want to wait on that," Maddox said. "It reminds me too much of the Xerxes System."

"Aha! Yes, Riker said something about that. Well, Captain, we succeeded again, didn't we? Even though I don't know what I had to do with it."

"We succeeded, and you're part of the team. You're part of the family, Professor. So you had plenty to do with it."

"You know," Ludendorff cocked his head. "That actually makes me feel good. Now, if you'll excuse me, I'm waiting for the nurses to return. I've been telling them stories, and they've been, well, they've been helping me recover."

"Right you are, Professor."

With that, Maddox got up and headed for the exit.

Star Watch had defeated Leviathan. He had rescued the professor, which was a serious mystery and there was a new problem with a nearby star system. That could wait for next time. This time, they had succeeded by thwarting Leviathan's invasion.

He would have to deal with the three missing crewmembers. He'd made a hard choice and kept his word. He'd never said anything about letting Becker keep the women for as long as he wished. Maddox would have to rescue them, and do so soon.

Maddox sighed. He would miss Cook and Stokes. Yet, that was the nature of life. As Maddox walked down the hospital corridor, he realized that one should enjoy life to the fullest while he was alive. For there would come a day when he no longer was alive.

Maddox nodded to himself. Then he increased his stride. It was time to take his family out for a big dinner. It was time to take a vacation with Meta and Jewel, having fun with his daughter, and with his wife. Maddox regretted that he spent so much time away from Jewel, not seeing her enough. It was time to rectify that, at least for a little while.

-78-

Several weeks later, Dax and Mu reached the tail end of the mauler formation heading for the Scutum-Centaurus Spiral Arm. They hailed the giant warships; one mauler detached from the fleet and waited. At that point, Mu lost her nerve.

"I can't do this," she told Dax. They were in the ready room off the bridge of the saucer ship. "I'm afraid to leave this spiral arm. I feel as if I'll never come back if I do."

"Aren't there Spacers in the next spiral arm?" Dax asked.

"That's not the point," Mu said, "and not Spacers from the Third Fleet." She twined her fingers together and bit her lower lip. "The truth is my blood chills at the thought of being in an empire run by cybers. I saw what your cyborg trooper could do." Mu shook her head. "It's too frightening to think of living among your people."

"The choice is yours," Dax said. "Will you return to the Spacer Third Fleet then?"

"I don't know," Mu said. "I feel like a pariah."

"Are you evading my question?" Dax said.

Mu turned and stared at him through her black-tinted goggles as some of her former arrogance returned. "If I am, I'm certainly not going to tell you about it."

"Fair enough." Dax became thoughtful, glanced at her and said slowly, "What then of the phase ship?"

Mu quit biting her lower lip as they firmed. "You remember that, do you?"

"I would be remiss if I didn't," Dax said. "The phase ship was my responsibility."

It seemed she was staring at him, although it was hard to tell with the goggles. "With the maulers near, you have the power to commandeer it."

"I do have the power," Dax said.

There was a subtle stiffening of her shoulders. "Will you use the power to take the phase ship?"

Mu asked because she was no longer able to read his thoughts. Dax had convinced her a week ago to dismantle the process she'd installed earlier, in his brain, under Venna's direction.

Dax debated with himself. Taking the phase ship would be the wisest policy, especially if he returned it to the Leviathan High Command. Returning without the phase ship might be a dubious prospect. Still, he wondered if Mu might kill him here at the last minute in order to keep such a prize.

He would never have to worry about Leviathan High Command if he died today. Such being the case, Dax decided to insure the greatest prize of all, his life.

No one else held his life in such high esteem. There was another consideration. Mu had helped him against Venna when she could have worked against him. She had worked against him in the beginning, but not at the end when it finally counted.

Considering the odds, risks, and rewards—

"The phase ship is not mine to command," Dax said. "Therefore, I will not enforce my right to it as a representative of Leviathan. The phase ship is yours."

"Do you mean that?" Mu asked, sounding dubious.

"I do, and I will not break my oath on it."

Mu stared at him, turned away and seemed to think. The phase ship represented power and a unique ability in the Orion Arm. She faced him. "I'm not going with you. I'm staying with the saucer ship and in this spiral arm. It's the only home I know, and I don't feel like changing it. I will do nothing to hinder you leaving, however."

Dax felt a wave of relief. He was going to live today. He could worry about tomorrow another time.

"Goodbye, Mu. Despite all you did to me, in the end, you sided with me when it counted."

"I hope I made the right decision doing that," Mu said.

"You most certainly did," Dax said. "Don't doubt yourself on that."

"I don't."

Soon, an orbital from the gigantic mauler docked with the saucer ship. Dax took his leave of Mu.

The cyborg trooper no longer existed in any meaningful way. It was spaced junk. Thus, Dax boarded the mauler alone and began the long trip home as it sped to catch up with the formation. There was no sign of the *Python* or the other two *Kraken*-class warships Dax had used to come to the Orion Spiral Arm. He had no idea what had happened to them. Likely, the Spacer Third Fleet had them.

The long trip to Loggia, the capital planet of the Sovereign Hierarchy of Leviathan, took eight months and eleven days after leaving the saucer ship. It proved an uneventful journey.

During that time, Dax thought, rethought, and recalculated, learning everything he could from the War Master of the fifty maulers about what had happened to them. Dax used the information to refine the report he could give upon his return.

After having been away from Grand Strategist Enigmach for well over a year and a half, Dax was returning.

The cyber spy decided on his strategy for maintaining a long life and retaining his post as a senior spymaster.

Dax reminded himself there was no one in Leviathan's spy services that could have endured his torments. He was, at least in his estimation, the greatest spy Leviathan had ever developed. Therefore, it behooved him as a servant of Leviathan, to make the most of his talents and skills in the service of Great Leviathan. That meant he should remain alive, did it not?

Dax certainly believed his logic impeccable. No one could shatter it, except possibly for Enigmach. The Grand Strategist would have a stake in Dax's evil outcome, however. Should anyone trust Enigmach's judgment then? Dax decided: not in the slightest.

Therefore, Dax would go through with his plan. His survival mandated it. The most likely candidate wanting to hear his side of the story would be Grand Strategist Tactix.

When the maulers finally entered the Loggia System, Dax began his initial maneuvers for accomplishing this task.

-79-

The great metropolis planet of Loggia hove into view as the war master and other sub-commanders headed in orbital craft for the metallic planet.

The fifty-plus maulers remained in the outer system under super-mauler guard.

Loggia was unique from all other planets in the Sovereign Hierarchy of Leviathan. Throughout the centuries, it had been one hundred percent urbanized. That meant great towers, monumental structures, mansions, factories, sprawling amusement parks and museums covered the entire planet. That included many and varied parks, although none of those could truly be called forests. Most of the edifices were composed of metal. It made Loggia the perfect capital planet for a Cyber Empire.

On Loggia lodged Great Leviathan. He kept his exact whereabouts secret so that assassination attempts, even with antimatter missiles, would probably fail.

From his seat on an orbital, Dax looked out a small porthole as they neared one of the myriad spaceports.

Loggia, great Loggia glittered in space like a great metal jewel, like a great iron ring on some master warlord's finger. Cybers had uniquely created the planet throughout the centuries. Others brought more metals and ores down from the greater star system.

Far above the metallic surface floated sub-metropolises tethered to the planet by sky cables. They swayed in Loggia's near-perfect atmosphere.

Who could claim a planet like this? Surely, Loggia proved the greatness, the power, the uniqueness of the capital planet of Leviathan. The cybers were the greatest life force in existence. This Dax believed with all the others. The Spacers, the humans of Earth, and the ancient and extinct Aetharians with their Phantasma Synth Crystals had never been enough to thwart the greatest spymaster of Leviathan.

Dax considered himself such.

In his orbital seat, Dax swelled with pride, confidence and assurance. He partly achieved this by activating the cybernetic organs within him to induce these states. He was going to need every ounce of confidence, every logic circuit to help him persuade Grand Strategist Tactix of the rightness of his cause.

The year and a half of absence from the planet hadn't dulled Dax's cunning.

The orbital landed in Met-653 Spaceport. There, Dax passed through Truth Monitor Stations and a Debriefing Chamber. Through various tricks and sleights of hand, he evaded Enigmach's agents who would be keeping tabs for his eventual arrival.

The strategists of Leviathan, including the grand strategists who plotted the empire's invasion plans, were among the highest aristocracy of the cyber system. As such, many had clients who sought their help and provided aid in return. It was similar in political system to the Ancient Roman Republic of Earth. Even so, Dax slipped through the net and remained hidden from Enigmach.

After many magnetic train rides and subway passages, Dax found himself deep underground in a supreme sanctuary subterranean district. There, armed cyborg troopers brought him into a vast antechamber. A beautiful sky scene moved across the ceiling of the antechamber.

Dax knew it was an imitation, holographic sky, but it was impressive nonetheless, with three faint moons hanging in wonder.

Dax stood before several marble slabs as he waited. Zeroing in with optics, he spied cyborg troopers watching him from a distance. They aimed blast rifles at his chest. If he did anything unwarranted, they would fire.

Eventually, a long, lean cyber approached. This cyber had a vast and complex head with computer additions plugged into an otherwise bald noggin. A long, red, trailing cloak followed him as he walked.

Soon enough, this one stopped and towered over Dax.

"Yes," the cyber lord said. "You wished to speak with me?"

Dax strove to appear calm. "You are Grand Strategist Tactix?"

"You asked to see Tactix, did you not? I just said yes. Logically, then, you should know who I am."

Dax inclined his head. "Excellency, may I tell you the ill fortunes we encountered during the invasion of the Commonwealth?"

"This is the first anyone on Loggia has heard of this. That is despite the remnant commanders of the invasion fleet reporting to the Military Institute. Proceed with your tale. Wait, I have just detected an anomaly. Are you not Enigmach's premier spy?"

"I am, Excellency, but I feel—no, please let me rephrase. I do not possess your logic and computing power of mind. Yet I am certain that Grand Strategist Enigmach has failed Leviathan and I have the facts to prove it."

Go on," Tactix said. "You almost make this sound intriguing."

Dax proceeded to tell Tactix almost everything that had happened during the invasion. He left out any mention of the phase ship and other peculiarities that might throw him in a bad light. Surely, Tactix would learn of them in time, but that time wasn't now. Dax told the story, fixating on Venna the Spy and the evil entity entering her through the shattered Phantasma Synth Crystals.

"This strikes me as odd," Tactix said, interrupting the extended tale. "It appears that you are correct in your assessment, Senior Dax. I mean regarding Enigmach. You were right to seek me out and inform me of these infractions. What reward do you require for your action?"

Dax inclined his head. "I serve the Sovereign Hierarchy of Leviathan. I serve as a spy, and I feel I am a good spy. My wish is to continue in this capacity. But whatever you say—"

"No more," Tactix said, interrupting him again, holding up a thin metallic hand. "It is clear that you must become one of my spymasters. If you prove as adept for me as you did in forestalling utter disaster to our invasion and the possible revival of those on Ector—you have done me and the empire a grand service indeed."

Tactix withdrew a glistening computing cube from a chest cavity. "I have everything here you have said. It is all I need to rectify certain unseemly matters."

Dax bowed his head, certain that Enigmach's days were finished. In this, the old adage worked for him: Better you (Enigmach) than me.

"Be assured, Senior Dax," Tactix said, "that your days as a spy are far from over. I will reward you according to the service you do me."

"Thank you, Great One. Thank you. I am glad to serve."

"I understand," Tactix said. "I understand completely."

-80-

Several days later, the Grand Strategists of Leviathan met. Unfortunately, where there had been three Grand Strategists plugged into the great computer in the subterranean chamber, there were now but two: Tactix and Hyperion Codex. Of Enigmach, there was no sign.

"It is a pity that Great Leviathan saw fit to eliminate Enigmach, destroy him down to his component parts, and melt all of it," Hyperion Codex said. He was the senior of the pair.

"Indeed," Tactix said, "I had foreseen that happening to Enigmach when I gave the news to the High Command, but my patriotism toward Great Leviathan was such that I felt compelled to explain every facet of this disastrously failed invasion of the Commonwealth."

"Yes," Hyperion Codex said, "I understand your motivations, both overt and covert. I also concur with how you operated. Have you decided on a mission yet for Senior Dax?"

"You know about the spy?" Tactix asked.

"I believe it wise to keep up on such matters."

"I'm impressed at the breadth of your information service."

"One does not become the Chief Grand Strategist on his logical ability alone. A finely running network is mandatory."

"You have made your point," Tactix said. "You are first. I have no intention of challenging that."

"We understand each other then."

"We do," Tactix said. "As to Senior Dax, I am unsure how to utilize the master spy. For now, I will await the perfect assignment for him. Dax gave me priceless information and also became a traitor to his former master."

"That is a correct assessment," Hyperion Codex said.

"If Senior Dax worked for you," Tactix said, "how would you handle him?"

"That is a delicate issue," Hyperion Codex replied. "First, what is the senior's key motivation?"

"Ah…" Tactix said. "The key motivation to Senior Dax is his inordinate desire for advancement."

"You speak about ambition," Hyperion Codex said. "Or would you call it something else?"

"No. Inordinate ambition says it best."

"Now," Hyperion Codex said, "in your estimation, is that a bad attribute or a good attribute?"

"So far, it has proven to be an excellent attribute," Tactix said. "It drove Dax to prioritize advancement over loyalty to a fool."

"Then, I would remember that when giving Dax an assignment. He turned in Enigmach's hands. Make sure Dax does not turn in yours."

"Wisdom," Tactix said. "I would eliminate Dax immediately, but I wish to encourage similar actions from others and thus demonstrate that I reward them lavishly."

"A tricky operation," Hyperion Codex said. "Surely, it promises vast rewards while forcing one to move carefully with subordinates."

"That has been my experience."

"Do you have any last words regarding Enigmach?" Hyperion Codex asked.

"I do. I have always felt that Enigmach was arrogant, hasty, and unwise in certain of his procedures. He cloaked this arrogance in seeming logic, but we see the outcome of using ancient and alien shamans' tools."

"Yes," Hyperion Codex said, "you are correct, particularly in the last point. Taken as a whole, your logic is flawless. Enigmach is gone and good riddance to him. We two have gained greater status because of his ineptitude. He was a pretender and now we will have to choose another to take his place."

"If you permit me…"

"I do," Hyperion Codex said.

"I suggest we choose one who is less zealous in his efforts to rise above us," Tactix said.

"Are you suggesting we choose one who has more meekness?" Hyperion Codex asked.

"That might be the appropriate term."

"What about the Commonwealth in the Orion Spiral Arm?" Hyperion Codex asked. "What about Star Watch and Captain Maddox?"

Tactix thought for a time. "I believe we should continue with the spy missions. It is less costly than sending expensive assault fleets of maulers. Perhaps we should continue with the spy missions until the Commonwealth is weak, embroiled in conflict and battle."

"Through secession wars, perhaps?" Hyperion Codex asked.

"That would be the best outcome. Perhaps engineering a war between the New Men and the Commonwealth would also be advantageous. Then perhaps inserting the fleet of fifty maulers would finish the volatile situation for good."

"That is an extraordinary and vast thought indeed," Hyperion Codex said. "You are a true Grand Strategist of Leviathan."

"As are you, Hyperion Codex, as are you," Tactix said. "With the paring away of the dead wood named Enigmach, perhaps we should feast our brilliance and rejoice in having an ambitious fool take the fall for us."

"Ah," Hyperion Codex said, "you speak bluntly and forthrightly."

"Just this once," Tactix said.

"Agreed," Hyperion Codex said. "We will speak about this no more. It was a bitter, costly failure, but it was all Enigmach's fault."

"Senior Dax proved that for us," Tactix said. "Now, if you will allow me, what is the next matter on the agenda?"

"I allow it," Hyperion Codex said. "Let me see…"

The End

LOST STARSHIP SERIES:

The Lost Starship
The Lost Command
The Lost Destroyer
The Lost Colony
The Lost Patrol
The Lost Planet
The Lost Earth
The Lost Artifactt
The Lost Star Gate
The Lost Supernova
The Lost Swarm
The Lost Intelligence
The Lost Tech
The Lost Secret
The Lost Barrier
The Lost Nebula
The Lost Relic
The Lost Task Force
The Lost Clone
The Lost Portal
The Lost Cyborg

Visit VaughnHeppner.com for more information

Printed in Great Britain
by Amazon